Traitor

DAVID HINGLEY

Allison & Busby Limited
11 Wardour Mews
London W1F 8AN
allisonandbusby.com

First published in Great Britain by Allison & Busby in 2018.
This paperback edition published by Allison & Busby in 2018.

A CIP catalogue record for this book is available from
the British Library.

10 9 8 7 6 5 4 3 2 1

ISBN 978-0-7490-2124-5

Typeset in 10.5/15.5 pt Adobe Garamond Pro by
Allison & Busby Ltd.

The paper used for this Allison & Busby publication
has been produced from trees that have been legally sourced
from well-managed and credibly certified forests.

Printed and bound by
CPI Group (UK) Ltd, Croydon, CR0 4YY

Library and Information Centres

Red doles Lane

Huddersfield, West Yorkshire

HD2 1YF

This book should be returned on or before the latest date stamped below.
Fines are charged if the item is late.

23/04/19		

You may renew this loan for a further period by phone, personal visit or at
www.kirklees.gov.uk/libraries, provided that the book is not required by
another reader.

NO MORE THAN THREE RENEWALS ARE PERMITTED

For Brenda, Eliza, Bob & Bob
who laughed, played and taught

Dramatis Personae

THE KING'S WAR COUNCIL

Sir Geoffrey Allcot	ambassador for the Royal Adventurers
Sir William Calde	recently returned from America
Sir Stephen Herrick	advisor on matters that pertain to the Fleet
Sir Peter Shaw	advisor on matters diplomatic and general

THE WOMEN WHO COULD BE VIRGO

Lady Grace Allcot	Sir Geoffrey's wife, often absent from Whitehall
Lady Helen Cartwright	Sir Geoffrey's mistress, enjoys her entourage
Lady Anne Herrick	Sir Stephen's wife, protective of her husband
Mrs Cornelia Howe	Sir Stephen's niece, likes her clothing bright
Miss Lavinia Whent	Sir Peter's mistress, raised in the Barbados

PRINCIPAL ACTORS

Mercia Blakewood	transatlantic adventurer
Nicholas Wildmoor	her manservant; one-time sailor & farrier

Sir Francis Simmonds	her uncle; usurper of her manor house
Lady Margaret Simmonds	her aunt, Sir Francis's wife
Daniel Blakewood	her son
Julien Bellecour	envoy of the French
Lady Castlemaine	otherwise Barbara Palmer, the King's chief mistress
Thomas Howe	Cornelia Howe's husband; owns a trading concern
Giles Malvern	barber surgeon with other talents
Henry Raff	courtier, serves the Earl of Clarendon
One-Eye Wilkins	entrepreneur
Phibae	maidservant
Tacitus	in Lady Cartwright's service

THE ROYAL HOUSE OF STUART in order of succession

King Charles II	His Majesty the King
James, Duke of York	his brother, heir to the throne
James, Duke of Cambridge	infant son of the Duke of York
Her Highness the Lady Mary	infant daughter of the Duke of York
Her Highness the Lady Anne	baby daughter of the Duke of York

NAMED SENIOR MEMBERS OF THE COURT

The Earl of Clarendon	King's Chief Minister
The Earl of Arlington	senior Secretary of State

Chapter One

'Watch out!' came a sharp voice from above.

Mercia pulled back as the tallest wave yet dashed itself to nothing against the ship's weary hull. Fine droplets of mist soared into the air, the ring of gulls circling the mast shrieking their soaked disapproval. Clutching a sealed envelope against the splintered rail, she craned her neck towards the faint shoreline as another, smaller wave played out its lively welcome. Spray speckled her wet cheek anew, and she swayed on the warped deck, its planks damaged as much of the hardy ship had suffered in the storm on the long voyage home.

Home.

Briefly, she closed her eyes.

Home, after all.

'Don't you think you should open it now?'

A familiar presence approached from behind; she knew someone had been watching, but she had wanted to bear witness to the coalescing cliffs, the first glimpse of grass atop the jagged morass. The first glimpse for nigh on a year.

It had been a long year, these past twelve months.

'Mercia?'

The man was as persistent as the waves. She paused a moment more, breathing in the saltiness of the ocean that seemed somehow . . . English, and traced the pattern of a cleft in the bluffs, listening to the pervading caw of the gulls as they scoured the sodden deck for a sailor's charity. Finally she turned, grasping at her hat at a tug of the sharp Channel wind.

'Careful,' her companion warned. 'You've been waiting three months to read that letter. You don't want the sea to take it now.'

'No, Nicholas,' she said. 'But I promised I would only open it when we arrived home.'

'And you've been as patient as you vowed. Now break the seal.'

'Why I allow you to—' She shook her head. 'No matter. Suffice that I do.'

His green eyes flashed, the glimmering edge of the sun's unsure circle peeking from behind a ragged cloud. 'You've always said I should speak as I think.'

'Still.' She thrust the letter into the pockets beneath her dress as a boy ran to take her hand, nimble despite the rocking deck. 'My, Danny.' She staggered slightly as she reached to scoop him up. 'You are getting heavy.'

'It was my birthday last month, Mamma,' said the boy. 'Don't you remember? I'm growing up.'

His innocence charmed her. 'That you are. Past time I brought you back home.'

The ship continued on, edging through the Channel, heading for its long-sought destination: the busy port of Southampton on the English south coast. Mercia felt a twinge of agitation as the harbour of Plymouth passed by to the north, but nine weeks had passed since they had embarked in New York; she could wait a few hours more. Besides, her impatience was mingled with excitement; the thrill of seeing her homeland again after such a long journey abroad. But finally the westernmost cliffs of the Isle of Wight roved into view, and passing along the narrow Solent, the wharves and inns of the Southampton docks began to give up their features until individual sailors and dockhands could be seen roaming the jetties or leaping through the rigging of the many-moored ships.

The industry of the docks could be heard from afar, even as the ship was still some way out, awaiting the tug boat that was rowing towards them. Positioning itself at the battered bow, the tug's crew of two swore in jocund ribaldry at the sailors leaning down from the bowsprit, waiting to be thrown a sturdy rope to use to steady the ship into dock. Then as they manoeuvred into the harbour, a glint of sudden sunlight made Mercia wince. Arm shielding her eyes, she squinted to starboard to wonder at a floating behemoth, larger than any vessel she had seen. Its army of cannon sparkled in the bright spring day.

'God's truth!' swore Nicholas, coming alongside once more as she laid a restraining hand on Daniel, the young boy leaning too far over the railing for her liking. 'Never seen a ship that big before.'

'Not even when you were serving yourself?' she asked.

'Not that I remember. And look at that paintwork all along the side, that figurehead at the bow . . . 'tis brand new. I'd say about ready for launch.'

Daniel squirmed under his mother's grasp. 'The . . . *Royal Charles*,' he announced, reading the nameplate stretched across the expansive stern. He turned his eyes up to her. 'Like the King!'

'Yes,' said Mercia, taking in the golden ostentation that peppered the length of the magnificent ship. The red, the yellow, the blue; the gleaming ironmongery; the furled white sails towering high above. 'You are right, Danny. 'Tis just like him.'

* * *

It was the first step back on land after an arduous crossing. All around, Mercia could hear the sounds of home, breathe in the . . . stench, but it vanished from notice as her legs began to buckle, and at her side, Daniel fell to the ground with a bump.

'It will pass,' grinned Nicholas. 'This always happens after a long voyage. People not used to it get land-sick.'

As the uncomfortable sensation dissipated, Mercia was taken by an overwhelming emotion. The events of the past months had been hard, and to be back home, surrounded by a certain familiarity—

'England!' she cried, sinking to her knees in the middle of the docks. 'England, after all!'

As though unbelieving, she reached out a palm to the dirty ground, wavering her hand above the earth until with a sudden movement she drove it firm against the hard surface, compacted by so many boots. For a blissful moment she cast down her joyful gaze, then retracting her hand she drew herself up and took in her surroundings. The English people, the English port – the English frowns at the unexpected behaviour of this woman in her weather-worn brown dress.

'Perhaps get up now?' offered Nicholas, reaching out his own hand to help her rise.

She seized his wrist. 'No matter what people think. We are home. And no sense in waiting.'

'You still want to take the first coach I can find? No rest?'

'Yes, Nicholas. I must know if the King will do as he promised.' She looked at him, her travelling companion of many months' standing. Now the time was near, she realised she was more saddened that soon they would part than even she would have thought. 'Do you . . . still want to journey with us? You have fulfilled your obligations to me. I have no call on your service now.'

'I've come this far, haven't I?' He smiled. 'There and back again. I need to know how this ends.'

'And then? You cannot defer it any longer.'

'I don't know.' Looking away, he ran a hand through his blonde hair, ruffling it beyond its usual disarray. 'Shall I see to our luggage?'

'Thank you.' She caught sight of a stone bench at the end of the dock, its only current occupants a pair of fighting pigeons. 'We will wait there.'

As Daniel ran ahead, copying another boy by chasing the pigeons around the bench, Mercia watched Nicholas force his way into the crowd at the side of their abandoned ship, where a horde of grubby, disembarked passengers were clamouring with the one sailor overseeing the removal of their belongings from the water-sodden hold. Keen that Daniel exercise his legs after so many weeks at sea, nonetheless she ordered him to remain close. Then she took a deep breath and felt inside her pockets for the makeshift envelope, a sealed piece of paper folded around the letter inside.

She studied the writing on the front: just two words, her name. The initials, M and B, were written in a flourish, the whole beautifully copied out, each letter drawn with meticulous care. There had been no need for an address, the rider bringing the letter from Hartford well instructed as to who she was and where she had wintered. Beneath the words, a thick black stroke underlined the esteem of the writer in adorning the paper with her name.

She flicked the thin packet over. Now was the time, she supposed. But as she eased her finger beneath the flap, drawing her cracked nail towards the small blue seal, she paused. On the back, she looked again at the request that she not open the letter until she arrived home in England, but despite this injunction, why had she waited until now? True, she had promised herself she would comply with the writer's entreaty, but could she really not have broken that vow in her cabin as she broke the waxen seal now?

She withdrew a sheet of pale grey paper, folded in half along an immaculate crease. Had she been scared to read what was inside? Not dared take in the words while trapped on a ship at sea, nowhere to hide if they upset her as she suspected they might?

Or had she, as she thought was her correspondent's intent, merely wanted to wait until she was an ocean's distance from the hurt of her recent past? Whatever the reason, now, here in England, there was no longer any excuse.

She unfolded the letter and began to read.

My dearest Mercia, my friend, my love,

She stopped before she had barely begun. Already her breathing had quickened. Should she continue to read here in the open, or wait a while longer until she could be alone indoors? But now she had started, his writing drew her to the page as surely as if he were beside her speaking the words.

When you left Meltwater, you—

She broke off once more as a shadow fell over the page, and she looked up, startled, half expecting, half hoping, to see the man who had written the letter standing before her. Certainly she did not expect to be confronted by a soldier, armed with a halberd-like partisan and a grimmer expression.

'Mrs Blakewood?' he asked, his voice equally gruff. Over his shoulder, a fellow pair of guardsmen stood watching.

'Yes?' she said.

'Mrs Mercia Blakewood, of Halescott in Oxfordshire? Returned this day from America?'

A prickling anxiety teased her insides. 'That is me.'

'Then you are to come with us.'

'Why?' She looked from soldier to soldier, but their impassive faces told no story.

Their captain stood to one side. 'On the orders of the King, you are under arrest.'

The room was light, surprisingly. Fearing a small, dark space, she was taken to the top floor of a sizeable house that overhung a broad street in the middle of town. Three windows in the street-facing side flooded the floor with the sundered rays of the sun; the bed, although small, appeared comfortable, and the truckle in the corner was a sufficient resting place for Daniel.

And yet, the door remained as locked as the soldiers' mouths had been closed when she had pressed to know the reasons they had led her away. There had been no time to alert Nicholas; she had tried to shout over, but he had long since disappeared into the melee surrounding the ship. And so here she was, trapped in another chill room, at the behest of the King whom she thought she had served well.

'Why are we here, Mamma?' asked Daniel, no longer as subdued as before. 'I thought . . . aren't we going home any more? I wanted to see James. I wanted to play with him.'

'We are going home, Danny, I promise you that. I have come too far to be denied now.' She forced a smile. 'Come here, on the bed.'

She sat on the sheets – as comfortable as they looked – and waited until he dragged himself over to join her. She put an arm around his young shoulders and began to stroke his hair.

'Do not be afraid. Mamma will put this right.' She sighed. 'Whatever this is.'

His lower lip trembled. 'Is it because of grandfather again?'

'No, Danny. You must not think that.'

As she stroked his hair, she pondered the reasons for her arrest. People had died during her mission for the King in New York – was that it? Had she spoken to someone she shouldn't have? Or had her uncle, more recently returned than she, made insinuations about her conduct that the King wanted to investigate? Despite her reassurances to her son, her father had still been condemned a traitor the year before: one of Parliament's staunchest advocates in the civil war, he had served in Cromwell's long-gone Protectorate, unlike her uncle who had sided with the Royalists. But surely, she thought, her recent actions were proof of her family's loyalty?

The afternoon faded into dusk, then into gloaming; lanterns were lit outside, dotting the fronts of shops and houses with the swinging shadow of their quivering light. The prison-house stood not far from the dock, and constant shouting drifted through the thinly paned windows, lined with diagonal lead that had warped in places, allowing the cool breeze in. The port was crawling with sailors; Southampton had a great number of drinking dens, none of them nearly as restrained as those in the Puritan colonies of New England she had most recently known. And so she teased Daniel to bed, wincing every time a bawdy group swore its slow way past, until she realised one of the passing men was calling her name.

She eased open the window, wincing as it ground out a low squeak.

'Nicholas!' she said, leaning out. 'Thank the Lord.'

'What's going on?' he called up. 'I came back and you'd gone. It took hours to find out where you were.'

'I am not certain.' She squeezed her head through the narrow opening as far as she could; somewhat tricky with the topknot she had taken pride in maintaining throughout their long voyage home. 'Did you secure our belongings?'

'I've paid a fellow by the dock to look after them. The sailors say he does it for people all the time, while they wait to move on.'

'Can you trust him?'

'He can trust me to take against him if anything goes astray.'

She tried to lean out further, but all she managed was a sore shoulder. 'Nicholas, 'tis the King. He has had me placed in confinement.'

'I got that much out of the guards downstairs. But they won't let me see you, not even for coin, and I had to wait for dark to – hey!' For a moment he disappeared, but he quickly returned. 'Sorry,' he said. 'Some cloyer was trying to rob me. Listen, I don't know how long 'til the guards chase me off. I want to know what I should do.'

'I . . . do not know. If the King has changed his mind, I could be in trouble, despite all that I have done. Perhaps the best course is to wait.'

'Damn it, if I were Nathan, I could speak to someone, but you're lumbered with me. At least I know where you are now. Maybe I can find Sir William and get his help. He deigned to talk to me on the ship, but now we're back . . .'

She nodded, but sucked in through her teeth as her neck caught on the frame. 'I asked the guards if I could speak with him myself, but they refused. Can you get him a message? If you say it concerns me, he will listen.'

'I'll try. Stay calm. I'll come back when I can.'

She pulled shut the window, feeling more hopeful than before. If Sir William could help, she knew that he would, unless the threat of the King's retribution prevented even his noble person from acting. She nibbled at the remnants of the plentiful food and ale an untalkative woman had brought in, and persuaded herself to relieve her discomfort in the pisspot she found under the bed: a difficult operation in all her heavy clothes. Then she listened again at the door, hoping for any sign that Sir William had arrived, or that the guards were ascending the stairs, but all she could hear was the rolling of dice and the chinking of beakers.

A fire was burning in an alcove in the wall, lit by the untalkative woman, and she took a candle from a holder at her side, setting it down once lit. Now she was alone, and Daniel asleep, there was no reason to postpone a second attempt at the letter. She retrieved the crumpled sheet and glanced down.

My dearest Mercia, my friend, my love,

No. No reason.

When you left Meltwater, you took some of me with you. And so here, take some more, a piece of my heart waiting for you to unwrap as you arrive home. I hope you did wait to read this, for it is now that I think you will need it, but no matter if you did not. I know how you can be impetuous.

She smiled, remembering the man who had written those words. The man she had left behind.

After what happened in America, I know you are still in pain. The murders here have affected all our souls, but yours especially, I know. I hope in time you will learn to accept that none of this was your fault, and that your grief can start to lessen as once you helped me vanquish mine. For now, do as I asked when last we spoke – let yourself live, and let me into your heart, for I will find you when you need me. And if ever you change your mind to the question I asked, I shall swim the very ocean to be with you. But until that day, I shall remain in America to help the town through these still-dark days.

Now you are returned to England, you will face new trials. A merchant from New York told me how your uncle had sailed before you, and I know he will not let the matter of your manor house rest, for having once seized your family's lands he will desire to keep them. But believe in what you accomplished when the King sent you here, and in his promise that he would restore to you your home. For yourself and for Daniel, I hope my love will add its light to God's to keep you strong, and that we will see each other once more.

I am always yours.

Always.

Nathan

She sat back. Nathan, her friend, now so far away. At one time she had thought . . . but no. Lying down to rest, she plumped up the pillow, and passed into restful sleep.

A bang on the door forced her awake. As she opened her heavy eyes, a key turned in the lock, and the guards appeared in the threshold.

'Well,' she yawned, the grey light of dawn falling through the windows. 'Are you speaking with me now?'

'Not us, my lady. Someone much more important.' The guard's captain took a step forward, yesterday's long partisan replaced with a shorter, less brutal sword. 'Rouse your boy. You depart for London this morning. You are expected tomorrow at the palace.'

Chapter Two

She had planned to travel to London by public coach; at the least her captivity spared her that cramped trial. Instead the guards helped her into a spacious carriage emblazoned with the royal arms.

'But my luggage!' she protested.

'Leave that to your man,' said the captain, picking Daniel up in his turn. 'If he comes back, someone will tell him where you've gone.'

After a night's rest in Farnham, the coach made London late the following day, or rather it made Westminster, juddering down the side of the new royal park of St James. Reaching Charing Cross it sped right, heading for Whitehall, turning into the courtyard of the magnificent palace that had been Mercia's destination in any case. Leaving her to jump down by herself, the guards handed her to a teenage page, but they told her not to worry when they insisted Daniel wait behind with a maid. Reassuring him she would return, she was led deep into the heart of the palace, if not in triumph then in . . . what?

Following the page through the bewildering maze of passages, Mercia recalled the first time she had visited Whitehall, on the heels of another young servant much like this one; indeed, it could well have been the same swift youth, recovering on that occasion from a celebration the evening before: the day of her wronged father's execution. And then she wondered, as she walked, whether the object of her mission to America was yet hanging in the palace, for like her uncle it too had arrived before her, and despite her trepidation she was anxious to see it. But there was no sign of the great portrait yet.

After an age of corridors, the page reached a door in that section of the palace that perched above the Thames, but in place of the expected guard, a young lady-in-waiting was watching for their arrival. The page winked, and she shook her head, but her smile was clear enough.

'Please,' she said to Mercia, eyes roving her face and clothes. 'Enter.'

She waited for Mercia to pass through to the room beyond, but she did not follow, pulling shut the door to leave her seemingly alone. The room was dim; despite the brightness of the afternoon, the sole visible window was small, the others covered with thick drapes. A fire burning in the grate was the only other aid to vision, and that was scant enough from the doorway. But then a figure stirred beneath the undraped window, and Mercia realised she was not in truth alone.

'Good morrow,' she offered, uncertain what to say.

The figure rested a book on an adjacent table: directly beside the window, that spot at least must have enjoyed sufficient light.

'Welcome, Mrs Blakewood.' A woman's voice cut through the gloom, youthful but full of practised confidence. 'Shall we have more light? I prefer to see those with whom I speak.'

A silhouette developed, standing and bending to the fire, at which a small flicker sprang up as a taper caught. Slowly, the woman passed around the room, lighting several candles until the whole space was well lit. Shaking out the taper, she threw the remnants into the fire and turned, revealing her notorious face.

Startled, Mercia only just kept from stepping back, instead

21

dropping to the floor in a curtsey of sorts. Was that how you were supposed to greet this woman? In truth she did not know, but she had to hide her discomfort somehow.

The woman smiled in evident satisfaction. Her luscious chestnut hair was tied in a near-impossible topknot: a multitude of thick strands, meticulously curled at the tips, cascaded down her cochinealed cheeks. She was in her mid-twenties and intensely beautiful, her eyes aflame, her lips red and full. On her face she wore a decorative black patch, made of three pointed stars, their curious darkness a contrast to the pale radiance Mercia knew this woman employed to entrap many a willing man of the Court.

'I . . . My Lady Castlemaine,' she tried, resuming her curtsey. 'I was not expecting to be received by such a noble hostess.'

A rustling of Lady Castlemaine's many-folded dress accompanied a wave of her hand. 'Oh come, Mrs Blakewood, you need not bother with such flatteries. I insist that we talk eye to eye.'

Mercia raised herself up, eager to look more on the celebrated woman, renowned countrywide as the most beautiful in the kingdom. She was entirely dramatic, her orange dress and sky-blue scarf a piercing of colour, her pearl and ruby jewels dazzling. Certainly, the King valued her splendour, for this was his most favoured mistress, partner in his bed, and more formally, thought Mercia wryly, Lady of the Bedchamber to the Queen.

Lady Castlemaine laughed. 'You seem surprised, Mrs Blakewood. Were you expecting a mysterious spymaster, intoning brusque orders from his humourless seat, a dark secretary arms folded at his side?' She inclined her head. 'That would be a little . . . obvious, no?'

Recovering herself, Mercia blinked. This may be the King's mistress, and de facto queen of the Court, but she had her pride, and she would hold her own in her presence.

'Assuredly, my lady, I did not expect you. Nor my treatment likewise.'

Lady Castlemaine chuckled, a bright, pleased chord of teasing delight. 'Of course not. But Charles – that is, the King – agreed this would be more advantageous to us, and I . . .' She shrugged. 'I thought it could amuse.'

A slight indignation rose in Mercia's chest, but she kept her thoughts to herself. Was locking her in overnight, hiding the truth, this woman's idea of fun? But there was little time left to wonder on the reason for her brief arrest.

'I will be candid, Mrs Blakewood,' said Lady Castlemaine. 'The King was most pleased when he received the painting you recovered overseas. He truly believed his family portrait lost for all time. He would hang it near his bedchamber were it not for the thought of his mother being close during certain . . . private acts.'

She paused, but Mercia made sure to keep her expression constant.

'Indeed he has come to hold you in no small esteem,' she continued, a slight frown emerging on her forehead. 'And so he wishes you to accept another task.'

Aghast, Mercia looked up. 'But my lady, if I may . . . what of my manor house? His Majesty agreed he would restore it to me if I aided him as I did.'

'I believe he agreed he would consider it.' Lady Castlemaine arched a fine eyebrow, taking time to brush a thread from her bulbous silk sleeve. 'And I will speak truth. He is troubled at how he was convinced to permit your father's execution. But you remain his servant and he needs your mind for another matter. One, I may add, of significant delicacy. Aid the King in this, and you will be back in your manor with little delay.'

Mercia met the younger woman's gaze. 'May I speak with His Majesty myself?'

'In time. For now, I am to explain the undertaking, and when you have heard me, His Majesty wants you to be free to acquiesce or to decline.' Her smile resumed its faint mockery. 'Of course, if you say no . . .'

'Then I suppose I am to understand that His Majesty may take longer to . . . consider.'

Lady Castlemaine's face twitched. 'Less bold, Mrs Blakewood. I have said how the King is thankful, but he is the King and you are . . . merely you. Now pay me heed, for much has happened since you departed.' Her eyes gleamed in the candlelight. 'Finally, we are at war with the Dutch. True war, I mean: much more than the seizure of colonial backwaters like New York that you witnessed. All Englishmen – Englishwomen – must play their part.' She gave Mercia a penetrating stare. 'Your uncle already is.'

'Sir Francis?' Despite the warm fire, a chill set in.

'He returned from America some weeks ago now, in a foul temper no less. I fear you have much to do with that.' She smiled. 'I never much liked the dour man, but his injury has made him yet more intolerable. He is obliged to walk with a cane, and is always in poor humour and discomfort. The result of events in New York, I believe?'

A picture of her uncle came to mind, lying injured in a meadow, a sword wound in his side. The same uncle who had usurped her manor house and set her on her journeys in the first place.

She glanced down. 'He was near death, it seems.'

'Much livelier now. And eager to help the King with the matter I am about to divulge to you. As for me, I think you can do better.'

Mercia took a deep breath. 'Does this mean the King is inclined to refuse me his support?'

'The opposite. Let us merely say that if you help him in this, he will be inclined to refuse you little. We think you are the perfect trap.'

'Trap?'

'Must you repeat what I say? You proved adept at seeking out the King's inheritance. Now he needs you to seek out a spy.'

'A sp—?' She felt herself reddening. 'Surely there are men in His Majesty's service who are trained in such . . . arts?'

'Trained, yes, but competent – who can know? In this climate of war, 'tis so difficult to know who to believe and who to trust.' There was a sparkle in her cheeks, in her eyes, as she spoke. 'Someone at Court is passing information to the Dutch. Charles wants you to find out who.'

Mercia's mouth had fallen half-open, but she found the wit to reclose it. 'Why me?'

'I shall come to that.' Ignoring her shock, Lady Castlemaine pressed on. 'The King debates matters of war in a specially created council. Matters he does not discuss even with me, and yet it seems the Dutch commanders know more than they should. Recently, he gave the council a report he knew to be untrue, and yet the information found its way to Amsterdam, according to our people there. This, even though it was false, and no one but the council had heard it.'

'Meaning someone on the council had to be passing it on.'

'So it would appear. Naturally I am not privy to the intricacies of these affairs, but you seem to grasp the problem as well as I do. Although the council is not the precise matter the King wants you to address.'

'Oh?' said Mercia, intrigued despite herself. 'Then what?'

'The traitor he seeks is not a man of the council. Not a man at all, indeed. No, the spy I speak of is a woman, Mrs Blakewood. What do you make of that?'

She paused, her slender chin jutting forward, her right eyebrow raised, and only when she could see Mercia was fully ensnared did she continue.

'A coded message has been intercepted of late, and after some effort, its meaning has been deduced. The message is brief, but makes plain that a woman is the one gathering the information. That she has close ties to a member of the council, either as a relation or a mistress, perhaps. And that her name is given as Virgo.'

'The virgin,' mused Mercia, her mind already dissecting the possibilities. 'An allusion to this woman's chastity?'

Lady Castlemaine scoffed. 'The only virgin here is that insufferable Frances Stewart, the vixen. And I really do not think her tiny mind could be so capable. But whether Virgo's name is literal or no, it is from her that the reports to our enemy start. We do not know from which council member she acquires her information, or whether that man is complicit or simply deluded, but Virgo is the principal actor – or rather, actress. I have convinced Charles that setting a woman on a woman is a prudent course. And so he has been awaiting your return.'

'Indeed, my lady.' She swallowed. 'Your confidence in me is most gratifying. But are there no other women to ask?'

'Perhaps, Mrs Blakewood, but you have entrapped yourself with your success. And you have another advantage no other woman has.'

Again, she paused. Again, Mercia waited.

'The King,' Lady Castlemaine pursued, 'wishes to discover Virgo by placing a spy of his own in the Court, one who should arouse a minimum of suspicion. If the worst is true, and the council member is complicit, then he is likely privy to knowledge about many of those we could use for this task, and he will seek to protect Virgo accordingly. Whereas you, Mrs Blakewood, can enter Court in an entirely different manner that neither he nor Virgo should ever suspect.'

Mercia frowned. 'I should have thought the whole Court would view me with suspicion. Even if the King does repent my father's death, my family has never been much in royal favour, not until my voyage to America, at least.'

'Which is why I . . . why we have devised a ploy. I do not know if you will like it, but it removes all such suspicion at a stroke. It involves your friendship with Sir William Calde.'

Mercia studied her face, attempting to read there her plan, but she could think of no obvious answer, unless—

No! Not that!

Lady Castlemaine smiled. 'Your reaction suggests you may have unmasked our scheme. Do you approve?'

'My Lady, I do not know until you speak. But I venture to presume I have divined your intent, and I am not certain I can consent.'

'You may have to. 'Tis the only sure means of explaining your arrival at Whitehall. And I hear you so loved the theatre when you were a girl.' She winked: a calculated hint, Mercia thought, that she knew more about her than her childhood pleasures alone. 'Now is your chance to act a fine role indeed. You are to play the mistress of Sir William Calde.'

She closed her eyes. 'So I was right.'

'You must agree, 'tis the perfect subterfuge. The whole Court knows how Sir William has pursued you these many months. How difficult is it to surmise that the two of you became close on your mutual journey to America? Particularly after the . . . unfortunate death of his wife.'

Mercia looked her full in the eye. To her credit, she did not flinch. 'May we be frank, my lady? Are you saying that unless I pose as Sir William's mistress and unmask this Virgo then my manor will be denied me?'

'The King thinks you have more chance with the women of the Court than any man. That is why he has sent me to talk with you, to offer my guidance.' She toyed with the tips of her fine white gloves. 'But I have intimated your uncle knows too of this plot. Should he discover the traitor in your place, then naturally the King may be more disposed, shall we say, to reconsider Sir Francis's own claim on the manor house.'

By the Lord, swore Mercia in her mind. *Am I to find no peace?*

'Say I agree. Will Sir William expect that we . . . ?'

'How far the two of you take this pretence is entirely your affair.'

'And my son? What am I to do with him?'

'Mrs Blakewood, do this and your son will want for nothing again. He will see his inheritance restored, enjoy the best tutoring while you are at Court, mingle with the sons of the noblest families in the land. Perhaps even a title to go with his manor one day, if you play your part well.' Her lips curled upwards. 'Yes, I thought that might interest you. And you have a manservant, do you not? Install him in a servant's chambers. He can wait on you here.'

Thrown by the proposal of a title, Mercia cleared her throat. 'He is not my manservant any longer. I can scarce call on his time now.'

'He has no choice, if you will it. And I shall furnish you with a maidservant to help you dress, provide you with the finest gowns and jewellery. You will need to convince, and you will need help with the fastenings. They are so complicated, these clothes, do you not think?' She held up a fold of the opulent dress she must have known Mercia could never afford. 'But keep your attentions to Sir William, do you hear? The King is inclined to younger women than you, however beautiful.'

And you, thought Mercia. *How long now until you are usurped?*

'But His Majesty seems to trust that you can achieve his purpose here. Accept it for the honour that it is, Mrs Blakewood. The King has had little call to put his faith in many, besides his brother the Duke – and myself, of course.'

'No other person?' asked Mercia.

The younger woman's beauty vanished into the narrowing of her eyes.

'Lady Castlemaine? If I am to do this, I shall need to know everything of import.'

'Just that . . . jackanapes.' The grinding of her teeth was audible. 'Hyde.'

'The Earl of Clarendon?'

'Him.' She held up a quivering finger; even through the layers of her dress, it seemed her whole body had turned rigid. 'But be sure not to trust him yourself. As Charles's chief minister, he is free to attend the war council, and he receives its reports.' She pursed her red lips. 'You must be aware how he arranged for Charles to take a barren bride. He intends his own grandchildren to inherit the throne.'

Uncomfortable, Mercia looked to the fire. 'I know, my lady, that the Earl's daughter is sister-in-law to the King. But to be so devious as intentionally to—'

'Devious?' All the restraint in Lady Castlemaine fled, replaced by a rampant fury. 'You have no idea. Not about Clarendon, nor any of the men at this Court. Surviving in the palace . . . 'tis every bit as hard a battle as on the soldiers' fields.' She sighed and shook her head, as if to clear her angst. 'I merely urge caution. And to report to no one save myself or those I say we can trust.' Her dress brushed the floor as she turned to collect her book. 'Now I will see you installed forthwith, so you can best your obsequious uncle and return to your manor house.' She bestowed her with a piercing look. 'Where you belong.'

'Yes, my lady.'

'And remember, Mrs Blakewood. You may be here on the King's business, but I am in charge of the women of this Court. Take care not to cross me in mine.'

She broadened her smile as she swept from the room.

Mercia returned none of her own.

Chapter Three

The apartment was spacious, she would concede that. Huge, indeed, comprising three separate areas: a sitting room in which to pass the time, or to receive guests; a smaller space with a table, perhaps for dining, or playing at cards; and a bedroom, equipped with the largest silk-canopied bed Mercia had ever seen. Off the bedroom adjoined a partitioned wardrobe awaiting clothes and finery, and in the opposite corner, a sparse closet with a pot and an ample-sized hole in a wooden bench.

'Do you approve?' asked the richly dressed man at her side, switching his ostrich-feathered hat between his gloved hands.

''Tis somewhat different to the quarters we have been used to on board ship of late, Sir William. Much grander than the room I was given last night.' She looked up at him. 'These were not . . . were they?'

'My wife's?' A sadness passed his face. 'No. That would not have been proper.'

'Well then. I suppose I shall make the most of them.'

'This was not my idea, Mercia.' He bit his lip. 'I hope you realise that. I would have intervened in Southampton, had I known you had been led away.'

She ignored his beseeching look. 'It matters not whose idea it was. I am here.'

'Still, you must agree it is an excellent disguise for the mission at hand.' He drew himself up, his usual confidence reasserting itself. 'The King must value your wits indeed to grant you such a vital task.'

She approached the window to look through the diamond-paned glass. The view gave onto the Privy Garden below, familiar to her from a previous meeting with Sir William, its multiple grassy squares intersected by gravelled paths.

'Do you suppose the sundial is still . . . yes, it is. I had thought the King might replace it.'

'Oh, no. He has a passion for scientific pursuits.'

'I meant he might want to improve it.' She turned back round. 'Sir William, I think we should discuss my role here. For that is what it is – a role, not a truth.'

'It could be both.'

'I do not . . .' She took a deep breath. 'Even if I were . . . so inclined . . . I do not think it would be appropriate beyond what will be expected to maintain the pretence. You will have to visit me from time to time, but I hope for no further expectation on your part.'

'Mercia.' He smiled. 'We have been through much these past several months. May I be frank?'

'Of course.'

'Then you should know how my opinion of you has only increased. You have aided the King in a matter of import, uncovered a murderer and saved my own life. I cannot think of you in the same way as before. Our friendship is more than that now.' He cleared his throat. 'I expect nothing of you, save to enjoy my company and to accept my admiration. And then we shall see where our mutual benefit shall lead us. For now, I suspect you shall want to change your attire.' His eyes roved her drab-looking dress. 'I am told a maidservant is on her way with an array of clothes. But Mercia, heed me when I say Whitehall can be a dangerous place. It is full of suspicion and intrigue.'

'Lady Castlemaine said as much yesterday.'

He snorted; an unexpected reaction she had never heard of him before. 'Indeed. She is the expert.'

'You do not like her?'

'She is the King's mistress, Mercia, and so I am bound to like her. But you see how she toyed with you in bringing you here. I do not have to approve of her, and nor does all the Court, which fawns in her presence or else tolerates it.' He sniffed. 'But there are other, equally pretty women growing old enough now to catch the King's eye. She meddles in political affairs. One bad move on her part may be her downfall. Separate this task from her person. Take care not to become too involved.'

'No doubt there are those here who would work to expedite that fall.'

He replaced his hat, straightening a limp feather. 'You learn quickly, Mercia, as I knew you would. But believe me when I say be careful. Not solely your uncle will seek to undermine your presence.' He held her gaze: as often, a moment too long for her comfort. 'You are an attractive woman, I will never stop telling you that. But there are others who will not welcome such a new rival in Court, whether you intend to play that game or no.'

A muffled knock sounded at the door, or rather a kick, for as it swung open a pile of clothes seemed to enter of its own accord, obscuring the person carrying them in.

'Well.' Sir William stepped out of the servant's way. 'I shall leave you, then.' He gave Mercia a swift bow. 'If you need anything – there may be a thousand souls living in this palace, but truly I shall not be far.' He looked over the small tapestries dotting the walls. 'My, 'tis good to be back.'

He disappeared into the corridor, leaving the door ajar. Mercia turned to the new arrival, watching through an inner doorway as, her back turned and head down, the maid deposited the clothes on the bed, deftly ensuring no sleeve was left overhanging the sides. Then she re-entered the principal room and dropped to a curtsey. To her immediate embarrassment, Mercia felt a flash of unintended surprise.

'My Lady Blakewood,' the servant said.

Recovering herself, Mercia smiled. 'I am not a lady by title.'

The maid looked uncertain. 'That is how I have been told to address you, my lady, and so if you please, then I must.'

As she talked, she held her eyes averted. Mercia imagined how foolish she herself must have appeared on meeting Lady Castlemaine. Fawning, as Sir William had said.

'If those are your instructions.' Wondering why her curious spymaster was so keen to upgrade her standing, she tilted her head. 'You are the maidservant Lady Castlemaine promised me?'

The servant bowed lower.

'Then please, stand up in my presence.'

The maid raised herself up. She was pretty, her brown eyes keen, her skin and hair black under a loosely-tied coif.

'What is your name?' Mercia asked.

'Phibae,' she replied.

'And you are to serve me while I am here?'

Another low nod.

'Well, Phibae. What have you brought me in the other room?'

'Let me show you, my lady. I hope you approve of—'

'Hey!'

Mercia frowned as a tumult in the corridor carried her attention to the open door. To her astonishment, Nicholas was standing in the threshold, rubbing at his arm. But instead of entering, he set his face and disappeared into the corridor.

'Hey!' he repeated. 'Come back here and do that again.'

Motioning to Phibae to remain where she was, Mercia followed after him. Where the corridor turned left beside a splendid porphyry vase, two guards had halted in comical fashion, their boot heels suspended above the floor. As one they turned, but broke off their retort as they noticed Mercia hurrying towards them.

The taller cleared his throat. 'Another parcel for you, my lady.'

'Another what?'

'Another parcel.' The guard jerked his head at Nicholas. 'Delivered on the orders of Lady Castlemaine. She said we should call him that if you asked.'

The annoyance deepened on Nicholas's face. 'Did she also say to use your fists?'

'If you will permit us, my lady.' The guards bowed, continuing on their way. Nicholas made to pursue, but she held out a cautioning arm.

'This is not Cow Cross,' she warned.

'No.' He halted. 'No, it's not. At least I had a chance to go back there – for all of two hours, mind. I got off the coach from Southampton, went home, and before I knew it those shabberoons turned up to bring me here.'

She squeezed his arm. 'Did you see your daughter?'

'Yes.' He broke into a smile. 'Growing bigger now. She turned five while we were away.'

'I am so glad, Nicholas.' A deep warmth coursed through her. 'Truly.'

'My old lodgings are taken, mind. That bastard Dapps stole them as soon as he could.' He looked around. 'My, Mercia, I've been to some strange places with you. New York, New England. Now here. My old mother would have died with the surprise of it, if she was living still.'

'This will probably be the strangest.' She lowered her voice. 'What happened? Lady Castlemaine suggested you might be able to attend me here, but I did not think . . . have you been told why they brought you?'

'Of course not. All I know is those . . . guards said I would be dressed up so fine I should watch my arse.' He looked at her, his sharp expression a mixture of accusation and relief. 'When I went back for you in Southampton, you'd already gone. I had to force my way onto the first coach to come after. Good thing I had some coin. Sir William took care of your luggage.'

'I know.' She sighed. 'Nicholas, Lady Castlemaine has made clear I have little choice in the matter she has required of me. But you do. There is no need to stay if you do not wish it.'

'I can hardly refuse the King. The guards told me that, at least.'

'I see.' Pleased he was there, she rested a hand on his shoulder to steer him towards her rooms. 'Then I shall explain later. Come, meet the maid I have been given. You should see the clothes she has brought.'

Removing her hand, she led him through the door. The tiniest exclamation escaped from under his breath.

'Nicholas,' she said, 'this is Phibae. Phibae, this is Mr Wildmoor. He has assisted me before and it seems is to do so again.'

'Pleased to meet you,' said Nicholas.

Phibae bowed. 'Mr Wildmoor.'

'Well,' said Mercia, after a brief silence in which the two studied each other. 'Do you know where your lodging is, Nicholas?'

'Not as such. And – damn, I forgot.' He glanced at Phibae. 'I just need to . . .' – he jerked his thumb behind him – 'in the corridor.'

He disappeared again, leaving Mercia to stare. 'Phibae,' she said as she followed. 'Perhaps if you could hang my clothes?'

'Very good, my lady.'

Nicholas was loitering outside the door, looking nervously back the way the guards had gone.

'What is this?' she said. 'I should think a man who has seen the Indians would not be much troubled by—'

'God, no.' He shook his head. ''Tis not that, not at all. I forgot to warn you who I passed when I was being marched over.' Then his face fell. 'Too late. He's already here.'

She turned to look at the reason for his discomfort. Her own expression plummeted to a darker state than his.

'Well, Mercia,' came a man's steady voice. 'Still consorting with this churl? And here I was thinking you had finally taken my instructions to heart and taken rooms near Sir William Calde.'

A sharp rigidity raced through her being. But she held herself well, unsurprised he had found her so soon. At the end of the passage, a soberly dressed man was staring from beside the porphyry vase, and behind him, an entourage of women.

Steeling herself, she took a deep breath.

'Uncle.'

'So the rumours are true.' He sniffed as he approached, his perfumed gloves scenting the air. 'You are returned, at last.'

'As you see, Uncle.' She glanced down at his side, at the cane he was gripping. 'I am pleased to see you are recovered.'

'Recovered?' He barked out the repeated word, causing his cane to slip, and for a moment he lost his balance. Pushing aside the maid beside her, the woman hovering nearest spoke in his place.

'I would not have believed it,' she said, 'had Francis not told me himself. As soon as you are back in England, you install yourself at Court. Did your father's disgrace not dissuade you from such brazenness?'

'Aunt,' said Mercia, not rising to her taunt. 'It would appear that affairs have changed.'

'Not by much.' Her voice was cold and slow, as much a contrast to her husband's anger as her white hair contrasted with the darkness of her maid's. 'You would do well not to forget yourself, or whose patronage your uncle enjoys.'

'I know he has powerful masters. But I count others as my own support, as you know.'

Lady Simmonds' companions shared a worried glance. In the ensuing silence, Mercia studied her aunt's face. Her speech was forthright, but there was something uneasy in her demeanour, however much she was trying to hide the disquiet through her bitter words.

'I was about to change my clothing, Aunt,' she said. 'You see how I still wear my travelling dress. If you will excuse me.'

'We will not.' Recovering his wits, Sir Francis turned his head, commanding with a brisk nod that his wife's friends leave. The younger of the two frowned, but she did as she was told, the other following close behind.

'Go to my rooms, Nicholas,' ordered Mercia, as her aunt dismissed her maid. 'I will arrive presently.'

He hesitated, but then retreated through the open doorway. At the same time, the threshold seemed to brighten, as though a shadow had lifted from the opposite side. Paying it little heed, Mercia turned around.

'What then, Uncle, did you wish to discuss?'

By now Sir Francis had drawn himself up. Lady Simmonds parted her lips, but a rap of his cane on the floor cut off her reply.

'It would have been easier for you if I had died of that wound,' he said, his jaw lightly trembling. 'Alas, I am merely wounded. Forced to walk forever with the aid of this poisonous stick of wood, obliged to return from America before I could aid the King in furthering his ventures. All because you disobeyed me.'

His knuckles whitened as he tightened his grip, but Lady Simmonds laid her hand on his, calming his shaking somewhat.

'Uncle,' said Mercia. 'I never wished you harm, but if we cannot speak with civility then perhaps we should not speak at all.'

Shrugging off his wife, Sir Francis sidled closer. 'You may think you have the King's support, but His Majesty listens to his brother, and I am yet in the Duke's favour. I will not allow you to shame me, not in this, or in anything.' He steadied his voice. 'I know why you are here. The Earl of Clarendon has informed me of the . . . problem. You may think your mind is quick, but you are no match. Keep yourself to Sir William. I am much more practised in affairs of the Court than a novice like you.'

With a ferocious glare of hate, he returned the way he had come, leading his wife out of view. Her anger stoked, Mercia rubbed at her temples, tracing her fingertips across the tiredness of her eyes. Then she raised her head and re-entered her rooms. A scuttling sounded from further along the corridor, but nobody was there when she flicked up her eyes to look.

Taking short breaths, she crossed the principal room. Nicholas was standing apart, leaning against a fine oaken table, clasping his hands as he watched Phibae through the bedroom door. Hearing her enter, he turned his head, absent-mindedly tucking a loose shirt fold into his breeches.

'Is all well?' he asked.

She blew out her irritation through her cheeks. 'In a way, I am glad he came, as I was not looking forward to our first encounter. Now I can stop worrying how it might unfold, for I know it went ill. But let us not dwell on that now.'

She looked into the bedroom herself. Phibae was busy holding up dresses, examining them for defects and, finding none, hanging them in the closet.

'My God.' Despite herself, Mercia could not help but laugh. 'I cannot . . . really, those are too splendid. But no.' She shook her head. 'I must remember 'tis but for a short while, as part of the disguise.'

Nicholas smiled. 'I should find my lodgings, leave you to settle in.'

'Let me spend a half-hour with Phibae, to wash and put on one of these fine dresses, and then I will ask that she help you find your way. Just sit down and . . . admire those miniatures over there.'

'Oh yes.' He took a seat. 'Just what I like!'

It took a little longer than she thought, but an hour later, Mercia was staring at an armchair beside the bed draped with the drab brown dress she had been wearing for weeks. In contrast, the outfit Phibae had conjured up for her was magnificent, and she felt refreshed – properly refreshed, not the half-hearted comfort of a splash of water that had been all she could administer of late. She smelt of rose and lavender, her hair was brushed, and although not yet styled to perfection for lack of time, the ends were more finely curled than they had been for months, while the simple addition of two slender pieces of wire above both ears was holding up seamless rows of ringlets on either side of her rigid topknot. Her face was painted, made up in simple reds and whites, although she had refused Phibae's suggestion that she don a diamond-shaped face patch, not wanting to take that step yet.

But it was her dress that enthralled her the most. It was blue, cerulean blue, as though she had wrapped herself in the very ocean she had been crossing these past two months. The stays underneath were fresh and crisp, her bodice was blinding white, and her collar was folded in a multiplicity of fabric as bright as the silver necklace that finished it off. On her fingers, beside the mourning ring for her father that she wanted to wear still, she added a second band, gold with a ruby at its centre. And this, she thought in astonishment, was merely one of many such outfits Phibae had carried in.

'My, Phibae,' she said, examining herself in a mirror. 'Who is this person you have created?'

'The clothes fit you well, my lady.' Phibae took up the old brown dress; Mercia could see every stain, every small rip in it now. 'Shall I take this to be laundered?'

'Please. And would you help Nicholas find where he is to sleep?' She turned her face, examining her side profile. 'I should like to spend some time here by myself.'

Phibae curtsied. 'My lady.'

Hearing them pull the door to the corridor shut, Mercia set down the mirror and wandered in her finery to the sitting room window that overlooked the Privy Garden below. If she craned her neck, she could just about see the corner of the palace where she knew Daniel was being smartly dressed in his turn, ready to be introduced to the boys of the Court. That she could see a little of his chambers was happy comfort, and unlike last year in New England, this time he was close at hand, and she could see him whenever she chose.

But for all the advantages, she knew where she would prefer him to be: home, at the manor house in Halescott, where he belonged – where she did. For all the fanciness of her clothes, of the splendour of her position at Court, all this was but temporary, and it did not feel quite right. True, she had worn fine dresses before, but never this dazzling, and not often in her adult life, conditioned as it had been by Cromwellian-leaning relatives. For all the opulence, she felt somehow naked, as though the real Mercia inside were covered by some fake varnish. But that was what this was, a disguise: a false image to delude the world into believing she was someone she was not.

Forgetting her outfit, she cast her eye around the bedroom, her gaze settling on Nathan's letter. Placed carefully on a side table, it was resting against a Venetian glass vase of as many pretty hues as the flowers within it.

She sat in her silk on her leather-backed chair, listening to the ticking of the nearby clock, and felt of a sudden alone.

Chapter Four

'And that woman, there, is Lady Grace Allcot, Sir Geoffrey's wife.'

Through the slits of her simple red mask, Mercia looked on yet another grandly dressed woman, this one draped in scarlet, her dress swallowing up the floor.

'She appears bored.'

Sir William laughed. 'Lady Allcot has too much wit to tolerate more than an hour of obsequious Court chatter. But then that wit has caused her trouble in the past.' He glanced down. 'In the same way you would cause trouble, I think.'

'Oh yes?'

'Asking questions. Wanting to . . . know things.'

'How awful of her,' she said, lowering her mask. But Sir William was smiling.

'You know as well as I do that while husbands seek their wife's advice in private, they prefer she keep her opinions silent in public. Sir Geoffrey is one such man.'

'My husband never much minded.'

'No. But then you have a way of bringing men around to your way of thought.'

'Sir William,' she admonished, sipping the last of her drink. 'What is this wine? I have never tasted it before. It – tingles.'

'Do you like it? Champagne, I believe it is called. The French insist it should be still, but if it ferments long enough it fills with bubbles, and that is the way many here prefer it.'

'Then I count myself among them.' She restored her mask. 'Now, you will have to take me through these women again. I can scarcely remember their names, let alone much about their persons, and if I am to believe one of them is Virgo, I needs must recall it all.'

He took her empty glass, setting it on a table, holding her gloved hand in front. 'Let us play our pretence a little first. It is expected that guests talk at these gatherings. And that way you can meet your quarry face to face.'

'Or mask to mask.'

She allowed him to lead her into the den: the Court of King Charles the Second, sovereign of England, Scotland, Ireland and, so asserted the tradition of his coronation title, France, although she wondered what the Comte de Comminges, the current French emissary to the Court, standing by the fireplace, thought of that – that, and the unnaturally sparkling wine. Like the French delegation, she and Sir William had been loitering at the sides of the gargantuan ballroom that was the King's stone Banqueting House, the great man pointing out who was married to whom, and who had which position at Court, as the various nobles assembled.

It felt awkward to touch the hand of the man who had at one time desired her for his mistress – and finally succeeded, she thought wryly, if only in deception. As they moved towards the centre of the ballroom, he let drop her fingers, lightly brushing his against hers. Did he still want deception to become truth? She did not know, and did not much care to find out.

'Sir Peter,' said Sir William, as they approached a chuckling quintet. 'A magnificent gathering. Is the King due soon?'

The unmasked man broke seamlessly from his conversation. 'Is this . . . ?' he wondered, eyes flitting to Mercia, ignoring Sir William's question. 'Sir Rowland's daughter, returned from America?'

Mercia gave him a slight bow. 'I am honoured you know me, Sir Peter.'

'I knew your father. I am . . . sorry for what happened to him. When we found out the truth of his dishonour . . . how he was betrayed . . . it was a most appalling discovery.'

'What is this?' perked up a young woman at his side, veiled by a sumptuous turquoise mask.

Sir Peter glanced at her and smiled. 'Nothing that need trouble you, my dear.'

The young woman's mask slipped as he turned to Sir William, revealing her flushing cheeks. She appeared scarcely into her twenties, her unblemished skin taut and surprisingly tanned. Mercia sympathised with a conspiratorial roll of her eyes.

'A great success in New York, Sir William,' Sir Peter was continuing. 'The King and the Duke are mightily pleased. The first prize in this war, all told.'

'Although strictly said, we were not at war at the time,' smiled Sir William.

'And a prize of a different nature for you, it seems.' Sir Peter again looked Mercia up and down: at her face, at her dress, at her chest. Now it was the young woman's turn to bestow a reassuring wink.

Sir William laughed. 'Indeed. It would seem persistence pays in the end.'

She did not like the way the conversation was going. 'Sir William was telling me, Sir Peter,' she interrupted, 'how you serve on the

King's new war council. That must weigh much on your mind.'

His eyes never wavered from her chest. 'Do not worry, my dear. You can rest safe at Court, sure we will bring this war to a swift conclusion.'

'And I see another member of your council over there,' she persisted, 'standing on his own. The man with the green doublet. Sir Stephen Herrick, I believe?'

'Oh, yes.' Looking up, Sir Peter's smile faded. 'I do not know why, but he is always in green. Still, a fine admiral. This war will be fought at sea, my friends, and Sir Stephen's expertise will be invaluable.' He leant back in. 'Or so says Sir Stephen. But now I think I see . . . yes, the Duchess herself. That means the Duke will be arriving soon . . . come, my dear, we should pay her our respects while we can.'

With a waggle of his finger, he beckoned at his companion to follow. As the pair walked off, their former group broke up, leaving Mercia and Sir William alone.

'Sir Peter Shaw,' said Sir William. 'You might remember him. When Sir Francis brought you to Court that time, before you eluded him to intercept the King – Sir Peter was one of the men you saw in the corridor with the Duke of York and myself.'

She thought back to the previous year. 'Yes, I remember. As pompous then as he remains now, it seems. Did you say before that the young woman with him was his mistress?'

'So I am told, although she was not so when we left for America. He has had several since the death of his wife, but I have not seen Miss Whent before today.'

'Lavinia Whent,' she recalled from his earlier description. 'A shame you know little about her, given what she might be.'

'To speak true, I am rather behind with happenings at Court. 'Tis nigh on a year since I was last here. But I do know Sir Stephen. Shall I introduce you?' He retook her hand and she replaced her mask. 'He is still on his own, the poor devil. I do not think he likes these gatherings much.' He laughed. 'He was ever a Puritan at heart, if not in deed or in thought.'

Mercia clicked her fingers. 'I knew I had heard the name before. When my father served Cromwell, Sir Stephen was a senior officer in his navy even then.'

Sir William looked impressed. 'You remember much, Mercia.'

'Merely some trifles. As I recall, Sir Stephen was highly thought of.'

'He fought for the King in the war, with fervour, but his first love was always the fleet. When Cromwell took power, Sir Stephen accepted the situation and thrived in it. But now the King is restored, he need not hide his preferences.' He stepped aside to allow a golden-wigged partygoer past. 'He commands much loyalty among the sailors. If you ask me, he knows more about the navy than his master the Duke, though 'tis the Duke who is Lord High Admiral.'

She looked at him askance. 'For a man who claims unfamiliarity with the Court, it has not taken you long to become reacquainted.'

'A compliment, Mercia. I must be doing something right.'

By now they had reached their prey. Sir Stephen Herrick was a tall, slender man of imposing bearing, his celadon-green doublet the spark of colour in an otherwise subdued outfit. Unlike many of those present, who were following the King's lead in donning extravagant wigs, he had chosen to flaunt his real head of hair, as thick as any of the artificial pieces. When he turned to Sir William to respond to his greeting, his unmasked eyes were as sharp as his manner was bright.

'Sir William!' He clapped the great man on the shoulder, evident pleasure in his smile. 'I had hoped to see you tonight. I want to hear of your travels across the ocean. And you will be joining us on the war council, no?' His eyes roved to rest on Mercia. 'But forgive my prattle. Who is your companion?'

Sir William smiled. 'A delight to see you again, Stephen. This is Mrs Blakewood – Mercia. You may recall she accompanied us to America.'

Sir Stephen thought for a moment, his eyes darting left to right as though reading from a list. 'Ah, yes indeed.' He gave Sir William a complicit glance. 'And now returned with you also.'

Mercia bowed. 'An honour to meet you, Sir Stephen. You served with my father at one time, I believe.'

'Your father was a good man, Mrs Blakewood. We disagreed much, about most things indeed, but on the need to keep this country strong we were of one mind. I am sorry for the fate that befell him. The King is troubled by it, as are we all.'

'Thank you,' she said, hoping she would not have to endure the same pitying conversation with every man of the Court. 'But I hope some of that can now be put right.'

'You are here, are you not?' Sir Stephen looked between them as another guest joined them. 'Ah, Mrs Blakewood, allow me to present my wife, Anne.'

Mercia turned to see a woman of senior years standing directly behind them. Like all the women, she was splendidly attired, her golden dress and silver jewellery a more glittering imitation of the patch of sun and stars that adorned her left cheek. Her auburn-flecked grey hair cascaded so smoothly over her shoulders it was as though a waterfall were gliding over its precipice, the tips splayed as if the foam in the pool below.

'Lady Herrick,' said Mercia. 'You look magnificent.'

'I look as good as my maids have made me.' She lowered her mask. 'My husband and Sir William have no idea. They have never been required to haul around a bushel of silk in the guise of a dress.'

'It suits you well.'

'Yours also. As is to be expected of Lady Castlemaine's new favourite.'

'Oh, I do not think I am—'

'That is what everyone is saying. And so it must be true.' She smiled. 'Stephen, take my hand and lead me to Helen. 'Tis much easier to walk with your support.'

Mercia watched them across the room. 'Is that what people think?' she said. 'That I am Lady Castlemaine's . . . pet?'

'I am afraid you will encounter such condescension,' Sir William replied. 'Any woman newly arrived at Court can expect resistance from those who are established. And you being so—' He chuckled under his breath. 'By the Lord, Mercia. You must see this.'

He nodded in the direction of an emaciated woman who was entering the hall, hand in hand with a more simply attired man. Impossibly thin, she was draped in a lurid yellow dress, an oversized collar sprawling awkwardly over her shoulders. Atop her brown hair perched a gaudy silver tiara, but it was impossible to see her face, for a rose veil covered her looks.

'That is Cornelia Howe,' he said. 'Sir Stephen Herrick's niece, and by all accounts a woman with a fiery temper.'

'That is Cornelia?' said Mercia, watching as the couple glided off. 'How can you tell?'

'Because she is with her husband, Thomas Howe, and . . . because of the way she is dressed.'

'Indeed? I had not expected her to dress like that.'

'Then what did you expect?'

'Someone less . . . extravagant, from what you told me earlier. You seemed to suggest she was unappealing.'

'I should say that was unappealing.'

She laughed. 'My, Sir William, you had best be careful, or people might take you for a spiteful tattler.'

'I hope not. Ah.' He raised a finger to point at the far side of the room. 'Look there. Sir Geoffrey Allcot.'

She craned her neck to observe two men as they retreated from a loud group of highly coiffured women. One put his hand on the other's shoulder, turning him towards the wall, and they began to talk.

'I wonder what they are discussing,' Sir William mumbled, more to himself than to Mercia. 'The war, no doubt.'

'Which one is Sir Geoffrey?'

'What?' He glanced down. 'Forgive me. He on the left is the Earl of Clarendon, the King's Chief Minister. And the other is Sir Geoffrey. The fattest man in England.'

'You do not much like him?'

'You may call me old-fashioned, but I think if you wish to serve on the King's war council then perhaps you should have at least some experience of war.'

'Then why is he on the council?'

'Because he makes the King rich, Mercia. Or more rightly, the King's brother the Duke. He is a man of enterprise, an ocean trader, one of the new breed at Court. A man of vast profit and riches, rather than of soldiery and honour.'

'A trader in what, to bring such wealth?'

He hesitated. 'In people.'

'People?' Her mask slipped. 'You do not mean . . . ?'

'Slaves. Africans. 'Tis the Duke's new venture. It has developed somewhat even while we were away, and Sir Geoffrey is one of its strongest advocates.' He sucked in his lips. 'He and his fellows style themselves the Royal Adventurers. They send ships to the west coast of Africa, load them with men, with women and children too, and they send them to our colonies across the Atlantic. It is extremely . . . profitable. Especially now sugar is in such demand and needs their labour to work it.' He looked at her askance. 'Can you guess which other nation claims colonies in Africa?'

'I know the Dutch control much of the Guinea coast.'

'Precisely. But if we were to oust them, then we would have access to the whole of that coast, and with it, its pitiable bounty. And that, my dear Mercia, is why Sir Geoffrey is on the war council. The Royal Adventurers have a powerful stake in this conflict, and their master is the Duke.'

The image of the Indians she had met in America came to mind – of the abuses they had suffered, of their warnings of conflict. 'My father used to say that whatever their provenance all men should be free. And after what we saw in New England . . .'

'That is not for me to say, Mercia. There are those who oppose it, but they are few. What price the life of a heathen black when power and profit stand to benefit? And do not forget, it afflicts the white man also. Think of the Barbary slavers on the edges of the Mediterranean. I knew men myself who were taken captive there and never returned.'

Uncomfortable, she restored her mask. 'That aside, it would seem Sir Geoffrey and his like would benefit nothing from passing secrets to the Dutch.'

'While war rages there can scarcely be trade at all, and if the Dutch win that coast, it will cease for the Adventurers completely. But men's motives are often duplicitous, as you well know.' He took another glass of wine from a passing page and sipped, speaking with his mouth against the rim. 'So besides myself, the King and the Duke, those are the three men of the war council. Sir Peter Shaw, Sir Stephen Herrick, and Sir Geoffrey Allcot. Whether intentionally or through Virgo's manipulation, one of those must be the source of her intelligence.'

Bubbles fizzed on her tongue as Mercia took a sip from her own fresh glass. 'Lady Castlemaine said Virgo was close to the man. So I will begin with the obvious, and simply speak with the women she could be. She has to be near to compile her reports so promptly.'

'It still leaves five, so you said.'

She nodded. 'Sir Stephen's wife, Lady Herrick, and his niece, Cornelia Howe. Sir Geoffrey's wife, Lady Allcot, and his mistress, Helen Cartwright – Lady Cartwright, moreover, who is absent tonight. And finally Lavinia Whent, Sir Peter's mistress. Nobody else is close enough at hand. Sir Geoffrey's daughters are abroad or in the North, and Sir Peter only has sons.'

'While the Herricks are as childless as I am. I doubt Anne Herrick will appreciate being thought a suspect.'

'Unless she is the guilty one, she need never know. Nor that young woman with Sir Peter. But they must all be considered if I am to consolidate the King's favour and rid myself of my uncle for good and all.' She shook her head. 'The noble Sir Francis. There he is now.'

She looked to the far side of the room where her uncle was standing amidst a group of well-dressed men, deep in conversation. Staring directly at her, one of the younger in his company caught her eye. He lowered his mask, breaking into a growing smile; even at this distance she could tell he was attractive, his thick, black hair and penetrating eyes exactly the type she admired. She found herself inclining her head in acknowledgement of his interest, until she remembered Sir William was at her side and she made herself look away.

Where was her aunt, she wondered, unable to find Lady Simmonds near her husband, but then she jumped as a trumpet droned from a balcony directly above, and a malicious part of her was glad her aunt had committed the error of missing the King's imminent entrance. Too glad, she chided herself: was the intrigue of the Court rubbing off on her so soon?

The call of another trumpet joined the first, and through an entrance barely ten feet down, two pages stood aside as a grand couple walked in: an immensely tall man in a vibrant black wig, and a much shorter woman, her attire so elegant she was almost floating at his side. Mercia stepped from behind Sir William, curtseying as the regal pair strolled by, and flicking up her eyes she beheld the man who held the power over her future, the King walking with his Queen. Had he noticed her as he passed, or was that her imagination?

After the King and Queen came the Duke of York, joining the Duchess his wife, and in their train a number of ladies-in-waiting, Lady Castlemaine at their head. Presently the royal group halted, and the elderly man who had been conversing with Sir Geoffrey took a pace forward and bowed.

She could hear Sir William scoff. 'Still she makes her own father bow in her presence.'

'Who?' she whispered.

'The Duchess of York. It may be required, but she could spare him the embarrassment in his elder years.'

Mercia looked again upon the Earl of Clarendon. He was pulling himself up from his excessive bow, clutching his waist.

'Why is not Clarendon on the war council?' she mused, relaxing as the King's party moved off. 'Does the Duke seek to bar his influence as Lady Castlemaine would intend?'

'He is not a member as such, but he can attend if he wishes. Indeed it was he who suggested I retake my own seat, for my knowledge of the Dutch that I learnt in New York. He sits rather on the Foreign Affairs Committee, to which the war council reports. The King and the Duke are naturally free to partake in both.'

'So the war council has no real power?'

'But massive influence. And the council members are . . . should I say were . . . Mercia? Are you listening to me?'

Ignoring Sir William's pique, Mercia was staring at a commotion in the corner of the room, where a gradual murmuring was taking flight, growing in volume alongside a series of frowns and a shrugging of confused shoulders. At its epicentre, a footman was leaning against a liveried servant; even from here Mercia could tell how he was agitated, his head shaking, his face pale. Then another, more certain servant broke from the group, and unheeding the demands of his betters, he strode across the room, halting directly before her uncle. As she raised her eyebrow in surprise, the servant bent in to speak to him in confidence.

On his new cane, Sir Francis stumbled. Applying too much force, the stick shot out from beneath him and he staggered to the floor. Swiftly, the efficient page stooped to help him up, and placing himself as a substitute staff, he led Sir Francis away while the Court looked on in bemusement. Then in echo of the growing murmur, a series of gasps spread from where he had been standing, until the waves reached Mercia, looking towards the door through which Sir Francis had been led in obvious confusion.

''Tis Lady Simmonds,' said the first person she could overhear.

'What of her?' said a second.

'She is grievously hurt. A blow to the head. It seems she has been attacked.'

Chapter Five

Despite the warm comfort of her bedsheets, she lay awake for much of the night, agonising over her aunt. When morning came, she splashed rosewater about her body and put on bodice and dress, this time choosing a more subdued, purple outfit, slit down the middle to reveal a fine lace petticoat, its whiteness seemingly taken from the pattern of snowflakes Phibae applied to her cheek.

Aiming for her aunt's chambers, she strode out into the palace, but she quickly became lost. Whitehall was huge, comprising thousands of rooms, stretching for half a mile along the course of the Thames between its slow curves at Westminster and Charing Cross. Rooms were built on rooms, corridors atop stairs, balconies jutting over the river, some with a view of the King's moored yacht. She was sure the courtiers she passed were laughing as she hesitated at each junction, wondering which way she should turn.

Conceding defeat, she found a helpful page, who told her the way: back from where she had come. And so she resumed her dance, waltzing left down this passage, carousing right down that, until finally she came to the closed door she was almost hoping not to reach.

With a light knock, she groaned open the heavy wood, sliding her head through the gap. It was dark within, the curtains drawn, but in the adjoining room a candle was burning, the light shining beneath the connecting door. As she crossed towards it a figure stirred to her left, and she paused as her uncle awoke with a single grunt of a snore.

'Is that you, Faith?' he asked, his voice lightly shrill.

''Tis Mercia, Uncle. I hoped to see my aunt.'

'Mercia.' The three syllables dripped with his bitterness. 'I thought you were that new servant of Margaret's.'

'How is she? My aunt.'

'Not well, if you care. She was struck devilish hard.'

'Of course I care. Do you know who did it?'

Grasping the cane at his side, he staggered to his feet and hobbled to the window.

'No.'

She waited in vain for more. 'But she will live?'

'Yes.' He opened the drapes and stared through the glass. 'Now you can go.'

'Uncle, I merely wanted to find out how my aunt was faring. I have lain awake all night worrying—'

'Worrying?' He spun on his cane to face her. 'Worrying – you?' The morning light accentuated his reddening face, his eyes narrowing to slits of black. 'Mercia, follow me into the corridor.'

She did as he bade her, walking behind him as he limped down the passage to enter a smaller room stuffed full of books and charts. He stood by the doorway, looking into the air, anywhere but at her, and when she had come through he pushed the door shut.

'Mercia,' he said. 'Let us have this discussion once, and once only. I am ashamed to call you my niece.'

'Must we act like this?' She sighed. 'I told you last year, I would not abandon my home to your illegitimate claim. Return it to me now, as is my right, and this animosity can be over.'

His knuckles blanched on the head of his cane. 'You be done with it. Move in with Sir William, as I wanted from the start.'

'I have, it would seem.'

'Not in pretence,' he scowled. 'In truth. You want wealth and houses – take it from him.'

'Sir William and I have become close these past months, Uncle, but not as you would wish it. Your hopes of using me to win his influence are over.'

'Listen hard.' His fist shook as he tightened his grip. 'I will not be undone by you, the child of my sister! Halescott Manor is mine now in law. The King is not likely to force me from it.'

'Only one person here has pleased the King of late. Nor is your infirmity my fault, even if you have convinced yourself that it is.'

'Dare you speak to me of the King?' He raised his cane, only to strike it against the floorboards. On a shelf behind him, a pile of musty papers jumped. 'You sailed to America to spite me, nothing less. I shall not forgive it. Not while I remain master of this family, while you are bound to obey, or you should be.'

She folded her arms. 'If you say I have tried to spite you, you have brought it upon yourself. But I have lived through too much now to be cowed by you, relation or no.'

His face trembled, and he made to move towards her, but he stumbled after one pace and was forced to stop.

'Mercia, I swear – it shall not be long now before I am rid of you. The King will never grant you back your house.'

She cocked her head. 'My house?'

'Get out!' He abandoned all composure, his raised voice sure to be heard in the adjoining rooms. 'Perhaps when you have pried further into this ring of spies it will be you lying hurt, and not my precious Margaret. Except perhaps you will be dead!'

She looked at him open-mouthed. 'You are changed, Uncle, even for you. I no longer care to . . . I will not—'

But words were impossible. Sickened at his hatred, she marched from the room, striding fiercely along the corridor to the foot of a marble staircase, clutching the edge of a granite-topped table with such force she could feel its sharpness digging into her ungloved palm. Head bowed, she breathed in and out, willing herself to be calm.

'Are you well, my lady?' asked a passing maid.

She took a deep breath, eyes closed, before nodding and forcing a smile. She continued on, wanting to walk, turning this way and that. Her uncle's fury had stoked an urgent need for action – to do something, anything – and she decided to set her inflamed zeal to good use by seeking out the women she wanted to question. And besides, she reflected, it was not just her uncle that could inspire her passions. She was English, by God's truth. If there was something she could do to help protect the nation, she would strive her utmost to do it.

But which woman to attempt first? There were five principal suspects, as far as she could tell, and while four of those five she had seen at the ball, she had spoken with but two. Determining to build on her modest complicity with the mistress of Sir Peter Shaw, she selected Lavinia Whent as her initial target. Another bored page indicated the way, and she mounted what seemed to be an everlasting staircase, catching her breath as she finally came out onto the magnificent landing at the top. Recalling how the last time she had climbed such a height had been along a spry waterfall in the wilds of New England, she was about to press on when a tittering of court women made her pause and turn her head.

'See,' one of the party was observing. 'How he is handsome, for one of his sort.'

'Somewhat thin,' replied another. 'But charming.'

'I think he goes well with me,' said a third. 'Although he is slow, and must learn to accept his place. Quite incapable of reading a thing.'

Hovering a little back, Mercia craned her neck to view the object of the women's discussion. Sitting at the side of the last to speak, beneath an Italianate statue of a perfect male youth, a teenage boy was staring out onto the landing. Although finely dressed, the agitation in his widening eyes was apparent.

'Yes, Helen, he goes well with your outfit,' said the first woman. 'Much better looking than that fool of Rebecca's.'

'Shall I keep him, then?' said the third. 'These blacks can be irksome, but they match well with a ruby necklace, and they behave better than those dogs the King is so fond of.' She laughed. 'Heaven knows how they behave in Africa, but at least here they are trained not to shit all over the palace. He is getting old, I suppose, but I can use him for a year until I find another.'

The women looked on the boy as on a misbehaving cat. Still incensed by her uncle's behaviour, Mercia spoke up without much thinking.

'He is not a pet, you know.'

The women turned, their faces a kaleidoscope of combined amusement.

'That is precisely what he is,' said the boy's supposed mistress.

'And yet it would do you well to treat him with some dignity.'

'My, I should take care how you address me.' She leant forward and frowned. 'Are you not that middling churl who sailed to America?'

'I had that pleasure.'

She looked around her group and smiled. 'Then it would seem the ways of the savages there have infected you.'

'Savages?' As the women laughed, Mercia stepped forward. 'If you mean the Indians, then I grew to have a keen respect for their ways. They have as much nobility as—'

'Do you think I care to know? Go, leave us be.'

'So you can abuse this poor child some more?' Mercia's anger was now decidedly piqued. 'Perhaps I should stay until you learn manners of your own.'

One of the woman's friends sucked in through blackened teeth. 'Do you not know with whom you speak?'

'I care little with whom I speak. Be she the Duchess of York herself.'

The principal of the group rose. 'Come, ladies. Let us leave Mrs . . . Blakewood, I believe, with my black. They can converse in whatever base language they both share.' She threw Mercia a contemptuous glance. 'You will learn who I am soon enough.'

Without a thought for the boy, she walked to the staircase, affecting a deliberate gait: when she tripped on the top step, even her friends had to stifle a hasty laugh. But eventually the harpies vanished, leaving Mercia alone with the teenager.

'Hello,' she said. 'I am sorry about them.'

Perched on the edge of the plinth, he was as rigid as the statue above his head. Like the half-naked youth, his eyes were firmly fixed. She adjusted her dress and sat beside him.

'What is your name?' she asked.

'Tacitus, my lady,' he replied after a silence.

She smiled. 'Your name is as peculiar as mine. I am Mercia.'

'My Lady Blakewood.' He nodded, the slightest of bows. 'I heard you speak.'

'I hope I have not caused you any trouble with your mistress.'

'No, my lady.' He swung his feet against the plinth.

'How long have you been here, Tacitus? At the palace.'

'About a year, my lady.'

'With your mistress all that time?'

'Lady Cartwright is my second. I . . . am a gift from Sir Geoffrey.'

'That was Lady Cartwright?' Mercia threw back her head, narrowly avoiding the outstretched finger at the end of the statue's arm. 'By the Lord, I should have known. Sir Geoffrey Allcot's mistress. It gets worse.' She glanced at Tacitus askance. 'Her chambers are near, are they?'

'That is right, my lady.' Of a sudden he looked right at her. 'But I must return to her now, or she will be displeased.'

'Yes, of course.' She got to her feet, but Tacitus stayed put. 'Then you may go.'

The boy bounded from the plinth, his polished shoes echoing on the slippery floor, and he hurried after his mistress. Mercia was watching him leap the stairs when another voice made her jump.

'He is sixteen, you know. And they treat him like a piece of jewellery. An animal to coddle or chastise.'

The woman she had been hoping to find was standing almost alongside her. 'Miss Whent,' she exclaimed. 'I did not notice you approach.'

'I heard the commotion from within my rooms. I was trying to read, but this sounded more . . . entertaining.'

'Miss Whent,' she repeated. 'I am pleased to remake your acquaintance.'

'And the pleasure is all mine, and so on, and so on. Call me Lavinia, or else nothing at all.'

'I am sorry if I said—'

'I am jesting. Do not look so appalled.' She folded her arms. 'Now would be when you tell me your name. I did not get to learn it yesterday night.'

Mildly thrown by her abruptness, Mercia stammered her response. 'Mercia. Mercia Blakewood, Miss Whent.'

'I have already told you, Mercia, to call me Lavinia. I cannot abide these covers of formality. Miss this, Sir that.' She flicked at the lace of her wrist. 'Why do you care for what happens with the blacks?'

'I suppose . . .' Mercia stared into the distance, caught in an immediate reverie. 'I suppose 'tis because I have travelled. But a half year since, I was talking with the chief of a tribe of Indians, a majestic figure draped in a vast pair of eagle wings. How can I be like the women of this Court when I have seen that and they know nothing but their comforts?' She shook her head, dispelling her vision, of a sudden embarrassed. 'Forgive me, Miss – Lavinia. I do not mean to offend. I have been in a temper. I do not include you in that over-hasty judgement.'

'You do not offend. But you do entice. If you have the time, I should like to hear of your journeys. I grew up across the ocean myself.'

'Indeed?' For an instant, Mercia forgot why she had come. 'Where so?'

'In the Barbados, until I was sent to London to learn the art of being a lady. Now I have the joy of serving in the Duke of Cambridge's nursery.'

'The Duke of York's son. How old is he now?'

'Not far off his second birthday. Would you care to join me in my chambers?'

Pleased at the ease with which she had ingratiated herself, Mercia accompanied the young woman into her apartment. She was of an age with Lady Castlemaine, perhaps younger, and looking at her beauty, Mercia suddenly felt quite old. But then she reminded herself she was only thirty-three. Still life in me yet, she thought.

'Would you sit down?' said Lavinia. 'The armchair is quite comfortable.'

'Thank you,' said Mercia, glad to accept. 'Your chambers are most appealing.'

'They are, are they not? And not a single black boy to adorn them.' She winked. 'You acted boldly, speaking up for Tacitus. Although I am sure his mistress will not be best pleased with it.'

'She will not hit him, will she?'

'Hit him?' Lavinia furrowed her brow. 'That would affect the prettiness of his looks. And that, in turn, would affect Lady Cartwright's.' She removed the pointed top of a shining decanter. 'Some wine? 'Tis French, the best.'

You are supposed to be questioning this woman, thought Mercia. But she had endured a hard morning, and so—

'Why not?'

'Excellent.' Lavinia poured out two glasses of a grassy-coloured wine; the smell of hay filled the room, of gooseberries. 'I wager you did not drink much of this in America. It is simply superb.'

'Over there it was mostly ale, or water if we had to. Some rum from time to time. At least, that is what Nicholas liked to drink.'

'Nicholas?'

'My manservant.'

'You have a maid also, I hope?'

'Phibae is her name, although I doubt you know her.'

'But I do. Lady Castlemaine's jest, I take it?'

She frowned as she accepted a glass. 'I am not sure what you mean.'

'Oh come, Mercia. You are the woman who has consorted with Indians. Do you not see how she mocks you?' She took a seat beside her. 'These women little understand the difference between anyone who does not share the pallor of their skin. But it scarcely matters, for you have done well of it. Phibae is a fine maid, from what I have gathered.'

Mercia took a sip: the wine was as good as her hostess claimed. 'Do you know all the servants, Lavinia?' she asked casually.

Lavinia's jaw seemed to twitch. 'One or two. I would talk with the . . . servants, at home. I was interested in their ways.'

She nodded. 'Phibae has served well so far. Intelligent, it seems.'

'But no black boy to go with her?'

'Why, no.'

Lavinia tutted. 'All the best women at Court have them now. They compete for the most beautiful, the most charming. They want the boy who most enhances their looks.'

'But not yourself?'

'No. There was enough of that in the Barbados.' Her smile faded. 'If much worse.'

She examined her glass, turning it around in her many-ringed fingers. Her nails were flawless, and a diamond bracelet jangled against the base. But her eyes were motionless, staring at the wine as she swirled it.

'Why is he called Tacitus?' asked Mercia. 'That cannot be his true name.'

'Hmm?' Lavinia blinked. 'Heaven knows what his real name is. The fashion is for mistresses to give their blacks a classical name. Livy, Pliny. Virgil. Tacitus. The Lord alone knows why.'

'In America, the settlers often give the Indians a Christian name.' She took another sip. 'But they are like us, Lavinia: clever and proud. That boy, too. Tacitus. Treat him as Lady Cartwright does, and he will spend his life resenting the English, just as the Indians begin to do in America. War threatens there as surely as here.'

'They treat all of them like that. 'Tis an accessory to their costume, no more. They acquire the boys, lead them like hounds, and when they are grown too old, sixteen, perhaps seventeen if they still look young, they discard them.'

'What happens then?'

'What do you think? If they are lucky, they find service in London. If they are not, they are shipped to the Indies to join the rest of their sorry race and forced to work. You should see it there.' She turned away her face. 'I have stood at the docks of Bridgetown, watching hundreds tumble from the ships, withered and afraid. And then bought like cattle by men of vast wealth, who seek merely to be wealthier still. Put to work in the heat of the sun, given little nourishment, flogged at any transgression.' Her rings chinked loudly on her glass. 'Killed when their masters think they have gone too far in their requests to be treated like men. That is the fate that may await Tacitus and his like. That he serves in the palace is a temporary blessing, and a humiliation nonetheless.'

'In New England,' ventured Mercia, 'there were those who wanted to live in harmony with the Indians. Perhaps the same can happen in the Barbados, in time.'

'And what of those who would sooner wipe them all out? Did you not meet any of them?' She took a long breath. 'Forgive me. You did not come to talk of this.' She looked back and smiled. 'Tell me about Sir William Calde. He is an attractive man, for his age.'

Mercia studied the younger woman's face, but despite her impassioned speech she seemed perfectly tranquil. 'He is the same age as Sir Peter. I came to know him well on the ship back home.'

'A powerful man, too. I hear he has been reappointed to the war council?'

'I . . . believe so.' She held herself still. 'Sir William talks little of such matters with me.'

'Sir William?' Lavinia laughed. 'Does he make you call him that? With Peter, it is simply Peter, pompous though he may be.'

'Another man on the war council,' tried Mercia.

'Indeed.' Now it was Lavinia's turn to stare. 'He may be a fool at times, but he is a rich one. A widower, with the ear of the King. I am well rewarded for my . . . patience.'

'How so?'

'You know.' She held up her dress. 'But there are many incentives to being at Court, besides Peter. As long as the master does not know, eh?'

The wine was making Lavinia candid. 'Are you, then . . . with someone else too?'

She leant back in her seat. 'I will admit, I have a weakness for a tight doublet and breeches. But I would not worry. It will not take long for the men to sniff you out. You are quite the beauty.'

Mercia reddened. 'You make me sound like a dog.'

'Some of them would treat you like one, if you wished it. Even if you did not.'

'No doubt.' She realised she had half drained her glass. 'But no, I have no lover. Just Sir William.' She put a hand to her chin. 'What is it? I have not spilt . . . ?'

'No. 'Tis just that you suddenly seemed rather distant. When you said that, about not having a lover.' Lavinia pulled her knees towards her chin, as much as she could in her splendid dress. 'What then of your adventures? I long to hear of them, and I think this might play a part.'

Mercia looked across, unaware she had drifted into thought. But she would not miss this chance to prolong their conversation.

''Tis a long story, Lavinia.' She held out her glass. 'I suggest you replenish the wine.'

Chapter Six

Despite her request, Mercia took care not to drink too much more – it was still morning, after all – and although Lavinia clearly liked to help herself, nothing incriminating passed from the young woman's lips. Mildly disappointed, but determined to pursue her investigation, Mercia left an hour later to choose a second target, this time Lady Allcot, the woman whose husband was embroiled in the human trade of which Lavinia had so passionately spoken. But her luck had little changed, for Lady Allcot's chambers were empty of all but a maid.

'She was distressed at the attack on Lady Simmonds,' the girl explained. 'She left for Hampton Court this morning. She wants some country air.'

'With her husband?' asked Mercia.

'No. He's still here.'

'I do not suppose . . .' She leant against the wall, affecting her best smile. 'That is a pretty trinket you are wearing.'

The servant broke into a broad beam. 'This bracelet? Thank you, my lady.' She looked around. 'I shouldn't really be wearing it, but 'tis from my betrothed.'

'How lovely. Does he work in Whitehall?'

'No, my lady, he sweeps chimneys in town . . . oh. But you aren't wanting to know about that.'

'Still, 'tis a beautiful band.' She pretended to admire its weak lustre. 'Lady Simmonds, as you mention her, is my aunt.'

'Oh, my lady. I am sorry.'

'I wanted to speak with my uncle about what happened, but . . . well, he is distressed, as you can imagine. If there is anything you may happen to have heard, from any of the servants . . .'

The maid pursed her lips. 'Well, my lady, I'm sure I don't know the truth and all, but I heard some rumours from Faith this morning, Lady Simmonds' own maid.'

'Indeed?'

'They say' – her eyes roved left and right – 'they say she was struck with the hilt of a dagger, one of them ceremonious ones. Good thing it weren't the tip, is what I say. Who would do such a thing?'

'Who is "they"?'

'Well.' She folded her arms. 'Just people. Maids.'

'And how do they know about the dagger? It seems a strange weapon to use to land a blow.'

''Tis just what I heard, my lady, as you asked. But Lady Simmonds . . . she's been wandering the palace of late, and that ain't like her. She keeps herself to her rooms, most like. Especially while her husband's been overseas, the poor man.' Her eyes flicked away. 'I'm sorry for that too, my lady.'

'For what?'

'For your uncle. For him coming back with a cane and all.'

'I see. And is that all you know about my aunt?'

'All as I know, my lady.'

'Then thank you.' She made to move off. 'Do you know when Lady Allcot will be returned from Hampton Court?'

'She'll only be gone two days, my lady, perhaps three. She's away there often, but never for long.'

She nodded in thought. 'Is Lady Herrick's apartment near?'

'Very near.' The maid pointed along the corridor. 'Turn right at the end, then halfway down. Neighbours with my mistress, almost.'

Unwilling to pry more lest the maid grow suspicious, Mercia smiled and strolled away. She turned right at a collection of paintings, pausing to admire a portrait of a young boy and his dog: Lavinia Whent's charge, the Duke of Cambridge, dressed in his baby's swaddling, his pudgy face reminiscent of all infants of such tender years. The adjacent images of his mother and father were less appealing, but leaving the young family behind, she soon came upon the closed door to Lady Herrick's apartments, painted a distinct bright white.

She knocked and waited, but there was no response. Consulting a clock set into the side of a miniature ship – eleven o'clock – she reasoned Lady Herrick should no longer be abed and so she knocked again, somewhat louder. This time the door swung open, a savagely young maid's face peering out.

She put a finger to her lips. 'Sorry, but the mistress is not to be disturbed.'

'No matter,' said Mercia, turning to leave. 'I will return later.'

'Stay!' bawled a husky voice from within, causing the maid to jump. 'You may as well enter now you are here.'

The maid stepped back, holding open the door. Mercia passed through to the bedroom where Lady Herrick was sitting in a blue silken robe on the edge of her grand four-poster. Her long grey hair was as unmade as the bed, a stark contrast to its perfection of last night. A red Bible sat on a side table, but the leather spine was not much creased.

'Oh.' Lady Herrick yawned. 'I thought you would be Helen. Lady Cartwright.'

'You seem tired,' said Mercia. 'I can come back.'

'I cannot imagine you will be here long.' She picked up a mirror and examined her aged face. 'Not too ghastly, do you think? Considering I did not retire until three.'

'The festivities continued long?'

'Did you not hear them? After that . . . interruption, we were able to get on.'

'I am afraid I did not stay. You were not concerned at what happened?'

'Why should I be? If some madman were roving the Court intent on attacking its ladies, I should think he would have chosen a more illustrious target.' She sighed and set down her mirror. 'The problem with your aunt is she can say the wrong thing to the wrong person. You clearly know this.' She took a brush to her fingernails. 'She is still with us, I take it?'

'Yes.' Mercia studied her seeming indifference as she continued to work her brush. 'Then who could have struck her, do you think?'

'How would I know?' Lady Herrick paused in her administrations. 'This does in the end grow tiresome. Tell me why you have come and then leave me to my rest. There is another gathering tonight I shall be forced to attend.'

'I merely came to introduce myself more fully, Lady Herrick. We did not much have chance to converse last night.'

The brush resumed its steady work. 'This is scarcely a convenient time, Mrs Blakewood.'

'I offered to come back.'

'Yes. You did. Perhaps I should speak plainer.' She looked up, the dark bags under her eyes almost flaring. 'Lady Calde was my close companion. Well before she married Sir William, we were almost like sisters.'

'I do not intend to replace her, Lady Herrick.'

She flung the brush carelessly on the table. 'Then what do you intend? Why come to Court as Sir William's mistress, if you do not seek to make him your husband and take the money that used to be his wife's?' She jiggled her bare foot. 'Is it not true what is said about you? I pay such rumours little heed, but sometimes they turn out correct.'

'Rumours?' frowned Mercia.

'She died, did she not, when you were with her? Lady Calde?'

'Well, yes, but—'

Lady Herrick gave her a searching look.

She gasped. 'People cannot think that I . . . ?'

'Your father was executed, you lost your inheritance, but still Sir William had an interest. Such good fortune considering your family's disgrace. But Lady Calde yet lived, and so you swooped and cleared your way. And when you return to Court, Lady Simmonds is attacked, the wife of the man who took away your house.' She ran her tongue around her lips. 'Such beautiful vengeance, Mrs Blakewood. I shall have to be certain not to cross you myself.'

'But none of that is true!'

'Perhaps.' Lady Herrick sat back, rubbing her temples in deliberate circles. 'Perhaps not. But I really must insist you take your leave now. It takes so long to prepare oneself for Court, as well you must know.'

Undone by Lady Herrick's mischief, Mercia remained rooted to the spot, thoughts of her mission vanquished. Did the women of the Court really believe those falsehoods of her? That she was a . . . a harlot? A heartless pursuer of men?

'Mrs Blakewood.' Lady Herrick cleared her throat. 'Send in my maid on your way out.'

The encounter had left her needing air. Leaving the palace, she meandered through the Privy Garden, mingling with the other courtiers who, like her, were in want of the freshness of the outdoors. But the garden soon grew too small, and so she crossed the street, aiming for St James's Park, the same route she had taken every noontime since she had arrived. Stuck in the enclosed palace after weeks on the open ocean, both her body and her mind craved the cheer of daylight. Today the sky was blue, the barest wisp of white drawn across the vista, and Mercia found her mood immediately lifting as the warmth of the sun bathed her face.

Strolling amongst the aviary on the southern side of the park, she forced her thoughts from the intrigue of the palace. Daniel at least seemed to have settled in well, but she never worried on that account, for he swiftly made friends in any group. And it was good for him, she thought, for his prospects, to get to know the boys of the Court. It would almost be a shame to take him away, but if all went as well as she hoped, there would be more such opportunities in his future.

Nicholas came next to mind, the loyal manservant who had proved his valour in America, even if their relationship had not enjoyed the strongest start. But she trusted him now, implicitly, and she knew she would miss him when he finally escaped to his old life, for despite who he was, the strangeness of their journeys had made him her friend, and the norms of society had crumbled.

She continued through the Physic Garden, stopping to admire the small orange and lemon trees, tracing her finger along their rubbery fruit to release their tangy citrus scent. The surrounding herbs were an intoxicating combination, and now she found herself thinking of Nathan, the friend who had remained over the ocean, the friend who could have been more. And she realised, so thinking, how she missed that wilderness, the pine-infused breeze, the vastness of the sky. But it was Nathan she missed most, and as she walked towards the canal that split the park in two, she promised herself she would reply to his letter tonight.

Further along the canal, she paused to admire four huge birds that had appeared since the year before: four white birds with enormous, distended beaks, lolloping their saggy bulk across the grass as they emitted the occasional caw. She had seen strange fowl abroad, strange beasts, but never a bird as odd as this. As every morning that week they had gathered quite a crowd, a host of children pointing in delight, the adults beside them no less entranced.

'Do you like them?' said a man she had not noticed come alongside. 'A gift from the Russian ambassador last year. Pelicans, they are called. And I am called Henry Raff.'

'Mr Raff,' she said, turning to look. He was around her age, wearing fashionable clothes of colourful hue, his doublet slashed to reveal the silk beneath. He was . . . extremely attractive, jet-black hair and immaculate beard, and she realised she had seen him before.

'I saw you at the ball last night,' he confirmed. 'From across the room. A shame you had to leave.' He held out an arm, keeping the other behind his back. 'May I?'

Taken with his appearance, she accepted. She allowed him to steer her from the mesmerised crowd until he halted in the shade of a tree.

'I shall not long disturb your stroll,' he said. 'But I was told by my friend you were walking in the park and I could not ignore the chance to approach you.' Releasing her arm, he pulled a yellow rose from behind his back. 'For you. It will go well with your dress.'

'Thank you.' She could not help but smile. 'Mr Raff.'

'Henry,' he said, and then he leant in, arresting his lips an inch from her neck. 'I know you are close with Sir William. But do not forget, there are other men about you. Younger men, more able to . . . please.' He retreated a pace. 'Look for me in the palace whenever you want. For now, let me bid you good day.'

He bowed and walked away as quickly as he had come, falling in beside another spruce courtier who laughed and clapped him on the shoulder. The pair ambled off, leaving Mercia to the rose and the pelicans, but a short way along Raff paused and turned his head, giving her another broad smile. She watched him as he disappeared towards the palace, and smelling the fine scent of the flower in her hand, a surprised satisfaction coursed through her. But then she shook her head, for she knew well the stories of the men of Whitehall – the bored and competitive men of Whitehall – and she resumed her canalside stroll, although she swung the carefree rose by its stalk.

Keen to soak up the sun a half-hour more, she reached the park's limits, the pell-mell courts where men played at ball and hoop stretching out to her right. And then, her legs finally tiring, she dragged herself back, sauntering along her usual line of beech trees, wanting to prolong the enjoyment of the early afternoon breeze.

Up ahead, a woman in dark clothing emerged from behind one of the beeches. Disarmed by Raff's charm, Mercia took less notice than she otherwise might have, and she stepped to one side to pass by. But as she drew level, the woman coughed.

'Good morrow, Mrs Blakewood,' she said. 'How agreeable to see you in London once more.'

Mercia stopped still. It had been almost a year, but she recognised that voice.

'And he was such a handsome man,' the woman continued. 'Aren't you going to pick that up?'

The rose, loosely held, had dropped to the ground, one petal fallen from the rest. Betraying none of her mounting emotion, Mercia turned to take in the creased visage, the narrowing eyes, the well-worn folds of skin. The woman was wearing a man's broad hat, but she knew underneath would be a clutch of white hair, for she had seen this person before.

'Mrs Wilkins,' she managed.

'I'm touched,' said the woman. 'You remember old One-Eye.'

The warmth of the day had all gone. 'I remember.'

'Then it will be pleasant for us to talk together a while.'

Mercia looked along the line of beeches. Now that she noticed, she could see a man leaning against one of the trunks.

'One of yours?' she asked.

One-Eye shrugged. 'The sooner we talk, the sooner you can return to your newfound comforts.'

'I cannot be seen with you here.'

'You have little choice. But if you prefer, we can talk in the shade of that big tree over there. Don't think to walk away. We have matters to discuss.'

Thinking it best to comply, Mercia led the way to the indicated spot, somewhat hidden from the canal. It was all she could do to keep her face set.

'Well then,' said One-Eye. 'Your trip to America was quite the success, I am told.'

She frowned. 'Told by whom?'

'By one of a hundred sailors, Mrs Blakewood. As soon as the first men returned, they spoke of you in the taverns. Not quite the usual thing for them, was it, to have a beautiful woman on their ship? You delayed your own return, I see, but here you are at last.'

'So it seems. How did you know where to find me?'

One-Eye cackled. 'I am master of a host of smugglers. I know men in every port. Those in Southampton learnt of your arrest and found out where you were taken. I have had Whitehall watched ever since. You have taken this same walk in the same park at the same time for the past few days. You are wearing the finest clothes. If you do not want to be found, you should take more care.'

'You live up to your name, Mrs Wilkins. It seems you do have one eye on everything around you.'

'Thank you, my dear.'

'Now what do you want?'

One-Eye grinned, her chipped teeth showing through the gaps. 'My men have a temper, Mrs Blakewood. They do not like to see me talked harshly with. And after I helped you with your little task for the King last year. How ungrateful.'

'Mrs Wilkins, I am grateful. I merely ask what you want of me now.'

'You recall our bargain, Mercia?' One-Eye leant against the tree. 'That if I were to give you the name of that man you sought, I might come to you for some favour in return?'

Could chills freeze over? Mercia grew as icy as the canal must do in winter.

'I recall how you extorted that promise with a knife at my manservant's cheek.'

'A deal is a deal, my dear. When I heard where your fortunes had taken you, I knew I had to redeem your vow without delay.'

'That will depend on what you ask.'

She shook her head. 'There is no question of dependence. I ask and you do, that is how this works.' She hacked up a cough, but then the cough turned into a fit, and she beat at a spot below her neck until she stopped. 'Yes. I ask, you do.'

'Not unwell, I hope,' said Mercia.

'Quite well.' But then she coughed again, and had to clear her throat several times before she could continue. 'Now, my dear,' she said at last. 'You are in a rare position, wouldn't you say? Living at the palace. Taking up as mistress to Sir William Calde.'

The leaves above them fluttered in the breeze. 'How do you know that?'

'That I do is all that matters. I want information, Mrs Blakewood. Information you can provide me.'

'I am hardly about to do that.'

'I've wanted someone inside the palace for years. I admit, perhaps, I have someone who . . . tells me things now and then. But you can get close to the powerful. Give me morsels of intelligence I can use if ever I need to . . . persuade them of anything.'

'You mean bribe them.'

'My business is not without risk, Mrs Blakewood. Sometimes life becomes simpler if the men with the power can make lesser men look away.'

Mercia stared. 'I do not know if you have noticed, but we are at war with the Dutch. I know full well that you ferry . . . cargos to Holland. I will not make it easier for you to smuggle to our enemy.'

'Such fervour, my dear. But you must comply.'

'And if I refuse?'

'You recall my rules. Actions, even lack of them, lead to consequences.'

'No, Mrs Wilkins.' She shook her head. 'If you insist on payment for your scant help last year, you will have to devise some other form of compensation.'

One-Eye pushed from the tree. 'This is the payment I require. I want nothing else.'

'Then you will have to think harder.' She could feel the sweat forming on her back. 'Or better still, cancel the debt in its entirety. You should know I have the ear of the King himself.'

'A threat?' She laughed. 'And so this is your answer?'

'There can be none other.'

'Then consequences it is, Mrs Blakewood.' One-Eye nodded at her man, and for an instant Mercia thought she was going to order him to strike. But he merely lingered to one side.

'Enjoy what remains of your day,' said One-Eye, as she led him into the sun. 'We will talk again soon. Of that you can have no doubt.'

Chapter Seven

'I couldn't see her.' Barely out of breath from his brisk search of the park, Nicholas was still seething. 'But she was never going to stay around.'

'I said there was no sense in you looking. What would you have done if you had found her?'

'Warned her to lay off. I may have been away a while, but I still have mates.'

'Mates.' Mercia shook her head. 'Nicholas, she is a renowned smuggler. She must use scores of men.'

'Yes, and it was me who got you involved with her, when we wanted her help last year.'

'At my request.'

He growled. 'I should have known she'd show herself, making her threats. I should have made it my business to chase her off as soon as we came back.'

'God's truth, Nicholas, I have seen too much death of late to be concerned for the words of a self-appointed queen of smugglers. I told her I would not do as she asked.'

'Well, I am worried. We're not dealing with frontier settlers here, or nobles acting alone. These are nasty people if you get on their wrong side. You'll have to stay in the palace until I can get Martin to ask around.'

'One of your – mates?'

'The one who arranged the meeting with One-Eye for us last year. He . . . deals with these things.'

'You mean he is part of them.' She looked at him but he chose to keep silent. 'I am not going to be put off my walk, Nicholas. I cannot stay in the palace the whole time.'

'Then you'll have to let me come with you. Maybe take Phibae too.'

'Have to?' She raised an eyebrow. 'I do not have to do anything.'

'And I suppose I'll be the one struggling to write to Nathan to explain what happened, shall I? I made him a promise to look out for you, and I don't mean to stop now.'

'Why is it men think we need their help with everything?' She sighed. 'I know you mean well. But do not fret so.' Her eyes flicked to the door and she put a quick finger to her lips. 'She is back. Not a word more.'

The door pushed open and Phibae entered, a smile on her face.

'Here it is, Nicholas. It was not hard to find.'

'Thanks for looking for it,' he said, taking a shirt from her outstretched hand. 'I knew I'd left it in my room.'

'And I see Cerwen did launder it. I told you she would.'

'Yes.' He cleared his throat. 'Cerwen.'

Mercia looked at him askance; she could not help but notice how his cheeks had lightly flushed.

'Thank you, Nicholas,' she said. 'You may go, if you wish.'

He opened his mouth as if to protest, but then he nodded and vanished, leaving Phibae to shut the door.

'Follow me into the bedroom,' said Mercia, her hems swishing across the floor. 'I am to see Sir William later. I want to change into something new.'

Phibae smiled. 'I promise you will look magnificent.'

She sat at her dressing table, similar to Lady Herrick's, but made of oak rather than walnut. 'Perhaps the red dress this afternoon? I wish to surprise him after his council meeting. It will be well to take his mind off matters of war.'

'Very good,' said Phibae, reaching into the wardrobe for a beautiful silken dress that would rival anything Lady Castlemaine could wear.

'But I am troubled, Phibae.'

She set the dress on the bed. 'How so, my lady?'

'About Sir William. He is so recently returned from overseas I fear he is at a disadvantage with his fellows on the council. They must know much more of events in England than he.' Gently, she pulled the silver wires that supported her ringlets from out of her hair. 'I thought if I could know their wives better, their mistresses, I might help ease his way back into Court. Lady Cartwright, Lady Allcot, and suchlike.'

Phibae loosened the folds of the dress Mercia was wearing, enough to heave the heavy garment over her head in one assured movement. 'What would you like to know, my lady?' She leant in. 'Or would like me to find out?'

Mercia laughed. 'I see you understand me, Phibae. You have served at the palace long?'

'Near ten years, since I was a girl. First under Cromwell, now the King. I know most of the maids here, and they know their mistresses.' She untied the bow holding up Mercia's bodice. 'My, I tied this tight before. It didn't dig in during your walk, did it?'

'Not that I noticed.'

'And your stays are comfortable?'

'Yes, no need to change those.' Unencumbered by her heavy dress, she twisted her neck to relieve the trapped tension. 'I suppose I want to learn anything of interest about these women. What they like, whom they meet. What they favour. And do you know a maid named Faith? She serves Lady Simmonds, my aunt.'

'Arms up, please.' Phibae deftly removed the floral bodice, lying the patterned garment beside the discarded dress. 'I have seen her, my lady. But I don't think she's been here long. About a month, if that. Lady Simmonds dismissed her last girl over some row or other.'

'Why so?'

'Nobody really knows. Nobody really liked her, in truth.' She puffed out air through her teeth. 'Mary, her name was. Folk said she was stealing, but I think there was more to it than that.'

'Where was Faith before?'

'Upriver, I think, at Hampton Court. Now hold still.'

Splashing a little rosewater on Mercia's arms and neck, she pulled on a new bodice and tied the fastenings at the back. The material was firm against her skin, even through her stays, but when Phibae pushed the whalebone down the front to hold the ensemble in place, all she could feel was its unyielding discomfort.

'And now stand up, please,' the taskmaster continued.

Mercia obeyed, holding up her arms so that Phibae could haul on the new dress. 'Why do we put ourselves through this pain, Phibae?'

'I wouldn't know, my lady. Keep your head straight.'

Embarrassed at her thoughtlessness, Mercia chose not to protest when the expensive dress stuck in her hair – soon set right with a sharp tug of the delicate silk.

'I am sorry, my lady. If you sit again, I can straighten that out.' Phibae took up an ivory comb, brushing Mercia's curls into place before firming up the topknot with deft skill. Finally, she reinserted the silver wires to trail her ringlets over her forehead, applied cochineal, and adhered a decorative patch to her left cheek: a tiny minstrel serenading from a boat.

'Lady Cartwright won't be able to find fault in this,' said Phibae, regarding her creation with satisfaction. Then her face fell. 'I only say as you mentioned her, my lady. And . . .'

'What is it, Phibae?'

'I . . . heard of your argument. I'm sorry if I speak out of turn.'

'Heard from whom?'

'From her . . . boy. Tacitus, they call him.'

'I see.' She craned her neck, as best she could with the whalebone jutting into her chest. 'What do you know of her, then? Of Lady Cartwright?'

Phibae's eyes flicked away. 'I shouldn't like to say.'

'Phibae, you may speak as you find. I told you it would help me to know.'

She hesitated. 'Well, I know little of Lady Cartwright. She doesn't much speak to her own maids, let alone to me.'

'She is not a pleasant person?'

'Not to people like me.'

'What does that mean?'

Phibae smiled sadly, tracing a finger along the skin of her hand. 'But Tacitus is a good boy, my lady. Clever.'

'But his mistress treats him badly?'

'I cannot say.'

'Hmm.' She gave her a glance, but Phibae chose to stay silent. 'Then how long has Lady Cartwright known Sir Geoffrey Allcot? She and he are close, I understand.'

'Several months, I think.'

'And her husband?'

'He is not often at Court. And . . .'

'Yes?'

'And when he is, he is not often in her chambers. But really, my lady, that is all I know.'

'Then what of Lavinia Whent?' she tried.

'Oh, the opposite, my lady.' Her taut shoulders seemed to relax. 'Miss Whent is most generous.'

'She says she knows of you.'

'She has talked with me, once or twice.'

'And what do you think of her?'

She began to tidy the dressing table. 'I think that . . . I think she means well, my lady.'

'But?'

'But she is young.'

'Indeed.' Mercia waited for more, but again Phibae had fallen silent, and in all honesty, Mercia could little blame her. 'And Lady Allcot?' she prompted. 'I tried to see her this morning, but her maid said she was away.'

'All I know of Lady Allcot is that she spends half her time at Hampton Court.'

'Do you know why?'

She walked to close the door to the wardrobe. 'For the same reason many ladies of the Court spend time away from their husbands.'

'She has a lover, you mean?'

Phibae stopped still. 'You say I may speak as I find, my lady?'

'Please.'

'Then I think . . . she and her husband . . . they do not get on. She . . .'

'Go on.'

'She doesn't like him meeting Lady Cartwright. And I've heard, perhaps, she wants her revenge by doing the same herself.'

'Revenge? That is an interesting notion, Phibae.'

'I am sorry, my lady. I did not—'

'No, that is helpful. You have said nothing wrong. Can you tell me anything similar of Lady Herrick?'

She frowned. 'Lady Herrick is loyal to her husband. Good to her maids too, as he is.'

'She seemed a little sly to me.'

'I wouldn't know about that, my lady. Her maids speak of her fondly.'

'And Cornelia Howe, Lady Herrick's niece? I know she does not live at Court, but she attends its balls and so on. She was here yesterday evening, in a remarkable outfit.'

'She stayed overnight, I believe. Her maids talk to the rest of us while they are here. But none of them much like her.'

'Oh?'

'She just isn't . . . she's not like you, my lady. If her maid caught her hair like I caught yours in the dress just now, even though by mistake, she'd near strike her with whatever she had at her side. But then her maids think . . .'

'Yes?'

'They think maybe her husband treats her badly, and she takes it out on them. Sarah who does her clothes, poor girl, only just fifteen – she hears things. Knocks, thumps. But we don't know for certain.'

Mercia set her face. 'I shall have to recall that when we speak.'

'They're still here, my lady, if you're interested.'

'I did not know that. Thank you.'

'They like to sit out on the terrace when the weather is fine. Not that they're often at Court together, mind. More so now, with the war started, but Mr Howe used to go abroad a lot, so Sarah says. Spent a lot of time with the froglanders.'

'With the Dutch, you mean?'

'Yes, my lady. They say trading with Holland's where he made his money. So now the war's begun, he's not best pleased.' She shook her head. 'I'm sorry, my lady. I'm talking too much.'

'That is quite acceptable, Phibae.' Patting down her topknot, Mercia rose to her feet. 'You are a maid of many uses indeed.'

Sir Stephen Herrick's position as close counsellor to the King had made life easy for his niece Cornelia Howe. No children of his own, he had been eager to use his influence to provide her with access to the Court, eager too to promote her husband's trading business, securing him ready patronage among the wealthy and the great.

The day's brightness had continued through afternoon, and as Phibae had suggested, Cornelia was lounging in a comfortable chair, her legs stretched out, enjoying the shade of the east-facing terrace. At her side, a man in a red doublet sat with eyes closed, seemingly as relaxed as she.

Mercia sauntered to the balustrade at the edge of the terrace, overlooking the Thames to the Southwark side. Across the water shimmered a faint smattering of sawmills, the same she had visited last year. How was Tom Finch, she wondered, the boy she had met? But then a breeze picked up, and she snatched for the bonnet Phibae had brought out. She need not have worried: it was tied as securely as the bodice.

Looking down the river, feeling the warmth of the pleasant spring day, she took in the sprawling urbanity to her left. In the distance, she could make out the hulk of St Paul's Cathedral, near where she knew London Bridge must lie, its teeming mass forever at risk of caving in, and yet somehow it always stayed up. To her right opened out a different picture – the marshes of Lambeth on the opposite shore, and the curve of the river on this, the many wherries and barges roaming back and forth.

Breaking from the view, she turned to face the relaxing couple. The woman appeared stern, largely the fault of her large, patrician nose; curved slightly towards a freckled mark on her cheek, it dominated an otherwise attractive face. Her outfit, in contrast, was as brash as last night's, a melange of bright greens and yellows. The man seemed oblivious to much around him, his head lolling on the back of his seat, even humming a casual tune that carried to Mercia's perch.

Adjusting her bonnet, she strolled across the terrace and paused, faking a gasp of recognition.

'Mrs Howe, is it?' she asked.

Cornelia had been working on an embroidery, but she set it down to study Mercia's innocent face. 'I do not think . . . have we met?'

'Not in person,' said Mercia. She indicated a vacant chair. 'May I join you? 'Tis such a fine day.'

'That is meant for my aunt,' said Cornelia, as the man looked on from under disinterested eyelids. 'I am expecting her shortly.'

'Oh, I do not intend to stay. I have an appointment with Lady Castlemaine.' Mercia smiled. 'She and I enjoy a friendship.'

'Ah.' Cornelia jiggled her head. 'Mrs Blakewood, I take it.'

'I thought you implied that we had not met?'

'My aunt has mentioned you. And of course, we all knew Lady Calde.'

Mercia pulled up the empty seat. 'I can assure you, Mrs Howe, those mistruths about Lady Calde and I are just that – untrue. I may be . . . enjoying Sir William's company, but that is little wonder after becoming so well acquainted during our time abroad.'

'Sir William is a fine man,' broke in Cornelia's companion. 'A fine eye for ladies too.' He rested his fist on his chin. 'That dress suits you well, Mrs Blakewood. Don't you think so, Cornelia? Clearly an acquaintance with Barbara Whore-Roy brings most everyone benefit, except you.'

Cornelia glared at him. 'You will have to forgive my husband. His tongue can be somewhat loose.'

Mercia gave a slight bow. 'Mr Howe. You do not approve of my Lady Castlemaine?'

'Tsk.' Howe studied his hand, adorned with one simple ring. 'All that woman's children are named Fitzroy, for being bastards of the King. So why should she style herself Castlemaine, by virtue of her cuckolded husband? Surely Whore-Roy is more apt?' He let out a deep belly laugh, pleased at his own wit. 'But yes, you must forgive me. I am merely enjoying a jest. Perhaps last night's wine is still in my humours.'

She indulged him with a smile. 'Sir William tells me you have a shipping business, Mr Howe?'

'I have that honour. A substantial concern, indeed. But it occupies me less for the while.'

'Because of the war?'

He nodded. 'I should be eager to join the fleet myself, all told, until trade resumes.'

'He served with my uncle some years ago,' said Cornelia, a hint of pride now in her voice. 'Until he inherited his company from his father.'

'It does well?' asked Mercia.

Howe shrugged. 'Cornelia does not want for fine things.'

'Forgive me, but I am curious how matters are changed of late. Did you much trade with the Dutch?'

'Every trader did,' he said. 'And no doubt will again.'

'But if we win the war, and the Dutch are diminished, then—'

'Then merchants will still have goods to sell, and I will still ship their produce. The American market too is promising. Tell me.' He leant across his wife. 'I hear Boston and New York grow fast. Did it seem so when you were there?'

'I did not see Boston, but New York, yes, I should say it will begin to expand now. But does the war not—'

'Thomas,' interrupted Cornelia. 'This talk of commerce bores a woman.'

'I do not mind,' rejoined Mercia, but Howe nodded.

'My wife is right. Please, Mrs Blakewood, do not let us keep you from your own business.'

I am on my own business, she thought, and then she recalled what Phibae had said, how this couple did not get on. But that did not match the picture before her.

'You have been married long?' she asked.

Howe pulled a face. 'Trust a woman to bring up marriage.'

'Five years,' said Cornelia.

'And do you have children?'

She knew straightaway she had made a mistake. Howe's face darkened, while Cornelia's blanched, and her jaw shook.

'We do not talk of that,' she said.

'I am sorry,' apologised Mercia. 'I should not have asked.'

'No, 'tis a common enough question,' sighed Howe. 'But we do not have children, and we never will.'

Cornelia banged her fist on her chair: the unexpected violence made Mercia jump.

'It is not my fault, Thomas!'

'I did not say it was.'

'But you always think it!'

'This same act, Cornelia?' Howe turned his bleak visage on his wife. 'You embarrass yourself, yet again.'

Cornelia snatched her embroidery and jumped to her feet. 'I think I shall meet my aunt inside. I am sure Mrs Blakewood will make a more suitable companion for you. She has a son, I believe.'

'Go, then. Back to your relations, as is your wont. Do not concern yourself with your own husband.'

Her hand trembling on her needlework, the look on Cornelia's face could have blacked out the lowering sun. She turned on her heels and vanished out of sight.

'Well, that is my wife, Mrs Blakewood.' Howe stood in his turn. 'My life, indeed. And she wonders why we—' He clenched his fist. 'I trust your day will improve now.' He reached for his hat. 'Mine will not.'

He bowed and followed, leaving Mercia to stare at the vacated seats. Just a half-minute before it had been going so well, and then . . .

She returned to the river where, elbows on the balustrade, she pondered how one misplaced question had undone her planned technique.

Chapter Eight

Mournful trees glided by on the greying riverbank. Pearls of water drained from their drooping leaves as the insistent downpour lashed the misty landscape. Dry in the cabin of a palace barge, Mercia watched Nicholas press his face against the window, squashing his stubbled cheek on the steamed-up glass.

'Seemed a good idea at the time,' he said. 'Still, better than being caught in a storm at sea. And to think it was hot just two days ago.'

'I feel sorry for the men rowing us,' said Mercia. 'They will be drenched.'

'Don't worry about them. Anyway, the tide's with us. Takes us almost the whole way, so they said when we boarded.' He chuckled. 'I can't stop thinking it should be me out there, instead of keeping warm in all these fine clothes.' He tugged at his well-fitting doublet, and in truth Mercia had never seen him look so smart.

'It suits you,' she said. ''Tis nice to see you with your hair combed for once.'

'I prefer it messy.' He ruffled the front of his hair. 'See. Better.'

'If you say so. Where are we now?'

'No idea. I don't know round here at all.' He opened the cabin door, only a few inches, but the wind still made its intentions felt. 'Hey,' he shouted. 'Where are we?'

'Putney,' came back an ethereal voice, almost deafened by the pattering of the rain. 'Two hours left.'

'Two hours,' she heard Nicholas mutter. Then he slammed the door, struggling against the gusts, and smiled. 'Only two hours to go. Time enough to prepare what to say to Lady Allcot.'

'The only thing I have decided on thus far is my excuse for coming all this way, and that is weak enough. I suppose I will say I wanted to enjoy the country air.'

'Do you think she could be Virgo?'

'I do not know. Her husband is on the war council, because of his stake in the Royal Adventurers—'

'The slave traders.'

'Indeed. But if the Dutch win the war, the Adventurers lose their foothold on the Guinea coast. Sir Geoffrey would stand to lose a fortune, as would his wife. Then again, she vanished straight after the assault on my aunt.'

'If her maid said she was upset, that's probably right. I'm surprised more people weren't, to speak true. And we don't know for certain if that attack is related to Virgo.' He scratched at his stubble, thinking. 'You say Lady Allcot is angry her husband has taken a mistress?'

'So it would seem. Phibae suggested she was involved with another man, if only to spite Sir Geoffrey.'

'Then perhaps she's hoping to spite him further. If he loses his fortune in the war – and maybe his mistress with it?'

'You mean she may deliberately be trying to ruin him?' She drummed her fingers on the bench. 'Perhaps, Nicholas, but taking a mistress is commonplace at Court. Think of the King, and where we are going now.'

'What of it?'

'Hampton Court is where the King first received the Queen when she came to England. It was there he presented her with her Lady of the Bedchamber, all well and good until she turned out to be his principal mistress.'

He smirked. 'Funny how that's all so decent at Court. The King can have as many bastards as he likes, but when I have a daughter out of wedlock, 'tis frowned upon.'

'By all accounts, the Queen became crazed when she found out the King was forcing Castlemaine on her, even falling to the floor and crying out her heart. But His Majesty was having none of her tantrum. Mistresses are a fact of life in his Court.' She sighed. 'The truth is we know too little. But Nicholas, now I have started on this task – I know I serve at the King's command, but I do want to unmask this woman.'

'Because you can't resist a puzzle.'

'A failure of mine, perhaps.'

He grinned. 'Do you think if we succeed, the King will reward me too?'

'I would not be too hopeful. But when I am restored to my manor house, I will give you a reward. My eternal friendship.'

He cocked his head. 'You seem much more cheerful even than a week ago, when we got off the ship. I think perhaps, 'tis having something to do?'

'That, for certain, as well as being back in England. And I must admit, I am pleased Daniel is able to take advantage. He is making some useful friends, I hope. But there are still moments, Nicholas. When I feel sad.' She wiped a circle in the steam of the window. 'Still raining. At least we are closer now. We will continue our search with Lady Allcot.'

* * *

92

The rain had eased by the time the boat moored at Hampton Court, and she followed Nicholas into the courtyard of the palace, informing the page who received them why they had come. The officious young man led them inside, where a large fire was belching its heat into the dimness of the wainscoted hall.

'If you would wait here,' he said. 'I will enquire after Lady Allcot.'

While they waited, Mercia explored the length of the impressive room, admiring the portraits and busts. Nicholas, conversely, slumped onto a bench beneath a pair of fearsome antlers, and although he won some inquisitive looks, in return he paid nobody much heed. Then the page came back, a troubled expression on his face.

'Mrs Blakewood,' he said. 'I am sorry, but Lady Allcot appears to be missing. Her maid says she has not been seen since yesterday.'

'Since yesterday?' Mercia frowned. 'Did her maid not become concerned?'

'Not until this morning. She says Lady Allcot often retires early, or rises late.' He shrugged. 'Some people like their sleep.'

Mercia jerked her head at Nicholas as an order to join them. 'I assume her maid has checked her bed.'

'The bed appears slept in, but . . . I am not sure. If you would like to come with me?'

The page led them through the palace; smaller than Whitehall and more comfortable, they reached their destination sooner than she expected. He entered through a half-open door, manoeuvring his stocky frame through sideways. Mercia followed, stooping to enter a small, dark room the solitary window could never have hoped to brighten. The light of several candles was illuminating a girl wringing her hands beside the fireplace. Nicholas shut the door with an extended creak.

'Well.' Mercia peered around the overcrowded room, the small space overflowing with a selection of glasses and decanters. 'Would somebody explain?'

The maid opened her mouth, but nothing came out. Instead her cheeks reddened and began to tremble. She was so young, thought Mercia. Only what – about thirteen?

'Alice.' The page's tone was abrupt. 'You have been asked to speak.'

Mercia shot him a glance. 'Alice, is it? What has happened to your mistress?'

'I don't know, my . . . my lady,' the girl managed. 'I thought she was in her room.' She bit her lip. 'Am I going to lose my place?'

The page folded his arms. 'You will if you don't answer.'

Mercia could see the look in Nicholas's eyes, but she held up a staying finger. She didn't want to frighten the girl, but if a little anxiety forced her to focus, perhaps that was for the best.

'I'm sorry, my lady.' Alice dropped to a pitiful curtsey, but when she raised her eyes, they seemed a little calmer. 'My mistress went to bed early last night, even for her. She sent me for a pitcher of the ale she likes, told me to leave it outside the door, but she never came for it. I thought she'd gone to sleep and forgot, for her door was locked when I tried it. But then this morning when I came it wasn't locked, and she wasn't there, nor any of her things she brought with her, and I know she never came out, I'd have heard. I have to be up early, see, light the fires, gather the clothes and . . .'

'Mrs Blakewood knows well enough the duties of maids,' intoned the page.

Mercia ignored his pomposity. 'All her things were gone?'

''Tis as if she's left, but she never does that without saying goodbye. She's nice like that, see.'

She glanced at Nicholas. 'Alice, how long were you away, fetching the pitcher last night?'

'About ten minutes, my lady.'

'And do you know where she might have gone? Is there . . . anyone she likes to spend time with, say?'

The girl looked down. 'Well, I'm sure it's nothing, but . . .'

'Don't worry,' said Nicholas. 'Nobody's going to be upset with you.'

Still the young maid looked as if she would burst into tears. 'I'm not supposed to say.'

'It could be important,' said Mercia. 'Alice.' More firm. 'I need an answer to my question.'

The girl looked up in fright. 'She . . . there's a man she meets from time to time. Speaks foreign with him.'

'Foreign?' Mercia's head jerked up. 'Do you mean Dutch?'

'I don't know, my lady. I only know English.'

'And that none too well,' smirked the page.

Mercia glanced at him. 'Perhaps you should . . .' She put a finger to her lips. 'Alice, when does she see this man?'

'Often, this past month.' Mercia's chiding of the page had given her confidence. 'Always at Hampton Court. She comes at least once a week, often don't tell her husband, but he don't much care. Don't even notice she's gone half the time, and her maid up at Whitehall helps her keep it quiet. She says she needs to get out of the city.'

'God's wounds,' Mercia swore. 'Alice, if she was with this man now, where could she be?'

The maid thought for a moment. 'There's a summer house in the grounds she likes to go of a morning. It's out of the way in the woods, so she lets me stay here, to save me the walk. But all her things are gone!'

'Every morning, Alice?' she persisted.

'Yes, most mornings when she's here.'

'Then if you were worried, did you not think to go there and look?'

'I can't.' Her eyes moistened. 'I'm told I must stay here, my lady.'

95

The page snorted. 'Can't you think for yourself? If your mistress has vanished, then—'

'Did you think to ask?' said Nicholas.

'Well no, but . . .'

'Then keep quiet.'

Alice rallied once more. 'Do you want me to show you, my lady?'

Mercia shook her head. 'Your mistress is right. Someone should stay here in case she returns. Your young friend will take us.'

She snapped her fingers and signalled behind her. Nicholas suppressed a grin as the page scuttled to open the door to usher them through, leaving Alice in the room alone.

'Annoying cove, isn't he?' he said in the corridor, the page walking some way ahead.

'A little,' she agreed.

'And this is all a mite obvious, no? She sent that maid on a fool's errand last night, locked the door and went to see this man of hers. And now she's sneaked away again. They're probably at it all the time.'

She looked at him. 'Quite possibly, Nicholas. But we had better find out who this man is. And whether Lady Allcot is mixing treason with her pleasure.'

Head held high, the page led them into the palace grounds, weaving his way through a number of unknown courtiers who stared as Mercia passed, wondering who she was, no doubt.

'A pleasant aspect,' she said of the view towards the river. 'The palace too. I prefer it to Whitehall. The air is so much cleaner here. It feels more like home.'

'Not to me.' Nicholas wrinkled his nose. 'I was getting used to the stench of London again.'

'I enjoy the park, of course, but go into the city itself and –

horrible smells, everywhere, horrible. If I had to spend much time there, I would be forced to walk around with a posy. Rosemary or some such.'

'That's probably wise, in truth. They say there's one or two cases of plague about. I hear the *Intelligencer* reckons 'tis all over Europe, and you know what that means.'

She shivered as they passed by a lithe pair of statues. 'That it is on its way here.'

''Tis only the odd case, so perhaps we'll be spared. But remember that comet last winter? Eve – my sister – said yesterday when I saw her that it flew over here the same as it did in New York.'

'Is she worried?'

'If it comes, they'll take their chances with the rest of them. So will I, once I go back.'

'Through this gap here,' the page called from up ahead, waiting for them to catch up. 'Do you see the curve in the river, the other side of this hedge? Just past there a path leads into the woods. That's where you'll find the summer house, but it's not well kept. No one much goes there.' He cleared his throat. 'Might I return to my duties, my lady?'

Mercia nodded, and he bowed and walked off, but not before Nicholas lunged at him; the page emitted a squeak and scurried away.

'You did not have to do that,' she admonished, turning towards the gap in the hedge.

'Doesn't hurt to give that sort a fright.'

'Still.' Not stopping to wait, she passed through the hedge, flicking off a stray leaf that settled on her shoulder. There was still a fair walk to the bend in the river, but the rain had given way to sunshine, and she enjoyed the few minutes it took to amble down. Just after the bend, an earthen track headed for the trees, and she scuffed at the dirt as she headed along it. At the edge of a sprawling wood, a lone white structure could be seen off the path.

'The summer house,' she said as they approached. 'It has a good view of the river, but that page is right, 'tis quite out of sight.' She raised her hand. 'Wait. I think . . . can you hear something?'

Nicholas lifted his head. 'Yes, a sort of—'

Of a sudden his eyes lit up, and he stole towards the summer house, taking great care not to make any sound. A circular window was set just above head height, and he reached to peer through. Then he shot to the ground, clutching his stomach with his right hand and swatting at the air with his left.

'What is it?' she whispered as she crept beside him, startled at the silent laughter creasing his face. But then standing on tiptoe she dared a glimpse through the window and swiftly understood. Eyes wide, she fell to join Nicholas on the ground.

'By the Lord!' she said. 'Anyone could walk in on them!'

'Like us,' he managed. 'I have to . . . quick . . . before I—'

Struggling to maintain control, he crawled through the long grass until he was out of earshot of the summer house. With more decorum, Mercia stood and walked.

'Well,' she said. 'That is one way of furthering foreign relations.'

Nicholas was breathing steadily in and out, struggling to calm his mirth. 'My, that was some sight. Did you see how she was—?'

'Nicholas! I saw. Now what do we do?'

'Well, I'm not sure we should interrupt.'

'But what if they are – what if she is telling him things?'

'Passing the King's secrets?' He almost choked on his laughter. 'I don't think they were talking much, Mercia. Are you certain it was Lady Allcot? You could only see from one side.'

'I did not much look, but – yes.' She glanced towards the summer house, hand to her mouth. 'But this is too sordid. I can hardly speak with her straight after . . . that.'

'Why not?' He giggled, a ridiculous sound from a grown man, she thought. 'And we do need to know who's with her.' He beat at his chest, taking hold of himself. 'Right. Wait down there by the river, as though you're resting from a stroll. Watch the ducks. I'll stay closer in, keep my eye on the summer house, and wave at you when they . . . finish.'

The waterfowl did not hold her attention for long. Two ungainly geese were coming in to land, their orange webs outstretched in comical descent, when Nicholas motioned across. As he darted behind a nearby bush, she sat on a flat patch of grass between river and wood, pretending to rest, feeling vaguely ridiculous. Subtly – she hoped – she turned her head, peering at the two figures emerging from the summer house, Lady Allcot and an unknown man.

Now fully dressed in a plum-coloured outfit, her hair slightly askew, Lady Allcot reached to kiss the man, grasping his hand before letting it drop. Then she turned alone towards the river, kicking at the grass as she strolled along the path. Mercia buried her face, feigning renewed interest in the geese as Lady Allcot headed the way they had just come, walking in the direction of the palace.

Outside the summer house, the man was holding back; she hoped Nicholas was close enough to get a good look, but even from her viewpoint she could make out his face. His hair was intensely black, his nose intensely long, and he seemed somehow familiar. Then he stretched his white-sleeved arms high into the air and, rotating his shoulders, inhaled deeply. But instead of following the path to the river, he walked into the wood.

'Was it her?' mouthed Nicholas, appearing from his hiding place.

'Yes,' she replied as he approached. 'I assume she is returning to the palace. But where are the belongings she has taken from her room?'

'Shall we follow her?'

'I want to see who the man is first.' She set off in pursuit, talking as they went. 'I think I have seen him before, Nicholas. Recently. At Whitehall, but . . .' She paused to close her eyes, picturing the layout of the palace, positioning its courtiers in the locations she had seen them, her mind flying through the corridors and hallways until it emerged into the grand space where—

'The Banqueting House!' she hissed, starting up again. 'Alice said he was foreign. I think he was with the French delegation at the ball the other night. Against the fireplace.'

'You are sure?'

She closed her eyes again to picture him: a tall, black-haired man in a tight doublet, the allure of his face deepened by the strength of his Gallic nose.

'Yes. His mask was lowered. He and Lady Allcot may even have exchanged a few words.' She sighed. 'So this man she meets is not Dutch, after all.'

'Still, I wonder what he sees in her?'

'What?' The man had passed out of sight. 'Just because she is not the most attractive—'

'That's not what I meant. But a handsome Frenchman at the English Court . . . there are so many pretty women for him to choose, if that's what he wants.'

'Maybe he prefers older women. Maybe those with wit. But this is beside the point.'

'Not if he's interested in certain – connected women. Say, those with a husband on the war council.'

She looked at him askance. 'But he is French, Nicholas. What would they gain from betraying the King's trust?'

'I don't know, but . . . Mercia, while we talk he's getting away, and your dress isn't the plainest. Why don't I follow him, and you go back for Lady Allcot?'

She looked down at her bright-green dress; even amidst the trees, she supposed it stood out.

'Very well. Just try not to be seen.'

'I'm used to that,' he said, speeding off.

Left on her own with the birdsong and the breeze, she felt a sudden and unexpected apprehension. The appearance of the Frenchman had put her senses on alert, the closeness of the woods making her cautious. She hurried back to the river; the water was sparkling in the playful sun, but her disquiet was no less uneasy.

She looked towards the palace, where a flash of plum was disappearing through the gap in the hedge. Picking up her pace, she ascended the slope, squinting to search for Lady Allcot. As she reached a series of herb-filled patches of earth, she saw her rounding the side of the building, and despite her prior misgivings she continued her chase, hopeful Lady Allcot might be more receptive to her questions, flush from her morning's enjoyment.

She was nearing the palace when a man's cry rang out.

'Mercia!' he shouted from behind, and she realised it was Nicholas. 'Mercia, watch out!'

Caught by surprise she turned, only to be confronted by a blur of a man as a dark figure ran into her before she had a chance to react. She tumbled to the ground, jarring her arm, but the man merely stumbled and hurried on. Her arm throbbing, she lifted her head to see a white-sleeved individual running round the corner of the palace.

'Are you hurt?' said Nicholas, extending his hand as he came alongside, barely out of breath.

'Get after him!' she ordered, trying to ignore the pain. 'Quickly!'

He hesitated, but then sprinted away, avoiding the crowd of courtiers and servants gathered along the miscreant's route. He dodged the startled onlookers as best he could, vanishing in pursuit. There was no sign of Lady Allcot.

As Mercia tried to shuffle to a sitting position, another man ran up, and when he held out his hand, she accepted it. But she cried out in agony as he pulled on her injured arm.

'I think 'tis sprained,' she said, offering him her other hand instead. This time he tugged more gently, but there was no discomfort, and she managed to get to her feet.

'What happened?' he said. 'Are you much hurt?'

'Someone pushed me. My manservant is chasing him.' Clutching her injury, she attempted to walk, but the pain pulsed through her and she had to stop. 'Damn him!' she cursed. 'Why has he done this?'

'May I?' Gently, the stranger squeezed her forearm, feeling it up and down. 'I do not think it is broken. Most likely you are right and 'tis sprained, but you should rest it awhile.'

'I have no time for rest. Can you help me to the front of the palace?'

The man frowned but nodded, and using his shoulder as support she managed to bypass the assembled crowd, reaching the drive that led up to the palace entrance, where she looked to find Nicholas. As she cleared the last of the chattering watchers, she finally saw him, running towards a waiting carriage. Two small cases were tied on top, the horses and driver waiting to depart.

'Stop!' she heard him cry. 'Come back!'

He was nearly at the carriage when the driver cracked his reins; the steeds lurched forwards, directly into his path. He had just enough time to jump to one side, landing on the gravel with a crash, before the horses whinnied past. Further down, Mercia forgot about her arm and strode forwards, just as the carriage drove by. The leather blind was raised, and although it passed quickly, a flash of plum betrayed the sole occupant.

'Lady Allcot!' she called out.

She raised a hand at the coach in a futile instruction to stop, without thinking: she sucked in through her teeth as she gripped her wounded arm. To her right, Nicholas got to his feet and made to pursue, even though it must be in vain. But then two men stepped from behind an embankment near the gates at the head of the drive, and this time the driver did slow his horses. Nicholas took advantage, accelerating hard, while the driver began to converse with the men who had caused him to halt.

Hooded men, Mercia noticed. Hooded men, each holding a gun.

And then the men each fired one shot, the one shattering the window of the coach, the other forcing the driver back into his seat. Two loud cracks echoed off the palace walls. A host of birds ascended from the trees.

And all around, the people screamed, as the shooters walked away through the gates.

Chapter Nine

She found herself in three places at once: the world outside the palace, where the aberration had happened; the world inside the palace hall, where she sat with Nicholas on a hard and cold bench; the world inside her head, her own racing thoughts hemmed in by a throng of agitated murmurs. The whole of Hampton Court had ceased its daily business, servants and noblemen congregating on the drive to stare in paralysed shock at the overturned carriage now blocking the iron gates, the panicked horses thrashing on their flanks. Inside the hall, nervous maids lingered in the entrance, whether slumped against the walls, or holding each other for comfort, or curling their fists against the innocent wainscot. Inside Mercia's head, she was struggling to understand the horror she had witnessed.

'You would think it would be easier by now.'

'Easier?' Nicholas looked at her in sympathy. 'What do you mean?'

'Another death. Another two deaths. And yet it is still painful to see.'

'Mercia, if it wasn't painful then something would be wrong. There's no shame in it.'

'I suppose.' She pulled herself up. 'What are we going to tell the

King? We have nothing to show for this . . . travesty. Did nobody manage to find those two men?'

He shook his head. 'They fled into the woods. Some people went to look, but so far – nothing.'

'And the Frenchman?'

'No sign of him either.'

'Hell's teeth,' she swore. 'This is my fault. If I had not fallen so strangely, you would not have thought to stop your pursuit to help me and you might have caught him.'

''Tis not your fault. When I saw the carriage, I made a choice to go for that instead. But . . . I don't know if the man who pushed you was the Frenchman.'

'What? Then who?' She winced as a dart of pain shot through her. 'Nicholas, I do not seek to blame, but why were you near the palace? What did happen in the wood?'

'He saw me, simple as that. I think he must have noticed us after he left the summer house. Pretended to stretch and all and then headed into the wood. Then when he saw me catching him, he panicked, and before I knew it, I'd lost him in the trees.'

'Then who was it pushed me, if not him?'

'I don't say it wasn't him. I couldn't see for certain, but . . .' He blew out his cheeks. 'I was coming back to you, in case he'd run in a loop towards the palace. Then I saw someone running right for you, head down.'

'But why knock me over at all, unless to prevent me from reaching Lady Allcot?' She thought back to the blurred moment. 'In truth, I cannot say either. I recall he was wearing white somewhere on his person, like the Frenchman. But that is hardly unusual.'

'What if . . . Mercia, what if he wanted to be sure you couldn't stop her leaving? And so be sure you couldn't prevent her death?'

'You mean if he was aiding the killers?' She stared at the dusty floor. 'God's truth, Nicholas. Shot at close range before a score of witnesses. And that poor driver. How can anyone be so bold as to do that?'

He shifted to face her. 'I'm not sure the driver was so innocent, Mercia. He was very keen to get away from me. So why did he slow down when those other two turned up, even though he could have ridden on? He could see they had guns, but it didn't seem to bother him. No, I fear he knew what was about to happen.'

'But he was killed himself.'

'Simplest way to be sure he never talks. I tell you, this isn't the first time those men have killed. They stepped into the open, no thought to anyone, and fired their shots like that.' He snapped his fingers. 'Nasty and precise.'

'There is another question.' Her mind was beginning to reassemble itself. 'Is this related to our hunt for Virgo? People are not murdered without reason. Perhaps Lady Allcot knew something of Virgo somehow. Or . . . what if she is Virgo herself, killed to ensure her silence, like your driver? If that were so, it would suggest a wider conspiracy than one woman acting alone.'

'Or at least panic on the part of her Dutch masters. But how could these men have known you were pursuing her so soon? Then again, she could have been killed for another reason entirely. Say . . . a jealous husband, if he knew what she was up to?'

'That seems too much.' An approaching movement caught her eye. 'But enough of this now.'

The man who had come to her aid in the grounds was walking in their direction. Now that she had the chance, she could see he was well dressed, a courtier of sorts, but he was not wearing the finest silk shirts of the highest nobility. Instead he was more soberly attired, a woollen jacket hooked into simple breeches. In his hand he held a bandage, and on his lightly freckled face, a pitying concern.

'Here,' he said. 'This may help.'

'Thank you,' she replied. 'I am sorry to trouble you, Mr . . .'

'Malvern. Giles Malvern. And it is no trouble, not after what you have witnessed.' He weaved the bandage in dextrous loops, tying it gently into itself. 'This will keep the sprain from catching.'

She looked at her wrist. 'You have some skill, Mr Malvern.'

'I should have. I am a barber surgeon in the King's fleet, or I was.' Smiling, he got to his feet. 'When I see someone hurt I am drawn to help.'

'My manservant was a sailor at one time,' she said. 'On the *Hero*, Nicholas, was it not?'

'That's right,' he confirmed. 'As farrier to the horse.'

'Edward Markstone's old ship,' said Malvern. 'Then you have left the fleet, I take it?'

Nicholas nodded. 'I found employment with Mrs Blakewood.'

'Well, my man. Make sure you take care of your mistress. This must have been a terrible fright.'

'I am quite well, Mr Malvern,' she said.

'Still, I would rest for a few days. Stay in your bed, take a walk in the park. Nothing more wearing.'

She indulged him with a short bow.

'And you, my man,' he repeated, looking again at Nicholas. 'This Dutch war will be fought at sea. Strong tars like you are always needed.' His face faltered. 'But I am sorry, my lady. I should not be encouraging your servants to abandon you. Please forgive me.'

'There is nothing to forgive. I wish we could have met in less dreadful circumstances, Mr Malvern.'

He bowed. 'I hope you can forget this . . . incident, in time.

107

Keep the bandage tight for a couple of days, and if the pain is easing, then remove it.' His freckles seemed to dance as he smiled. 'And remember. You should rest.'

The bandage helped, in truth, but the shock of the murders may have had more to do with distracting her mind from the pain. As for rest, that was impossible. While everyone else was still stood on the drive, waiting to get a glimpse as the bodies were brought out, Mercia spoke again with Lady Allcot's maid, but the devastated girl could barely speak. Nor did anything come of her search of her rooms, and with nothing else they could do at Hampton Court, they left the awful scene behind, in place if not in thought. The boatmen who had brought them upriver broke off their excited conversation to glance at her bandaged wrist, but they said nothing as she stooped inside the cabin of the barge, drawing the blind half-shut.

Dusk was enveloping London as they arrived into Whitehall, but the trials of the day were not yet over. Returning to her chambers, Phibae handed her a freshly sealed summons to attend Lady Castlemaine that same evening. It seemed news had travelled fast, but then the day's events had ensured that it would.

Wanting to calm herself beforehand, she took a quick stroll with Sir William in the Privy Garden, but not only to soothe her fractured spirit. The nobleman had just returned from an interview with the French delegation at Court, enquiring after their missing compatriot from the description Mercia had been able to impart.

'His name is Julien Bellecour,' he said, as they circumvented the magnificent sundial. 'But the French will say nothing about his affair with Lady Allcot, save they see nothing wrong in it. And they would be right.'

'What of Sir Geoffrey?' she asked.

'He refuses to talk of it. When he was told of his wife's indiscretion, he turned red in the face and walked straight from the room, the pompous rogue, as though that were more offensive than her murder.' He sniffed. 'Still, if she had been more discreet, then—'

'Then what, Sir William? The woman has been killed.'

He peered from under his ostrich-feathered hat. 'Are you sure you are well? Witnessing such an act must have been—'

'I will be,' she snapped, but then she sighed. 'I am sorry, Sir William. I know you are asking from kindness.'

He set a hand on her shoulder. 'Do you think she was Virgo? You will be asked.'

She thought a moment. 'I think 'tis possible. Her maid confessed how Lady Allcot had been seeing this Bellecour for at least some weeks, but he is French, not Dutch. Still, he did not flee without a reason. If he is involved, the most likely explanation is he is as much in their employ as she was.'

Sir William sucked in his cheeks. 'Mercia, if you are proposing Bellecour could be complicit in spying for Holland, His Majesty will not take kindly to hearing so. He needs French support for the war.'

''Tis just a notion. There is no evidence.'

'Even if there were, the King would need persuading to broach the subject with the French, for fear of appearing untrusting.' He scoffed. ''Tis a secret and charmed life, that of a diplomat. I have had to deal with many such sneaking characters in my time.'

'Suitable protection to liaise with spies at a foreign Court, then,' she mused. 'In the meantime, I will continue to consider the other women suspect. And hope I can convince Lady Castlemaine that her faith in me was well placed.'

* * *

On opening the summons, she had swapped the dress that had been scuffed in the tussle for an inoffensive ensemble of blue and white, although the neckline plunged enough to show off her ample necklace. As ever, Phibae had set her topknot tight, her ringlets tumbling anew over the silver wires, but she had declined a face patch as too frivolous for the mood. As for the bandage, she made sure it was hidden beneath a pair of black gloves.

She approached the room where the summons had bid her come, but in place of a lady-in-waiting, a pair of liveried guardsmen stepped to the side to allow her in. Uncertain, she entered the well-lit room and dropped to an immediate curtsey. But when she raised her face, her stomach gave out from beneath her. Expecting Lady Castlemaine alone, she was confronted by a much more awkward prospect.

'Your Majesty,' she managed, resuming her curtsey, eyes trained on the hems of her dress.

'Mrs Blakewood. Returned in triumph from America. Please, rise.'

It was the King himself. There was something warm in his acknowledgment, but her heart was still pounding. She knew better than to look up yet.

'My brother and I would like to thank you for your efforts,' he continued. 'And to atone for what has been a day of considerable distress, I should like to share with you this.'

She rose to stand, making sure to hold herself erect. Keeping her gaze averted from the King's, she saw matters were yet worse than she had thought. Beside him stood his brother, the Duke of York, behind whom a third figure, supported by the aid of a cane, looked down with undisguised contempt. Ignoring her uncle's scorn, she dared a glance at Lady Castlemaine, staring out on the river, looking for all the world bored. But then her eyes followed the line of the King's outstretched arm to a portrait above the fireplace, an intricate work of art, and her heart beat faster still.

'The painting!' For an instant she forgot about Lady Allcot. 'Your Majesty has received it!'

'Three months ago.' The pleasure in his voice was evident. 'It was sent from New York while you were visiting the Governor of Connecticut, I believe.' He walked into her line of view. 'Hard to believe this child is me, no?'

At last she looked on the King, his rich black wig falling over his shoulders much lower than her own hair covered hers, before she looked anew on the painting on the wall, a family portrait she knew intimately: the same the King had so desired, the same she had crossed the ocean to retrieve.

'It is magnificent, Your Majesty,' she said, unable to keep the wonder from her voice. 'Especially so here at Whitehall, where it should always have hung.'

'And I have you to thank for it,' said Charles. 'My father's family portrait, thought burnt and now restored.' He looked at her and smiled. 'I have stood here, Mrs Blakewood, every day since it was returned to me. I am filled with a mixture of contentment and sorrow: joy this picture is mine again; melancholy to see myself as a happy boy with my family, before all the troubles began and most of them were taken unto God. But now I, like this painting, am back in the palace, where I belong.' And then his tone changed; he held out his tanned hand towards a leather-backed chair. 'But now sit. My brother and I wish to discuss the obscene events of today. And you, Sir Francis. You will join us also.'

Taking his own seat, he beckoned with bent finger for Sir Francis to come forward. Unseen by the King, her uncle's face twitched; he hobbled towards them, lowering himself with the aid of his cane into the narrow chair at the Duke of York's side, who was looking on her presence with equal enthusiasm. Lady Castlemaine had not ceased staring through the window, but Mercia knew she was listening to every word.

'Barbara there,' the King began, 'has told you of the delicacy of the situation we face. We are gratified you agreed to help so soon after your arrival home.' He glanced at Sir Francis, an unwelcome reminder that her own fate hung in the balance. 'But I am not accustomed to hearing of public murders in my palaces. What can you tell me of the death of our Lady Allcot?'

'Thank you, Your Majesty,' she began. 'May I say, 'tis an unexpected honour to be in Your Majesty's presence, as well as that of the painting you have desired these many years to find.'

Sir Francis scoffed lightly under his breath. The King turned his head, the smallest amount, enough for Sir Francis to resume his deferential posture, but the Duke's lips were curling well enough.

'Speak then, Mrs Blakewood,' he said. 'We have little time for such obsequiousness.'

'Your Highness.' She bowed to the Duke. 'Then I believe what happened today is likely connected to the endeavour His Majesty has asked me to pursue.'

'Likely?' said the King. 'It should be extraordinary if it is not. A woman who is suspect of treason and who is then shot down.'

She nodded. 'Your Majesty knows that the woman you have set me to unmask is close to a member of the war council. That means one of five women, as far as I can see, one of whom was Lady Allcot, may the Lord protect her soul. I had been hopeful of speaking with her today, before her untimely death prevented it.'

'Look up, Mercia, please,' said the King. Startled at his use of her Christian name, she blinked, but complied. 'Tell us what you suppose. I shall ask Sir Francis to share his knowledge likewise. You will know that he and his wife have been considering this matter also.'

Sir Francis's cheeks convulsed. 'I had thought, Your Majesty, that—'

Again the slight turn of the head; Sir Francis bowed, leaving Mercia to continue.

'Lady Allcot's murder is heinous, Your Majesty. But you will have been informed, I believe, that she had travelled to Hampton Court to meet a man.'

His face set. 'I have been so informed.'

'While we cannot know the connection this may have with the killing, I think it possible there might be such.'

'I hope not.' The King glanced at his brother. 'Nor do I want my enemies twisting this outrage. Enemies at home, I mean. I do not want to see false stories spread.'

'Charles,' said Lady Castlemaine, still looking through the window. 'I scarcely believe people will think you had a hand in her death.'

'I would not be so hasty. Even if they do not think it, they may be led to believe that others in my retinue are not so scrupulous. You know full well how matters stand. Yet we believe in the rule of law here, unlike the usurper Cromwell.' He leant forward, his large hands gripping the finely carved hawks' heads that finished the arms of his chair. 'Mrs Blakewood, your enquiries have taken a sinister turn. I need you to tell me if Lady Allcot was the spy, and if not, then who is. Moreover, I need you to tell me why she was killed.'

'Mrs Blakewood will do so,' said Lady Castlemaine. 'Will you not?'

Mercia swallowed. 'Yes, my lady.'

'See, Charles.' She smiled. 'You shall have your answer, and by the end of next week. Unlike Clarendon's man there, whose wife was dissuaded by a simple threat.'

The King gave his mistress an unreadable look. Mercia glanced at her uncle, but his face was equally impassive.

'My Lady,' she said. 'I am not sure if I can—'

'By next week,' she repeated, and Mercia fell silent.

The King looked at her. 'Thank you, Barbara, for that confidence. But it is now past four of the clock. You have summoned Mrs Blakewood and she has come. I believe you are expected with the Queen?'

Lady Castlemaine's head jerked back. 'Indeed, but—'

'Then I shall see you later.'

Mercia looked on as Lady Castlemaine cleared her throat, swept out her dress with an exaggerated flick of her wrists, and stood. When she had left, no farewell of her own, the King continued as though she had never been present.

'But this matter of Lady Allcot's lover,' he said. 'You must forget it. You are to confine your investigations to the women of the Court.'

'If I may offer an opinion, Your Majesty,' she said, recovering her wits after Lady Castlemaine's sudden dismissal. 'The Frenchman may have information about the death of Lady Allcot, even if he knows naught about Virgo. Would not that be incentive to seek him out?'

'Perhaps on that point you are right. But listen well. We have discussed how this matter is delicate. I do not want your involvement to compromise any work that may already be in train.'

She raised the slightest eyebrow. 'Other work?'

'Conducted by men in my employ, shall we say, more accustomed to such affairs.' He gave her a meaningful nod. 'But let us return to the problem at hand. Your uncle has made no headway in determining the source of our breach, and as Barbara so subtly reminded us, you know what happened to your aunt.'

She dared not look at Sir Francis. 'At this juncture, I would not want to accuse any of the women of being—'

'So you have made little headway likewise,' he sighed.

'It is merely that, Your Majesty, more time is needed to know—'

'More time during which our fleet and our interests are in danger.' The Duke had been toying with his doublet; now he walked to rest against the mantelpiece. 'We shall have to abandon the council if we cannot stay this leak. I knew this idea was folly.' He scoffed. 'Setting any woman on the task was dubious, but a woman whose father was an enemy of the Court, even more so.'

'We are maintaining the council so that we can uncover this spy,' said the King. 'And we agreed with Barbara that a woman would have more liberty than a man. In a state of war, it is doubtful that Virgo is the only spy in the city, and I do not want information she may have on that point frightened out of reach by an overhanded approach.' He tapped on the arm of his chair. 'Mrs Blakewood, you are well aware of what is at stake here.' He fixed her with a look, and she knew he was not referring to the war with the Dutch. 'You have been at Court near a week thus far. You had the ingenuity to find that painting above my head. You must have learnt something.'

Wanting to show confidence, she made sure to hold his gaze. Despite the King's plea for information, she could tell it was reassurance he required now, not enlightenment.

'Your Majesty, we know Virgo's intelligence comes from the council. We know Virgo is close to a man of that council. Whether he is passing her that information inadvertently or no, in the end it makes little difference, for just as she will soon be held to account, so too must he be. Whichever Virgo is, I will find her out, and you shall have your spy, and the security of your council restored.'

'Bold words, Mrs Blakewood,' said the King. 'I find it hard to believe any of those men could be untrue, but I have learnt in my life how fragile a commodity is trust.' He reclined in his seat, crossing his tightly stockinged legs. 'I think, Sir Francis, now would be the time to repeat for us all what you told me and my brother just before.'

Sir Francis seemed caught off guard by the sudden request. 'Your Majesty . . . you will recall . . . that the man I spoke of . . .'

The King scratched at his wig. 'Which man was that?'

'Sir William, Your Majesty,' he conceded.

'What?' Mercia could not help herself. 'Sir William Calde?'

'The same.' The King nodded sagely. 'You were concerned at his trade interests, if I remember rightly, Sir Francis.'

'He . . . yes. He has dealings that lead to the Dutch West India Company. And of course, he sits on Your Majesty's war council.'

Mercia stared. 'If you insinuate that Sir William could be connected with this affair, you should recall he was only appointed to the war council last week.'

'That is not strictly true,' he droned. 'The war council has existed for over a year and Sir William was never discharged from it.' Unseen by the King, he narrowed his eyes. 'You realise you are not privy to most of what goes on at Court. Sir William has associates he has never before revealed. Perhaps you know him less well than you think.'

'I merely advise caution,' said the King. 'Be mindful of what you divulge, and to whom you divulge it.' His eyes drifted to Lady Castlemaine's vacated seat. 'A sad state of affairs, but as I am oft told, 'tis unwise to assume a thing.'

Chapter Ten

Sir Francis's revelation about Sir William was intriguing, if only because he had never mentioned his Dutch interests before, but part of her wondered whether her uncle was merely being mischievous.

'Sir William cannot be the source of Virgo's information,' she explained to Nicholas, walking beside him on an hour-long stroll around the palace – or rather, an hour-long march. 'He was sailing home with us when the King's false report was finding its way into enemy hands.'

'Then likely 'tis nothing to worry on. A reminder to be careful, is all.'

'As the King said.' She sighed. 'Damn Lady Castlemaine. She more or less made a promise on my behalf I doubt I shall be able to keep. Success by the end of next week, she said.'

'Can you do it?' He smiled. 'Can we?'

'We shall have to make a discovery of some sort. I tell you one thing, mind: she was not pleased when the King ordered her from the room. Perhaps her position is not so secure as she likes others to believe. And we still have no idea who Virgo is. I shall have to speak with the other women again. I mean to start with Lady Cartwright.'

'The mocking woman with the servant boy? I thought you said you'd offended her.'

'Remember the first Indians we met in New England? Well, they had been offended too. I plan to ambush her, as they did to us in the forest.'

Nicholas laughed out loud. 'Will you also throw a head on the ground at her feet?'

'And she is Sir Geoffrey Allcot's mistress. She might have some notion why his wife could have been murdered. But truth be told, none of these women are much like me. It is difficult to find a way into their lives at all.'

'I wouldn't worry about fitting in. I certainly don't.'

'I suppose not.' She glanced at the extravagant sleeve of her pale-yellow dress. 'I must admit, I sometimes wish I could be back in the simplicity of my attire on board ship.'

'You didn't say that at the time. You said you wanted to throw them in the sea, if I remember right.'

'Yes, Nicholas.' A passing courtier gave them a snide glance, and she lowered her voice. 'But you should temper how you address me here. These people do not care we have spent months together, crossing the ocean and back, or realise what we have lived through. Any closeness on our part will not be understood, or will be deliberately misconstrued.'

He held up a hand. 'Back to the gutter for me, then.'

'I do not mean that. Take care not to be conspicuous, is all.' She cleared her throat. 'What will you do while I am trying to make progress? It must be dull for you here.'

'I . . . promised Cerwen a turn in the park.'

'Cerwen?'

'The maid who washed my shirt that time, when Phibae brought

118

it back. She has a spare hour this afternoon, and as she doesn't leave the palace much, I thought . . .'

'I see.' She raised a playful eyebrow. 'Then enjoy.'

Arranging the ambush was not hard. Once a day at least, Lady Cartwright met her cohort of admirers at her vantage point beneath the Italianate statue, the whiteness of the youth's harsh pallor gleaming in the candlelight that lit up his handsome face. Just out of sight, Mercia spread herself across a comfortable bench, reading over and again the same lines of Wroth's poetry, waiting for the women's banal conversation to end. Hours seemed to pass, though it must have been minutes, until a baying of raucous laughter caused her to raise her head. Then Lady Cartwright's morose boy Tacitus came round the corner, staring at the floor, his eyes glum.

'Tacitus,' she said, setting down her book.

He bowed and made to move on. 'My lady.'

The boy's wretched expression tugged at her heart. 'Stay a moment. Why so sad?'

His whole frame sagged. 'There is no reason, my lady.'

'Come, sit beside me.'

He hesitated, but did as she asked, installing himself on the bench. The candlelight in the sconce above seemed to find reflection in his darting eyes.

'Is it your mistress, Tacitus?' she asked. 'Do not worry. She cannot hear if we speak low.'

He glanced back the way he had come. 'She is my mistress, my lady.'

'That is not much of an answer. Do you like being in her service?'

He blinked. 'Then yes, my lady.'

'In truth?' She leant in. 'She does not like me. You have seen that for yourself.'

'That is . . . not for me to say, my lady.'

'Perhaps not. But I can. I think she is a vain wretch who would last not ten minutes outside of the comforts of this Court.' She smiled. 'Look at me, Tacitus. I am not trying to trick you. I am merely trying to say that there are people who do not think as she does.'

He stared at the floor, the smile she had hoped for nowhere to be seen. But then what had she expected? As far as he was concerned, she was a lady of the Court, and he was but a servant. A young, mocked servant at that. The gulf between them was greater even than that between herself and the King.

'What is your name?' she ventured.

'Tacitus,' came the response.

'I mean your birth name. Not the one these women have given you.'

At that he looked up, and there was something new in his eyes.

'Are you like Miss Whent, my lady?'

'Miss Whent? Why say that?'

'Because . . . I am sorry, my lady. I should not speak.'

'Has your mistress ordered that you must remain silent? Tacitus, if you talk with me I will not say. Why speak so about Miss Whent?'

He swallowed, but this time he answered. 'She is the only other person who has asked me my name. She is . . .'

'She is what, Tacitus?'

His hands were gripping the edge of the bench; he looked as though he wanted to flee. 'She is kind, my lady, nothing more. I mean no offence.'

'There is no offence.'

'Then you are kind too, my lady.'

'I am . . . understanding, that is all. So what is your real name?'

He wrung his hands, but his voice caught a little firmer. 'I do not speak it here.'

'Oh? Why not?'

'Because it is mine, my lady. While I am Lady Cartwright's, I am Tacitus. If one day I am someone else, then perhaps I will have my old name once more.'

The notion appealed to her. 'I understand. It is something that is yours alone. Then tell me how old you are.'

'Sixteen, my lady. But . . . do not think I am complaining. I am well treated, have good clothes and food.'

He seemed in a state of perpetual anxiety. *What can I do to help?* she thought. *There must be something.* Then she glanced at her book and had an idea.

'What of entertainments, Tacitus? Do you have friends?'

'Yes, my lady. Some boys outside the palace. And – I know your maid, my lady, Phibae. She talks to me sometimes because . . . Well. Because.'

'That is good. And with your friends, do you play games, or read together also?'

'No, my lady.' His eyes widened. 'I cannot read.'

She would have been astounded if he could. 'Would you like to be able to, Tacitus?'

He looked away. 'Sometimes we try to teach each other things, like some letters, but . . . read, my lady? That is not for boys like me. Boys like your son read.'

'You know I have a son?'

'My mistress has talked of it with her friends.'

'Of course.' She smiled. 'There was a time, Tacitus, when nobody in England was allowed to read the Bible save for priests. But now all who can read are able to follow its teachings for themselves. It is a noble thing to read, and a good one. To enjoy beautiful poetry, or to understand what others think. History from across the ages, written by men such as a long-dead Roman called Tacitus himself.' She looked at him. 'While I am here, I have promised to help Phibae improve her reading, just a little. If you wish it, I could teach you as well.'

The look of wonder on his face caught at her soul. 'You would do that?'

'While I help one, I may as well help two.'

'Not even Miss Whent would do that!' He frowned. 'Why so gentle?'

'Because I like to help, where I can. Some would say because I like to interfere.'

'My lady, I would like . . .' But his sparse frame wilted once more. 'I cannot go anywhere without my mistress's permission.'

'You are not with your mistress all the time. You are not with her now, for instance. You can come when you have your spare time.'

He thought a moment, then of a sudden looked right at her. 'My lady, Phibae says you have sailed the seas. Have you seen my people, as Miss Whent has? She tells me things. Bad things.'

She shook her head. 'I have not much seen them, no, not outside of London. But Tacitus, I believe we are all God's creation, wherever we are from. It is strength of action and of mind that separates one man from another, or one woman. I think you, too, have a strong mind beneath. Can I ask Phibae to arrange for you to join us?'

He looked away, and then –

'Yes.' He nodded. 'Yes, my lady. Please.' But then his body turned rigid, and he leapt to his feet. 'Mistress! I was just . . . I was . . .'

Mercia glanced round to see Lady Cartwright hands on hips before them, glaring with obvious pique. Much more slowly, she stood herself.

'Lady Cartwright,' she greeted. 'I did not hear you come up.'

'Mrs Blakewood, I might have known. Why are you keeping my boy from his duties?'

'The blame is mine. Tacitus walked past while I was reading. I made him sit with me awhile.'

'Why? Because you cannot afford your own black?' She clicked her fingers. 'Boy, go back to my chambers and wait for me there.'

Tacitus's wide eyes darted from woman to woman in a sort of sympathetic fright. He scurried away, but not before Mercia raised the slightest eyebrow, giving him a complicit glance. Then she took a deep breath and turned back to Lady Cartwright.

'It is pleasing to see you again, Lady Cartwright. Pray, may we talk a short while?'

Lady Cartwright pursed her lips. 'I have been talking this past hour. And your conversation was not the most appealing when last we met.'

'I was affected by the assault on my aunt that day. You will understand my mind was not itself.'

'Oh, I think you were perfectly lucid. And the insult was taken nonetheless.'

'It was not meant to be as such.' She tried a warm smile. 'Come, let us sit and talk.'

'Then let me be plain, Mrs Blakewood.' She folded her arms. 'You may think you can inveigle your way into Court, but however much you feign it, you are not one of us. Once Sir William is bored, you will be on your way. Now kindly stand aside. I must prepare for tonight.'

'Another party, Lady Cartwright?'

'Another you shall not attend.'

Attempts at civility were getting her nowhere. 'And yet you were not at the ball in the Banqueting House. Why ever not?'

Anger flashed over her face. 'What concern is that of yours? I was elsewhere, that is all. But know this. I should take care that what happened to your aunt that evening does not happen to you.'

'Assuredly, Lady Cartwright? What does that mean?'

'Nothing at all. A mere observation that those who pry tend to come undone.' She brushed Mercia aside with a rustle of her dress. 'And now, Mrs Blakewood, goodnight.'

* * *

All the more pleased with her offer to teach Tacitus, Mercia made her way back to her rooms, pondering the force of Lady Cartwright's words. Had they been a mere observation, as the bitter woman had implied, or had they been more of a threat?

Reaching her chambers, she heard the sounds of laughter from behind the closed door, a man's voice and a woman's. She pushed it open to find Nicholas jutting out his chin, sharing a joke with a maid she had never before seen, while Phibae sat in a corner altering a dress. He held out his hands and waved them around in imitation of some creature or other, making the woman laugh louder as she brushed a hand through her deep brown hair.

Hearing Mercia enter, she abruptly ceased her mirth. Nicholas turned his head and coughed, tucking a fold of his shirt into his breeches.

'Hello,' he said. 'Er, this is Cerwen.'

The maid curtsied. 'My lady. I was . . . helping Nick pass the time.' She retreated to the corridor. 'Goodnight, my lady.'

She left, pulling closed the door. Over Nicholas's shoulder, Phibae lightly shook her head.

'You told me to wait for you here,' he explained, 'and I thought I'd welcome a bit of company. Phibae is . . . that is, I didn't want to disturb her from . . .'

'Indeed, Nicholas,' said Mercia. 'But I would rather you be careful whom you invite into my chambers.' She looked behind him. 'Phibae, I happened to speak with Lady Cartwright's boy, Tacitus, just now. I had a thought I should like to discuss with you later.'

Phibae nodded, not breaking from her work. 'He is a good boy, that one.'

'Nicholas, would you come with me a moment?'

She walked into the bedroom. Nicholas followed her in, shutting the door.

'Nicholas,' she began, 'I know you want to make friends, but you must heed what I said before. I should have thought what we have experienced these past months would have taught you the value of caution.'

His eyes widened. 'We were talking, is all. Phibae was there the whole time. I'm not going to—' He shook his head. 'No matter.'

'Not going to what?'

He sighed. 'Suspect everyone I ever come across. 'Tis not right.'

'And you think I do, is that it?'

'No, Mercia, but . . .' He glanced briefly away. 'I've served as your manservant for months. Aside from . . . that once . . . I've acted faithfully. I've stood by you, risked my own life . . . God's truth, I was nearly killed in America! I sat idly by as Nathan was left behind—'

She folded her arms. 'Left behind?'

'All I mean is I've done a lot for you, and I've been glad to do it. But I don't think it wrong to expect I might be allowed my own life into the bargain. Now I've taken a woman for a walk in the park, and I've talked to her here in your rooms. If you'd rather I didn't bring her here, then I won't. But I'd think I'd be allowed a little freedom.'

'What has brought this on?' She stared at him. 'You know I am grateful for everything you have done. And it was not me who forced you to come to the palace. You think I want to be here? I want to be home, with Daniel, as soon as I can. All I said was, we need to be discreet.' She lowered her voice. 'Which presumably includes not arguing while Phibae is near.'

He took a deep breath. 'You're right. And I'm sorry. But I am . . . frustrated, if truth be told. I was looking forward to seeing my daughter again, my family and my mates. Instead I'm stuck here with all these . . . precious coxcombs, and if a pretty woman wants to spend some time with me, what harm is that?'

'None, Nicholas. I just meant you should—'

'You may have given up on all that, but I haven't.' He looked to the ceiling, tugging at his already ruffled hair. 'Damn it, Mercia, I'm sorry, again.' He turned his sad eyes to her. 'I'm sorry, Mercia.'

She nodded, but the backs of her eyes were burning. He was right, she knew, but what he had said still hurt.

'Perhaps you should go,' she said. 'We can speak another time about what we do next.'

'I said I was sorry.' He took a step forwards. 'I mean it.'

'And I know you speak the truth.' Annoyed with herself, she scratched away her nascent tears, but then the words began to flow in their place. 'Why cannot everything turn out right? Why do I have to struggle like this, my whole life? My brother, my mother . . . by the Lord, I have not seen my mother since we returned! All I want is a normal life, Nicholas, like other women have. All I want is to be with Daniel and with . . .' She shook her head in angst. 'But that is too late. After what happened in America . . . it hurt, Nicholas. It hurt, and it goes on hurting.' She jabbed at her chest. 'Here, in my heart. In my mind. I see them over and over, all the deaths! And I have nobody to turn to but myself.'

'Yes, you do.' He came round to her, and he placed his hands lightly on her shoulders. 'You have me, in spite of what I said. But you cannot rely on me forever, not like that.' He smiled. 'I'm from the alleys of London, Mercia, and you're a fine lady of the gentry. We're a very odd twosome. May I?' He reached into his pockets and withdrew a clean handkerchief, wiping the moisture from her eyelids. 'But you need someone else to share some of this with, as I need someone too. I've lain awake myself at night because of what we've seen. You aren't alone in how you feel, but . . .'

'Yes?' she said.

'You are strong, Mercia. The bravest woman I've known. But there's no shame in admitting that it's hard to live alone.'

'Strong.' She bit her lip. ''Tis hard for you to understand, perhaps, but I have to fight, every single day, to be taken as seriously as my brother would have been taken in my place. When I tell those who doubt me of the hardships I have endured, of the things I have done, they oft refuse to believe them, solely because of who I am. But I mean to go on ignoring those naysayers until the day I join my brother in heaven.' She eased herself from his touch, and she forced a smile. 'I am well, Nicholas, truly. Now, 'tis not too late. Why not join your friends in some tavern or other? Spend tomorrow with your daughter, or with Cerwen, if you like, if she can be spared the time. Come back the day after. You need the rest.'

'That's . . . are you sure you don't mind?'

'Go. I shall want my bed soon.' She shooed him away. 'I mean it. Have a day apart.'

'A whole day?' He grinned. 'Thank you. That means a lot.'

'Leave, you old rogue. I will be better after sleep.'

He returned her kind look, and when he had gone she imagined him drinking with his friends, or walking with Cerwen, or any of a number of things he could be doing with his life. As for herself, she sat on the bed, thinking that tomorrow she would make sure to see Daniel, for she would welcome the comfort of her son.

But tonight she was alone, and as she looked at the flowers dying in the vase, at the wavering flames of her fire, at her waiting pen and ink, she felt the rawness of bruised emotion, and she longed for the days when she had enjoyed friends of her own. And yes, she was strong, but still she felt bereft, and the call of her tears could no longer be denied.

Chapter Eleven

She watched, happier now, as Daniel talked with another boy slightly older than himself, and she was proud, too, to see him so finely dressed in his little grey suit, his doublet remarkably free of stains.

Yes, she thought, this was all worth it. Even when her son spent all of five minutes with his mother before returning to his new friends.

'He does you credit,' said the young woman at her side. 'He has only been here a week and yet see how quickly he has made friends. The tutors already speak of him as capable.'

'Thank you.' Mercia beamed. 'He is a curious child, that is certain.'

'Inquisitive, I take it you mean, rather than strange.'

She laughed. 'Indeed, Lavinia.'

'I only hope that one day my charge proves himself the same. Between us, I fear the little Duke is somewhat mindful of his status, even though he is not yet quite two. A little too much like his father, the Duke of York.' She touched Mercia's sleeve. 'If you can tear yourself away, I will introduce you.'

Dressed in a simple red dress outdone by her opulent hairstyle, Lavinia Whent led Mercia along a corridor to a massive oaken door barred by two sturdy guards. She winked at the guard on the left, a strong youth of about her own age; the guard smiled, standing aside to let them in.

She progressed through an outer chamber, filled with the paraphernalia of a one-year-old infant – a cradle, small clothes, tiny toys – into a larger room, the floor strewn with the sweetest doublets Mercia had ever seen. In the corner, an older woman was tending to her charge, a rather podgy child.

'Good day, Your Highness,' said Lavinia, crouching down to look into his eyes. 'Did you miss me?'

The boy laughed.

'Yes, you missed me.' She brought her face close to his and scrunched up her nose, making him laugh still harder.

'Miss Whent,' said the other. 'I have cautioned you before against such frivolities.'

'Forgive me, Lady Plaidstow.' She rose to her feet. 'I cannot help it.'

'Perhaps you would do well to learn how. And who might this be?'

Mercia bowed. 'Mercia Blakewood, my lady. An acquaintance of Miss Whent's.'

'Mercia's son is currently tutored at Court,' explained Lavinia. 'I knew she could not resist a look at the Duke.' She pulled a face at the young child, who laughed once more. 'How could anyone?'

'Your Highness.' Despite the infant's tender years, Mercia dropped to a curtsey. 'It is an honour to meet you.'

The boy squealed.

'Hard to believe this fragile creature may be King one day,' said Lavinia. 'Such a delicate aspect, and so very young.'

'Miss Whent,' admonished Lady Plaidstow, clearly her superior in the nursery. 'The Queen may yet conceive.'

'She may. But Mercia, all the talk is that the Queen is barren. I am not sure you knew that, being away for so long. Should matters stand, 'tis likely the Duke here will be crowned one day.'

'His Highness is healthy?' asked Mercia, unable to take her eyes away, wanting for all the world to copy Lavinia by blowing in his face and making absurd noises. Why do we do that to babies, she thought?

'Very,' answered Lady Plaidstow. 'Too healthy, at times, bouncing around all over the place.' She held out a finger, which the young Duke gladly took. 'Are you not, my precious?'

He squawked, and the women laughed.

'I remember when my Danny was that age,' said Mercia. 'He had none of the responsibility His Highness has, but he was just as vocal.'

'He is the new boy?'

'Yes, my lady.'

'Then my husband says you have a gifted son, Mrs Blakewood. He is tutor to the boys.'

'Thank you, Lady Plaidstow. His Highness is a remarkable child, I can sense it.'

Lady Plaidstow inclined her head. 'Indeed he is. I dare say it will not be long before he is learning with the men himself.'

'Come, Mercia,' said Lavinia. 'Let us leave His Highness to his amusements and talk some more outside.'

With a broad smile at the Duke, Mercia followed into the antechamber, shutting the inner door behind them. The high-vaulted room let in less light, but was airy nonetheless.

'What do you think?' said Lavinia. 'Beautiful, no?'

'Quite. Are his sisters healthy also?'

'Mary is. She is five now, and seems in rude health. As for Anne, she is but two months old, so 'tis still early to say. I do not much know of her, but from what I can gather, she seems free of sickness.' She drew up her seat. 'Do not underestimate the importance of these children. You heard what I said. The King spreads bastards across the land, but his wife produces no heir. Surely she is barren, and that means his young nephew in there will just as surely be King.'

'And yourself, Miss Whent?' asked Mercia, settling into an upholstered chair.

'I told you to call me Lavinia.'

'Forgive me. Do you intend to marry Sir Peter and have children of your own some day? He is . . . advancing in years.'

'As is Sir William, Mercia, but then you already have your own boy.' Lavinia scratched at her calf. 'My, these boots are uncomfortable.' She smiled. 'Yes, I should like children, but not necessarily with Peter.'

'Then with whom?'

'It is hard to say. But when I have children, I hope it will be as a wife, not as a mistress. There is enough of that around here already.'

Mercia studied her blank face. 'You do not strike me as a disapproving sort of woman.'

'I have morals, Mercia. Strong ones, betimes. But this Court can be a little . . . uncomfortable, shall we say. Staid, for all its pleasures.'

'I understand. Do you miss home?'

'If you ask if I miss the Barbados, then yes. If you ask if I miss my family, then no.'

The answer intrigued her. 'Why so?'

'In short, I despise my father. Does it shock you to hear me speak so?'

It did, a little. 'I do not know the circumstances. I make no assumptions one way or the other.'

'It was my father who sent me here. It was he who asked his friends at Court to secure a position for me. And so I was placed in the young Duke's household, under the watching eye of my . . . cousin's wife's aunt.' She counted the relations on her fingers. 'I think that is right. Lady Plaidstow.'

'Then it did not turn out badly. What do you miss?'

She draped her hand over the edge of her chair. 'The sun. My friends. My own nephew. Then again, I do not miss the heat, I do not miss the insects, I do not miss the constant risk of dying from some unheard-of disease, and I do not miss being forced to witness the treatment of the blacks.'

Mercia nodded. 'I spoke with Tacitus yesterday. Lady Cartwright's servant.'

'You mean toy.'

'Servant. He speaks well of you.'

She shrugged. 'I know the blacks better than most here do. I lived with them, remember, and am prepared to speak with them.' She leant towards her. 'Did you know, there are more blacks in the Barbados than there are of us? If ever they realise that, men like my father will be in trouble. It will be they who are flogged until their skin is but a sliver of mangled puss.'

The image made Mercia no less nauseous than Lavinia's seeming detachment. 'The way you describe it is most graphic,' she said. 'In America, I saw an Indian boy shot before me, with no hearing. And yet he was not owned as chattel.'

'Nobody wants to know. Not as long as men like my father own the sugar plantations, or men like Sir Geoffrey Allcot and the Duke of York are prepared to engage in this . . . trade.' She glanced at the inner door. 'Can you believe that sweet child in there is the son of such a man?'

'I have found the Duke of York to be unpleasant in many circumstances.'

'And the King?' She looked at her. 'You have his ear somewhat, I hear. What thinks he of matters such as these?'

The question gave Mercia pause. 'Why do you say I have the ear of the King?'

'He sent you to America, did he not? To retrieve that painting.'

'You are well informed.'

'Mercia, this is Whitehall. Everybody knows everybody else's business, or at least the most of it. When that painting arrived, His Majesty made certain the entire palace was paraded before it. Not that he mentioned you, of course, but the word soon spread all the same.' She set her palms on her lap. 'The daughter of a supposed traitor sailing the ocean on a secret quest, vanquishing the real villain to see him dragged home in his place. And now installed at Whitehall as consort to the rich and powerful Sir William Calde. Quite the story, is it not?'

'I had not thought of it like that. But Lavinia,' she said, keen to divert the conversation back to her companion, 'aside from your duties with the little Duke, are you happy here at Court? And with Sir Peter?'

'Yes, Mercia, I am. Peter is a little pompous, but he provides for me well.'

'You spend much time together?'

'As he is widowed. You and I are not like other women, who have to share their master with his wife, or who are married themselves, like Lady Castlemaine.'

'Or Lady Cartwright.'

'Her?' She almost spat. 'I would not pay much heed to that foulness of a woman.'

She frowned. 'What makes you say that?'

'Come, you have met her. She spends her time being fawned over by those ridiculous followers, growing rich and fat on the profits of Sir Geoffrey's insidious trade.' She smirked, dispelling her looks. 'She will have to take care not to get too fat, or like Lady Castlemaine, she will be on her way out.'

'Lady Castlemaine?'

'The King has his eye on young Frances Stewart now. Who is beautiful, lithe – and seventeen.' She tapped her forehead. 'Not much up here, mark, but whenever are men much interested in conversation when their breeches start to swell?'

'Lavinia,' whispered Mercia. 'The Duke is next door.'

Lavinia laughed. 'I do not think his young mind will yet be offended by such talk. Besides, that door is thick. Nobody can hear through it.'

'And the guards beyond this other door?'

'They are guards, Mercia. They have their place and will let me mind mine. I speak as I want.'

She tugged at a ringlet of her hair. 'Does Sir Peter too speak as he wants, do you find?'

'Why ask?' Lavinia blinked, but then reclined into her seat. 'Do not all such men like to prove their worth, to their women as much as to each other?'

She made sure she laughed. 'I suppose that would depend on the boast. Sir William talks well enough, if he keeps his opinions hidden at times. But I am intrigued. We both enjoy the company of trusted men. Is Sir Peter much the same as Sir William?'

'As I said. He likes to talk.'

'And this war with the Dutch?' She decided to venture a bolder question. 'What says he of that? What say you?'

'It grows hot in here, does it not?' Lavinia fanned the air before her face. 'Oh, this tiresome war. 'Tis all everyone has been baying for. I leave such matters to men like Peter, as I must. If you are concerned, I doubt we are in danger in London. No, we face a much more deadly threat.'

'And what is that?'

She shuddered. 'The plague. They say the first few families have already been taken. If we are not careful, it will spread, and we shall have to move from the city.'

'Is that likely?' A chill took her as she thought of Nicholas on his day out.

'Outside the palace and the park, the air in London is foul. My knowledge may be slight, but I fancy I know something of how sicknesses begin. If the stench of the city is not lessened, then the plague will spread through the miasma and infect more and more. Many of the poor are at grave risk. Indeed, at risk of the grave. But I suppose when 'tis our time, God will call regardless.'

She fell silent, and Mercia recognised the look in her eyes, the look that takes the mind to some unfathomable place. She was on the verge of asking more when the door behind them opened, and Lady Plaidstow called for aid. Bidding Mercia farewell, Lavinia disappeared into the happy room to care for her precious young charge.

Returning to Daniel, Mercia dragged her reluctant son to spend a half-hour together in the park. The time over too soon, she kissed him goodbye and walked back to her chambers to plot her next move. But she did not get far before she came across an onlooker leaning against a pillar, one leg crossed over the other, watching her approach.

He stepped forward and smiled.

'Hello.'

Recognising his handsome mien, she was about to nod a polite greeting and walk on, when she thought of what Nicholas had said the evening before.

'Good morning, Mr Raff,' she greeted.

'Henry. And yes, it is a good morning now.' He held out a hand. 'Would you care to walk with me a while?'

She looked at his expectant face. She knew better than to think he was purely interested in her company, but he was. . . very good looking. Surely a few minutes would not hurt?

'Lead on,' she agreed.

He broadened his smile and set off towards the Privy Garden, engaging her in idle chatter as they strolled. But it was drizzling by the time they reached the atrium that led outdoors, and so he sat her in a window seat, from where she could see the garden's splendour through the rain-spotted glass.

'I know how you like the park,' he said. 'But as you cannot walk out now without spoiling your dress, I hope this view will be a substitute. And perhaps my company, if I do not flatter myself overmuch.'

She eased herself into the cushioned seat. 'Your friend is not with you today, Henry?'

'James? He would be in the way.' He sat beside her, close, but not so they were touching, his jet-black breeches tight against his legs. 'I have some time before I must attend to work, and I should like to become better acquainted.' His eyes flashed. 'I serve under the Earl of Clarendon.'

'And what do you do for him?' she asked, amused at the way he sat back, pretending not to puff out his chest.

'Oh, this and that.'

'Very precise.'

'Just somewhat dull. I should rather learn about you.' He leant towards her. 'I was saying to James, when I saw you at the ball earlier this week, how I had never seen you at Court before.'

She held his gaze. 'Are you not married, Henry?'

'What does that matter?' He shrugged. 'But no. There is time enough to find a wife. In the meanwhile, there is much to admire here.'

The younger man's flattery was as ridiculous as Sir William's, but she could not help but smile.

'I am not sure Sir William would approve of such boldness.'

'And I said before, Sir William is an old man. Enough of him.' He inched a little closer. 'Tell me of yourself. The woman who travelled the ocean.'

'So you do know about me.'

'Only that. How you did not rest until you succeeded. I admire that, Mercia, very much. But I want to know about the woman.' Closer. 'Who you are and why.'

He was near enough now that she could feel his presence in the space around her, a tingling, erotic sensation that made her guard slip. She looked into his eyes, bluer than hers, and saw his pupils were dilated. And he was so . . . damn it, so handsome, and she began to think, why not just . . . enjoy the attention? Until a voice inside reminded her where she was, and how she had to be cautious.

She pulled back. 'You will find, Henry, I am not the sort of woman who merely accedes to a man's wishes.'

'Whatever sort you are, you are a woman. You have the same needs any woman does. But that you are different is what makes you so exquisite.'

She did her best not to react, but her shoulders betrayed her. Yet Raff was unabashed.

'Why not allow this?' he said.

'Because . . .' Unable to think of a reason, she rose to her feet. 'I enjoyed our talk, Mr Raff.'

'Must you go?' He leapt to stand beside her. 'May I see you again, at least?'

She looked him up and down. 'Perhaps you may yet.'

'I take that to mean yes.' He reached to touch her cheek, the lightest of caresses from the very tip of his finger. 'Then I will speak with you soon, fleeting temptress.'

He pulled a hand across his shirt, casually, but she knew he had done it to draw her eyes to his chest. And then he smiled, and as he walked off, she realised her breathing was coming a little faster than she would have liked. And she realised, also, how she had not shirked his attention, how – yes, how she had enjoyed it, and as long as she stayed in control, keeping Raff at a suitable distance, then what could be the harm in savouring his appeal?

Chapter Twelve

Nicholas, due back at Whitehall following his day out in the city, had still not returned by the morning after. Cerwen, his maid friend, had not seen him either, not since he had left her to stay overnight with his family, and she claimed he had expressed no intention of spending another day apart. Come that next evening, a worry was settling in. Mindful of the plague, an irrational panic made Mercia think of Nicholas's daughter, but no sooner was she convincing herself she should go out tomorrow in search, than she saw the note propped up against her bedroom mirror.

'What is this, Phibae?' she asked.

'A letter, my lady. A page brought it this afternoon, when you were trying to talk with Lady Herrick. One of the postmaster's lads.' She bit her lip. 'I've always left letters for my mistresses untouched. I don't like to be thought of as prying. Did I do wrong?'

'No, Phibae.' She turned the sealed paper over in her hands, studying the unfamiliar handwriting. 'You said mistresses. Are you passed around so often?'

'From time to time, my lady.'

'How did you come to work at the palace, then?'

'I had a friend who worked here, my lady. She said they often want new maids – younger ones – so I thought I would try. That was, oh . . . years ago now.'

'I am curious.' She set the paper on her lap. 'You have a comely name. Does it have meaning, as mine does?'

'It means I was born on a Friday, my lady. It should be Phibba by rights, two b's and no e, but my mother preferred it the way she named me.'

She smiled. 'My father named me. After an old English kingdom, many centuries old, from where I was born. He thought it important we learn from the past. And you, Phibae? Have you lived in London your whole life, like Nicholas?'

'Yes, my lady. Going back, my family's lived here since Good Queen Bess was alive. Seventy, eighty years now. Not that we haven't had some tough times.'

'People can be harsh, that is certain. And always in service, since childhood?'

'That's right. My grandmother used to say that when she was my age, well before the war – the civil war, that is – it was hard for . . . people like me to find work. She told me once there was a petition to be rid of us, but that came to naught when folk realised how hard we worked.'

'And during the war? Do you have older brothers who fought, or your father, perhaps?'

'My father died a while back, my lady, same as both my brothers. I only have a sister left, her and my mother. My husband, of course. We had a girl of our own once, but . . . she died.'

'I am sorry.'

'Maybe we'll have another child soon. With talk of all this plague about, we might wait a while, and then we'll see.'

140

'I understand.' She took up the paper, easing open the seal. 'I do not suppose you know where Lady Cartwright's servant boy is from? Tacitus, I mean.'

Phibae's chattiness vanished into a monotone. 'Near the Guinea coast, my lady. Or what you would call as such.'

'I take it he did not come here by choice.'

'No. He was brought here, my lady, picked out for his role. And I worry . . .'

'You worry he will be sent elsewhere once his mistress is finished with him. To the Barbados, perhaps.'

Phibae hesitated. 'We hear . . . that is, we know . . . but that is not for me to say.'

'Perhaps not to everyone.' Mercia nodded her encouragement. 'But you can to me.'

She looked to the side, as though considering, but then she seemed to make up her mind.

'Then we are free here, my lady. In England. If we choose to be in service, 'tis most often our decision, although there is much work we are not allowed to do, and there are masters who like to think they own us. Sometimes they go too far, but little is done, and a servant is forced to run away.' Her face hardened. 'But in the Barbados, or in Jamaica, it is not a choice. Men and women, children – they are taken in Africa, they are put onto ships, and that is the last time they see their homes. Those who survive the crossing are made to work for no reward.' She bowed her head. 'Sometimes I think that is how things must be. Other times I feel a great sadness. That there is little I can do.'

Despite all her compassion, Mercia did not know what to say. 'Maybe Tacitus can stay in England,' she tried. 'In service somewhere, like you.'

141

'Maybe, my lady. But there are many boys besides Tacitus. Their mothers . . .' She trailed off, struggling to maintain her composure. Her arm was twitching, and she blinked more than once.

'Phibae.' Mercia reached out her hand. 'I believe there is always hope. I know that is small comfort, but it has often sustained me. And I know it sounds foolish, and unwanted, coming from a woman wearing this expensive dress. But please, and I would say the same to Tacitus. Never give in.'

Phibae gazed sadly up. 'But my lady, on those ships, they have no hope.'

Mercia looked on, and felt a barren helplessness, aware there was nothing worthy she could add. So she limited herself to a futile smile, and turned back to her letter, unfolding the sheet of paper to reveal its contents. As she did, a barely noticed fragment dropped to her lap.

It was a simple message in poor handwriting, although the words were correctly spelt. She read it in five seconds, and within those five seconds, her helplessness had given way to a newborn terror:

Mrs Blakewood,
If you care to see your man again, you will come to me this evening at eight of the clock, at The Partridge in Whitechapel.
If you fail to attend, alone, your inactions will have consequences for his pretty face.
You will find a token of my sincerity enclosed.
One-Eye Wilkins

It was as if the room had become loose from the palace to arise in the midst of the stormy ocean. The table before her seemed to buffet in the doom-laden maelstrom roaring to life inside. She looked down, searching for the token of which the letter spoke, and found nestled in a crease of her dress a small, hard object that could easily have been thrown aside. She reached to retrieve it, but as soon as she examined its coarseness she threw it to the table, only just keeping from being sick.

'My lady!' Phibae's voice was pierced with shock. 'What is it?'

'A . . . Bad news, Phibae. Most terrible.'

She stared at her ashen reflection in the mirror, then forced herself to look back at the table, at the ragged, flat object cast against her box of jewels.

At the torn-away fingernail, stained with congealed blood.

There was no question she had to obey the terrible summons. Nicholas's life was in danger, of that she was certain, and not only the physicality of the fingernail confirmed it. One-Eye had not hesitated to use the threat of violence when they had met last year, and Mercia knew the smuggler-queen would not long be content with a mere nail.

From the back of her wardrobe she dragged out a hidden dress from her long ocean voyage, the drab garment better suited to the dirty streets of London than were the opulent gowns of the Court.

'I need to find Nicholas,' she explained to Phibae. 'I need to go into the city.'

'Then let me go, mistress. You shouldn't be walking the streets alone.'

'I have done so before, Phibae. Could you help me on with this dress?'

'Of course, but—'

'Not a word more. Not a word to anyone, come to it.' She looked at her. 'I trust you, Phibae. Not a word.'

Phibae opened her mouth, but then she nodded and got to work, turning Mercia into the familiar, less colourful woman she had been these past several months. When Phibae had finished, most of the make-up had gone from her face, she was wearing no decorative patches, and her hair fell down her cheeks, depleted of stiff wire for her ringlets. By then it was after six, and she hurried from the palace towards Charing Cross, making for the row of sedan chairs she knew would be waiting for trade.

'The Partridge,' she muttered to the two men at the head of the line. Their arms were massive, the result of years of carrying heavy passengers, no doubt. 'In Whitechapel.'

The men glanced at each other. 'Sorry, my lady,' said one. 'Did I hear you right?'

'Yes.' She climbed into the small compartment. 'Please.'

She pulled shut the door and lowered the leather blinds, steadying herself as the lead carrier took up the poles at the front, and his fellow the same poles at the back. Despite the combined weight of the sedan and its occupant, they set off at a swift pace. Although the ride was long it was not uncomfortable, once she grew used to the constant bouncing left and right, and the frequent swearing whenever the carriers lamented the many obstacles in their path. Soon enough they arrived at their destination, and the chair was lowered to the ground.

'Half-crown, my lady,' said the lead carrier, as his partner stood to one side, rubbing at his aching biceps.

She reached into her pockets, feeling for a coin of the right size, and handed it over with a few pennies more. Looking up, she saw she was directly outside an inn with the sign of a faded plump bird swinging in the wind, and surmised she was at the correct place.

'Thank you,' she said, striving to ignore the stench of the street. Pulling up her jacket to cover her nose, she glanced at the surrounding buildings, a collection of run-down houses and shops that had seen better days. A few candles were set above the doors, but the locale was mostly dimly lit. Still, nobody glanced at her as she approached the inn – at least, nobody that she noticed – but it felt like the sort of place where somebody should. The two girls in the alley opposite, perhaps, or the link-boys waiting in the shadows for anyone who should wish to pay for their light – or be pickpocketed if they ignored their calls for business.

Taking a deep breath, she entered the inn, but it was not nearly as bad as she had supposed. There were scarcely any customers, for one, just a group of men playing at dice, and a couple of women laughing as they slugged on their tankards of ale. It was extraordinary, Mercia thought, how but thirty minutes earlier she had been inside the royal palace. Different shades of life, alien the one from the other, and yet finding a strange way to co-exist in this city of many layers.

Trying to be inconspicuous, she looked further into the room, unsure whether One-Eye would be waiting. Then she locked eyes with the tavern keeper, and she crossed the sticky floor towards his warped bar.

'What's your name?' he demanded, his hands resting on the wood.

'I am looking for someone,' she said.

'Tell me your name,' he repeated. 'And I'll tell you if you're expected.'

There was little to lose from being honest. 'I am Mercia Blakewood.'

He nodded, and as he did, a smirk seemed to grow on his face, or was that just the candlelight flickering above?

'Through that door there,' he sniffed.

She followed his mocking eyes, passing round the bar to reach a narrow opening, more a hanging collection of splinters than a functioning door. She sidestepped behind it, coming into a small storage space stacked full of barrels, lit by a broad candle atop a chest. Water dripped onto her sleeve as she made for the staircase at the back of the room, and she ascended the creaking steps, a spider

145

scurrying from her boot, to find a larger, more open space upstairs. Seated opposite, two people were playing cards, a woman and a man.

'Here she is,' said the man, setting down his hand. 'It's been a while, Mrs Blakewood.'

She peered forward, studying the man's rough features.

'Jink,' she said.

'That's right.'

'And Mrs Wilkins.'

The woman leapt to her feet. 'Mercia, Mercia, welcome.' She turned to her companion. 'Of course she came. She merely needed the right incentive.'

'A shame, all told,' said Jink, twisting one of his fingers. 'Could've sent her more gifts.'

The room was sparsely furnished, a loft beneath the rafters of the tavern. Mercia could see to the end, but Nicholas was nowhere in sight.

'Where is he?' she said.

Jink made a feint of looking around. 'Not here, love, is he?'

'Jink,' said One-Eye. 'How about you leave the talking to me?'

Jink sucked in his cheek, but he kept his silence, slinking back into his chair.

'Wildmoor is safe,' continued One-Eye. 'And mostly intact. I see you received my token.'

Mercia narrowed her eyes. 'You need not have done that. It was cruel. Barbaric.'

One-Eye scratched at her clutch of white hair. 'It was nothing compared to what could have happened. He is your man, and you scorned my request. When people scorn me, their property tends to suffer.' She threw her a meaningful look. 'Would you rather I had visited your mother in Warwick?'

The threat turned her cold. 'Please, tell me where Nicholas is.'

146

'We have matters to discuss first.' Returning to the table, she took up her threadbare hand of cards, laying her choice onto a central stack. 'Now, would you sit? 'Tis somewhat chill in this loft, but I thought you would prefer secrecy to the warmth of the fire downstairs.'

She was going to refuse, but the roof was low, and standing to the side she was having to stoop.

'How did you know where to find him?' she said, lowering herself onto a stool.

'I told you.' One-Eye lifted her own seat and brought it alongside. 'I have someone at Court.'

'Who?'

'I'm hardly going to tell you that. But I trust this misunderstanding is now resolved?'

'I am here, am I not?'

One-Eye laughed. 'You promise your aid, I return your man. You give me what I ask for, no one loses anything more. Not Wildmoor.' She licked her lips. 'Not your son.'

A raw anger flared. 'You go too far if you think to threaten my son.'

'I am jesting, my friend. I would never harm a child. Most like.'

She looked on One-Eye with utter disdain. 'What do you want?'

'Information, as I said before. Custom, if you can get it. There are many at Court who would want the goods I can provide, legal or no. But there is one thing in particular you can do.'

'Well?' She could hear the muffled voices from the tavern below.

''Tis this war, Mercia. Trade has come almost to a halt, yet there are still keen buyers in Holland. I mean to help the flow of commerce. For an increased price, of course.'

'Must I say it again? I will do nothing to advantage our enemy.'

'Presumptuous talk, Mrs Blakewood, as I still have your man.'

She hesitated. 'Then what is your – particular – request?'

'Nothing beyond the wit of a woman such as you.' One-Eye waved a careless hand. 'Merely information on the deployment of the fleet. In the North Sea and Channel.'

The legs of her stool slipped. 'That is unthinkable!'

'Plans for blockades of Dutch ports. Ship movements. Anything that will tell me where the fleet is and when.'

'No!' She widened her eyes. 'If that were to fall into enemy hands . . .'

'I want no contact with the fleet, English or Dutch. As long as you give me true reports, I shall sail nowhere near either. I shall go to Holland to sell my cargo, and anything I bring back I shall sell to others here. And if you give me bad reports, well . . . Should I be apprehended, your part in this might come to light, and I should not think much for your family's standing after that.'

'One-Eye.' She swallowed. 'What you ask is impossible.'

'Impossible, unthinkable . . . such melancholy, Mercia! But you have no choice. If you refuse, those close to you will lose more than just a fingernail. And so I think our talk here is done.'

'Mrs Wilkins. I am telling you I cannot—'

'You will receive a letter in a week or so, telling you where you should bring your report. Heed its instructions or face the consequence once more. Remember there is someone watching at Court. Do not think to delude me, for I shall know.'

She bared her teeth. 'Then give me Nicholas. Where is he?'

'That's for you to find out.' Clapping her hands on her knees, One-Eye stood and grabbed her stool, slamming it down next to Jink's. 'You thought to play games with me, by refusing my request in the park. So now I shall play a game with you, in pleasing symmetry. The directions to your man are on that bench behind you. 'Tis a most simple game, so do not be perturbed.' She took up her playing cards, studying them intently as she fanned them into a semicircle. 'And this time, I shall let you win – or perhaps let you think you have won. But let it be a reminder that any who seek to play games with me will find themselves toyed with in far greater measure.'

Mercia stared at the back of One-Eye's head, near overcome with ire, but there was little she could do against the smuggler-queen in the heart of her own territory. So saving her energies, she walked to the bench, snatching a small paper from under a beaker, and focussed on the problem at hand.

'This is it?' she said.

'Simple, no?' said One-Eye, as she played a faded King of hearts. 'You know the way out.'

Turning away, Mercia descended the creaking stairs, thrusting the crumpled paper into her pockets. Her head spinning with fury and fear, she made a vow to herself there and then: whatever One-Eye said, she would play her at her own games and win. She had bested worse enemies before.

As for the present game, One-Eye was insulting her. The directions solely read:

Why tall, say you?

Whitehall, she seethed. He had already been returned to the palace.

Chapter Thirteen

She forced herself to look again at the red patch of skin, raw at the tip of his finger.

'I do not believe you,' she said. 'It must hurt.'

Nicholas wrapped the wound in a tiny bandage. 'Very well, it does. Not as much as it did at the time, though. Those pliers did their work.' He curled his hand into a fist and winced, but he managed to close the fingers. 'I promise you this, she's going to pay for it.'

Mercia glanced away, towards the window. 'My, I dearly want to know who she has watching us at Court.'

'Could be anyone.' He rested his elbow on her dressing table, setting his chin on his fist. 'I feel like . . . going out there and doing the same to her. Worse.'

'I cannot give her what she wants, Nicholas. If I were to be discovered, I would be taken for treason. She wants me to become the very woman I am trying to unmask. Virgo. A beautiful irony, do you not think?'

'Irony?'

'An . . . unwelcome similarity.'

He grunted. 'And if we report her to the constables, she'll hit back all the harder. Not that most of them would do much. You can take a wager as to how many of them she's already bought.'

'I have to outwit her, Nicholas, or she will have a hold on me forever. If I do not do as she says, and she snatches you again . . . or Daniel . . . I cannot bear to think of it.'

He sucked at his bandage. 'Damn it, Mercia, 'tis like . . . taking on the Duke of York. She has power and men, lots of them. You think it was her knocked me over the head on my way to my sister's and locked me in that room? Overnight, without a pisspot?'

'But she gave the orders. And if she is a Duke in her own world, then she must have enemies.'

'Yes. Us.'

'Other people, I mean. Let's find them out. Ask them to help.'

'How? You want to post a notice on the city gates? Wanted – helpful townsfolk to fight notorious smuggler.'

She sighed. 'I suppose you are right. What of that friend of yours who introduced us to her last year? Martin – was that his name?'

'I doubt there's much he can do. Unless you want to flout the law, or even . . .' He looked sharply up. 'But I doubt you would want to do that.'

Through the window, the darkness seemed absolute. 'No, Nicholas. I would not.'

The murder of Lady Allcot had been a shock, but not, it seemed, for everyone. Her husband, Sir Geoffrey, was still parading about the palace, carrying on his business much as before, and although his doublet and breeches were black, the armband on his sleeve the optimal thickness, his superior expression was uncompromised, his shabby gait strangely light. But was his crude behaviour a mark of unfeeling, or a desperate cover for his grief?

Standing outside his rooms, she paused to consider the propriety of her visit, but Lady Castlemaine's demand for results was ringing in her head, and she held out her fist to knock. But then the door opened anyway, and just in time, she stayed herself from striking a manservant's curious face.

'Oh,' she recovered. 'I understand from Sir William Calde that your master is in his chambers. I should like to speak with him, if he is willing, about his terrible loss.'

The servant looked at her. 'I was just leaving on some business for Sir Geoffrey, but I suppose I can ask. Can I say who you are, my lady?'

'Mrs Mercia Blakewood. A friend of Sir William . . . and of the King.'

Friend of the King was stretching it, she knew, but it did not hurt to overstate her importance. Yet the servant seemed quite unimpressed.

'If you wait inside,' he said, 'I shall enquire.'

She nodded in dismissive condescension: while she disliked treating servants with indifference, this man seemed to demand it, and here in Whitehall she had found such attitudes were expected. As he vanished into the adjoining room she sat on a narrow bench, perching beside a side table adorned with a beautiful plate: blue and white Delftware, from Holland. The idealised scene depicted a man standing tall before a windmill, two labourers sowing seeds at his feet. The figures were blue, but the features on the workers' faces left little doubt of their African provenance.

'Mrs Blakewood.'

She looked up from the plate to find Sir Geoffrey on the threshold of his private chamber, a sharp compass in his hand of the sort navigators used to determine distances and bearings on a chart.

She rose to her feet. 'Sir Geoffrey. Please forgive the unexpected visit, but I wished to speak with you about . . . what has transpired.' She glanced at the servant, who was staring from behind his master. 'Alone, if we may.'

Sir Geoffrey pondered a moment, but then he nodded, and keeping his gaze fixed on hers he held his free hand over his shoulder, pointing to the door with a flick of his wrist. The servant turned side on to press past his ample frame, and with a bow, he departed in silence for the corridor.

'Well, Mrs Blakewood,' said Sir Geoffrey. 'Would you come through?'

She followed him into his private room, where sure enough a large map was laid out on a table, its frayed edges held down by a series of glass paperweights. She examined the crisp chart: a wavy, thickset line dotted with place names towards the left, but which faded into nothing towards the right.

'The Guinea coast,' she observed. 'I saw such a map as this on His Majesty's yacht once.'

The namedropping was outrageous. 'Indeed,' he said. 'Helen told me how you enjoy elevated company.'

She looked up. 'Helen?'

'Lady Cartwright. You have met her, so she says.' He stabbed his compass into the table beside the chart. 'And you are right. This is the Guinea coast.'

Something in his curtness gave her pause. 'I hope you do not mind that I have come, Sir Geoffrey. But I wanted to say how appalled I am at your wife's terrible—'

'You were there, were you not?' he interrupted. 'When she was . . . taken?'

She bowed her head. 'I was nearby.'

'Then death does seem to follow you, Mrs Blakewood, as I hear.'

'I am not sure that—'

'You need not apologise. Death is a necessity of life. Some die sooner than others, that is all.' He held out his hand to indicate a chair. 'What may I do for you?'

Thrown by his seeming indifference, she took the offered seat as he squeezed into his own. 'It is as I said. I desired to convey to you the measure of my sadness. I did not know your wife, but as you intimate, I was present at her end. I felt a measure of urgency to express my sorrow.'

He looked at her much as she had perused the Delftware plate. 'Thank you, I suppose, but you need not be sorrowful on my account. Grace and I scarcely got on. We may have been husband and wife, but we saw each other little, and spoke even less.'

'Nonetheless, she was your wife. To lose her in such a way must be—'

'Do not misunderstand me, Mrs Blakewood. I shall mourn, in my way. As you must mourn in yours, although you did not know her.' He drummed his fingers on the arm of his chair. 'Why were you at Hampton, really? I am told by her maid that you had travelled there to find her.'

'Her maid?'

'Anna, is she called? Perhaps Alice? The poor child was most distraught.' He rested his hands on his corpulent stomach. 'She said you had asked where my wife could be found, not long before she was killed.'

'I—' She cleared her throat. 'I had heard how she was upset at the attack on my aunt. I wanted some country air myself, and . . . Sir William had suggested I travel upriver. I thought I would call on your wife while I was there, to ask how she was faring.'

'Hmm. Then that was generous of you. My wife is well known for her melancholic airs. I leave – left – her to them.'

'Sir Geoffrey, I wanted to say that she died most quickly. She would not have been in pain, or even aware. When the men . . . attacked . . . there was no time to realise what was about to happen.'

'Then she was as unmindful in death as she was in life.' He sighed. 'No, that is not fair. She did have wits in life. Just of a different sort to what one would expect of a wife.'

She frowned. 'What sort is that?'

'No doubt Sir William will have told you how my wife liked to air her opinions on matters that hardly concerned her. He faced her incessant questioning often enough.'

'You will forgive me I hope, Sir Geoffrey, but should we not speak more kindly of the dead?'

'She was my wife, Mrs Blakewood. I shall speak of her as I choose.'

The lack of empathy broke through her shell. 'As you chose to speak to her in life, perhaps?'

'My, Helen was right.' He peered from over his sagging cheeks. 'You are a tempestuous mare. You remind me of her in some way.'

'I doubt she would welcome the comparison.'

'Neither do I. Perhaps we should become better acquainted, after all.'

'Sir Geoffrey, I hardly think . . . What of Sir William?'

He laughed. 'If men at Court refused to share their mistresses, there would be much greater discord between us than there is over matters of state. And as we mention Helen, she tells me you have allied with Lavinia Whent. She, too, has opinions she should keep to herself.'

'Miss Whent?' She blinked at the rapid change of subject. 'I have spoken with her once or twice, nothing more.'

'Why do you object to Helen owning that black of hers? Do not tell me you are one of those wearisome miscreants who cry foul at such dealings.'

'She scarcely owns him, Sir Geoffrey.'

'No, I do. Or as good as. I gave him to her mother last year to appease her temper, but she tired of him, and so I gave him to Helen.'

'And afterwards? What will you do with him then?'

'I had not considered it. Would that the war ended swiftly and allowed us to resume our business.'

She glanced slyly at the unfurled chart. 'That is what this war is about, is it not – the Guinea coast, at least in part? I understand you have made much wealth there. The Royal Adventurers, I believe your enterprise is called.'

He snorted. 'I would leave such matters to Sir William and the council, Mrs Blakewood. Keep your woman's mind to affairs that more befit your sex.'

'Forgive me, but if we win the war—'

'When we win it.'

'When we win the war, will not that increase your company's standing? All those Dutch outposts on your map will be yours.'

'They will be our patron's, the Duke's, but yes, perhaps, and in the meantime we lose out. I should rather we . . .' He cut himself off and smiled. 'Let me give you some useful advice. Do not antagonise Helen. She may be young, but she is determined – and most beautiful.'

She studied his gleaming face. 'You are much taken with her, it seems.'

'What man would not be? She is every bit as alluring as her Trojan namesake.'

'Helen of Troy,' she mused. *Or perhaps a Trojan horse*, she wondered? *A dazzling gift, planted by the enemy to deceive the credulous?* She inched forwards in her seat. 'I wonder. Is Lady Cartwright much disturbed by the war, as I am?'

'She frets, as all women are wont to do. But I have told her what I told you. Not to worry herself over concerns that need not trouble her. Still, I fancy she likes to be mistress to a man who has the ear of the King and the Duke.'

'I understand.' She faked a complicit smile. 'To hear a little of what Sir William does is exciting. I wager Lady Cartwright feels the same?'

'I knew it! You women cannot resist men of power.' He ran his tongue around his lips, staring in a way she did not much like. 'Mrs Blakewood, I tell you, when Helen and I are together . . . it arouses her, she says, to hear me talk of my duty. And yet I scarce remember what we talk of at such times. There is Helen, and little else.'

He breathed slowly, in and out, his head lolling to one side. Mercia had the uncomfortable feeling he was imagining some other activity entirely. The thought made her vaguely nauseous.

'Sir Geoffrey.' She rose. 'I should leave you to your work. Allow me to say again how sorry I am for the loss of your wife.'

'What? Oh yes, my wife.' Taking his time, he got to his feet. 'Thank you, Mrs Blakewood, for your visit.' He winked. 'I shall tell Helen you came. It will do her good to think she has a rival, eh?'

Back in her chambers, she pulled the patch of stars from her cheek, irked at Sir Geoffrey's chauvinistic bearing. There were so many such opinions in the palace, she thought, so many expectations of a particular person's place, or a particular group's. How was she going to find Virgo in the face of such rigidity? How, moreover, when most courtiers did not even acknowledge her right to ask the simplest of questions?

His nonchalance towards his wife's death both disgusted and intrigued her, just as Lady Cartwright's amorous interest in his responsibilities intrigued her, for she never would have thought such curiosity likely from the petulance of their brief encounters. Or was Helen Cartwright, like Mercia, playing a covert role, weaving different appearances to different audiences as befitted the particular scene?

Or, she thought, is it I who am judging without cause? Is it I who am expecting overmuch?

A firm knock behind heralded an appearance at the door. Sure to hold herself straight, she looked around to see Sir William come in, his familiar ostrich-feathered hat dangling from his fingers. For some reason, it made her wonder why he never once chose to emulate his peers by donning an elaborate wig.

The whimsical thought made her relax, but then she noticed his laboured breathing, remarked the redness in his face. His steady look told her this was no polite visit to enquire after the success of her interview.

'Mercia,' he simply said. 'Lady Allcot's Frenchman is back at Court.'

Chapter Fourteen

'Julien Bellecour?' Her heart raced. 'Since when has he returned?'

'Is your maid here?'

'No. I am alone.'

'Good.' Sir William closed the door. 'I do not know. There was a meeting of the French delegation with a group of our own men, and Bellecour was in attendance. I had asked to be told if he should make a reappearance.'

'Then let him be arrested and asked what he was doing with Lady Allcot.'

'He is not the King's subject, Mercia. You know this. We cannot even question him, let alone throw him in the Tower. And when the King wants French help in our war with the Dutch – you can see how this is delicate.'

'Has anyone asked the French for permission to talk?'

'We are . . . deciding on our best approach.'

She scoffed. 'He was the last person with Lady Allcot before she was murdered. He fled from Nicholas and possibly knocked me to the ground. Then he vanished. Is it not simply a matter of setting that out before the French and demanding they accede to our sensible request?'

She sighed. 'Of course not. Hell's teeth! Why did he have to be foreign?'

He looked at her in a sort of sympathy. 'Perhaps you should forget about Bellecour. Concentrate on Virgo instead.'

'But what if Lady Allcot was Virgo, working with Bellecour to export her secrets? His immunity gives him the perfect cover, no? To say nothing of his own access to the Court.'

'Or perhaps, Mercia, he is utterly innocent. Lady Allcot too, and this is but a distraction. You should know, her belongings have been thoroughly searched since her death, on the highest orders. Nothing has been found to suggest her involvement, and if she were Virgo, you would think there should be.'

'Quite possibly. But we will discover nothing without asking.'

'He could lie.'

A chink of doubt entered her mind as she recalled the King's warning about Sir William's trading interests. But then she watched as he passed his hat from one hand to the other and set the notion aside as frivolous.

'Then what can be done?' she said. 'Set a watch on him?'

'A request will likely be submitted to the French emissary. Not to arrest Bellecour, but to put it to him what he was doing at Hampton Court.'

She raised an eyebrow. 'I saw what he was doing.'

'Besides his liaison with Lady Allcot.'

'How long could all that take?'

'Some time, I fear.'

'Then I shall have to find a way to speak with him myself. Subtly, outside of official purview.'

'Mercia, listen.' Sir William took a step closer. 'And I mean this. If you do anything that offends the French – anything – you will be in a great deal of trouble with the King.'

'I cannot merely do nothing, Sir William.' She shook her head in exasperation. 'Lady Castlemaine has put me in a difficult position with her demands for swift answers. And yet talking with these women can be like . . . trying to encourage a plant that refuses to flower. They mistrust me, or know me too little, to truly open up. But Bellecour offers another possibility, a route into Lady Allcot's death. If I do not pursue him, I am not fulfilling the task I have been set to do.'

'Damn your thoroughness.' He sighed, then scratched at his neck. 'Make sure you are very careful. Do not tell me what, for I shall be bound to stop you, but whatever you intend, you must not be caught.'

He fell silent, but his eyes darted about, settling on anywhere but her.

'What is it?' she asked.

'What is . . . ?'

'You seem to have something else you wish to say.'

'Oh.' He gave her a nervous smile. ''Tis merely that, when I was speaking with Sir Stephen Herrick just now, there was a young man who asked after you. He says he helped you at Hampton Court, after the . . . trouble there. He gave his name as Malvern.'

'Giles Malvern?' Mercia rubbed at the wrist he had tended after she had fallen: still sore, but now free of its bandage. 'He is at Whitehall?'

Sir William pulled a face; a peculiar look on the nobleman, she thought. 'With the war, there are navy men coming and going all the time. Malvern is but one of many.'

'And was that all he wanted, to ask you how I was?'

He jiggled his head. 'He . . . may have asked to speak with you directly. But only if you had time.'

'Yes, I should like to thank him for his help. Is he still in the palace?' She looked at him. 'Sir William?'

'Forgive me. As far as I know.'

'Where?'

'Near the . . . Banqueting House, I think.' He cleared his throat. 'But he will most likely have left by now.'

'Sir William.' She took his arm, and he glanced down at her hand, surprised. 'I have met him once. He is hardly a rival. And we both know my presence here with you is merely a deception.'

'That may be, but . . . I had hoped, perhaps, that we were getting along well.'

'And I am glad of it. But nothing has changed. Save that maybe, I hope, I have gained a friend?'

His arm froze in her hand. 'I never intended to . . . But no. It does not do well to talk of it.'

'Talk of what?' She looked up at him, and was startled to think . . . could he have – after all these months? Had the lust he had thought to bear on her last year morphed into something more? But then he turned to face her, and his eyes showed only kindness.

'Go.' He squeezed her uninjured arm. ''Tis only proper you be polite. And thank him from me, would you, also?'

'For what?' she said.

'For looking after you, Mercia, when you were hurt. For making sure you were well and safe.'

She found him where Sir William had claimed he would be, beneath a white portico at the edge of the Banqueting House, the newest part of the palace where the ball had taken place. As she paused in an archway she took in the grand columns, the bustle of courtiers and supplicants filling the gleaming space, and she thought back to

162

the time when this construction was new, to before the civil war that had set King against Parliament, to when the world was simpler, less crowded with bloody death. Or perhaps that was merely her child-self speaking, back through the years when she need never worry where she was or whom she met.

Who could have thought then, when she read cross-legged in her father's study, that she would ape the heroes of the stories she loved with the patterns of her own life? Who could have thought then, when many still held to the divine rule of Kings, that the first Charles would be ended, so near this very spot, with the docking of his head by that harsh and fearsome axe? Who could have thought then, after a decade of republic, that his sons would be restored with the docking of a ship, the new King welcomed home on a tide of rapturous glory?

Such times she had lived through . . . but she was drifting again. Shaking her head of its nostalgia, she brushed down the sleeves of her bodice – flawless already, but even so – and walked to the waiting surgeon, a smile on her face, when—

'Good day, Mrs Blakewood.' A different man stepped from the archway to her left. 'A delight to see you once more.'

'Mr Raff,' she said in surprise. Looking over his shoulder, she could see that Malvern had noticed them. 'If I did not know better, I should say you are following me about the palace.'

'If only I had the time to do just that, life would be sweet indeed.' He leant against a nearby pillar. 'What brings you here?'

'Can I not walk where I please?'

'Of course.' He held out his arm. 'Why not walk with me? 'Tis not raining today.'

'I fear, Henry, I have another engagement.'

'Not one you can interrupt?'

'That would be ill-mannered.'

He leant into her ear. 'Then be ill-mannered.'

'Alas, Henry, I am too . . . polite.'

She locked eyes with him a moment before inclining her head and continuing towards Malvern. As she approached, she was sure she could feel Raff's stare burning into her neck.

'Mr Malvern,' she said, seamlessly shifting from one man to the next. 'It was an unexpected pleasure to learn you were at Whitehall.'

'The pleasure is mine.' He bowed. 'I hope you do not mind my asking Sir William to enquire after you.'

'Not at all. It gets so dry in my chambers. I am glad of the diversion.' She indicated a vacant bench. 'Shall we sit?'

Leading him to the bench, she could see Henry Raff loitering behind his pillar, pretending not to look. But even on the third time she glanced across, his eyes were quickly turning away.

'A friend of yours?' asked Malvern.

'An acquaintance. Well, Mr Malvern. What brings you to Whitehall?'

'Giles, please.' He shrugged. 'I am here because of the war.'

'Sir William suggested as much. I did not think a barber surgeon would have reason to attend Court?'

'Not every surgeon, no.' He looked at her intertwined hands. 'How is your wrist? And . . . how are you faring? It cannot have been easy, seeing what you did.'

Not easy, she thought, although more common than you would think. Sir Geoffrey had been right on one point at least. Death did seem to follow her of late.

'My hand is much improved,' she said. 'I have you to thank for attending to it so swiftly.'

He smiled. 'I merely bandaged it.'

'Still, it hardly compares to what you will have seen on the ships.'

'Indeed, but I shy from discussing that in front of a lady.' He sat forward on the bench. 'Sir Stephen Herrick tells me your father was Sir Rowland Goodridge. I had no idea. I am sorry for what befell him.'

Yet another pitying look. 'Thank you. It was a difficult time.'

'You did not let it cow you, though. I should love to hear your tales of the ocean. We men endure the cramped quarters because we must, but a lady like yourself . . . it must have been uncomfortable.'

'I will not lie. It was. But I managed.'

There was a brief silence. 'Forgive me if I overstep the mark, Mrs Blakewood,' he said finally, 'but if you are willing, I should like to accompany you to dinner some time. I should like to help you recover from the terrible scene at Hampton Court.'

'That is most kind, Giles.' On instinct, she found herself querying his motives as she looked at his hopeful face. But then she thought of Nicholas, about his warnings of being too wary; and also she looked at Henry Raff, pretending still not to observe them, and—

'Yes,' she said. 'I should like that. But only to eat and to talk.'

'Do not think me untoward, for I am widowed, like yourself. And I know that you and Sir William Calde are . . .' He cleared his throat. 'Will you be free tomorrow, perhaps? I am only in London for a week or so more, until I rejoin my ship.'

'Why not?' The excitement at accepting his invitation coursed through her; how long had it been since she had last done that? 'But I fear you shall have to choose the eating house. I have been too long away from London to know which are the most fashionable spots.'

He thought a moment. 'Does fish too much remind you of the sea?'

She laughed. 'Unless you wish dried biscuit as an accompaniment, I should welcome anything, truth be told. The food at Court becomes a little rich for my taste.'

'Then shall we say noon? I will arrange for a carriage to collect you at the gates.'

'There is no need. I can take a sedan, if you send me a note to say where you will be.'

'A carriage is more comfortable,' he said, getting to his feet. 'I insist. And shall see you tomorrow.'

He doffed his hat and strode head high through the nearest archway. She stayed where she was, surveying the crowd, and she noticed how Henry Raff had vanished also. And then again she pondered – dinner with a strange man. Was that wise? But then she laughed out loud, startling a passing servant. At least, she thought, Nicholas would approve.

With the threat of One-Eye Wilkins prevalent, Nicholas did, however, insist on accompanying her to the eating house, riding beside her in the carriage. She allowed him to follow her into the spacious dining room, where she craned her neck to seek out Malvern, finding him rising in greeting from his table in the farthest corner. Satisfied she was safe, Nicholas withdrew to the crowded street, there to remain on watch.

'Good day, Mr Malvern,' she said, as he dashed to pull out her chair. 'Thank you.'

He eased her into place. 'Good day, Mrs Blakewood. I trust your carriage was waiting on time?'

'And thank you for that also. The driver told me I owed no fare.'

'It was I who invited you to join me.'

She looked around the vaulted space; it was full of expectant diners, some tucking into fish or lamb, others waiting for their orders, but all deep in conversation. Frantic conversation, at that.

'You know what they talk of,' he said as he sat. 'The Dutch

fleet has set sail. Seven squadrons, with over one hundred ships.'

She nodded. 'I heard mutterings about it at Court this morning. You think they will come?'

'Not to London, so do not be alarmed. They may merely seek to make a show of strength. Our own fleet is being readied in response, but . . . let us not dwell on that here. What will you drink? Wine?'

'Still, it seems strange to think the Dutch are on their way.' She sighed. 'Ale, I think. I have drunk so much wine at the palace that I long for something simpler. Truth be told, I am not used to it. We did not get much wine aboard ships.'

'Ale, then. You are fortunate, for here they serve one of the best.' He raised his hand, waving it back and forth; a teenage boy shot across, took their order, and dashed away.

'That was quick,' she said. 'Either London eating houses have become more proficient of late, or else you have a favourable reputation here.'

He laughed. 'I hope the latter, for the chances of the former are slight indeed. But yes, his father serves on the ships. As young Andrew hopes to in his turn.'

She looked at the harassed boy, already speeding back with two tankards of frothy ale.

'Do you think . . . thank you.' She waited for him to move away. 'Do you think the war will last long? For boys like that who know little of battle . . . how hard it can be – I do not much care to think of it.'

'There are reasons for war, Mrs Blakewood, good and bad. Sometimes when the cause is just . . . but you are right. That is scant comfort to the wives and mothers left at home.'

She lowered her head in reflection. 'My husband died in his soldier's dress. Not in a battle, but . . . shall we talk of something more cheerful?'

'Of course.' His taut cheeks sagged. 'War seems to be all there is in my thoughts right now. War and the reasons for it.' He looked at her. 'I wonder – could I tell you something that might affect your opinion of me? At the least, prove I am not a common soldier?'

She held his gaze a moment, and then found herself roving his face. Like Raff, his hair was black, but his eyes were a hazel hue. His forehead was strong, devoid of worried creases, and his jaw traced a rectangular shape. His ears stuck out the smallest amount, in an endearing way, and his lips were thick, his mouth an ellipse. His skin was smooth, aside from a light beard and moustache that complemented his wavy hair.

She reached for her ale and took a sip. 'You are right. This is good. And in answer to your question, yes. You can tell me what you will, and I shall tell you how I respond.'

'A sensible and noble proposal.' He took a sip of his own drink and paused. 'You may not like it, mind, but I think it better to be honest at the start.'

She raised her eyebrow. 'At the start of what, Mr Malvern?'

'Of our friendship, I hope.' He lifted his tankard, and she chinked it with her own. 'Which I venture to presume might flourish, provided you do not shun me after my revelation.'

'You presume much, Mr Malvern.' She smiled. 'Especially for a man who knows little about me.'

'You must forgive me for being forward in my discourse. I know more about you than you think.'

In an instant her body turned rigid. 'What do you mean?'

'That I did not ask you here merely to eat, but also to confess. Nor did I meet you merely by chance, either.'

The serving boy Andrew chose that moment to approach, asking if they wanted to eat. Malvern shooed him away, but

Mercia's face was set, little caring for who could hear her.

'So, Mr Malvern. It seems I was right and my manservant was wrong. I am correct to be mistrustful of the motives of others.'

'That is always prudent.' Still he looked at her. 'And yet I cannot help but notice you are not leaving. You would like to know the reason for my interest, I am certain.'

'Do you perceive that through your study of me also?' She narrowed her eyes – juvenile, perhaps, but she was suitably incensed. 'How long have you been watching me? For whom? My uncle?'

'Sir Francis?' Now he blinked. 'No, but . . . in truth I cannot say much. But I want to be fair, and I will say that I work for . . . certain people, on certain matters of interest to the state.' He leant in. 'Do you understand me?'

She lowered her voice. 'You mean to say you are a . . . spy of sorts?'

'Of sorts.' His voice was as quiet as hers. 'As are you, it seems.'

'And not a barber surgeon?'

'I am that, and good at it, I hope. But this is a time of war, and as I have been before, I can play the other, when it is needed.'

She frowned. 'Why are you telling me this?'

'Because I think we are working to the same end, and I should like to cooperate. Especially now a lady of the Court is murdered. For we both serve England, do we not?'

She remarked his calm face, his calm movements. He did not appear to be lying, but others before had seemed honest. And so who could truly tell?

'Say I believe you.' She took a drink of her ale: a long one. 'If we are working to the same end, what is your part in it? Why have I been asked to do so at all?'

'The same end, not the same task. Besides, you were recruited by Lady Castlemaine. Whereas I am in the service of . . . others.'

'I see. Others that Lady Castlemaine may or may not like.'

'I am afraid we are caught in a game of favourites, Mrs Blakewood. Should you unmask your quarry, you vindicate your patron's choice and earn her favour. But I think, perhaps, our Lady Castlemaine merely wishes to annoy my employers. It matters little that she enjoys a friendship with their own master, the Earl of Arlington.'

She thought of her uncle's benefactor. 'What of the Earl of Clarendon? Lady Castlemaine has told me how they do not see eye to eye.'

'Clarendon is the King's Chief Minister. Arlington is the senior Secretary of State, with overall charge of . . . these affairs. What you see here is how all things unfold at Court. Clarendon and Castlemaine vie for influence, while all around them play their own games.'

'That seems petulant.'

'I suppose I should not say so, but that is the level on which these persons of high rank operate. I think, if I read you right, that you are as unimpressed with their petty fights as I am.'

She could not help but feel she was being challenged, somehow. 'Perhaps. You were at Hampton Court for this reason?'

'I was supposed to be observing, as I think you were.'

'Observing whom?'

'That scarcely matters. But I was not going to hide from you when you needed help.' He pushed his half-drained tankard to one side. 'I am acting without permission in speaking with you, Mrs Blakewood. But you intrigue me in ways that are not solely connected with my work.' He laid his hands on the table. 'I have a further confession. I did not ask you here only to discuss our mutual task.'

'Then what?' she said.

'I am a man. You are a woman.'

'I can see how you were chosen for this kind of work.'

He laughed. 'I mean I find you . . . captivating.'

'Other men have called me that, Mr Malvern. It may turn the heads of certain women, but it does not work with me. Perhaps I am under your observation, after all.'

'Only in so much as I desire it. Others are watching you more properly, no doubt. They are most likely watching me also.' He shrugged. 'We are from the outside, unlikely to arouse suspicion in what they have asked us to do. But when all is finished, they will cut us adrift as it suits them. I have asked you here also to advise you to be cautious.'

'I am not a fool, Mr Malvern. And so you will forgive me if I am cautious with you.'

'I do not expect you to be forthright with me yet. But there is more at stake here than one woman's treason. Whatever the pamphlets bleat, the war is finely balanced. The Dutch fleet is strong and swift. One wrong move may court disaster.'

'Then we must all play our part as best we can, assuredly.'

'Then play it carefully, is all I ask. And now let me prove my sincerity in some other way.' He clicked his fingers at the serving boy. 'By allowing me to do what I came here for most of all.'

'And what is that?' she asked.

'To buy a beautiful lady her dinner.'

Chapter Fifteen

She was out in London and had the rest of the afternoon free: she was going to make the most of it. Retrieving Nicholas from his observation post outside the eating house, she hailed the nearest hackney carriage and asked the driver to take them to the docks, downriver past London Bridge.

'Pleasant meal?' asked Nicholas, as the carriage jolted its way through the crowded streets.

'Interesting, at least.' Quickly, she filled him in on Malvern's revelations. 'What do you think?'

He tapped his bandaged fingertip on the wooden seat. ''Tis convenient he was at Hampton Court at the exact time Lady Allcot was killed, loitering near the exact place you were pushed.'

'Hmm.' She looked through the dirty window, splattered with dried rain spots. 'I thought the same. And yet he sounded sincere. He did not have the manner of a brute sent to put me off. There were no threats or anything like. Quite the . . . opposite, indeed.'

'Oh yes?'

She ignored his curiosity. 'And he did not encourage me to

abandon my pursuit. More a warning to take care. But whatever Giles's motives, I shall—'

'Giles?'

She flicked her wrist. 'Mr Malvern, then. But whatever his motives, I shall continue as intended. Starting with going to the docks.'

'And why are we going to the docks?'

She laid a hand on the rough ceiling as the carriage lurched right. 'Because of Cornelia Howe. I have learnt that her husband's enterprise is based there, in a warehouse where he manages his business, including—hell's teeth, this journey is uncomfortable!' She wedged herself into the corner of the seat. 'Including ships to Holland. I want to see if there is any connection to Virgo's interests, or any reason else Cornelia might be involved.'

He glanced at her. 'Won't a well-dressed lady walking into a warehouse look a little odd?'

'Indeed.' She shuddered forward as the carriage jerked to a standstill. 'Which is why you will go in for me, if ever we make it through these streets.'

Now it was her turn to wait while Nicholas disappeared indoors. A gloomy half-silence permeated the salty air, the tidal lapping of the river licking at the bank below her swinging feet. Although she had chosen a spot out of the way, the paucity of workhands was nonetheless surprising, evidence she supposed that the Dutch war was impacting on trade.

Still, she received a few strange looks from over the crates that powerful arms were hauling about, the sweaty faces of the dockhands creasing into frowns or else leers. Although her black cloak covered the finest flourishes of her outfit, her ensemble was still uncommon. But thankfully none of the men gave her much trouble, and as she watched the rain form ripples on the water, the transfixing swirls caused her mind to drift along as naturally as they carried the barges and the wherries, leading her to thoughts of Giles Malvern and Henry Raff; and she thought too of Virgo, of her uncle, and of the King; and her imagination lifted her to those lofty realms of fantasy to which her mind often ascended when she had little else to do, to a fancied scene of Virgo sailing from the palace in the King's own yacht, laughing at the Court as she ferried her secrets to the canals of Amsterdam itself.

But Lady Allcot's death had rendered such fantasies too unreal. The drizzle moistening her exposed cheeks woke her back to the Thames, and she turned her head, looking for any sign that Nicholas was emerging, but the dockhands continued to lug their crates, and the door to the warehouse stayed shut.

She got to her feet: doing nothing was hard. She had only asked him to make some pretend enquiries about a potential shipment for a made-up master. Another five minutes dragged by. What was taking him so long? A cold feeling began to take her as the recent troubles of the past toyed with her reason. She called a halt to her agitated pacing, determined to enter the warehouse herself.

She approached the door, waiting for a dockhand to pass before resting her hand on the wood. She listened within, but heard nothing. Tentative, she pushed, but immediately jumped back as the door swung open, and she scurried aside to avoid a man coming out, but too late – he had noticed.

'What are you doing?' whispered Nicholas.

'Oh.' She breathed out. 'It is you.'

He studied her face. 'Not now. Come, let's get out of here.'

Head down, he scuttled away along the side of the wharf, halting only when they had left the waterfront and come out onto the street. The usual London chimney smoke seemed to waft not far above his head.

'What has happened?' she panted, chasing as swiftly as she could.

He looked back over her shoulder. 'Let's get further into town.'

He pressed on through the city gates, dodging an ox cart to turn into a busier road full of pedestrians with a singular purpose: walking directly in her way. Just about managing to keep up his pace, she weaved through the gauntlet, passing various signs of diverse businesses swinging in the ever-strengthening breeze. Not far down, she found him waiting beneath one of the smartest, a peculiar depiction of a small, green amphibian, the sign of the Leaping Frog.

'There's a table,' he said as they entered the inn. 'Pull your cloak about you and wait. I'll fetch a couple of ales.'

Unused to following his orders, the insistence of his tone nevertheless made her comply. Taking an empty bench, she watched as he fetched two brown beers from the landlord, the purpose in his gait a match for the sureness of his words.

'Here you go,' he said.

He set the ales on the polished table, pushing the closest towards her. It spun a little as it caught on a knot, the white foam of its bubbling head dribbling down the side.

'Now will you speak?' she said.

'I'm sorry. But I couldn't take the chance they might see you.' He sucked in through his teeth. 'I just hope they didn't see me. I had to hide for a bit.'

She gripped the wet tankard. 'Hide from whom?'

'Guess.'

'Do we have to play these games?'

He took a swift glug of his beer. 'I just think you won't guess.'

'Mr Howe, then.'

'No.'

'Cornelia?'

'No.'

'The Queen.'

He chuckled. 'Don't be silly.'

'No more absurd than you are in making me guess. Come, Nicholas, tell me.'

'Very well.' He puffed out his cheeks. 'It was—'

Of a sudden his eyes bulged, and his head lurched forward, hitting the table with a bump. A gurgling noise rose from his throat.

'Nicholas!' She shook his forearm, fallen next to his matted hair. 'Nicholas!'

And then just as suddenly he raised his head, a huge grin on his face.

'Don't worry. I'm well.'

Her heart was beating fast. 'What in God's name?'

'There was nobody in the warehouse. It would have been chance indeed if Howe had been there at the same time I went in.'

'Then what was this . . . display for?'

'To lighten the mood, is all. I could tell you were worrying about that Malvern cove all the way here in the carriage. And when I saw your face when I came out of the warehouse . . . sometimes, I have learnt that the best way to stop you brooding is to startle you out of it.'

She stared at him, annoyed, but by now his grin was infecting her own humour, and she could not be angry for long.

'You know me too well,' she said. 'But do not do that again. 'Tis not seemly.'

'Also, I simply fancied a pint.' He took a long swig. 'I'll tell you what, though. There truly was nobody in the warehouse.'

'Nobody at all?'

'Not one person.'

'At this time of day?' She thought back to the scarce dockhands. 'Maybe the war truly has affected trade.'

'I doubt it has that much. There are always means.'

'Then what were you doing in there? You took your time.'

'Looking around, of course. Seeking out evidence.'

'And did you find anything?'

'Something quite interesting.'

'Well? Do not make me suffer one of your irritating . . . prolongations.'

'What?'

She sighed. 'Do not go on about it.'

'Would I ever?' He leant towards her. 'They have a room at the front of the warehouse. An office. You'd think it'd be locked, but' – he coughed – 'it wasn't.'

'Nicholas . . .'

'There was a ledger inside, in a desk. Nice desk, too, walnut and—'

'I said no prolongations.'

'The ledger lists all the people and so on that use Howe's company. I still find it a bit hard to make out the writing, but . . .' His eyes shone. 'Guess whose name was on the list?'

'Not this again.'

'The Frenchman.'

Startled, she pulled back her head. 'Bellecour?'

He nodded. 'And the destination. The letters A-M-S.'

'My God. Amsterdam?'

'No indication of what his cargo was, mind.'

'Well.' She drummed her fingers on the table. 'What does this mean?'

'That the man who fled before Lady Allcot's murder is shipping to Holland, through a company owned by the husband of another of your suspects, Cornelia Howe.'

'Curious, no? Malvern said he was at Hampton Court to watch someone. I have been wondering . . . do you think that could have been him?'

'It might well have been, if this Belco—'

'Bellecour,' she corrected. 'With the "r" at the back of your throat.'

'Him. If he is part of this somehow, then yes, 'tis possible he was watching him.'

'Except he was not doing a very good job. He should have followed him to the summer house as we did.'

'Maybe he was being . . . discreet.'

'Perhaps. And besides, there is nothing preventing Bellecour from shipping what he likes – or else not before war was declared. Was there a date in the ledger?'

'There were two entries by his name. Early February, then the first of March.'

'Just before the war, then.' Thirsty, she drained a full third of her ale. 'On the other hand, Howe's business must be well known to people connected with the Court, his wife's uncle being Sir Stephen Herrick. Perhaps he was recommended to Bellecour, nothing more, and all Bellecour did was send a couple of shipments to a friend.'

'Just because there are no more entries in the ledger doesn't mean there weren't more shipments. People hide what they're doing during war, even respectable traders. Or perhaps Bellecour used Howe's company until war broke out, then turned to other means.' He stared at his tankard, already almost empty. 'There's something I don't understand, though. If Cornelia is a nobleman's niece, how is it she's married to a mere shipping agent?'

'Money, of course. Howe owns a profitable trading concern. That would bring a pleasing sum to Cornelia's family, and the prestige of noble connections for an aspiring merchant. Indeed, my own grandfather was a wool trader, on my father's side, while my mother is descended from nobility.'

'I suppose.' He finished the last dregs of his ale. 'So what are we saying – that Bellecour is part of this?'

'How would the sequence go?' She counted out points on her fingers. 'Virgo acquires her information from the man of the war council. She passes it to Bellecour. Bellecour ships the intelligence to Holland, hiding it in some cargo or other, maybe using Howe's company, at least before the war. I suppose that could work.'

'If so, could it mean Virgo is Cornelia Howe?'

'Then why go through Bellecour at all, instead of sending the information directly herself?'

'So her husband doesn't know what she's doing? She could give the information to Bellecour, then use her knowledge of the company to be sure it gets out safe.'

'But are not all goods checked on leaving the country?'

'Not necessarily. Bribes, agreements, they're more common than folk admit.' He eyed up the tavern keeper, who was serving another customer his drink. 'Aren't we forgetting Lady Allcot? I still think it's unlikely Bellecour was just . . . seeing her. Why can't she be Virgo?'

'She still might be, although Sir William told me nothing has been found to suggest it. But if she is not, and Bellecour is involved, then he may have been trying to seduce her for a particular purpose – to add to whatever intelligence he learns from the real spy.'

He rubbed the stubble on his chin. 'I hadn't thought of that.'

'We know Mr Malvern was at Hampton Court for a reason. The King himself told me that other work, as he put it, was already underway in that regard. No, there is much that points to our

179

enigmatic Frenchman. I will have to try to speak with him myself.'

'How? Will he not recognise you from Hampton Court?'

'That may not matter. We never established who pushed me over. He may never have seen me. Besides, I could gauge how he reacts.'

'Still, it could be dangerous.'

'More difficult is how to approach him. Sir William told me that making representations to the French would be difficult. But . . . I wager there is some other means I can employ. One that none of the King's men ever could.'

'What's that?' he asked, only half listening as he waved expectantly at the tavern keeper.

'If he is attempting to glean information from the women of the Court – women close to men with power – it should not be hard to use his own devices against him. If I am right, all I have to do is hasten matters.' She smiled. 'Though from the look of your thirst, that might take a long while yet.'

Maybe she had it all wrong. But there were two connections now between Bellecour and the women who could be Virgo: his liaison with the murdered Lady Allcot, and his use of the trading company owned by the husband of Cornelia Howe. Coincidence, maybe, but she was convinced Bellecour was more intricately tied up in events than that, all the more because Giles Malvern had been present at Hampton Court at the same time she had been hoping to meet her own quarry. Malvern had not wanted to discuss his mission at the eating house, but she would not be surprised if her suspicions were confirmed, that he had been assigned to watch Bellecour just as she had been pursuing Lady Allcot.

It struck her, also, as she sat in the palace, looking for signs of Bellecour near the rooms assigned the visiting French, that Malvern could have been watching her. Checking on her progress, making sure she did not make errors that would need to be straightened out. No doubt there were those in the shadows of the Court who were unhappy that the King had entrusted to her this task; no doubt their paranoia that she could blunder may have encouraged them to set a watch, and now, with Malvern's identity made known to her, a more explicit warning to take care.

She smiled to herself. She was the woman who had travelled the ocean. As if she ever needed such advice.

'You seem cheerful,' came an unexpected voice.

'Miss Whent,' she said, looking up. 'Lavinia. I was . . . thinking about something.'

'A man?'

'Why that?'

'It was that sort of a look.'

'No. Well. I suppose it was about a man. But not in that way.' She moved up on her window seat. 'Will you join me?'

'Thank you. I will.'

As she sat, Mercia looked past her. 'Where have you come from? There is not much down that way, besides rooms for the use of foreign envoys.'

'Oh, I was speaking with someone. A friend of sorts.' She winked. 'And this was a man.'

'What man?'

'One of the French.' She frowned. 'What of it?'

'Not Julien Bellecour?' she said, before she could stop herself.

As quickly as she had sat, Lavinia stood. Two embroidered cushions tumbled to her feet.

'You know him?'

'No, but I—'

'Then why mention him, specifically?'

'Forgive me. I just meant . . . I had heard he was . . . and I wondered if—'

'You do know him, don't you? Mercia, I have to go.'

Turning aside her face, she hurried down the corridor in a blaze of bright blue. Aghast, Mercia watched her round the corner, thinking . . . surely Bellecour was not involved with Lavinia Whent too?

She got to her feet. Enough was enough. It was time to uncover the truth.

He was desirable, she would give him that. No wonder Lady Allcot had been drawn to him. There was something in his dark eyes, in the way that he leant that little bit too far over when he passed her a drink; something in the cut of his breeches, in the way his shirt was that little bit undone, and something, above all, in his damned exotic . . . Frenchness.

But that wasn't going to work with her. Or so she told herself.

'*Je suis heureuse de vous faire la connaissance, Monsieur Bellecour,*' she ventured, trying to recall the scant French she had learnt when she was a girl.

'*Sir William m'a dit que vous parlez français,*' he replied. '*C'est excellent.*'

'*Il exagère. Je ne parle qu'un peu. Mais j'aime bien . . . essayer.*'

'Let us speak in English, then,' he conceded. 'Language hardly matters when one has other senses.'

She looked about her. 'This is a pleasant apartment, Monsieur. Your emissary must be in favour.'

'Julien, please. And I hope so.'

'Have you been at Whitehall long?'

He reached for the decanter of wine: crisp and white, its bouquet reminiscent of wheat fields basking in the sun.

'About four months myself. But you are not so long here, I think. I did not see you before.'

'Whereas I am certain I have seen you.' She made sure to examine his face. 'At the ball, I think, when you were standing with your delegation. And then . . . at Hampton Court.'

But he betrayed no reaction. 'I have not been at Hampton Court since the day that poor woman was killed.'

'You did not know her?'

He shook his head. 'Lady . . . Alton, was it not?'

'Lady Allcot.' *Interesting.* 'May the Lord protect her soul.'

'Ah yes, that is right. You were there?'

There was nothing in his eyes to suggest duplicity. 'Indeed, I refer to that same day. I was walking in the grounds, and . . . To think if I had been a few seconds earlier in my walk, I could have seen it all.'

'I had left by then. But this is hardly a topic for conversation. You did not come here to resurrect such horrors.'

'No.' She smiled. 'But I believe, Julien, it was you who asked me to come.'

He took a sip of his wine, never abandoning his persistent gaze. 'I flatter myself I know something of the women of this Court. Your Englishmen are so dull, so . . . soft. You like something a little more . . . firm.'

She nearly coughed into her wine. Had he meant to say that?

'Julien, I think you are ahead of yourself. We have only just met.'

'Then we should waste no time in becoming better acquainted.' The candlelight flickered as he pulled his chair closer to hers. 'I am glad we met in the garden yesterday.'

The image of their meeting flashed into her mind; how ridiculous it had been, how contrived, how . . .

'Are they coming?' she had asked, the dusk breeze across her face.

'They're coming.' Looking over her shoulder, Nicholas had been watching for the party to emerge. 'The whole delegation, it seems. I still can't believe Sir William's allowing you to do this.'

'I can be persuasive when I need to be. Lady Castlemaine's insistence on quickness may have helped.'

'But 'tis all still . . . what did you call it?'

'Conjecture. But surely, Nicholas, you do not disappear from the vicinity of a shooting unless you have something to hide? His status may protect him from the law, but – the King's wishes for a French alliance aside – it is not going to protect him from me.'

'Well, here comes Sir William now. And . . . yes . . . he's stopped them. He's bowing. He's started to talk with one of them – the ambassador, most like.'

'Very well.' She straightened herself up. 'That is our signal to proceed. Are you ready?'

He screwed up his face. 'I am.'

And then she slapped him.

'How dare you address me in that manner!' she shrieked, loud enough for her voice to carry across the garden. 'Get you gone, before I have you whipped!'

He widened his eyes; clearly, she had hit him harder than she had intended – that, or he was amused at her choice of language. Either way, he fled as planned without another word. Dramatically shaking her head, she turned around: on cue, Sir William was huddled with the French, gesturing towards her, asking the young man at the back of the party to find out if she needed help.

The young man at the back being Julien Bellecour.

'Madame,' he said, wasting no time in coming across. 'I saw what happened. Do you need assistance?'

She smiled, looking him up and down with deceitfully roaming eyes. 'Do not mind me. I have had words with my man, that is all.'

'The *bâtard* in the hooded cloak? I could not see his face, but I shall be happy to fetch him back, if you wish it.'

'Do not be concerned, sir.' She blinked her painted eyes. 'Your accent . . . you are French?'

'I am. And you, may I say, are enchanting.'

She faked a laugh. 'I see it is true what they say.'

'What is?'

'That chaste ladies must be on their guard around Frenchmen.'

He grinned. 'Do they say that?'

'But you should know, Monsieur, that the nobleman there is my love.'

He turned his head. '*Vraiment?* Sir William Calde?'

'Indeed so. He is the King's close advisor, so you had best take care.'

'Sir William . . . Yes, I know who he is.'

'You should hear the tales he tells of . . . but I am talking too much.' She rolled her eyes. 'I am always talking.'

'Not at all.' He looked at her. 'You have a charming voice. It is pleasing to hear it.'

Enough, she thought. *Time to lay the snare.*

She teased the lace of her plunging neckline. 'Thank you for your gallantry, Monsieur . . . ?'

'Bellecour. Julien Bellecour.'

'Monsieur Bellecour. You should know that Sir William is not a jealous man.'

'No?' He leant in. 'Then I see 'tis true what they say of the women of this Court. That they need little encouragement.'

'I walk in the park most days around noon. I should not be averse to finding you there – tomorrow?' Pulling back, she held out her hand. 'Goodnight, Monsieur.'

'Perhaps I should like that.' He bowed and kissed her fingers. 'Goodnight, Madame.'

She inclined her head, giving Bellecour a smile she cringed from as too obvious, but the Frenchman did not seem to notice. A moment more, and she broke off to join Sir William. The great man glared at Bellecour in feigned offence before taking her arm and leading her away. Yet somehow, she managed to look back.

Utterly ridiculous, as she later thought. But then, the absurd plot had worked.

Chapter Sixteen

'Where were we?' said Bellecour, thirty minutes after he had welcomed her to the French emissary's assigned rooms. 'Would you like more wine?'

'Just a little. It is too good to drink quickly.'

The wine licked the sides of her glass as he splashed it inside. 'I thought you English did not much like wine. But in my time at the Court, I have observed that not to be true.'

'Whitehall courtiers and Englishmen are different. We like wine well enough here. But tell me, Julien. How long have you served in your country's employ?'

'But a few years. I am still young, I hope.'

'This is your first time away from France?'

'No.' He stretched to set the empty decanter aside. 'I have been elsewhere.'

'I too have spent time away,' she ventured. 'But never to the Continent. When I was in New York . . . it used to belong to the Dutch, you know . . . I decided I should like to visit Holland, but I suppose I shall have to wait a while now.'

He sniffed. 'I should not bother. Too full of water. Too flat.'

'Ah. You have been there?'

'Only from necessity.'

'You have acquaintances?'

'So many questions.' He smiled. 'Why ask?'

'Only because I have an interest in other places. Sir William and I discuss such matters often. We talk about a lot of things, indeed. But I am sure you do not want to hear about him.'

'Oh, I do not mind. When did you meet?'

'We were introduced last year. Now we have established . . . beneficial relations, shall we say.'

'And so he brought you to Whitehall.' He reached for a second decanter; where had that come from, she wondered? 'Fortunate for me.'

'Fortunate for me you were sent at this time.' She placed a hand over her glass as he tried to top it up. 'But I do not think you can live here, at the palace, Julien. You must have lodgings elsewhere?'

He nodded. 'In the city, not far from St Paul's.'

'Watling Street, perhaps?'

'Gutter Lane. A garret atop a tanner's shop.' He screwed up his nose. 'A good reason to spend more time at the palace than in what passes for a place to sleep.'

'The accommodation is small?'

'Very. That is why the ambassador allows us the use of these rooms when we need to . . . receive guests.'

She staged a sympathetic frown. 'It must be difficult for you here, especially with the war. Or perhaps that is why you have come, to offer our King your support?'

'You are quite unusual, Mrs Blakewood. I have found most women are not so curious about these affairs.'

'Oh, come, I talk of them with William most every day. Do not all such couples do so? It is what keeps the men sane, surely?'

He held her gaze, and for a moment she thought she had played the role too far. But then he smiled.

'Perhaps it is.'

'I should say so. But I should not speak of it here.'

'And let a Frenchman take your secrets back to Paris.' He held up his glass, looking at the clear liquid as he swirled it inside. 'I can assure you, Mrs Blakewood, that is not why you interest me.'

'Not even a little?'

'Maybe . . . a little.'

'Then I shall have to take care.' She chinked her glass against his. 'What is your life like at Court? I imagine you have gatherings every night. Soirées, I suppose you might call them.'

He shook his head. 'Not every night. But as long as we do not disgrace King Louis, we have a certain freedom.'

'It sounds fascinating. I have always wondered what it would be like to attend such an event. I hear you have one this evening?'

'I do not think so. Where did you hear that?'

'Oh.' She feigned astonishment. 'Then I must have heard wrong. When is your next?'

'Tomorrow night, but it will not be an entertainment.' He sidled beside her. 'A droll conversation of tedious men, more like.'

'A pity.' She looked into his eyes. 'Then the next occasion, perhaps.'

It had taken half the second decanter before she was able to slip away. While Bellecour had not much incriminated himself, nor had he disproved any connection with Virgo either. Regardless, she had discovered the two things she had hoped to learn from their meeting: where in London he lived, and when he was not going to be there.

The evening after, she was outside the Gutter Lane tanner's shop, closed up for the day, but the stench of treated leather was still making its presence felt.

'Dear God,' she said to Nicholas, holding her scarf over her nose. 'No wonder he spends so little time here.'

'Smells normal to me,' he replied. 'Are you sure you want to go in alone?'

'Stop asking. I need you out here in case anything happens.' She nodded at a group of men loitering near the entrance. 'Can you make them look away?'

'I'll try.'

He walked towards them, then pretended to slip, sliding his way to drape his arm around one of the startled men.

'I know you,' he said, deliberately slurring his words. 'You were just in The Lion.' He nodded, giving the man a cheer. 'Yes, The Lion.'

The man looked at his fellows. 'I don't think so, friend. Too much ale, eh?'

'Yes you were. You came out after that woman, didn't you?' He pointed down the street. 'Huge – you know. She went that way.'

The men craned their necks in the direction he was pointing, allowing Mercia the chance to slip past unnoticed. Reaching the door to the tannery, she quickly went inside, finding a narrow staircase that led to the garret above and so the entrance to Bellecour's lodgings. As she had hoped, in such meagre accommodation there was no latch on the door: no need to signal for Nicholas.

Inside the room it was pitch black, the drapes drawn on the tiny window, but she dared not pull them back for fear of anyone seeing from the houses opposite. And so she waited for her eyes to adjust, until the black blurs of the few pieces of furniture sharpened into tangible shapes, abandoning their former uncertainty.

The room was as small as Bellecour had described it: barely enough space for a table and chair, a wardrobe and a bed, not much more than she had endured aboard ship. She went straight for the bed, feeling beneath the ramshackle frame, fingers brushing against what she assumed were discarded garments, a pile of towels, and a chest. Taking care to disturb nothing, she raised her head to listen, before pulling out the trunk. She set both hands on the twin clasps, and was surprised to find they sprang open, but when she felt inside there was nothing within, and she replaced the chest where she had found it.

There was another trunk on top of the wardrobe, and she clambered on the chair to fetch it down. This one was half-full, but only of folded clothes and a small box of jewellery. Balancing on the chair to restore the trunk, she nearly cried out as the legs slipped beneath her, but she grabbed at the wardrobe to arrest her treacherous slide in time. The wardrobe wobbled precariously, and for a moment she turned cold as she thought it would fall, but it teetered back into place, and as it did, a concealed object clattered to the floor behind it.

She got down from the chair, pushing it back before feeling behind the wardrobe for whatever had fallen, but although her fingertips reached the leathery object she was unable to drag it out. She searched the room for a tool she could use, and was beginning to panic she would be forced to leave the dislodged object where it was, in a place it could never have fallen by itself, when she realised she could use the length of a candle to apply pressure and tease it out.

Taking a candle from a drawer in the table, she turned her hand sideways to fit it in the gap, pressing the tip against the object. At first it slipped, coming away with nothing, and then the same, and again a third time, until on the fourth attempt she pushed down harder and eased the object towards her. Three more drags and it was close enough to set the candle to one side and grab it.

She had retrieved a thin notebook, of the sort she used herself to compile lists of things to do, or shopping for her maid to buy, and although she could tell that the first third was covered in scribbles, it was too dark to make out the writing. She squinted, holding the pages up to her eyes, but it was no use. Finally, her curiosity overcame her concerns, and replacing the candle in the drawer, she opened the window drapes the smallest amount to let in a sliver of moonlight. Over the rooftops of London it was barely enough, but she could now discern some of what she was reading.

The language was not French, that was evident. Nor was it English, or even Dutch. The letters were those of the Roman alphabet, all Qs and Ls and Ps, but which language placed impossible consonants together like that, or repeated the same vowel amidst overlong words that—

She closed her eyes.

Not again!

The notebook was written in code.

She had desired it, truth be told. Suspected it, even. If Bellecour was Virgo's conduit to send information to the Dutch, then any notes he had compiled should naturally be encoded. The existence of the book was vindication of her premise – or, as Sir William doubted the next day:

'They could merely be written observations on the English Court to send back to France. Or he could even be speculating on the women of the Court. You said yourself how he seemed to enjoy their company. I have known men before who like to . . . write down their qualities.'

'Evaluate them like cattle, you mean.' She blinked in the bright light streaming through the panes of Sir William's lead-framed windows. 'My, I think my eyes have still not adjusted this morning.'

'Mercia, I know you enjoy trouble, but I wish you would have considered better what you were planning. I explained to you before about the need to be delicate. Breaking into an envoy's lodgings could have brought serious consequences were you caught.'

She looked at him. 'I was not.'

'At least you left the book in his room. Could you translate it?'

She shook her head. 'It was too dark to make much out. Even if there had been a light, I doubt it would have been simple.'

'So what now?'

'Well, we know that Bellecour was with Lady Allcot before she died. We know he was eager to speak with me in the ambassador's rooms at Court. We know he has sent something to Amsterdam. And now we know he keeps a codebook. I suggest we put a watch on him.' She pursed her lips. 'Although I think someone might already have done so.'

'Who?'

'You recall that man from the other day, Giles Malvern?'

His cheeks reddened slightly. 'I do.'

'It turns out he is in the spymasters' employ. Under the Earl of Arlington.'

'Truthfully?' Sir William frowned. 'How do you know this?'

'Malvern told me so. He says he was at Hampton Court because he was ordered to go there. But then why are Arlington's men not looking for Virgo as well? Why permit my involvement?'

'You know why. The King thinks you can get close to her without arousing as much suspicion. Besides, there may be no connection.'

'The connection is strong enough. I cannot help but think that I may be being used. Me and my uncle both.' She looked up. 'Sir William, how are your relations with my uncle now? Do you know if he still pursues his own investigations?'

'I have no idea, Mercia. He keeps himself too close. But as you mention Sir Francis, I would advise you to be wary. No doubt he means to thwart you and keep hold of your manor house.'

She thought a moment. 'And what of the Earl of Arlington? Are you able to ask him about Malvern's purpose?'

'I can ask, but most likely he will not say.' He shrugged. 'He may not even know. It is his lackey, Williamson, who is in charge of these . . . secretive concerns. And he is even more guarded than his master. Now about this watch on Bellecour you propose.' He roved his eyes over her innocent face. 'I hope you do not think to suggest yourself for that duty. If others are already involved, as you imply, they will not thank you.'

'If that is my best means of finding Virgo, I am simply following my instructions. It is past a week already since Lady Castlemaine insisted I find swift answers, and so I shall have to provide them, and soon, or we shall all risk her displeasure.' She flashed him a mischievous smile. 'Do not worry, Sir William. I shall take great care.'

'Hmm.' He threw her a wry glance. 'I have heard you say such things before.'

'There.' Nicholas pointed out a hooded figure turning onto Trinity Lane. 'Got him again.'

'Thank the Lord. I thought we had lost him.'

'He's certainly being careful. Let's hope he isn't just trying to hide his shame at going into some fuddle-caps' drinking den.'

'Delicate as ever, Nicholas.' She set off again in pursuit of their quarry. 'Come, before he eludes us once more.'

'Ah, is that why you came this time? Four eyes better than two?'

'To speak true, I was bored waiting for you to return the other night.'

A young girl appeared from nowhere, hawking a bucket of dented spoons, but Nicholas brushed her deftly aside. 'At the weekend he wasn't being this careful. And it wasn't my fault if I was moved on. There isn't much you can do before you start to look suspect, even in London.'

'Is he walking in the same direction tonight?'

'Different. That was up near Holborn, now he's heading towards the Bridge. He has a purpose in his steps too. Something's going on, for certain.' He paused. 'I still wish you hadn't come. The letter One-Eye Wilkins promised you is due about now. Her men could be watching.'

'Then 'tis well I have you to protect me.' She smiled, feigning nonchalance. 'That letter might not arrive for days. Maybe even never. Come.'

They pressed on, craning their necks over the crowds. A fight had broken out ahead of them, ostensibly about who had the right to pass under the overhang of the houses above, and so be protected from the menace of thrown-down waste. Still, not worth losing a tooth for, thought Mercia, pulling close her hood as an angry combatant struck his adversary in the mouth.

Leaving the melee behind, they followed Bellecour right onto Garlick Hill, where the higher storeys reached out to each other across the narrow way, blocking what little evening light remained.

'He's heading down to the river,' said Nicholas. ''Tis more open there. He might see us, so stay by me and be ready to pull back.'

'Yes, sir,' she said.

'I wonder what he's—quick! Against the wall.' He thrust out his arm to arrest her passage, and the two of them retreated against the frontage of a butcher's shop. A pockmarked apprentice stared from the candlelit doorway, from where the stench of rotting meat assaulted their grudging nostrils.

'Ugh.' Keeping her eyes on Bellecour, Mercia screwed up her face. 'What do you see?'

'He's slowing. I think he senses danger. I recognise the signs. Let's just . . . yes, he's quickening his pace again. Out of here, we come over Thames Street by the river, so we shouldn't lose him.'

To a jeer from the apprentice, they ducked out of the narrow passage into a wide space before the river. Further down, boatmen were perched on a railing, jostling near their wherries to win fares. And they had spotted their latest customer.

'I hope he's not . . .' muttered Nicholas. 'God's truth, he is!'

Mercia watched as Bellecour followed one of the ferrymen down a series of wet steps. 'Damn,' she said. 'I think we shall have to—'

Without finishing her sentence she hurried to the lined-up boatmen. At once a trio leapt from the railing, nimbler even than they had been with Bellecour.

'Cheap price, my lady.'

'My boat's largest, love, more room.'

'Mine's fastest!'

She reviewed the three men in one quick glance; pointing at the second, she descended the steps to the rocking boats. She accepted the ferryman's hand as he steadied her into his craft.

'Him too?' said the man, as Nicholas got in. 'Pity. Where to, then?'

'You see that wherry that launched before us? We need to go to the same place, and quickly.'

Nicholas laughed. 'Follow that boat!'

The trip was a short one. Within two minutes, they were halfway across the river, following the dim shape of Bellecour's wherry, clearly heading for Southwark on the opposite side.

'Hell's teeth,' said Mercia. 'Is he only visiting the bear pit?'

'No fight on tonight, love.' The boatman sniffed in the stale river air. 'What're you following him for, anyway? Looked a bit foreign, if you ask me.'

'Nobody did ask you,' said Nicholas.

'Calm down, mate. Only trying to help.'

'Is anything else happening in Southwark this evening?' she asked. 'If not bears, then maybe cocks, or prize fights?'

'No, love. We haven't had much trade this way tonight at all. Bit of a pain, what with all them kids at home to feed, and their mother not so much as—'

'She said she would pay you well if you rowed us fast, not talked us to death,' said Nicholas.

The boatman sucked in through his teeth. 'That don't mean to say her man can't be civil. Or shall I leave you here in the middle of the river? That cove'll be clean away soon, you know, whatever your business with him, poor fellow.'

'You are right,' said Mercia, suddenly abrupt. 'He is foreign. He's crossed me, and I want my revenge.'

'Now we're getting to it! Bloody foreigners! Can't trust them, can you?'

'I could not agree more,' she said, ignoring Nicholas's amused expression. 'Good thing this war has started, now we can show them!'

'Right you are, my lady! I've said it all along, ever since the King returned, what we need's a good war to show them who's best.' He nodded as if agreeing with himself. 'I'll have you over there in a minute.'

She flicked her eyebrows at Nicholas, who covered his mouth with a well-timed hand, although the creases of his eyes told their own story. True to her word, when they disembarked not far up from London Bridge she reached into her pockets for a generous coin: the man's eyes fair bulged when he saw the silver crown.

'Shall I—' he stammered. 'Shall I wait here, my lady? Take you back, later on?'

'If you wish.'

She held onto Nicholas's shoulder as she climbed from the boat. St Saviour's church loomed close above, but it was the gloom of its deep shadow that drew her attention, for that was where Bellecour was disappearing, arrived just a short time before them.

Nicholas sped ahead. 'Don't worry, I'll keep him in view.'

She tossed the ferryman his coin and followed as fast as she could, but by the time she reached the church's western steps she had lost them. Cursing her misfortune, at first she failed to notice the beggar at her feet, but on the second tug of her hems, she shook the emaciated creature away.

'That way, is all,' the filthy man rasped, pointing to a nearby alley. 'Your man said to tell you.'

'Oh.' Red-cheeked, Mercia felt inside her dress to withdraw a penny. 'Thank you.'

She hurried in the direction the beggar had shown her: the alley was close, dirty sheets flapping out the scant moonlight, but candles had been lit in many of the storefronts, and she could make out Nicholas's cloak as he approached the thoroughfare's end. She squeezed past the few people standing about, making it through without incident, but then she found herself in a maze of streets, and each time she looked up, Nicholas was vanishing around the next corner.

At a four-way junction she halted to catch her breath. The road stretched on in each direction, but Nicholas was nowhere to be seen. Then she noticed two women chatting outside a doorway on her right, and she approached the animated pair, thinking to seek their help as the beggar had offered his.

'Excuse me,' she panted. 'Have you seen a man coming past? Two men indeed, one not long after the other?'

The women glanced at each other. 'What brings you down here, darling?'

'I am sorry, I do not have time to talk. Could you just—'

A hissing came from behind the women. She peered round to see a darkened hand, beckoning her approach the doorway. And then the hiss again.

'Here!' Nicholas called.

She looked at the women, who shrugged, before stepping to one side to allow her past.

'Nicholas!' she said, joining him on the threshold. 'Where is Bellecour?'

'He . . . came in here. Why don't you go back to the boatman and wait for me there?'

'Why?'

'I . . . just think you should.'

'Nicholas?' She glanced behind him. 'Is this not an inn? I can see down this hall that there are plenty of people drinking. Mostly women, besides, so I should not have any—'

She cut herself off with a gasp.

'That's right,' he said. 'Now will you listen?'

She put her hand to her mouth. This was no inn.

She was standing in the entrance to a whorehouse.

Chapter Seventeen

The women outside were smirking at her discomfort. 'Not quite your usual place, I'm thinking,' said the elder of the two. 'Perhaps you should leave your brother be.' She draped an arm around Nicholas's shoulders. 'I'm sure he can – handle himself.'

Nicholas shrugged off the whore's advances. 'I'm not looking for a woman. I saw a man come in here and—'

'God's wounds.' She exhaled a long breath. 'Well, I'm not sure. Simon might be willing to play your pipe for a shilling, but we don't much go in for that unnatural stuff here.'

He narrowed his eyes. 'I mean, I'm not looking for anything, damn it. A man came in here just before me. Are there any other ways out?'

The jilt cocked her head. 'You a harman?'

'A constable? Me? Do I look like one?'

'Not much. You sure you don't want a girl?'

'If I did, I wouldn't choose you. Answer my question.'

'Get this one.' The woman turned to her companion and pulled a mocking face. 'Must like them younger. You have a go.'

'I said I don't want . . . Hell's teeth!'

'What he means to say,' said Mercia, 'is could you answer his question?' For a third time that evening, she reached inside her pocket for a coin. 'It is important.'

The older whore eyed up the sixpence. 'What's it to you?'

'Does it matter? Here is money. Take it.'

Before the woman could react, the younger snatched the coin from Mercia's hand. 'There's one door round back, to the yard,' she said quickly. 'We use it if the harmans come knocking. But it's guarded. No one can leave that way.'

The girl sounded surprisingly erudite. 'So the man who just came in could not have come out,' asked Mercia, 'but by the same entrance here?'

She shook her head. 'No one's been past us since.'

'Does he often come here? Did you recognise him?'

'Yes, I seen him here before. He likes Mellie, but—'

The elder woman coughed.

'What?' said the younger. 'I'm just talking.'

'Mind what you're talking about, then. I've got better things to do.'

She disappeared inside. 'Ale to drink, more like,' shouted her companion. 'What was I saying?'

'About Mellie,' prompted Mercia.

'Oh yes. That man – he comes here, asks for Mellie, but there's never any noise coming from her room while he's in it. No grunting or anything.'

Mercia pulled Nicholas to one side. 'What could Bellecour be doing, coming here? He seems to . . . get what he wants at Court.'

'He's a man, Mercia. He'll have tastes, the same as any other. Coming to a place like this makes it easy. Some men like to think they have mastery over such girls.'

'But what if he becomes – spreads things, at the palace?'

'I should think there's enough of that there already. The quacks must have their work cut out.'

'So what do we do now?'

Nicholas turned to the young whore. Now Mercia looked more closely, she realised she could only be about sixteen, but then many of the women in this place would be as young. The same age as Tacitus, she reflected, suffering at the whims of others just as he did. But tonight was not the time for a pricking of conscience.

'Can you show me Mellie's room?' Nicholas said.

The girl smiled. 'What you going to do? Punch his face?'

'Something like that.'

She puffed out through rouged lips. 'Oh, go on, then. I never liked Mellie, anyway. I always said she was a queer one.' She set a hand on his arm, glancing at Mercia as she eased him inside. 'But your friend waits out here.'

She waited, inside the door. Left alone she felt exposed, especially when a well-dressed man of double her age slunk into the whorehouse and paused to leer. Before he could utter a word, she looked away in pique and shooed the client on. What did he think, she thought indignantly? That she looked like a whore? Even wearing her dowdy brown dress, nothing like the glamour of her fine Court attire, she did not have the air of one of those . . . base women.

The man growled and carried on, and she dwelt for a moment on the plight of those women, concerned her ready judgement was too harsh. Everyone had suffered in the war – the civil war, that was – and hardship was still prevalent, wherever in London she looked. Perhaps such work was all these women could find, if work it could be called, forced to deal with the cravings of men seeking their wanton release.

A shrill voice at her shoulder startled her from her thoughts, and she turned to find herself confronted by a penetrating scowl, the woman's face not so much painted as annoyed. Unlike the previous two, she exuded authority.

'What're you doing here?' she snapped. 'If your man's gone up with Susan, let him be. He don't need a chaperone.'

'He is not . . . we are just trying to find a man who—'

'I've heard all that. I'm not interested, and I don't want no ladybird like you loitering around. Mind your own, dear. Get it.'

'If I could wait for him to come down—'

'Do you want me to call Gunner for help?'

'Very well. No need to be impolite.'

She slunk out of the brothel and around the corner, hiding herself on the threshold of a closed-up storefront. A mangy dog padding past stopped to sniff the dirty step, but other than a quick lick of her boots it gave her little heed.

Five minutes passed. A breeze rose up, casting the litter of the day along the shabby street, and in the distance a group of drunks began a raucous song. Then a window opened above the crossroads, back at the whorehouse from where she had come. The squeak made her look up, and to her surprise she saw a pair of boots protruding through a first-floor window, soon followed by some breeches and the hooks of a man's shirt. Then a whole figure slipped through, gripping the sill before dropping to the ground with an intake of breath.

She pressed herself in to the darkness of her storefront, her brown dress merging with the evening gloom. Distracted by the jolt of his jump, the man rubbed at his legs and failed to notice she was there. But she noticed him.

'Bellecour,' she whispered to herself.

And then a commotion sounded from round the corner, as

a woman's accusing scorn chased another man into view. He careered on the spot in the middle of the crossroads, looking directly at the Frenchman.

'Nicholas,' she continued.

One look back and Bellecour shot into the Southwark dusk. Without hesitation, Nicholas set off in pursuit, soon followed by another man with a cudgel in his hand, stocky and utterly bald. But his bulk made him slow, and she could see even now how he was falling behind.

Tentative, she stepped out of the threshold, debating whether to pursue or to stay put, but she knew she could never catch up. Instead she decided to return to the riverbank, in case Bellecour made for the wherries there. As best as she could she began to jog, but not far past the whorehouse another figure leapt from the darkness and held her fast.

'Release me!' she cried, struggling in the man's grasp, but immediately he let her go.

''Tis me, Mrs Blakewood. Giles Malvern. What in heaven's name are you doing?'

'Mr Malvern!' She took a step back. 'I should ask the same of you.'

'What do you think? But there's no time now. Your man has likely ruined weeks of preparation.'

'You mean you were—'

'Wait back by the river. We can speak later.'

'I was going—' she protested, but he ignored her, sprinting away into the night.

By now a crowd of women had gathered at the entrance to the whorehouse. Keen to avoid their attention, Mercia marched off just as the madam was storming towards her, oblivious to the two men who were tucking in their shirts and slipping out of sight behind her back. But Mercia eluded her curses, following the streets towards the church, and thence coming out at the wherry rank. The boatman who had brought them over was sitting on a low wall, chewing some noisy substance around his mouth.

'Back across, love?' he called, spitting out a nut-sized lump.

'Not yet,' she said.

'You find that cove you were chasing?'

'Thank you for waiting, but do you mind if I just sit here and do the same?'

He shrugged and settled back onto his perch, but his presence was reassuring as she felt the tingling in her stomach, waiting for Nicholas to reappear. The lapping of the river against the moorings was eerie, the reflection of the waxing moon enhancing the effect.

She waited for what seemed an age, but the moon had barely moved by the time first Malvern, and then Nicholas, came into view. There was no sign of Bellecour.

'Well,' said Malvern, forsaking the niceties of the eating house. 'This is a problem. What did you think you were hoping to achieve?'

'I told you,' said Nicholas. 'We were following Bellecour.'

'I should rather you be silent and let your mistress speak.'

Mercia sighed; what did she have to lose by being honest? 'It is as he says. We think Bellecour might lead us to Virgo. We hoped his actions might provide us with useful intelligence.'

Malvern set his hands on his hips. 'Did I not tell you to be careful?'

'You did. But I did not think you would be here also.'

He beckoned her to one side, out of earshot of the clearly listening ferryman.

'I have been watching that . . . house for some weeks. Bellecour goes there from time to time, and not for the usual purpose. We think he meets someone there, or uses it to pass on information he has learnt. But I doubt he will return now.' He glanced at Nicholas. 'Did he get a look at you?'

'I'm not sure,' he said. 'I had my hood up, but I looked straight at him.'

'What happened in there?' said Mercia. 'The last I know was Bellecour jumping from the window.'

'Explain to your mistress,' ordered Malvern. 'While I search the streets once more. Even in that warren, there are only so many places he can hide. Mrs Blakewood, wait here.'

'I can help—' began Nicholas, but Malvern cut him off with a stiff shake of his head. Mercia waited for him to go before she turned to Nicholas and became forthright herself.

'Well?' she demanded.

He scratched at his ear. 'That didn't go as well as I'd hoped.'

'You could say that.'

'Susan – that girl – she took me upstairs. Tried to persuade me to . . . you know, but I kept telling her no, and she showed me the room where Bellecour was meant to be.'

'And was he?'

'I listened at the door while she watched out for me.' He winked. 'I think she liked me.'

'Your humour is not going to help you. What did you hear?'

'Not what you'd expect. Silence. But there was a small chink in the door I could look through. Susan said all the doors have a hole of some sort, supposedly protection for the girls. Then again, some men like to be watched, or pay so they can spy. So I've heard.'

'Nicholas, get on with it.'

'Well, that's certainly not what Bellecour was doing. He was fully clothed, sitting on the bed, while the girl he was meant to be paying was lying on the floor, reading.'

'She could read?'

'Looking at the letters, at least.'

She frowned. 'I know that face. You have done something.'

'Have I?' He held up his hands. 'Mellie – the girl in Bellecour's room – said something like she couldn't understand what she was reading, asking if it was French. Bellecour laughed and said she'd have a job to read it even if she could, it being no common language at all. Well, at that I burst right in.'

'Why?'

'To get the papers she was struggling to read. I covered my head with my hood, snatched the papers, and dashed right out before they knew what I was up to. Only trouble was, Bellecour came after me. I couldn't fight him, as I didn't want to risk showing my face, so I barked out the doors were being watched, but then he panicked. He ran back into the room, opened the window and jumped through.'

'He landed near where I was hiding.' She blew out her cheeks. 'Damn it, Nicholas, why did you have to say he was being watched? If he is Virgo's conduit, he will think he has been caught, and he will hide himself away. Clear his lodgings, maybe even seek to leave the country.'

'I doubt that. But he won't get far if he does try, will he? He'd have to get word to the French somehow, or if he decided to slip away alone, he'd have to make for the ports, where they'd just need to know to watch for him. Unless he used more dubious means, of course.'

'Like a smuggler ready to take him for a fee.' She narrowed her eyes. 'Why are you smiling? We may have scared away our only link to Virgo.'

'Because I still have these.' He reached into his pockets and withdrew two sheets of paper. 'The notes Bellecour gave Mellie. I haven't told Malvern about them yet.'

'You sly . . . well done, Nicholas!' More enthused, she took the papers and scanned the first sheet. 'Yes.' She nodded. 'In code, as I thought.' Then she glanced towards the end of the page. 'My God!'

For a moment she could feel her heart quicken, and she stared up at Nicholas, her eyes as bright as his.

'I was right! There is one word here not in code. This is proof of Bellecour's involvement, at last!'

He leant over her shoulder. 'What word?'

She allowed herself her moment of triumph.

'Virgo.'

'God's truth! But Mercia, why put everything in code and yet keep her name free for all to read?'

'I should think to avoid it being used to decipher the rest.' She lowered the papers to her side. 'Think about it. If we know the name of our enemy – Virgo – and we assume she will be mentioned in the message, then we can look for where her name might be written in the code. And if we deduce that, it becomes easier to decipher the whole.' She continued to scan, moving onto the second sheet. 'But 'tis already code, in its way. A substitute for the person's real name.'

'Clever.' Then he frowned. 'What is it? You've stopped breathing.'

'Nicholas, there is another spy.'

'What?'

'Here, halfway down the second sheet.' She jabbed at the papers with an urgent finger. 'Another word not in code. Gemini.'

'Gemini?' he repeated. 'The sign of the Zodiac?'

'As Virgo is a different sign.' She paled. 'Nicholas, if there are two words not in code . . . two words much like each other . . . and one of those words is the name of a spy . . . then surely the other must be too.'

'Could it be Bellecour's code name?'

'It might well be. Then again' – she glanced to one side – 'but hush for now.'

Giles Malvern chose that moment to return to the waterfront. She faced the river and hid the papers in her pockets before turning to meet him. Nicholas looked at her askance but said nothing.

'Did you find him?' she asked, remarking his perturbed expression.

'No.' He shook his head. 'He . . . he got away.'

'You seem troubled.'

'Can you much blame me?'

'I am sorry if we interfered with your work, Mr Malvern. But perhaps if you had described it more fully when we ate, matters would not have become so confused tonight. You knew my task; I did not know yours.'

'I did not want to burden you with unnecessary concerns.' He sighed, looking out on the dark river. 'It seems what they say of you is well earned, Mrs Blakewood. I shall have to think of a means of explaining this occurrence that does not reflect badly on yourself.'

'I can explain my own mishaps, Mr Malvern.'

'I am sure of it. But I think on this occasion it would be better to defer.'

'Indeed? We are on the same side, I hope.'

Slowly, he rubbed at his temples. 'Very well. I was watching Bellecour, as no doubt you suspected. The truth is he has troubled us for some weeks.'

'Us?'

'The men I work for. Do not expect me to say more.'

'Then will you at least tell me why you have been watching Bellecour?'

'We enquire into everyone who appears at Court. But Bellecour is not the usual sort to join a foreign embassy. Not disciplined enough. We are convinced he is helping the Dutch in some way, but why, we cannot say, other than for the usual reasons.'

'Money,' said Nicholas. 'Profit.'

'Quite so. Mrs Blakewood, I take it you have grounds to suspect Bellecour is involved with Virgo?'

'As we are being candid, I think she is using him. A go-between, to pass her secrets to the Dutch.'

'That might make sense, were it the other way around. I should rather believe Bellecour sought someone susceptible at Court and commissioned her services.'

'Why?' She folded her arms. 'Because to your mind, a woman could not be so devious as to outwit a man?'

'No, but—'

'It may be they are working together.'

'It may be,' he conceded. 'But I say it because we know that is how he operates.' He sucked in his top lip. 'I wonder. Is there any woman in particular you suspect could be Virgo?'

'I know she is one of five, and yet one of them is dead.'

'That one being Lady Allcot?'

'Indeed, but I doubt more and more she could be Virgo. I have been told how searches have been made of her belongings, and nothing suggestive found.'

'That is so. Because of her friendship with Bellecour, I was present at those searches myself. Her husband was not best pleased, but he had little choice.'

She stared at him aghast. 'And yet you said nothing of this when we ate?'

'Mrs Blakewood, I am supposed to say nothing at all. I cannot tell you much even now. But you are right. We are on the same side, and so let me help you with this. If Bellecour is involved with Virgo, that started long before he seduced Lady Allcot. The intelligence that revealed Virgo's existence at Court came to light before the first time they even met.'

'You are sure of this?'

'Completely. I may not know much of Virgo, but I do know him.' He smiled. 'No, Virgo is much cleverer than Lady Allcot. She hides herself well.'

She nodded. 'Then thank you, Mr Malvern. You have set my mind at rest on one point, at least.'

'It still leaves four women for you to consider,' he said, looking intently on. 'You will forgive my curiosity, I hope, but are you at all closer to finding any of them out?'

At last she reached for the papers in her pocket. 'Perhaps, Mr Malvern. Perhaps.'

Chapter Eighteen

She was not arrogant. By snatching Bellecour's coded message, Nicholas had turned a failure into a success, but she did not presume she could make headway with unravelling its secrets herself; nor, following her painful experiences in New England, was she in any way minded to try. Wanting swift answers, she knew the surest, most loyal response was to entrust the note to Malvern, but she made equally sure Sir William knew of her part, determined she not be abandoned at this crucial step. And at least she knew now that what she had suspected was correct: that Lady Allcot was not the spy she sought.

The great man was delighted, despite the contrary news of Bellecour's escape, and promised to make clear it was her man's courageous actions that had delivered the prize into the spymasters' embrace. Within a day, she had received another summons, but not from any secretive figure in the dark: Lady Castlemaine was demanding her immediate presence.

'The red dress again, my lady?' asked Phibae.

Thirty minutes later, clad in deep scarlet, Mercia was whisked inside her enigmatic patron's apartment. In contrast, the King's mistress was dressed all in white, staring once more from a window onto whatever scene was playing out below, but as soon as her lady-in-waiting withdrew, she turned slowly around, deliberate and sure. The look on her face was as unyielding as on so many gargoyles carved into any London church.

'Why did you not come to me?' she said. 'I had thought I made it clear you were working for me in this matter?'

'Forgive me, my lady.' Mercia swallowed, the abruptness of Lady Castlemaine's words disconcerting. 'I did not realise how much you wished to know. When I was before the King, last time, you seemed more concerned with quickness.'

'I keep my peace before the King,' she snapped, although Mercia did not much believe it. 'But now I hear from Arlington that you have made progress in finding out our spy. You gave certain papers to one of his men and talked with Sir William instead of reporting to me, and now Clarendon has found out. I wanted this all resolved before he—' She swept across the room, the fine drapes that covered the wooden pillars of her bed fluttering in her wake. 'You realise your uncle is working for him, do you not? Clarendon?'

'Indeed, my lady, I did.'

'Then 'tis well you remember it.' She stuck her tongue into her cheek. 'When he returned to England last winter, your uncle sought any means he could to encourage the King to your downfall. You have irked his preciousness mightily, Mrs Blakewood. That cane of his – he thinks it impinges on his supposed maleness. But in choosing Clarendon he has made a mistake. That man's days are numbered at this Court.' She narrowed her eyes. 'As for now, if Clarendon knows about the papers you found, so most likely does your uncle. Which means if Arlington's men decipher them, as I hear they will, he will know what they say as much as you do, and perhaps sooner. What do you propose in response?'

The onslaught over, Mercia bowed her head. 'That I have you as my sponsor, my lady, is preferable to serving the Earl of Clarendon in any consideration. I am certain there are matters in which you can offer your assistance in the pursuit of this task.'

The corners of Lady Castlemaine's lips turned up in pleasure. 'I see you understand well, Mrs Blakewood. You know where the power lies in this Court, even if you do not much care for it, or at least your father did not. You speak as nicely to me as to the King.' She wiggled her shoulders in a peculiar gesture. 'But it is for you to come to me, not the other way around.'

'In truth, my lady, I had hoped that I need not involve your person, but it would speed matters, perhaps, if you were to become engaged at this point. Nor did I want to accuse any of the women I suspect without just proof.'

'Most noble of you. But yes, now is the time to ask.'

'Thank you, my lady.' She made sure to bow once more. 'Then I have determined how Virgo must be one of four women.'

'And they are?'

Mercia paused. Did she really not know, or was this a test?

'Lady Herrick, Lady Cartwright, Lavinia Whent and Cornelia Howe, my lady.'

Lady Castlemaine grunted. 'I do not know Cornelia Howe.'

'And the others?'

'Somewhat.' She shrugged. 'Lavinia Whent is still new to the Court, arrived from the Indies with a loathing for slavers and a large dose of stupidity in her lustful mind. Lady Cartwright is her antithesis, other than in the bedchamber. Lady Herrick is a pompous old mare, devoid of looks as much as personality, but she is sharp as they come, and most loyal to her husband.'

'My Lady, Lavinia Whent may be given to her passions, but I do

214

not think she is as foolish as you perhaps suggest. She speaks of her youth in the Barbados with great erudition.'

'And yet still she is a strumpet of the first degree.' She sniffed. 'Lady Herrick is like her husband, the two of them parading their heritage as a badge of esteem. But they visited the King in his exile more than once.'

'And Lady Cartwright?'

'She keeps close with Sir Geoffrey Allcot. She, too, knows the rules of the game. She is not so beguiled by handsome looks and physiques as she is interested in wealth and power.'

'My Lady, what of the Frenchman Bellecour? I do not suppose you know if any of the women have been seen with him?'

She frowned. 'Who is that? I have not heard of such a man.'

'Oh.' This was a surprise. 'I had simply thought, given your interest in this affair, that you would have learnt of his connection with it.'

She blinked, a little too much. *Trying to hide your ignorance, my lady?*

'Perhaps you should tell me,' she said, her tone more subdued.

Quickly, Mercia summarised her findings. 'The coded message from the whorehouse is proof, it seems, that Bellecour is involved. I believe he was seeking to recruit Lady Allcot into providing him with information in the same manner he obtains it from Virgo. Indeed, I wonder if Virgo may well have suggested such a course. Lady Allcot would have been ideal, at odds as she was with her husband.'

'Then where is this man now? This Bellecour?'

'I do not know. But I doubt he will return to Court after what happened last night.'

'If you think he was using that house of whores as a place to leave his intelligence, then someone else must have been meant to retrieve them. Did you stay to see who?'

Her eyes darted aside. 'We did not have chance in the commotion. We stayed a while by the waterfront but nothing more happened. When Nicholas – my manservant – did return to the . . . establishment, the women there chased him off.'

'And whoever it is will be aware by now of Bellecour's unmasking.' She sighed. 'Still, you have done well, Mrs Blakewood. And you are right. I may be able to help you now.' She moved towards the door. 'Wait here.'

Left behind, Mercia's curiosity immediately won through as she realised she was alone in the private chamber of the most vaunted mistress in the land. With a glance at the door to confirm it was shut, she walked about the room, touching nothing, striving to gain an insight into the woman many claimed to be the power behind the throne. But all seemed too well ordered, as if deliberately concealing the real woman's nature. And then the door creaked behind her too soon; she jumped, walking to the window so as to feign looking out.

'I shall know if you moved anything,' said Lady Castlemaine as she came back in. 'Come here. You will be interested in this.'

'My Lady?'

'One of my ladies-in-waiting keeps notice of the women of the Court, shall we say. Who is with which man, what they have been saying, where it pleases them to go.' She inclined her head. 'Do you understand?'

'You like to be kept informed, that is all.'

'I did not rise to this position by virtue of my face alone. And men say we do not have the minds for it.' At this she smiled, and for once her mask slipped. 'But it is fortunate for you that I am so inclined.'

'You have uncovered something, my lady?'

'It seems I have been kept in the dark as far as Bellecour was concerned.' Her face set once more, and the momentary compact of sisterhood passed. 'But thanks to my own fastidiousness, I know something none of the men who would keep these matters from me do. It was not only Lady Allcot sharing a bed with Monsieur Bellecour. One of your other suspects is as well.'

Mercia blinked. 'You are certain?'

'She has not been especially discreet. Lavinia Whent has been seeing him for weeks.'

'Miss Whent? She seemed upset when I mentioned Bellecour to her before, but . . . I had no idea.'

'Nor did I, until now.' Clearly irked, Lady Castlemaine shook her head. 'This is why we women must work together. If I had been told of Bellecour's involvement earlier, the connection could already have been made.'

Mercia nodded in knowing sympathy. 'Do not be troubled, my lady. It was only last night I secured the proof. But let us be clear. Is your lady-in-waiting making an accusation, or relating a truth?'

'Of course it is truth. She has instructions to mark the movements of these . . . younger women of the Court. In case it proves necessary to persuade them, shall we say, to keep out of affairs that do not concern them. There is no doubt, Mrs Blakewood. Lavinia Whent has been sharing a bed with your Frenchman, and has been sharing it at length.'

'Lavinia Whent,' mused Mercia. 'Conducting a liaison with a man we now know to be handling coded messages that mention Virgo herself.' For a moment, the gulf between the two women counted for naught as she shared a complicit glance with her patron. 'She did tell me, my lady, how she likes to discuss Court matters with Sir Peter Shaw.'

'Sir Peter who sits on the war council.' Lady Castlemaine clapped her hands. 'My, Mrs Blakewood. Do we have our spy?'

'Let us not be hasty, my lady. Miss Whent does not much seem like a traitor to me.'

'Did your father?'

She felt her eyes narrow. 'No, my lady, he did not.'

'Then let us speak with her at once.'

'I merely advise that—'

'Mrs Blakewood. You tell me Bellecour is implicit in this matter. I tell you Lavinia Whent is implicitly connected with him. Do you doubt my judgement?'

'No, my lady, but – if you think to summon the guards, perhaps it would be prudent to insist they be discreet.'

'Oh, no.' Lady Castlemaine laughed. 'It is time to prove your reputed talents, Mrs Blakewood. You will come with me now, and you will question Miss Whent yourself.'

Lavinia was in her chambers, ostensibly perusing a red-backed book as her maidservant coiffured her hair. When Lady Castlemaine burst in, the servant's hand jumped, pulling on the long strand she was attempting to straighten with an ivory brush. Lavinia grimaced in shock; Lady Castlemaine barked at the servant to drop her accoutrements and leave.

Now the three women were alone. Rising to her feet, her hair unfinished, Lavinia's eyes had grown wide and uncertain. On the table behind her, unused cochineal sat ready to be applied, but the unannounced visit had rendered it unnecessary, her cheeks blushing as ferociously as a red-hot sun.

'My Lady!' she stammered. 'It is an honour to receive you.'

Lady Castlemaine snorted. 'A shame you did not say as much when you first arrived at Court.'

Lavinia's eyes darted to Mercia as though beseeching a friendly face. But the force inherent in Lady Castlemaine was too compelling. Like a planet entrapping its satellites, there was nowhere to look but at her.

'My Lady,' said Lavinia, recovering herself with an awkward curtsey. 'I did not know then that—'

'Scarce matter now.' Lady Castlemaine snapped her fingers, jabbing them at the seat Lavinia had vacated. 'I suggest you sit back down.'

Lavinia complied, but Lady Castlemaine remained standing. Positioned beside her, Mercia kept to her feet as well.

'And so.' Lady Castlemaine jutted out her chin. 'You have played quite the game since you arrived amongst us.'

'I cannot think what you mean, my lady.'

'Then ask Mrs Blakewood, who can think.'

The power in Lady Castlemaine's roaming eyes drew Lavinia's gaze towards Mercia.

'Mrs Blakewood?' she said.

Deeply uncomfortable, Mercia cleared her throat. 'Well, I . . .'

'Speak, woman!' ordered Lady Castlemaine. 'Make your accusation!'

'Accusation?' frowned Lavinia.

Of a sudden, Mercia's dress felt unnaturally heavy. 'Lavinia,' she began. 'I am obliged to ask you a question.'

Lavinia's hand reached for her untidy hair, but she paused midway, returning it to her lap. 'About what?'

'About a man you have been seeing.'

'And there are plenty enough of those,' purred Lady Castlemaine. 'No, Lavinia?'

There was no response. Mercia glanced at Lady Castlemaine, and chose to sit down.

'You know Julien Bellecour, I believe,' she said. 'We talked of him briefly before.'

Lavinia's cheeks blanched. 'I . . . suppose I do. What of it?'

'My God, Miss Whent, if you are normally this nervous, 'tis a wonder you seduce any men at all. What in heaven's name do you and Sir Peter talk of?' Lady Castlemaine folded her arms. 'But then I think we know.'

The gleam in her eyes was malicious and self-satisfied, jarring with the purity of her pristine dress. But then Lavinia sat up, took a long breath, and the simpering facade fell away.

'Yes,' she said, much more confident. 'I know Monsieur Bellecour. 'Tis scarce a crime to enjoy the company of attractive men.' Deliberately, she turned her head, meeting Lady Castlemaine's mocking gaze with newfound assurance. 'Or I doubt you would be long from the gallows yourself.'

The sudden insolence was staggering. Mercia gasped, looking on Lavinia with shock. But Lady Castlemaine merely laughed, holding thumb and finger a quarter-inch apart.

'Miss Whent, you are this near to the Tower. I advise you not to rile me.'

'I doubt that is possible, my lady.'

'My, my.' Lady Castlemaine shook her head. 'The vixen leaves her den at last. Continue, Mrs Blakewood.'

How do I do this? thought Mercia, frankly panicked. On the march to Lavinia's chambers through the palace, she had protested to her patron how she had no skill in interrogation, worrying that the wrong approach could cause Lavinia to keep her silence, be she guilty or no. But Lady Castlemaine had responded barely a word as she brushed courtiers aside to force their passage.

'Lavinia,' she recommenced. 'Could you tell us how long you have known Monsieur Bellecour?'

'Why?'

'Please.'

She sighed. 'I do not know. Two months, perhaps three? But I would not say I know him.'

'You just did,' said Lady Castlemaine. 'Not two minutes since.'

'I know who he is, is what I meant. I know some of what he likes. I do not know what he thinks, or all that he does.'

'But you have spoken with him often?' said Mercia.

'We . . . did not much talk.'

'No. But you talked a little. What about?'

'About me, mostly. Mercia, I do not understand the purpose of these questions.'

'Forgive me, but we will come to that. Tell us what you talked of, other than yourself.'

'But that is what he wants to know. If ever I ask about him, he smiles and turns the conversation back to me. He is interested, is all. For once a man places me above himself.'

'Sir Peter does not?'

'Peter treats me well enough, but he cares little for my opinions. At least Julien does care. He likes to hear me talk.'

A sinking feeling was settling in. 'About . . . ?'

'About the Court and the people in it.'

'Including Sir Peter?'

'From time to time.'

'And Sir Peter's work? His role on the war council?'

Lavinia pulled a strange face. 'You know, Mercia, how it is. When a woman is mistress to a powerful man, there are always other men, younger men, who want to prove they can win those same mistresses for themselves. You must have had the same, being with Sir William. I have seen you with Henry Raff. Of course, that attention excites us too.'

'And do you tell him, then, this younger man – Bellecour – what Sir Peter tells you?'

'Peter has a need to boast his importance. He need not do it, but I think he fears I will lose interest if he does not. But Julien says I am worth more than all those affairs of state we discuss. Frankly, I like to hear it. What woman would not?'

'Lavinia.' The sinking feeling had grown acute. 'Are you saying you speak to Monsieur Bellecour of matters that pertain to the workings of the state?'

'What?' She batted the question away with her hand. 'You cannot think . . . none of what I discuss with Julien could be harmful. Besides, the French are on our side, are they not?'

'You fool,' snapped Lady Castlemaine, as Mercia closed her eyes. 'Tell her, Mrs Blakewood. There is only one bed she is sleeping in tonight, and it is not Bellecour's, nor any at Whitehall.'

'Mercia?' The pallor in Lavinia's cheeks was worsening. 'I do not understand. What is this torment?'

'What my lady says is true,' she said, looking on Lavinia with a twinge of sadness. 'Julien Bellecour is working for the Dutch.'

'No!' Her eyes widened. 'That is not true!'

'I have seen him myself. But he is merely a conduit, acquiring information from a spy at the Court. A female spy.' She sighed. 'Lavinia, you know I sailed to America on a mission for the King. Now I am here at Court on another such task, to find this woman out.'

'Mercia, I . . . I grow confused. What has this to do with me?'

'Bellecour was with Lady Allcot, at Hampton Court on the

day she was murdered. I believe he was trying to seduce her into betraying her husband.'

'With Lady Allcot?' Suddenly, her eyes seemed unable to focus. 'But I thought he—'

'And now we learn that he has charmed you also, else you have charmed him.'

'But you cannot think I . . .'

'That you have spoken to him of matters Sir Peter has shared with you.'

'Mercia, whatever I told Julien, it was not out of malice.'

'But it is true? That you have passed secrets to this man?'

'Hardly secrets, but . . . no! You cannot be accusing me of—' Her words were assured, but behind them her voice was shaking. 'This is absurd!'

'I find it hard to believe you are this naïve, Miss Whent,' scoffed Lady Castlemaine. 'How do we know you have not orchestrated the whole affair and this act is merely a pretence?'

'My Lady, I swear. I would never betray my King. My country.'

'And which country is that?' She bestowed her with a look of total supremacy. 'Mrs Blakewood, fetch the guard. I shall remain with this treasonous slut and make sure she does not flee.'

'But these accusations are baseless!' Frantic, Lavinia leapt up. 'I have done nothing wrong!'

'Miss Whent, I suggest you retake your seat. And you, Mrs Blakewood – I gave you a command.'

'Yes, my lady.' Mercia backed towards the door, staring at Lavinia as she slumped in her chair. Was this innocuous woman before her the unknowing victim she was making herself out to be? Or was she the devious spy Lady Castlemaine's scepticism seemed so readily to believe?

At that moment, she did not know. Sweat down her back, it was all she could do to tear herself away, but she managed to abandon the charged scene for the coolness of the silent corridor. In her muddle, she forgot to curtsey.

But Lady Castlemaine paid the slight no heed, far too pleased with her vanquished prey to pay Mercia any notice.

Chapter Nineteen

Matters moved quickly after that. The guards Mercia alerted were hesitant at first, but when she dropped Lady Castlemaine's name they stiffened and followed, taking a distraught Lavinia Whent into their custody. Next, Lady Castlemaine led Mercia to an audience with the King himself, crowing at her protégée's efficacy where her uncle had supposedly failed: before the hour was out, Sir Peter Shaw, too, had been arrested on suspicion of treason, for whether Lavinia were Virgo or not, his loose tongue had imperilled the realm. Third, a royal command was sent to the constables of London and to the officers of the ports, ordering that Julien Bellecour be arrested on sight. Finally, in the face of the evidence, the French ambassador was summoned at last, but of that conversation Mercia learnt nothing, save the French professed to be as stunned as the English that one of their own could be complicit with the Dutch.

Meantime, the King's codebreakers made swift progress translating the message Nicholas had retrieved from the whorehouse. Barely a day had passed before Sir William had convinced them Mercia deserved to know its contents. But before she met with the shadowed elite, she realised she needed something else.

She realised she needed a break.

Just a short one, of course. A few hours at most. But Lady Castlemaine's ferociousness in attacking Lavinia Whent had so drained her spirit that an afternoon outdoors was an urgent respite. No matter that the sky was strewn with grey, or that the wind was more chill than she liked. And Henry Raff had been delighted to be asked.

'I knew you would come for me,' he said. 'At least, so I hoped.'

'It is kind of you to accompany me here.' Refusing his arm, she looked at the trees and the greenery around her. 'I realise I have never much seen Hyde Park.'

'Not even the May Day parade? A shame. We come here often, as does the King. There is space for our carriages to ride the paths, or to walk in even such weather as this.'

'The gallants,' she smiled. 'A colourful display for the people.'

'You talk as if you disapprove.'

'Not at all. I am as fascinated as anyone to know the latest fashions.'

'And do you approve of mine?' He twirled on the spot, opening his jacket to reveal the purple silk lining, the blue doublet beneath, the crisp white shirt. His breeches were similarly slashed, a long scar running down each leg; the light wind billowed through the material, causing the two large ribbons to flap.

'Indeed, it is most handsome. A shame you will be unable to wear such clothes when you leave to serve on the ships.'

'No, but I fancy we will still outsmart the Dutch, in clothes as much as in battle. We officers, at least.' He held up his hand, waving at the latest finely attired gentleman to descend from the procession of carriages arriving the one after the other: the same friend, she thought, she had seen with Raff when he had spoken with her in St James's Park.

'Are all the men of the Court off to war?' she asked. 'Your friend there, for instance.'

'James will be. It will be a pleasant change, a relief to escape the boredom. But not all will have a chance to serve with the fleet. There is word, too, that the King and his council will travel to the coast to witness the departure for themselves.' He grinned. 'To wave off the Admiral, the Duke of York. They wish to fete their valiant champion before he commands us in battle against the evil Dutch.'

'You sound like a news pamphlet, Henry. Have you fought before?'

His jauntiness faltered. 'No, but I know what I must do.'

'Let us hope the Dutch do not. Was it your master who gained you your commission? The Earl of Clarendon?'

'Mercia, all I want is to enjoy this afternoon with you, a last treat before I depart. Shall we walk down to join the rest?'

'The question is, why you would have such a wish? There are many younger women at Court.'

'None so alluring. Come, let us take our place in the parade, and prove the most dazzling of them all.'

She laughed; normally his self-assurance might annoy her, but after all she had suffered there was something about his confidence she found attractive, and she fell in beside him amongst the procession of gallants and ladies, as a number of Londoners stood on to watch the peculiar courtly display, a weekly occurrence for many. Even the arrival of Lady Cartwright and her minions did not impede the revelry, bereft of her boy Tacitus today.

After ten minutes strolling, or strutting perhaps, a seemingly never-ending number of cocksure gentlemen eyeing each other up,

227

another carriage arrived, depositing someone she had not expected.

'Giles,' she wondered out loud. 'What is he doing here?'

'Who?' said Raff, following her gaze. 'Oh, him. Well, I have the pleasure of your presence today, so he will have to wait.'

'It is not a competition, Henry. But he does seem to be coming this way.'

She watched as Malvern made his way along the line, a purpose in his steps as he made directly for her. He gave Raff barely a nod of acknowledgement before turning to speak.

'Mrs Blakewood.' He bowed. 'I was told I should find you here.'

'Mr Malvern. Told by whom?'

'By your man. Fortunate, for this concerns him as well as you.'

'Malvern is your name, is it?' said Raff. 'Well, friend Malvern, your business, such as it may be, can wait.'

Malvern ignored him. 'Mrs Blakewood, I am afraid I must speak with you.'

'Here?' she said.

'I should rather we return to the palace.'

Raff put himself directly between them. 'Cease bothering this lady, or I shall—'

'You shall what?' Malvern glanced up at the taller man. 'I think Mrs Blakewood can see through your swagger, Mr Raff.'

'You know me, churl?'

'Of you, yes.'

'Then I suggest you address me with more deference. I do not know you.'

The two men stared at each other, as if they were a miniature recreation of the civil war. Raff's long hair fell to his shoulders, his costume grand and stylish; although handsome, Malvern's outfit was more practical, shorn of flourishes and silk, his hat and jacket plain.

'Gentlemen,' said Mercia, 'I can speak for myself. Mr Malvern, you may have a few minutes of my time. Mr Raff, I shall return forthwith.'

'I must insist we retire to the palace,' said Malvern. 'I do not like to ask, but' – he lowered his voice a semitone – 'I have been sent to discuss matters pertaining to our mutual interest. Ours, and Lady Castlemaine's.'

Raff frowned. 'Lady Castlemaine?'

'Nothing of significant import, Henry.' She sighed. 'Very well, Mr Malvern. You had best return me to Whitehall in your coach.'

'No.' Raff laid a hand on Malvern's shoulder. 'Who are you to interrupt our day?'

Malvern tensed. 'Kindly remove your hand, Mr Raff.'

'I shall place my hand where I see fit. Mrs Blakewood and I are enjoying the afternoon, and I do not take kindly to some rogue arriving in his coach and insisting that she leave.'

'Perhaps you would do better to make ready for your commission.' Malvern shrugged off the other's hand. 'I hear we depart for the fleet in short order. But then I am sure noble officers such as yourself need little preparation, unlike we lowly . . . churls.'

'Is that so?' Harsh metal scraped as Raff drew his sword. Around their small group, an intrigued murmuring started up. An eager group of ladies flocked as if from nowhere to form a tight semicircle of encouragement.

Remarking their presence, Raff made a show of flicking his blade. 'Draw,' he said, 'and let us see who fights best.'

'I should be delighted, Mr Raff. But I do not have the time.'

The ladies booed. 'Be no coward,' called one, and 'shame,' another, who promptly laughed.

'Henry,' said Mercia, 'there is no need to impress.'

But by then it was too late, for the semicircle had become almost whole, the men joining the women in urging Raff on. His friend James threw Malvern his sword.

'Very well.' Malvern reached for the dropped weapon. 'Let us be quick.'

He looked to one side, and then in sudden, unexpected action, he lunged at Raff, striking the nobleman with the tip of his sword. But Raff's brazenness was not mere talk; he held firm, retaliating with an upward swing, pushing Malvern back.

'God's truth,' said Mercia. 'What way is this to behave?'

'The way your husband behaved, I am told,' said a voice. 'Men are men, after all.'

'Lady Cartwright,' she said as she turned. 'And your earnest companions.'

'It is true, is it not? What I implied?'

'That my husband died from a sword fight? It is not a scene I wish to see replayed.'

Lady Cartwright laughed. 'I doubt these two will kill each other. Let us enjoy their display.'

Malvern was parrying well, but Raff had the advantage. He forced his rival to the edge of the circle, which parted with an excited intake of breath to avoid his swift thrust. Malvern stumbled on a torn patch of grass, and the crowd gasped, but somehow he hopped to the side, balancing himself as Raff made to strike, and now it was Raff who was teetering over, the expected balance of Malvern's shoulder turned to thin air. Yet he too righted himself, and stabbed at his opponent once more.

Neither man was fighting as fiercely as surely they knew. Even though Raff had demanded the duel, it was clear he did not intend even to hurt; for his part, Malvern seemed happy to defend and attempt to disarm than to win with a shining blow. The two traded lunges and ripostes, circling each other in an elegant dance, until Malvern sighed in irritation. Raff took advantage, nicking his opponent's sword arm with a perfectly judged scratch.

Malvern jumped back, dropping his borrowed blade, but to the crowd's disappointment Raff chose not to pursue, instead holding his sword skywards and standing triumphant, awaiting, then obtaining, his cheer.

'Congratulations, Henry,' said Mercia. 'But I fear I shall still have to leave.'

'Oh?' he said, cheeks red with the thrill of the fight. 'I hoped I had won your favour.'

'And you have. But Mr Malvern speaks of matters that demand my interest. I . . . cannot speak of them, so I hope you will accept that this is no slight.'

Raff sheathed his sword. 'What is so vital you cannot speak of it?'

'Henry, please.'

He looked at her, his forehead not quite a frown. 'Very well. But I shall demand a fresh outing when I return from the fleet.'

'You shall have it.'

He smiled, then addressed the crowd. 'An easy fight, but worthy, to earn my lady's favour! Now I concede we must part, but first she has promised me this.'

Before she could react, he reached across to kiss her full on the lips. For a moment she was startled, but then she held herself against him a second or two longer than she needed. By and large, the group roared its approval, although Lady Cartwright gave her followers a stern look when they joined in.

'Farewell, sweet lady,' called Raff. 'You may leave with the loser, but the victor retains your heart.'

'Come,' she said to Malvern, trying not to smile. 'Does it hurt?'

'It was only a scratch. He fights well, I shall give him that. But I should have won.'

'You were distracted by the news of what you came to impart.' She walked him in the direction of his coach. 'Can you tell me now what it concerns?'

'I should rather be certain no one can overhear.' He opened the carriage door, stepping aside to allow her in. 'But I thought you should know as soon as I could fetch you. I have news of Lavinia Whent.'

She looked around the darkened room, but nobody was lurking against the fireplace, or hiding in the shadow of a heavy cloth drape.

'Is this it?' she said. 'Earlier I was led to believe I should be meeting the men who broke Bellecour's code.'

Standing behind a desk, Malvern stared across. 'I can tell you what you need to know.'

'I suppose you can.' She could not help but feel she had been brushed off, somehow. 'Then shall we sit?'

Nicholas was already present; she pulled up a grand, high-backed seat to join him, the chair finished in a fresh blue fabric that matched the colour of her eyes, as did Nicholas's choice of green, she noticed. Malvern, unable to pick hazel, was forced to make do with the red-upholstered seat behind the desk.

'Now we are here, Mrs Blakewood,' he said, 'I can properly applaud you.'

She straightened out her dress, caught on the leg of the extensive seat. 'I am not sure there is much to applaud.'

'But there is. You have helped silence Sir Peter Shaw and Lavinia Whent. Nothing further shall pass to the Dutch from their careless lips.'

'That at least is good news. Is Lavinia well treated?'

'We shall come to that in a moment. I fear there is less welcome news to broach first.'

She glanced at Nicholas. 'News you can share?'

'I have been ordered to do so, Mrs Blakewood. I did not want to tell you this in the coach, in case you became affected.'

She raised an eyebrow. 'Affected?'

'But now you are back in the palace, I have to tell you that Julien Bellecour is dead.'

'When?' An involuntary gasp escaped her lips.

'You are sure you wish to hear?'

'Mr Malvern—'

'Then he was found yesterday. Face down in a bucket at a stables in Southwark, but the knife in his neck might have been a more pertinent cause of death.'

'Only a day after we . . .' She looked up. 'Do you know why?'

'Our presumption is to ensure his silence. Perhaps by his Dutch contact. Or whomever was meant to read the papers you obtained.'

She thought of the affable Frenchman pouring her wine. 'Did he have a wife? A family?'

'We do not know. Now Bellecour's role is clear, the King can no longer pretend the matter does not exist, but as for the French, they tell us nothing. They prefer to say he was acting alone, and we are forced to believe them, for the King will not delve further into it, for risk of upsetting a needed alliance. Both sides want to forget Bellecour existed.'

'Most convenient.'

'But understandable.' He reached to his side, unlocking a drawer to retrieve a sheet of paper. 'It seems some of my own work is complete. As for yours, I have been instructed to reveal to you the content of the message you found. There were some who were not best pleased at that decision, but Sir William argued the case, and the King must have agreed.'

She inclined her head. 'His Majesty is gracious.'

'The code is the same we know from earlier interceptions, including that which alerted my masters to Virgo in the first place. It seems the Dutch are not aware we have broken that particular cipher, for which we can be thankful.'

She glanced down at the paper and frowned. 'This is the whole message?'

'You are . . . wondering why it seems shorter than the coded version you saw, no doubt.'

'I was wondering that, yes.'

He smiled. 'Most of that was simple padding. Letters that translated to nothing to hide the real message, but our men know the technique.'

'Nothing at all, then, to do with keeping most of the message for yourselves?'

'Quite. Would you like to read the translation?'

His eyes remained focussed on the paper. Shaking her head, she read out loud so Nicholas could follow.

'*Nothing of import from Virgo this week, but she promises fleet movements next. Her proposal to engage other women largely unsuccessful: attempt on Allcot aborted through her death while Whent has proven unreliable. Blakewood may be . . .*' her head jerked up '*. . . Blakewood may be possible, given family history, but seems now in King's favour. Gemini about to join his ship. Following report will thus be extensive.*'

'Well?' said Malvern, studying her closely. 'What do you think?'

She reread the message to be sure. 'You are certain this is accurate?'

'Our men do not make mistakes.'

'Then this means Lavinia Whent cannot be Virgo.' She sighed. 'Damn that woman, whoever she is. She mocks us yet.'

'I'm not sure I understand,' said Nicholas.

She turned to him. 'The note speaks of Lady Allcot and Lavinia Whent as two other women Bellecour was hoping to recruit. *Other* women. And so not Virgo.'

'It seems you were right about Virgo's active role in this intrigue,' said Malvern. 'She and Bellecour have been playing quite an operation – one that almost passed me by. Attempting to draw in Lady Allcot, Lavinia Whent – and now you.' He looked at her. 'You should have told me the two of you had talked.'

'At the time, you were sharing little with me, Mr Malvern. What should you have done in my place?'

'I suppose I have no defence to that accusation.'

'Then let us forget it. Could she have killed Bellecour? Virgo?'

'I suppose it is possible. It would mean she knew he was watched. Perhaps even that you are watching for her, Mrs Blakewood. You must take care. Greater than you have taken to date.'

She bit her lip. 'Will Miss Whent be released?'

'Not yet. She will have to be questioned further, and most certainly chastened. She will have to leave Court for a while, I suspect.'

'And in the meantime Virgo remains at liberty. Dear God, Lady Castlemaine will be furious.'

He sighed. 'To speak true, I am more concerned with this Gemini the note mentions. A spy at the heart of the fleet whose existence we knew naught of until now.'

'You infer that from this one reference?'

'And that is why you are here, Wildmoor,' he pursued.

Nicholas looked up. 'Me?'

'Some of what the pamphlets say is true. The Dutch fleet has already departed, and we expect a battle soon. If Gemini can get messages to Virgo or the Dutch, they could learn of our plans for attack and defence. Which officers are in charge of which crew. Put simply, men could die. Thousands of pounds of ordinance, to say nothing of the ships themselves, could be lost.'

'What has this to do with Nicholas?' said Mercia.

Malvern leant back. 'Just as Lady Castlemaine placed you at Court, we want to place a man in the fleet who should arouse no suspicion likewise. A common tar, if I may, to live in the bunks with the other men, all the while working for us. A man, moreover, already versed in this affair that is known to so very few.'

Nicholas stared. 'You want to use me?'

'You must admit, placing a man who was a sailor himself is a sensible choice. An advantage we do not think it wise to reject. And so I must ask you this, Mrs Blakewood. Do you trust your man to be true?'

'Why, yes, but—'

'Then it is agreed.'

'Hold a moment, Mr Malvern.' She held up a hand. 'Could you not take this part yourself?'

He shook his head. 'There is only one surgeon on board each ship, and I cannot be spared from mine. Besides, neither Virgo nor Gemini can be surprised if Wildmoor is pressed to the fleet. He is needed. We are at war.'

'At war, indeed. What say you of this, Nicholas?'

'He does not have a choice,' said Malvern. 'This has been agreed at the highest level.'

She looked sideways. Nicholas seemed pained, sucking in his lower lip as if he were keeping himself from speaking, and she suspected well enough what he wanted to say, that he was hesitant to leave London with One-Eye Wilkins untamed. But they could hardly talk of that here, much less dispute his commission, and so instead she turned to Malvern, seizing a chance of her own.

'Nicholas was never paid when he last left the fleet. Would there be some means of turning this service to his advantage?'

'Is not duty cause enough? I promise nothing, but I can propose it. Well, Wildmoor. Are you ready to serve?'

'I serve Mrs Blakewood,' he replied. 'If this helps her task, then I like it well enough.'

A proud feeling of fellowship came over her as he spoke those words, of moments enjoyed together and suffered, of happy and sad times beside firesides and rivers.

'Thank you, Nicholas,' she said. 'I know you will do well.'

Malvern nodded. 'We want you to join the *Royal Charles*, Wildmoor. The King's name but the Duke's command. It has recently joined the rest of the fleet.'

'The flagship?' he said, more enthused. 'We saw it when we arrived into Southampton. A beautiful ship. Huge!'

'As fine as the *Royal Sovereign*, if not finer. Larger, for certain. Used to be called the *Naseby* until it carried the King home from his exile and the name had to be changed.' He shook his head. 'Forgive me, Mrs Blakewood. Sometimes I . . . get carried away.'

'You are a true man of the fleet, Mr Malvern.'

'There is much truth in that.' Finally, he smiled. 'All manner of men are being recruited to the ships, but Wildmoor's past makes it easy for him to fit in. Whereas some of the newer recruits are not what I would call proficient.'

'Some of the lads like a bit too much rum,' agreed Nicholas. 'But then, don't we all?'

Malvern looked at him. 'You will take a hammock with the rest of the men. You will serve as the master orders, and in the meantime you will hunt for Gemini. I will give you a signal you can use to call for aid if you need me. My own ship will be part of the same guard.'

'Do you have any idea who Gemini is?' he asked.

'Alas, no.'

'But you must think he's on the *Royal Charles*. Or why put me there?'

'Very astute. But do not ask me why we think that, just accept that we do. Now, with Mrs Blakewood's permission, you will leave tomorrow.'

'That soon?' she said.

'I fear so. Wildmoor, you will have licence to roam the port as long as the ship is there and do whatever is required to find this man. When battle is joined, you will sail with the rest of us.'

He nodded. 'I'm ready.'

'Good fellow. I am sorry to take him from you, Mrs Blakewood, but you understand the import of this task. Do not be concerned. He will be safe.'

She smiled a sad smile. 'Battle is never certain, Mr Malvern.'

'Come now.' He winked. 'We are English, are we not?'

The reassurance helped; she found herself slapping the arms of her chair.

'Yes,' she agreed. 'We are!'

Chapter Twenty

Nicholas left the morning after, not before she had reassured him she would abstain from taking unneeded risks – but then that, of course, would depend on what occurred. She found she missed his flippant presence immediately he had gone, in that unsettling way that can seize those left behind when someone familiar is suddenly absent, if only for a short number of days. But her son was still close by, and as ever his youthful laughter brought her pride and comfort.

Not that she minded time alone. Indeed, she welcomed the chance to think, no longer enduring the loneliness of despair she had inflicted on herself after the deaths that had transpired in America. With a great sense of elation, she realised how the depths of her old melancholy were passed. And so she sat at her table with parchment and quill, wrote the letter to her friend Nathan she had so long postponed, and happy with its contents, she sealed the flap, waiting until she could send it on its long voyage to New England to be opened in three or four months.

By when, she hoped, Whitehall Palace would be behind her, and she would be returned in triumph to her manor at Halescott. But the restoration of her house still hung by a silken thread, for her uncle could yet strike to retain what he had stolen, and his actions could be unexpected, his associates powerful and rich. Yet she too had her allies, and not all as grand as Sir William or Lady Castlemaine. Not all as scheming, either.

She pressed her lips together to expel a vocal puff of air.

'B,' she pronounced. 'A straight back, and a half-circle at the bottom. That is the letter b. And then the next you remember, I think?'

She looked at the teenage boy sat cross-legged at her feet. He studied the paper in his lap, a simple rhyme she had asked Daniel to write out.

'A circle,' he said. 'O. And then . . .' He screwed up his forehead. 'It looks like . . . two v's together.'

'Yes, Tacitus. And that is called w, remember?'

'W.' He sat back. 'Yes, that's right.'

'Although why 'tis "double-u" eludes me, when 'tis more akin to "double-v". But that is complicating matters. What does that word spell?'

'B,' he said. 'O. And w. B . . . o . . . w – bow.' He pulled back his right arm, clenching his fist, while holding his left out before him.

'Excellent,' she said, as the clock struck eleven. 'Although now I teach you this, I realise how confusing language is. The same word is a weapon, and a rod with which to play the viol, and a flourish of material women wear in their hair, or men on their clothes. Pronounced differently, it means the front of a ship, or to lower your head, but then I suppose they all have something of bending in common, or curving, and—'

By now Tacitus's frown had grown very deep.

'By the Lord, I am an awful teacher,' she laughed. 'Ignore me utterly, Tacitus. B – o – w. Bow.'

In the corner, Phibae smiled. 'You are a good teacher, my lady.'

'And you are kind, Phibae. Tacitus is a quick pupil.'

'I am trying,' he agreed.

'You will learn. One day you will pass from simple words and children's rhymes to . . . Wroth's poetry or that fellow – what is his name? – Milton. Milton's texts. Although that might be thought of as disloyal.'

'Yes, my lady,' he humoured her. 'But for now I am happy with b – o – w . . . bow.'

'Now make another attempt of those first two lines, and we will come back to it later.' She stood and paced the room, rotating the stiffness out of her neck. 'One thing I will say – bowing my head to look at the paper is aching work.' She rubbed at a tender spot above the line of her dress, where a small mole decorated her neck. 'Although it is a pleasure, not work. I wish everything were as enjoyable.'

Phibae looked up from her needlework. 'Is there anything I can help you with, my lady?'

'Not in this, Phibae. Besides, you have your own duties to perform.'

'My duties are to assist you, my lady. That is what I was told, that Lady Castlemaine herself expected it. Now Nicholas has had to leave, are you . . . sure there is nothing I can do?'

There was something in her eyes that made Mercia wonder.

'Phibae, if you wish to say something, say it.'

She hesitated. 'I have heard you and Nicholas talk of . . . of a task of yours, my lady. Perhaps I should not mention it, and forgive me if that is so, but if I can help, I merely thought, with you being kind to us, I should like to, if I can.'

The words were garbled, but the sentiment was clear, as was that Phibae knew more than Mercia had thought: despite her attempts to be discreet, as ever the servants heard more than their mistresses often wished.

'What I need, Phibae, is to learn more of certain ladies, but they seldom talk with me.'

'Indeed, my lady, I recall how you asked me before. And I can tell you some of what their maidservants hear, but maids are not always in their mistress's presence during private conversations.' She looked across the room. 'Unlike some people.'

Mercia turned her head, her eyes meeting Tacitus's sudden grin. She glanced between the boy and the maid and narrowed her eyes.

'You two have been discussing this already.'

'But my lady, 'tis perfect. You say you cannot speak with the ladies of the Court. I can only hear what their maids wish to reveal. Whereas Tacitus, he can go with them anywhere.'

'You are not suggesting . . .'

'Why not? Not one of them pays him any heed. He sits at their feet while they talk of all manner of things.'

'And he tells you what they say,' said Mercia. Her eyes roved Phibae's face. Yes, she was more devious than she had thought.

'I can do it, my lady,' said Tacitus. 'If you wish it. Lady Cartwright, my mistress, and all of her friends. I sit with them every day. I cannot much read – but I can listen.'

'They ignore him,' said Phibae. 'They think him a mindless fool. But as you see, he is not. No, he does not ignore them.'

A knock sounded at the door. Phibae got to her feet, but the arriving page gave her barely a civil glance as he thrust a letter in her hands and scurried away. Taking in the poor handwriting on the front, Mercia's stomach began to churn, the ladies of the Court forgotten. Leaving Phibae with the letter, she hastened after the page, coming into the corridor just as he was disappearing from sight.

'Wait,' she shouted. 'Stop!'

Phibae put her head out the door, but Mercia continued towards the page as fast as she could, while he ambled back towards her at a glacial pace.

'That letter you delivered to my maid just now?'

'What, the blackamoor?' he said, hands in his pockets.

'Stand up smart while I address you. Who gave you that letter?'

The page stiffened. 'I don't know, my lady.'

'What do you mean, you do not know? Somebody did.'

'Yes, but only old Henton, in charge of the mail. I don't know who gave it to him.'

'The postmaster?' He nodded. 'Wait here. I shall return shortly.'

She hurried back to Phibae, taking the delivered letter from her outstretched hands. Ripping it open, she learnt her guess as to who had written it was right.

Mrs Blakewood,
Come to me at nine on Saturday evening with the information
I require. The map enclosed shows where. Do not come, and as
always there will be consequences. Come alone.
Wilkins

She took a deep breath. Although she had been expecting it, the letter still disturbed her. But she would not let it do so for long.

'Pass me that other there,' she instructed Phibae, indicating the letter she had written to Nathan. 'I might as well take it down.'

'Should not I—' returned Phibae as she handed it across, but Mercia had already gone.

'Take me to this Henton,' she ordered the page.

For a moment he was stricken with inactivity, but then he turned on his heels, making the polished floor screech. Quickening his pace, he led her through what seemed like half the palace before arriving at a windowless office adjoining a suite of stores, where an elderly man was sorting papers into piles, his wispy white hair lying thin over his haggard shoulders. In contrast, the room was the tidiest Mercia had ever seen: the recent motto of everything in its place, and a place for everything, seemed to have originated here. Stacked trays held papers where they could easily be found; pens and ink were laid alongside each other in immaculate rows. Even when Mercia coughed, the harmony of the room seemed little troubled, albeit the postmaster took a surprised step back.

'My lady.' The old man bowed low. 'Prithee, how may I be of service?'

'Arise,' she said, momentarily bemused at his antiquated language. 'You are, I take it, the postmaster?'

'I have that pleasure at Whitehall. Since the days of the King's late father himself.'

'Even through Cromwell's time?'

Another sagacious bow. 'I flatter myself I am a methodical man. Cromwell valued that. The present King remembers me from the days of his youth. He enjoyed hiding in this very room from his brother.'

'A charming image.' She passed him Nathan's letter. 'Could you be sure this is sent to America? Or should I find an alternative course?'

'You may leave it with me, my lady. Although I find 'tis usually a lady's maid comes with such requests.'

She waited for him to deposit the letter on one of his various piles, then she held out the other she had brought, the letter from One-Eye Wilkins. 'Could I ask – this was received here today?'

The postmaster glanced at it. 'Yes. I always send on letters as soon as I can.'

'And was it delivered to you by hand? There is no marking on the front.'

He brushed away a wisp of his hair. 'Is it from someone at the palace? I am often handed letters to pass on. It saves the servants the bother of walking the corridors themselves.'

'No, but someone at the palace may have been asked to deliver it. The sender has told me she has a . . . friend at Court. I should like to know who that friend is.'

'But surely the letter is signed, my lady?'

'Yes, but . . . do not ask questions, man! I know who wrote it. I want to know who delivered it.'

'Very good, my lady. Let me look again at the script.'

He took the paper and scanned the writing. Then he closed his eyes, feeling its texture, breathing slow breaths.

'Yes,' he said. 'I think this was delivered today.'

Her heart picked up a beat. 'By whom?'

'I have been here all day. There have been three – no, four – letters brought to me in that time.' He snapped his fingers. 'I have it!'

'Who?'

'I mean to say, my lady, I remember who brought it, but I do not know her name. I have never seen her before.'

'Even in your many years of service?'

'Even so. My lady, I fear I must seek your pardon. It was a young servant, dark hair as I recall, but as to her name I know it not. There are hundreds of servants here, arriving all the time.'

'Never mind,' she said, deflated. 'But if you see this woman again, find out her name if you would, and let my maidservant Phibae know. I am Mercia Blakewood.'

'Sir Rowland Goodridge's daughter.' The steadfast postmaster smiled. 'Yes, I know. I remember him well.'

The thought of her encounter with One-Eye was decidedly unnerving, but she was not about to let it deter her. Her true nemesis, Virgo, had still not been unmasked, Lady Castlemaine's wrath the perfect incentive to spend the intervening day on her trail. And the ploy she had devised was hardly unpleasing, for it gave her the chance to experience a diversion she had not enjoyed since she was a girl.

Theatre and all its frivolity had been banned in Cromwell's reign, but now the King was restored it had become a fashionable pursuit once more. On the bill of the King's Playhouse today was a drama entitled *Love's Mistress*, and she settled into her seat with excitement. A pity, then, when the play turned out to be a dull, obvious affair, little more than so many actors wailing laments and professing maddened love. Still, she barely took in the half of it, for it was not so much the play that intrigued her, as that Cornelia Howe and her husband Thomas were in the audience, with Cornelia's uncle and aunt, Sir Stephen Herrick and his wife Anne. A family outing, all told, for which Mercia had made sure she was present, her uncomfortable seat only two rows behind.

Not that the Howes and the Herricks were vastly more stimulating than the play. Sir Stephen was continually yawning, fidgeting in his seat; once, his wife even slapped him lightly on the arm as a command that he be still. Lady Herrick herself had to stifle her own boredom more than once, while Thomas Howe seemed to be asleep, as much as he could be when the man at his side was guffawing at anything that might pass for humour. Cornelia, on the other hand, appeared transfixed; she was leaning forward, gasping and sighing, chuckling and shaking her head, clearly enjoying the play.

Fortunately, all was soon over, and the players took their bow. The grumpy audience shuffled out, and in the hall outside the Howes and the Herricks paused to talk. Mercia took up position behind a nearby pillar and watched.

'Dear God,' moaned Lady Herrick, resplendent in a deep-blue dress, her tended hair flawless. 'Did you ever see anything so tedious?'

Sir Stephen shrugged. 'I thought it was not badly done.'

She laughed. 'How would you know, when you were scarcely looking at the scene?'

'I liked it,' said Cornelia, her own dress a gaudy orange affair. 'I liked the acting. The stage.'

'You like anything,' mocked her husband. 'Every other week we must sit through some awful nonsense.'

Cornelia's mouth turned downwards as she glared at him. Glancing at her husband, Lady Herrick cleared her throat.

'Would you like to come to the palace, to share a glass or two? We have not seen you both for some days.'

'Oh, yes.' Cornelia seemed to perk up. 'Very much.'

But Howe shook his head. 'I have much to do. Matters I must attend to at the docks.'

'The docks again, is it?' said Cornelia. 'Well?'

'Yes. The docks. Cornelia, these accusations grow tiresome, for your aunt and for yourself.'

'Then why do you spend so much time apart? Do not lie. Uncle, I have seen him.'

'You have seen me do what?' Howe smiled. 'Sir Stephen, I must apologise for these melancholies. It is not seemly to behave so in public, but all the same.'

Sir Stephen gave him a look. 'Cornelia,' he said, 'do not trouble yourself. Thomas is often with me. Talk of the upcoming battle and the like. Nothing that need interest or alarm you.'

'Uncle, you do not know how it becomes unbearable. All I want is . . . are we adjourning to the palace or no?'

'Thomas?' said Sir Stephen.

'I fear I cannot.'

'Not even for your wife?' frowned Lady Herrick.

'I am sorry, Anne, but the company suffers with the constant depredations of the war. I have to balance many considerations.' He took her hand. 'Anne. You know I love you. I will come next time.'

She inclined her head. 'See that you do.'

He reached to kiss his wife, but she pulled swiftly back. 'Cornelia,' he said. 'We will talk later.' Then he bowed to Sir Stephen and left, weaving his way amidst the crowds of spectators animatedly discussing the play.

Lady Herrick sighed. 'Cornelia, you need to comport yourself as the woman you are. If your husband must attend to his business, you should indulge it. That is what your mother would have said, I am certain.'

'Aunt, 'tis naught that concerns his business. I think he sees a woman.'

'Cornelia, listen to me. Whatever he does, you are his wife. You must behave as such.'

'As you do with my uncle?'

Sir Stephen rested a hand on his niece's shoulder. 'Cornelia, I think that is enough.'

'No,' said Lady Herrick. 'Let her speak.'

'Then I know the two of you scarcely spend time together. Is that how you think husband and wife must live? I should rather have a husband to cherish me than one who is continually absent.'

'My husband,' sniffed Lady Herrick, 'is occupied with his duties. Duties to his King, my niece. At times he is away for months. The

Mediterranean. The African coast. I endure it, because it is expected. And when he is here, mind how he advises the King and the Duke so that you and your petty husband can be safe.'

Cornelia shrugged off Sir Stephen's hand. 'What does it serve us being safe? We would do well to see the war over, and soon, so we can return to some notion of order.' She scoffed. 'Order! Whatever does that yet mean? Fighting amongst ourselves when I was a girl, then Cromwell, then the King, and now war with the Dutch! Are they not harmless enough? Let them keep their lands and let us keep ours.'

'Cornelia, this is too much, even for you.' Lady Herrick looked around. 'I have warned you before against your unnatural talk. And you have no idea what your uncle must contend with.'

'Do you, even?'

'He is my husband, child. I know well enough. But—ah.' Of a sudden, she broke into a smile. 'Look who is here. Did you enjoy the play, Mrs Blakewood?'

Mercia emerged from behind her pillar. The crowds had thinned, and she could no longer so easily hide.

'Not so much, Lady Herrick,' she said.

'Still, it was rather droll, was it not?'

'Indeed, Lady Herrick.' Mercia surveyed the nervous trio. 'An interesting performance, nonetheless.'

Chapter Twenty-One

It was time. While Tacitus sat and listened to the ladies' prattle, bedecked in his smart black suit, Mercia prepared herself to return to the streets of London, donning her dour brown dress. Declining Phibae's offer to accompany her through the dusk, at sundown on Saturday she left the palace courtyard to walk to the row of carriages waiting at Charing Cross. Skin prickling, she patted the comforting mane of a docile horse, asking the driver to speed her to the destination marked on the map One-Eye had sent her.

As she journeyed past the maypole in the Strand, and on through the stinking streets, the carriage jolting over straw and stones, or sliding through less salubrious detritus, she sank into her seat, pondering her dilemma. One-Eye had demanded information of her, and so information she would have to provide, but could she get away with the falsehoods she planned, or would the smuggler-queen see through her pretence?

She calmed her nerves by looking through the window at the darkening London streets. Here and there, homeowners and storekeepers were holding lit tapers to candles in their porches, wavy slivers of light dotting the swirl of mist that had descended from the hidden rooftops. Still, it was not a deep fog, the houses on either side clearly in view as the carriage thudded on its purposeful way.

A shout from up front caused the driver to swerve, and she slid down the bench, knocking with a grunt into the side of the coach. Rubbing at her shoulder, she heard a barrage of curses, and an equally vibrant response, but no fight broke out, and the horses cantered on. Soon they passed through the city walls, swapping the closeness of London for the fresher country air, both light and din dropping quickly away.

There was still some way to go through the darkness, but at last the driver reined in his horses and the carriage jerked to an abrupt stop. She opened the door and jumped out: an error, for the ground was muddy, and the hems of her dress became splattered with dirt. She paid the driver his fare and asked him to wait, hopeful her audience would not last long – and besides, she wanted an escape route if needed.

She looked up. Two dim lights were shining through the wavering fog, marking a path to a low building behind. The damp grass underfoot gave way to bare earth, her boots squelching in the shallow mud as she approached the silent facade. Somewhere nearby, a stream gurgled its passage through the surrounding field, and a fox screeched its foreboding call.

She reached the door, releasing the smell of sodden moss as she laid her hand on the broken wood, its unexpected springiness causing her to recoil. She took a deep breath, looking back to be sure the carriage was waiting, and she knocked, once, pushing open the door, its sinister creak welcoming her to the shadow-infested den.

The first room she entered was full of stacked tables and chairs, and in the corner was a dresser, adorned with blue and white plates. Candles were lit, and a fire was burning, while a half-open door in the opposite wall beckoned her through.

She passed into a smaller chamber, more sparsely furnished than the other; a fire was lit here too, and there was another, closed door in the corner. A chair had been set in the middle of the room, and around it a series of stools and upturned crates, on one of which rested a pair of flickering lanterns. Just as she reached them, the far door fell open and One-Eye appeared, flanked by her man Jink. At the same time, two others entered from the room behind, who must have been hiding outside the house.

'Welcome, Mrs Blakewood,' said One-Eye, indicating the chair. 'Won't you sit?'

'I prefer to stand,' she said, aware of the men behind her.

'It will not do you well to refuse my hospitality.' She nodded at Jink, who rested his rough hands on the back of the seat. 'I insist.'

Alone, surrounded by four smugglers, she had little choice. She sat.

'I see that handsome cove of yours is not with you tonight,' said One-Eye.

'You said to come alone.'

'That I did.' She pulled up a stool. 'But then I know he has left for the fleet.'

'How do you—oh. Your insidious helper at Court.'

'Perhaps.'

'The one who delivers your letters, no less. Who is she?'

Mercia observed closely, but One-Eye ignored the attempt. 'So, Mrs Blakewood,' she said. 'What have you to tell me?'

'There is little to tell. 'Tis not I, it seems, who am privy to the secrets of the Court.'

'And yet, my dear Mercia, you have enjoyed audiences with the

King and the Duke, with Lady Castlemaine and Sir William Calde. I am not sure I much believe you.'

'Does this woman of yours follow my every move?'

'What woman? Besides, it matters not. You remain in my debt and are aware of my terms of payment. Wildmoor may be away at the fleet, but you can scarcely doubt I have men on the ships. And your precious boy at Court . . . do not think I cannot reach him, even there.'

Mercia leant forward, striving to soften her voice. 'I have warned you before not to threaten my son. It was not a jest.'

'Then let us discuss what you do know. After all, Mrs Blakewood, the King has you on the trail of a spy. In the course of that search you must have learnt something of value to a woman like me.'

'Such fancies you have. A spy . . . I have never heard the like.'

'Deny it all you wish. But I tire of these constant games.' She beckoned to one of her men, her calloused fingers spinning a circle in the air. At once he sprang forward, laying his hand on the back of the chair, and although Mercia could not see it, the metallic noise she heard made clear he had drawn a knife.

'Base threats, Mrs Wilkins,' she said. 'But I have lived through too much this past year. I shall answer your questions in my own way.'

One-Eye chuckled. 'You always call me "Mrs". What makes you think I am married?'

'I merely supposed—'

'No, you presumed, and I have advised you before against that. Shall I tell her the story, Jink?'

Her henchman laughed. 'Aye, she'll like it.'

'I'm not so sure.' Slowly, she leant back in her seat. 'I was married once, Mrs Blakewood. Like you. Now I'm widowed, also like you. He was a smuggler, of course, always looking to be better than the rest, no matter who stood in his way.' She pulled up her right leg, settling it under her left. 'He wasn't a nice man. He used to beat his . . . competitors, can I call them? Maim them. Kill them, even. Used to beat me too, when he wasn't using me for . . .' She smiled. 'But unlike me, he wasn't clever. One day, when he came for his pleasures, I bit down on him, hard, and while he was clutching his parts in frenzied pain, I took the knife by my bed, and I slashed at him. Cut him a hundred times, I reckon, in a frenzy of my own, but you see, that's what he'd made me. And the man I paid to take the body away, I got rid of him too, drowned him in the Thames. But my husband's men found out what I'd done, and do you know what?' She lurched forwards. 'They feared it. From that day, it was me who was in charge, me who handed out the profit. Small wonder I care little for the lives of others after what used to happen to me.' She scoffed. 'But you don't look at the past, do you – people like you? You presume all of us here were born bad, or chose this life, but sometimes it just happens, and we make the best of what we have. So now tell me, Mrs Blakewood, do you still think it wise to cross me? Do you still think it wise to keep your secrets at bay?'

'Is any of that true?' said Mercia. 'All I heard was a very long story.' Then she raised her head, for she thought she could perceive a noise outside. One-Eye, too, rose to her feet and listened.

'Life is a long story, Mrs Blakewood,' she replied, looking at the door. Again, a muffled noise came from outside the house, this time more evident. 'What has happened to you in the past twelvemonth is only a small part of yours. My life has its own story. And yours, well.' She took a step back. ''Tis about to take an unexpected turn, I fancy. As might mine if —Jink. Go and see to that racket. I don't like it.'

Jink nodded, ordering his unoccupied fellow to follow him into the front, the door swinging shut behind them.

'What do you mean,' said Mercia, 'an unexpected turn?'

One-Eye ignored her, sidling to the fireplace. Setting a hand on the crude mantelpiece, she craned her neck. Her remaining man, his hand on Mercia's chair, cleared his throat.

And then a huge crash filled the silence as the front door was kicked in, followed by the clanging of metal and the thudding of heavy boots. From the front room Jink cried out, and a shot resounded, then a painful scream. Behind her the man keeping her captive removed his hand, and Mercia leapt up, first following his gaze and then looking to the fireplace, where One-Eye was backing towards the exit in the corner like a wary animal.

The door to the front room crashed open. A host of armed men in the livery of the King stormed through to surround her. Behind, the other door slammed as One-Eye fled; two guards broke from the rest to pursue, but they stumbled into the closing door, impeded by their swords. Utterly disconcerted, Mercia watched in panic as two more guards tramped in, throwing the captured Jink to the floor.

Then another guard entered, and the others seemed to stiffen: just a little, but enough. Their captain, it would seem. His blank face was as grim as the longsword at his side.

'What is going on?' Mercia exclaimed.

'I think it's I who'll ask the questions,' said the captain. 'Caught in the act of treason. The end of your hopes, I'd wager.'

'What?' She looked about her, but even had she wished to run, the guards were too close, and too well armed. 'I do not understand.'

He clicked his fingers at two of his guards, pointing at Jink and the unknown other. 'Who are these men?' he said. 'Mrs Blakewood. I am talking to you.'

'They are . . . I do not know.' She swallowed. 'I am not sure.'

'You'll have to answer better than that.' He waited for more, but in her confusion she could not think. 'Shall I tell you, then?' he said, drilling out the words as though feasting on her shame. 'They are smugglers. They ferry illicit produce between England and the Continent. Between England and Holland, betimes. That same Holland with which we are now at war.' He came up to Mercia and stared her in the eye. 'Illicit produce, and illicit secrets.'

'Captain, if you are after these smugglers, I can assure you I am not with them.'

'Then how have I caught you here, where I was told you'd be? How do you, a supposed lady, explain what you're doing in this reeking den?' He pulled back his scarred face. 'I'm not just looking for smugglers. I'm looking for you.'

'I had to come here.' Her protestation sounded hollow, and the captain knew it. 'If I did not, then . . .'

The captain signalled to the guard holding Jink. 'Bring that one to this chair.'

The guard pushed Jink forwards, far more roughly than he needed. Jink staggered into the chair, a line of blood seeping from his mouth.

'What's your name?' asked the captain.

'Charles Stuart,' Jink replied.

The captain sighed and nodded. His guard struck Jink in the face.

'Jink,' he hissed. 'That's what they call me. Jink.'

'Your real name?'

He wiped the blood from his reddening mouth. 'Sam. Sam Jinkin.'

'Seems as you're caught, Jinkin. Perhaps best confess, or it'll be the hangman's noose not far off.'

'I've done nothing,' he replied. 'We were having a talk, is all.'

'You were having a talk, is all. Sam Jinkin the smuggler and a lady of the Court. No, Sam. I don't think so.' He looked around him. 'Where's your lady boss?'

'Boss?' Jink frowned. 'What do you mean, boss?'

'You're in with the Dutch, aren't you? Boss is what they call whoever's in charge. Don't you call that woman your boss?'

'What woman?'

'One-Eye, she calls herself. That woman.'

Even through the dripping blood, Jink managed to smile. 'She ain't here, is she?'

'It seems not. Answer me one question, and we might not strike you again. Not that it would much matter with your disgusting face.'

'Captain,' tried Mercia. 'Please. Let me—'

Without taking his eyes from Jink, he held up a hand. 'Enough. I've been told not to let you speak over much, so keep quiet.'

She looked between the captain and Jink. The other guards were almost an irrelevance. She knew her face was pale; she could feel the apprehensive chill coursing through her cheeks. And in truth the captain scared her, for if he had orders, there was nothing she could say to dissuade him from his task. Nothing she could explain.

'Now, Jinkin,' he continued. 'Answer me this. Why is Mrs Blakewood here?'

'How do I know, you fucking princock, I'm not her—'

The captain nodded once more. This time the guard donned a sharp iron gauntlet and slammed it into Jink's mouth. His teeth crunched, and his cheek seemed to cave in. His eye bulged, and began to seep crimson.

'Bastard,' the smuggler managed, as Mercia looked away in horror. 'They were talking, right? One-Eye wanted information, and she was to give it.'

'No!' Of a sudden Mercia realised how much danger she was in. 'Captain, let me speak with Sir William Calde!'

'Didn't I tell you to keep quiet? Now, Jinkin, what were you saying? Did this woman, here beside you, give One-Eye information?'

The guard raised his gauntlet. 'Not yet!' slurred Jink, wrenching a tooth from his ruined mouth. A gushing of blood drained to the floor. 'But she said she was going to. She was going to tell us something about the fleet.'

'You are certain of this?'

'Course I am,' he snarled. He looked around, and Mercia could tell he was calculating how to leave the building alive. 'I was there, weren't I, when she promised? And now she's back tonight to deliver her side of it. Course, if she hadn't come, One-Eye would've—'

'That's enough, Jinkin.' Abandoning the smuggler, the captain turned round. The force of his hatred made Mercia quake.

'There's men fight in the army for their King, Mrs Blakewood. Men with nothing but their wives and their children, nothing but a tiny home. And then there's folk like you with everything, who live in the palace with all your pretty finery, who want to betray us all. Folk who care nothing if men like me die.'

'Captain, please, speak with Sir William yourself. Ask Lady Castlemaine. They know that is not true!'

'But then you've been caught out here, in the middle of not much anywhere, plotting with these smugglers exactly as I was told you'd be. What should I think? Besides, 'tis not my place to question, just bring you back. Right, men. Get these out of here.'

Immediately the guards complied. All the fight had gone from Jink; he allowed them to lead him away, but his unknown friend was less receptive, until a heavy boot kicked him hard in his stomach and he was dragged through the door on his knees. Left alone with the captain, the crackling of the fire seemed unnaturally loud.

'Captain,' she begged. 'It is the other way around. I am here to find a spy, not act as one. Please, ask Sir William Calde.'

He took her by the forearm. 'I shouldn't hope for much comfort from him. Time to go.'

'But Sir William—'

'Listen.' The captain narrowed his eyes. 'I was at your father's execution. I cheered, loudly, when his head was cut from his body. You understand? I despise traitors like you.' He looked ready to lash out. 'None of my men know this, but I've been told the truth. About the spy at Court. The woman spy, goes by the name of Virgo.'

'Yes! That is who I am seeking.'

The captain laughed. 'He said you might say that. Well, I do believe there's a spy. I believe we've caught her.'

She looked at him and gasped. 'You cannot think—'

'Oh, yes.' His eyes were full of loathing. 'Caught about to pass secrets to smugglers who sail to the coasts of the Dutch. This Virgo exists, no doubt, except she's right here with me.' He pulled on her arm, forcing her to the door. 'You are Virgo. The traitor is you.'

Chapter Twenty-Two

There was no sense in struggling. Dazed, she allowed the captain to lead her from the smugglers' lair, where out in the open she was pushed into a waiting carriage. The driver who had brought her there was nowhere to be seen, his own horse and carriage long gone.

Two subordinates accompanied the captain as escort for the short journey to London, but none of the guards responded to her entreaties, and she soon gave up trying, pondering with mounting anxiety the trouble she was in. She was not Virgo, and Sir William knew it, but would the King much care when she had been caught talking with smugglers, apparently on the verge of committing the very act for which Virgo was being hunted herself?

No matter she had not intended it. No matter she was hoping to pass on untruths. Her only hope was to convince Sir William why, and trusting that he would believe her.

But even if he did, would that be enough?

The ride seemed briefer than when she had come. Brutal fright had replaced her anxiety, and that may have spurred her mind to lose its sense of time. But when the horses were reined in, and the carriage door yanked open, it was clear they could not have travelled as far as Whitehall Palace.

Disdaining the hand of a guard outside, she tugged the hems of her dress over her boots and made sure to climb down with dignity. But then her eyes widened, and her head began to swim, for she could now see where she had been brought.

Huge stone walls, peppered with menacing turrets. A vast moat, a series of drawbridges and gates. A massive square-shaped keep at the heart of the enormous complex, the whole lit by hundreds of torches. Waiting to take charge, a party of uniformed warders armed with long partisans, a man she recognised from a visit last year standing tall in their midst.

She had been brought to the gates of the Tower of London, and the man was its Lieutenant.

She was taken to the Bell Tower, locked in a comfortable room with a bed, writing desk and cupboard. It was spacious for a prison, much larger than the Newgate cell she had endured for one night the year before, but the Tower was grand, a repository for captives of much more elevated status. Water and a platter of chicken and vegetables were waiting on a table beneath an arrow-slit window, and although she was not hungry, she gulped down the water to slake her eager thirst.

There was little to do now but wait, or else sleep. And so she slept, barely, until the light of dawn seeped through the narrow window to break her dozing state, the brightening sun stark contrast to the darkness of her mood. Hunger had come, and although the chicken was cold, she tore it from the bones and chewed the welcome meat.

There was a Bible in the cupboard and she turned to its strength, taking comfort in the creases of its leather-bound cover, reading from the New Testament as she sat on the bed, the letter to the Romans.

If only Sir William would come, she hoped, for surely he must soon be apprised of her detention. If only Sir William would come, she repeated, her prayers mixed with the teachings of Saint Paul.

Finally, the door opened. She looked round to see a guard, and somehow she knew it would be him, a sarcastic smile on his ugly face.

'Still here?' she got in first, before he could start.

'Well, well.' The warder folded his arms. 'I had to see it for myself. After all, you're right back where your daddy was.'

'I will not be here long, Dicken. Do not grow smug.'

It was the guard she had struck at the very beginning of her adventures, the act that had placed her in Newgate for that equally anxious night.

'Like father, like daughter, eh? Traitors both.'

She set down her Bible. 'Do you have some purpose here, or have you come to gloat?'

'To gloat.' He grinned. 'And to bring someone in I know you so like.'

He stepped aside as another figure passed through, one not dressed in armour or the striking uniform of the yeoman warders, but resplendent in fine Court attire. The look on his face was one of total satisfaction. His cane clunked on the floor in measured, slow thuds.

'So it comes to this, my niece,' said Sir Francis. 'Guard, you may go.'

Dicken leered at her, but he left, pulling the door shut. As they heard his footsteps fade, Mercia returned to her uncle's heartless stare.

'I should have known you would come. But your mockery is premature. When Sir William arrives—'

'Sir William will not come.' Sir Francis could not stop smiling. 'I shall see to that.'

'I do not understand.'

'Do you ever? But now I do, and soon so shall the King.' There was nothing but delight across his face. 'Sir William will find himself in the same predicament as Sir Peter Shaw. Held to determine what he may have told you.' He laughed. 'If only you had listened when I summoned you last year, the day after your father's execution. Had you accepted your fate, you could have been content. Instead you find yourself here, in this lonely room, learning at last that to betray me is to lose all.'

'This is absurd.' She got to her feet. 'We both know I am guilty of nothing, and nor is Sir William.'

'I do not know about him. But you, yes. You are guilty of being Virgo. I should think that is enough.'

She stared at him. 'How can I be Virgo when I have been abroad these several months? You cannot believe that, even you.'

'And yet you have been caught about to pass on secrets. Why should you not be Virgo?' He bobbed on his cane, incapable of keeping still. 'This whole time the answer was obvious to see, if we would only look through your twisted fakery and deduce how all was upside down. Yes, you are Virgo, and have been all this time. You have proved yourself a traitor as much as your father ever was.'

'My father was falsely accused, and you and the King know it. Your argument is meaningless.'

'We thought we knew. But it seems you have followed his example, ready to descend to any method to delude His Majesty and destroy his realm.' He drew himself up. 'You must have thought it such luck when Lady Castlemaine sought your help in seeking out your own crimes! You hoped to live at the very heart of Court, passing your secrets through that smuggler witch, but you did not reckon with me. And that cur you have been dragging around. Wildmoor. What will he say of you now?'

She took a deep breath. 'Uncle, I am not Virgo and I am certain you know it. You merely hope to discredit me through this chance turn of events and render my loyalty uncertain.'

'Scarcely a chance turn.' Sir Francis looked on her with glee. 'You bested me in America. You went all that way, solely to prevent me in my ends. And what happened, because of you? I was run through with a sword, and I was forced to use this cane. I swore to myself I would have my revenge. And now you have delivered it. Our game is finally over.'

'You have been fortunate, that is all. I cannot be Virgo. Nobody will believe it.'

He almost laughed. 'And yet you match her description precisely. Close to a member of the war council? Sir William is on the war council, as he was before we even left for America. Consorting with the Dutch? Who knows what happened when you were captured in New York, when the Dutch still held that place? What was the price for your release?'

She set her face. 'When I was captured, I was locked in a room until their commander freed me. God's truth, Uncle, how often shall I repeat it? I have not been in the country. I cannot be Virgo!'

He lifted his cane in the air and shook it. 'It shall soon become clear you have played at being Virgo for a very long time. Before you went to America, indeed. No doubt you hoped to subvert our colonies, learning information to pass to the Dutch, to help them retake what they have lost. To encourage our own people to revolt, perhaps, as happened while you were staying in New England.'

'This is ridiculous! Your mind is addled. You are twisting events to suit your false argument. I went to America to aid the King.'

'You used the King. You continue to use him, and take pleasure in doing so. But the simple truth, Mercia, is that I do not need the King to believe this whole tale. You know how he prefers to ignore difficult problems. All I need do is create enough doubt in his mind, and he will leave things as they are, with me in the manor house, and you – out of sight.'

'You seem to be forgetting the real spy remains at work. Even so, the facts—'

'Support what I contend. You were there when Lady Allcot was murdered. What, did she find you out too, and so you hired two ruffians to shoot her down? But then you panicked, did you not, and contrived lies about Lavinia Whent, thinking to hide your tracks.' He widened his eyes. 'Such deception, Mercia! But really, do you want your poor son to have everything taken away? Not only the manor house, but any chance of redemption at all? For if you do not submit, that is what will happen. He will become an orphan in this heartless world, no one to love or care for him, and—'

'You bastard,' she hissed, and she strode towards him, but when she brought back her hand she instead held it steady, and the fear in his eyes at that moment was enough.

'The real Virgo exists,' she said. 'When she is unmasked, your deception will prove itself false. And then it shall be you called a traitor, not me.'

'I do not think so.' He played with the fingers of his silken gloves. 'I doubt the real Virgo will ever be found.'

There was something in his expression that made her frown. 'What have you done?'

'Only what you have brought on yourself.' He rapped on the door. 'Open up! I am finished here.'

'Uncle, wait. What have you done?'

But his triumph had turned to silence. She had fallen into his trap, and there, in that room, there was nothing she could think of to do. And so he left, smiling, leaving her with her doubt.

* * *

More hours passed. She was brought more food and drink. She was not badly treated. But she was alone. She clung to the belief that her uncle was wrong. If only Sir William would come.

The sunlight began to fade before the heavy tread of boots echoed once again. The door creaked open, allowing an unknown man to enter. He had no weapon. No armour. No expression of any kind. As the door shut behind him, he pulled up a chair, indicating with a flick of his wrist that Mercia should do the same.

'You are Virgo,' the blank man said.

'I assure you I am not.'

'You are Virgo.'

'Sir, I am not.'

'You are Virgo.'

She stuck her tongue into her cheek. 'Who are you?'

'Who I am is unimportant. You are Virgo.'

'It matters not how often you repeat yourself. It does not make it true.'

'You are Virgo.'

'If you hope to madden me into a confession, then—'

'You want to confess?'

'There is nothing to confess.'

'You are Virgo.'

She made to push herself up. 'I—'

'You will sit when I tell you!'

She paused. 'As you wish.'

'You are a traitor.'

'Ah. Something new?'

'You are a traitor to the King.'

'I have aided the King.'

'Your past is irrelevant. Your present is what concerns me. You are a traitor.'

'I am loyal to the King.'

'Your father was a traitor.'

'My father was falsely accused.'

'He supported Cromwell.'

'That does not make him a traitor.'

'He was a traitor. He supported Cromwell.'

'He lived by his beliefs. He did not resent the return of the King.'

'He was executed on Tower Hill.'

'He was falsely accused. The King knows this.'

'Do not presume to speak for the King.'

'I merely say—'

'You are a traitor.'

A bead of sweat trickled behind her ear. 'Whatever I say will clearly mean nothing. If you wish me to confess, you will be—'

'You want to confess?'

'There is nothing to confess.'

'You are Virgo.'

'I will not be worn down by these constant repetitions.'

'There are other means.'

'So now you wish to frighten my confession?'

'You want to confess?'

'God's truth!'

'God is the truth.'

'You know what I mean to say.'

'I know you are Virgo.'

She took a deep breath, in and out, striving to calm herself. In truth the man was rattling her, as he must have intended.

'I am not Virgo,' she said. 'My Lady Castlemaine employed me to seek her out. Are you saying she is so deluded she cannot see what is truth and what is false?'

'Truth can be false.'

'What? Truth is truth. 'Tis falsehood that can be made out as truth.'

'You are a traitor. Your pretty statements do not count.'

'I am a subject of the King of England. What I think does count.'

'Can you count? One, two, three . . . ?'

'What is this? Of course I can count!'

'Then count for me the number of people who have died around you this past year.'

The sweat was now falling down her back. 'Why ask such a thing?'

'I said count!'

'I will not.'

'One – your father. Two – Lady Calde. Three—'

'Stop this! None of that is my doing!'

'What did you do in America?'

Her throat had gone dry; she stood to reach for a glass of water.

'Sit down!' The man rose to his feet. 'I said sit.'

'I will do what I—'

He pulled back his hand and struck her.

'Sit!'

Hand to her face, she stared in shock.

'When Sir William hears of—'

'What did you do in America?'

'I was sent on a matter of import!' She retook her seat. 'A mission for the King.'

'With whom did you speak there?'

'I do not know. Many . . . many people.'

'Dutch people?'

'Of course! They controlled the town before it became New York.'

'So you do wish to confess?'

'What?'

'You admit to speaking with the Dutch. What did you tell them?'

'I told them nothing.'

'All speech imparts something.'

'This speech does not.'

'What did you tell the Dutch?'

'I told them nothing.'

'Liar. You are Virgo. What did you tell the Dutch?'

'Sir, this is futile! I have never passed secrets. Never, let alone to the Dutch.'

'You have never held secrets?'

'Not in this regard.'

'But you have kept matters hidden?'

'Everyone has secrets!'

'Not everyone is Virgo.'

She gripped the armrest. 'I am not Virgo. I will not capitulate to this torment!'

'Torment is dying in war because a traitor has peddled secrets.'

'I demand to see Sir William Calde!'

'You killed his wife.'

'He knows what happened to his wife.'

'That you killed her?'

'No! My man tried to save her.'

'You made him kill her, so you could become Sir William's wife.'

'Then why have I not married him?'

'Because you are Virgo.'

'Damn you.' She looked away. 'I will answer no more questions.'

'Because you are guilty?'

'I am not guilty.'

'That was an answer to a question. You lie even to yourself.'

'This is absurd!'

'Confess and it stops.' The man bent forward, some of the intensity dropping from his face. 'I can sit here for hours, asking questions from whatever you say, never stopping, never ending, while your lips grow parched, your bladder grows weak, and your mind grows inflamed. Confess and it stops.' And then he leant back, the visor of impassiveness closed once more.

'You are not listening,' she implored. 'I am not Virgo. I am not going to confess to something I have not done. I am Mercia Blakewood, and that is all. Nothing else.'

'You are a traitor.'

'I am Mercia Blakewood.'

'You are Virgo.'

'I am Mercia Blakewood!'

'You are Virgo.'

'I know who I am!'

'I know who you are. You are a traitor.'

The back of her eyes began to burn. 'Please stop this.'

'I am a servant of the King. You wish me to stop in my duties?'

'I wish you to stop this.'

'The King is my master. Only a traitor would want me to disobey his will.'

'I am no traitor!'

'You are a traitor.'

'I am Mercia Blakewood!'

'No. You are Virgo.'

The interrogation lasted two hours. Her tormentor's repetitions clawed at her soul, his monotone drilling into her mind until a madness set in. And yet she managed to withstand it. She had to withstand it.

She was not Virgo.

She was Mercia Blakewood, and she was going to survive this. As she had survived all else before.

At last the man stood, no warning. Without a word he turned and strode to the door, banging twice, waiting on the guard as Mercia slumped in her chair, head in her hands, the monotone ringing inside. She was shaking, her stays were drenched in sweat, and her throat was utterly dry. Her jaw was trembling, but she forced up her eyes to the open door, feeling a chink of hope that her ordeal could be ended . . . and then the man came back in, and the monotone resumed once more.

Another hour. The man stood, banged on the door and walked through. This time he shut the door behind him, and Mercia slowly turned her head, scarcely believing what she had been made to endure, and she reached for the glass with trembling hand, spilling several drops on the hazy floor before she managed to take a sip, and then another, and then she drank with abandon, dribbling water down her cheeks, and then she put back the glass, and she reached for the pisspot – and the door reopened, and the man came in.

'Use it, if you must,' he said.

He watched, scarcely blinking, as she removed her dress and stays to relieve herself in front of him. And then he ordered her to sit back down.

Chapter Twenty-Three

Another hour dragged by until the blank man finally left. This time he did not return, but his work had been thorough, and at every slight noise, every creak, every knock, her heart began to pound, and she panicked he was about to reappear. But he never did, not while the night wore on, not while the moon passed over London and the people slept, not while Mercia lay awake, terrified and alone. And all the night, the monotone crowded her mind, the madness, and she found no peace, but two things she knew.

She knew she was not Virgo. She knew she was strong.

In the morning she prayed to God. Petrified the man would return with the daylight, she laid her left hand on the Bible, her right hand on the bed, and she begged God's forgiveness for the transgressions of her life. For the man had swayed her to insecurity, so that even though Virgo was not in this room, the troubles of her past became mighty in her thoughts. When the door did open, her chest began to heave, her breaths shallow and fast, but it was merely a guard with a tray of provisions. He left the food and drink with a pitying smile, and she took it as a sign that not all the world was bad.

At last, her prayers were rewarded. Mid afternoon, the door swung open, and Sir William walked in.

'My God, Mercia. What has happened to you?'

It took her a moment to realise she was cowering. 'I have been visited by a monster,' she said, and she got to her feet, brushing at her hair and her cheeks, oblivious to how she must look.

'By the Lord,' he said. 'What in heaven's name have you done?'

She felt her jaw tremble. 'Nothing. I have done nothing. Do not tell me you believe these lies?'

'I cannot believe them. I know you are true.'

'How is my son? Is he well?'

'Daniel knows nothing of this. The King does not wish him harm.' He looked her up and down. 'Have they mistreated you?'

'Not in my body. But in my mind . . .' She put her hand to her ear. 'I hear his voice, even now. Yours seems . . . loud.'

'I am talking normally, Mercia.' He came to rest his hands on her shoulders. 'Look at me. I am your friend. I will help you set this right.'

'But my uncle said . . . he implied you were in trouble.'

'Sir Francis underrates my position. But he is persistent. The King knows not what to think.'

'The King's doubt is what he seeks.' Sir William's presence was helping her restore her wits. 'For my uncle to succeed, all that must happen is the King do nothing. Should I become an embarrassment, then better to leave matters as they stand, regardless of what I have achieved. And so I must provide him with the indisputable truth. That I am no perfidious spy.'

He sighed. 'The truth is, if you are Virgo – which I know you are not – then you are getting your information from me. The King may know I am not treasonous, but he may think I am careless. Look at Sir Peter Shaw, still held not far from here.'

'Then help yourself, as well as me.'

'Mercia, I will help you solely for you. Now look me in the eye. Swear you have nothing to do with this treachery.'

She held his gaze. 'I swear it.'

His pupils moved left to right, up and down, back and forth, studying the blueness of her eyes. 'Then hold on here as much as you can,' he said at last. 'With luck, I will speak again today with the King. It will help that his brother the Duke has already left Court to lead the fleet.'

Despite her own plight, Nicholas came to mind. 'Battle is imminent?'

He nodded. 'If I am successful . . . you will need to be brave. I have a plan, but . . . the King is insistent that he and his council follow the Duke, and that includes me with them. You will have to be alone for a while. Everything depends on your unmasking Virgo.'

Guarded relief swept through her. 'I have to find her. I cannot stand another day of torment.'

'I hope you will not need to. For now, take heart.'

He reached down, and he kissed her forehead: a light, tender press of his lips. Then he withdrew his hands from her shoulders and went from the cell.

Aside from a second delivery of food, she was left alone after that. The guard who brought the tray even greeted her, and she wondered if Sir William's influence was already at work. When the sun again set, she lit three candles, positioning them around the room so as to give constant light. She thought to try sleeping, but her mind was too active, and although her ordeal had drained her, she did not know if sleep could come.

A scraping noise sounded on the other side of the room, and the key turned in the lock. Suddenly afraid, she looked on the door with trepidation, but it did not swing open. And yet someone knocked, before the sound of their footsteps vanished down the stairs.

She waited, but nothing further happened. Uncertain, she picked up the nearest candle and crept towards the door. She set her hand on the sawn-down knob that would have served as a handle, and pulled.

The door swung open.

With great deliberation, she held her candle outside the door, illuminating the middle of the stairwell: she was on the first floor of the Bell Tower, but aside from a host of unsettling shadows there was nothing to be seen. She eased back her head, wondering what could be amiss, and retreated into her room, afraid of a trap were she found out of her cell.

And yet . . . the door had been opened. Someone had knocked.

But no, she told herself. Even if she merely went down the stairs, surely a guard would be stationed at the bottom, and a score more between there and the entrance to the fortress. But still the door was open. There were no guards here. Could she not just – take a look?

She abandoned her candle; no sense in being spotted as a moving pinprick of light. Feeling an intense rush of boldness she dared to leave the room, pushing the door shut and, taking great care to be silent, she began to descend.

She reached the bottom. To her surprise, there was no guard. She put her head into the open air, and true, two guards were talking to her left, but they were some way off. To her right, the way towards freedom, all was clear.

She held herself back against the wall, pondering her options. There was no chance such negligence could have occurred by itself. The warders were not so careless. And so it meant one of two things: a ruse, to cement her guilt; or an opportunity, to permit her to escape.

275

Which was right? Or rather, who could sanction such a contrivance? Surely only the King himself, or the Lieutenant of the Tower, had the authority to give her that chance – or else to order the guards to swoop when she was far from her cell, a traitor caught evading her judgement.

But why do that? As a prisoner, she was already disgraced: only her uncle would stand to benefit from her further humiliation, and he could not orchestrate such a scheme without support. Did he know the Lieutenant of the Tower? She was not sure. But then why would the Lieutenant risk his position, having to explain to the irate King how her door came to be open in the first place?

For a moment she was paralysed with indecision. But then she thought of the interrogator's emotionless face, of the terror he had made her endure, and she determined it was worth the heady risk. Sir William had told her he had some kind of plan, that she had to be brave. And so brave she would make herself be.

She left the confines of the Bell Tower, emerging into drizzle, a temperate breeze blowing the damp into her face. With a steady glance around her she hugged the tall wall and slunk beneath the battlements, taking slow steps until she reached the two facing turrets at the wall's end, the so-called Middle Tower that protected the inner wards. And still there were no guards.

She continued on, sidling beneath a raised portcullis, and then across an exposed drawbridge over a dry moat. Yet again, there was nobody to stop her, but when she passed through the Lion Tower near the entrance to the complex a strange squeal made her pause, until she remembered this was where the King's menagerie was kept. Caged nearby would be all manner of beasts, but she did not mean to stop to admire them.

Now only the barbican ahead was keeping her from freedom.

Surely, she thought, there should be guards on duty at the Tower's outermost point, and sure enough, with a sinking stomach she saw that there were, but almost immediately one called to the others, and although they stayed at their post, they all turned their backs.

She crept ever closer, not daring to make a sound lest she were wrong and this was all incredible fortune, but by now it was evident she was being allowed to flee. She slipped past the guards, not one of them spoiling the deception by making any sign they could hear her. And then she darted round the entrance, clear of the Tower's supposedly impenetrable bulk.

There was no time yet to wonder why she had been so strangely released. Out in the open she hurried towards the city, intending to pass inside its walls and so lose herself in the darkness; best not to think of the folk who deliberately sought those shadows out. And then she thought, or was she imagining, that footsteps were pursuing, and she looked over her shoulder, fearing soldiers on her tail, but nobody was there. And then a hand reached out to grab her, and she gasped.

'Quiet, my lady,' came a voice. 'Sir William told me to wait for you here.'

'Phibae!' she said, startled. 'Come over here, in the shadow of the gate.'

'No, my lady. There are guards. Come this way.'

A shawl draped over her arm, Phibae walked briskly round the outside of the city wall, and only when they had gone five minutes did she stop.

'Are you well, my lady?' she asked.

'As well as I can be. Phibae, what is this? Sir William's doing, you say?'

'Yes, my lady. Sir William explained how you'd been imprisoned on a false charge. And that I was to tell you that the King has decided to . . . look the other way. He said you'd understand what that meant.'

'But why did they not just say I could go? Why all this secrecy?'

'I only know, my lady, that I was told to take you somewhere safe, and so I shall. 'Tis in the east of the city, not too far. Here, take my shawl.' She passed her the garment she had been carrying. 'Wrap your head and keep close. There are bad people about.'

Mercia took the shawl and cast it over her shoulders, pulling a fold over her head. She followed Phibae around the perimeter of the city until they came in sight of the Aldgate. Approaching the wall, she covered her face as best as she could as the guard at the gate stepped forward.

'What are you two doing out here at night?' He studied them closely. 'You don't look like whores.'

'We were visiting a friend,' said Phibae.

'Oh, it's you.' The man grinned. 'I keep on telling you, Phibae. I could be your friend.'

'And I keep telling you, Sam Earles, I don't think my husband would like that.'

Earles laughed. 'Well, you know where I am, daft wench. Get one of these lads to light your way.'

He clicked his fingers at the pack of link-boys mewling on some nearby steps. As one, the brood lurched forward, baying for business like so many half-starved pups.

'Just one of you,' said the guard. 'Toby, you'll do.'

The other boys howled but slunk back to their patch. The one called Toby, all of about twelve years old, picked up a nearby pole, lighting the lantern hanging from its end on the torch set into the gate. As the light caught, a sort of halo glowed around his face.

'Very pretty,' said the guard. 'Now take these two where they want.' He glanced at Mercia. 'Don't forget to pay him well.'

Because you'll take your share? she thought, but she remained silent, waiting for Phibae to give Toby her instructions and move on. But the boy had led them for barely three minutes before a pair of leering townsmen stepped from an alley, blocking their path.

'Told you it was,' said the shorter of the haggard duo. 'Two rum morts for us to share.' He licked his lips. 'Fuck off, lad, there's a good chit.'

'But they ain't paid me!' protested the link-boy.

'I said fuck off. You want to fight me?'

Toby shook his lantern. 'Aye, Joseph Dean. And I'd beat you, too.'

Dean laughed. 'You've got a ways to learn yet.'

'The only one who'll learn anything is you,' came another voice, hidden in the darkness.

'What's this?' laughed the taller of the ruffians. 'Someone else want to fight us too?'

Three men emerged from the doorway of a house, coalescing as if from nowhere. They surrounded the braggarts and folded their arms.

'Fuck me,' said Dean. 'Did we just set sail and land in Africa?'

He made a noise that would not have been out of place in the Tower's menagerie, a derisive, repetitive squeal. The newcomers glanced at each other, before one thrust his outstretched palm into Dean's mocking face.

'Bastard blackamoor,' said his mate, and he brought back his fist, striking out to begin a brawl. Phibae grabbed Mercia's arm, pulling her to one side as Toby swung his light with relish, seemingly on a side all of his own. But neither the link-boy nor Dean and his mate were much of a match for the well-built trio, and soon enough they fled in shame, abandoning their would-be prey.

'Should we run back to the guard?' said Mercia, making to return the way they had come.

'No, my lady. These men were waiting for us.' Phibae gave her a reassuring smile. 'I said there were bad people about. So we made sure there were more good than bad.'

The group's leader glanced across. 'This your mistress, Phibae?'

'This is her,' she said.

'Phibae's my wife,' the man explained. 'She says you're kind to her.'

Mercia looked at him, but it was difficult to make much out. 'I try to be.'

'Then we'll be kind to you. You need somewhere to hide, it seems. Follow me.'

With little choice but to comply, Mercia nodded her assent, and the group set off, the men surrounding the women. They forsook a light, trusting to their muscles and their evident knowledge of the streets to get them to their destination in safety. More than once Mercia cursed as she stepped in something soft, but she was glad of the men's presence whenever other late-night walkers cravenly stared, as if assessing who would most likely survive a fight.

After what seemed an age the group turned into a side street, where a line of forgotten washing swung from wooden beams above. At the end of the alley the men paused, looking back to be certain they had not been followed, and then one of the three knocked on the door in a pleasing rhythm: tap-ta-rap. The door opened, the men passed inside, and Phibae stepped back to allow Mercia in before her.

Inside the light was low, nothing more than the embers of a fading fire, and for a moment Mercia feared she had been led into a trap. But the men made no move to grab her, instead surrounding a hefty chest that was set atop a rug. Moving it to one side, they lifted the rug to expose a thin strip of light that marked out a rectangle cut into the boards. One of the men crouched, inserting his fingers and so easing the trapdoor up.

'Come, my lady,' said Phibae. 'Down here.'

This time Phibae went first, the man by the trapdoor holding out a hand to steady Mercia as she turned to follow. Placing one foot on the top rung of a ladder, she descended to a hidden room below. Phibae's husband came next, while his two companions closed the trapdoor and replaced the rug and chest, remaining up top.

At the bottom of the ladder, Mercia held her arm in front of her face, squinting in the unexpected brightness of the basement. A large number of candles were interspersed around the walls, while a fire was burning in a recess opposite that must have fed into the chimney in the entrance room above. But it was the people she noticed most: four of them in all, two playing at cards, two simply talking, but they broke from their activities as the newcomers stepped in. Everyone besides herself was black.

'This used to be a kitchen until we converted it,' said Phibae's husband. 'Those doors there lead to old stores, which we use as a pair of bedrooms. And that cupboard is now a makeshift latrine.' He shrugged. 'Not the comforts of the palace, I fear.'

'What is this place?' she asked, feeling as though she had walked into some hidden secret. In a way, it reminded her on a larger scale of the priest holes she had seen in one or two grand country houses.

'We call it Zion,' answered Phibae. ''Tis a place where servants who fear for their lives can escape their masters until they are able to flee.'

'A safe house!' she exclaimed.

'Indeed, my lady. There may be no slaves in England, but that does not prevent ill-treatment. Often folk have nowhere else to turn.'

'Come here, Mrs Blakewood,' ordered her husband.

'Ayo,' said Phibae. 'We talked about this.'

'I know what we talked of, but it still must be said. Lady, this place is sanctuary for those who need it. We endanger it by bringing you here. If once you leave you speak of its existence, and these people are captured, I shall see that you answer. Do you understand?'

'I understand,' she said. 'But you have nothing to fear from me.'

'She won't betray us, Ayo,' said Phibae. 'I told you how she's helping Tacitus to read.'

'Tacitus.' He scoffed. 'That boy is a fool. Can't we use his real name here?' He collapsed onto a rickety stool. 'Well, you might as well get some warmth from the fire, such as there is.'

'Thank you,' said Mercia. 'Believe me, I sincerely appreciate what you have done.'

He grunted and picked up a pamphlet from the floor. Although the basement was strewn with threadbare rugs, he still had to brush away specks of dirt.

'The *Intelligencer*,' she noted. 'Is there news of interest?'

He yawned, a deep intake of tired breath. 'The fleet is assembled. They expect battle soon. We should be safe enough in London.'

'So I am told.'

'All we'll have to deal with is the plague. Most likely you won't have heard how it's spreading. 'Tis only when the rich are threatened that anything is done.'

'Not now, Ayo,' said Phibae, suddenly appeared with a cracked mug: a sweet scent filled the enclosed air. 'Let's sit by the fire, my lady.'

Mercia took the proffered drink and sipped. 'Whey, just as I like. Thank you, Phibae. I should be glad to sit a while, now we are here. Will you introduce me to your friends?'

Quickly, Phibae circled the room, but aside from a few short pleasantries none of the group seemed in the mood for conversation. One young man refused to speak at all, shutting his eyes when Mercia tried to greet him.

'Don't mind them, my lady,' said Phibae, once they had sat. 'They have little trust in . . . your folk, but that's why they're here. They've been beaten or threatened too many times.'

'You do them a great service, then.'

'My husband does, but no one's really in charge here. 'Tis a common effort, my lady, of those who wish to help.'

'Phibae, I think now we are here, there is no need to call me "my lady". Please, use my Christian name. Mercia.'

'I am not sure I could, my lady. It does not seem right.'

'I do not mind.' A wave of fatigue came over her, and she set the mug in her lap, feeling the heat even through the thickness of her dress. Holding the mug with her right hand, with her left she rubbed at her aching temples and eyes.

'You need rest,' said Phibae. 'Do you want to sleep?'

'Soon. I should rather know more of what is happening. What did you speak of with Sir William?'

Phibae cast down her eyes. 'He came to your rooms. I told him you weren't there, but he ignored me, began to look around, and I . . .' She swallowed. '. . . I protested he should not be doing that. He got angry, said he was trying to help you. I said if you were in trouble, that I wanted to help too, and of a sudden he began to talk, said you had been falsely accused. To speak true, my lady, he seemed desperate. I have seen the look before, in many pairs of eyes.'

She nodded in thought. 'There was nobody else he could turn to. Do not misunderstand me, Phibae. But it must have been hard for him to seek your aid.'

'I told him I could help you hide. He wasn't sure until I said, who would think to look for you among people like me?' She smiled sadly. 'But I haven't told him where this place is, my lady. I trust you, but I cannot trust him. Even you would never have been brought here in the light of day. But please, if you tell anyone . . . I just wanted to repay your kindness.'

''Tis you who are kind, Phibae. In truth, you know me so little, and yet you have done this. I have seen so much that is wicked this past year, but when there are people such as you . . . the compassion you show – truly, it humbles.'

'No, my lady.' Phibae glanced up. ''Tis only how people should be.'

Chapter Twenty-Four

She was surprised, the next morning, to realise she had passed the
night deep in sleep. Having to share with two other women had made
her worry she would not much rest at all, but her ordeal in the days
before had lulled her into the void almost as soon as the sheets had
embraced her in their warmth. For seconds on waking she could not
remember where she was, but as she took in the bunks about her, and
the snoring of one of the women, with a heavy heart she remembered
the misfortunes that had brought her there and the urgency of her task.

She pulled herself from bed. A lit candle was burning in a holder
on a stool, clearly recently placed to assist the sleepers when they
woke. Beside it was a discarded hand mirror, and she studied her
reflection as best as she could in the dim light; she looked tired, the
first sign of heavy skin under her eyes, and her hair was unkempt,
an unruly clump sticking out to one side. A pail of water had been
provided with the candle, and she dipped her fingers in the cool
liquid, dabbing at the offending strands until they were tamed.
Then dusting down the dress in which she had slept, she entered the
common room just as Phibae arrived from above, bearing bread and
ale in a large bag across her back.

'Good morning, my lady,' she said, setting down the bag to lay out five wooden plates. 'Did you sleep?'

'Like I would not have thought possible.'

'I left you a candle before I went out.' Phibae shared out the bread. 'Have some breakfast. 'Tis not much, but it keeps hunger away.'

Mercia took the nearest plate, and when Phibae had finished pouring, she added a beaker of weak ale. The room was cold, the reborn fire struggling to keep itself alight, last night's grey embers littering the hearth. But she was thankful for the meal, however sparse, and she sat in a chair, devouring her bread.

'I have spoken again with Sir William, my lady,' said Phibae. 'At dawn. He said to give you this.'

She reached for her sack and rummaged inside, withdrawing a coin purse and a sealed envelope.

'But this is not for me,' said Mercia. 'It is addressed to a Sir Malcolm Stine.'

Phibae frowned. 'He said it was for you. That and the coins.'

Mercia hesitated, but then broke the wax seal. She teased open the white paper and, reading the greeting, found it was meant for her.

My dear Mercia,

Forgive the invented name, but I needed to be certain that if your maid was stopped she would not be relieved of this letter by an overzealous guard. I have spoken with the King. Your absence in America, your previous loyalties, and the interrogation you suffered have helped me persuade His Majesty how you cannot be Virgo. But you have still been caught meeting a smuggler, and in the face of conflicting opinions (your uncle!), he has ordered you secretly freed so you may be judged by your actions. I suggest you dare not disappoint him.

Reports have reached London from the Duke at the coast sooner than I had hoped, and we are ordered to travel today to the fleet, where as far as I know, your manservant remains trusted. I do not like to leave you, but in lieu of my presence, I have given some coin to your maid. Take great care. Burn this once it is read.

Your servant,

W

'Well,' she said, dropping the letter on her lap. 'Perhaps things are not so bad as I supposed.'

'Good news, my lady?'

'I see now why I was allowed to walk free from the Tower. If they had simply released me, I would have had to return to the palace, there to await the King's command. Whereas now I can pursue my mission in secret, without my uncle questioning why I have been freed at all. When he finds out, he will be furious. And when he is furious, he acts.'

'Is there anything I can do, my lady?'

'Indeed there is.' She ran her finger around her plate, amassing the last few crumbs of bread. 'You can fetch me Tacitus.'

Sir William's letter had rekindled her hopes, just as she now used it to kindle the stuttering fire, the tentative flames growing in confidence as she added more wood to strengthen the blaze. Gradually, the runaway servants woke and collected their bread, but none of them spoke, preferring to sit apart. Instead she flicked through yesterday's *Intelligencer* that Phibae's husband had left on the floor.

'WAR!' shouted the provocative headline, emblazoned across a whole third of the front page. Underneath followed a supposed description of the preparations for battle, although none of the quoted figures had much credibility. But then the pamphlets had never been about fact so much as about emotion, and this edition certainly excelled at that.

The Dutch turn tail before a Single Cannonball has been Fired! Van Wassenaer leads his ragged ships back across the Sea as the brave Duke of York rides for the Fleet with His Majesty the King. The butter-boxes scare of our English roar!

She smiled, for although she doubted matters were as simple as that, the sentiments still resounded. Then a dull scrape drew her attention to the ceiling; of a sudden, no one in the room was breathing. But when the trapdoor was heaved open, and a pair of boots appeared, everyone relaxed.

'Tacitus,' greeted Mercia, as the servant boy jumped the last rung of the ladder to the floor. 'You came quickly.'

'It is my pleasure, my lady,' he replied, as Phibae followed him down. In the room above, an unseen person closed the trapdoor and dragged the chest across.

'Do you not have duties with Lady Cartwright? I had thought it would be hours, maybe tomorrow, before we could speak.'

'Lady Cartwright is still abed, my lady. There was a gathering last night, to see off the King.'

'Another gathering.' She rolled her eyes in an attempt at conspiracy. 'How fares your reading?'

'Not badly. But my lady, although my mistress sleeps . . . I don't know how long I can stay.'

'Of course.' She pointed out two stools in the corner of the room. 'Shall we sit?'

He hurried across the shabby rugs, some more hole than fabric, the frayed threads clearly chewed in parts. Waiting for the women to take the stools, he tumbled to the floor in a gymnastic sweep, crossing his legs and leaning against the wall.

'Do you not want a seat?' Mercia asked. 'There are plenty of others.'

'No, my lady. Would you like to know what I've found out?'

'I can see you understand why I have summoned you. Yes, please tell me what you know.'

He hesitated. 'You have been gentle to me, my lady, but . . . I won't get into trouble for this, will I?'

'He is worried he will be dismissed from service, my lady,' said Phibae. 'Or worse, if Lady Cartwright decides to punish him by asking he be sent to the Barbados.'

Mercia looked him in the eye. 'Tacitus, I swear I will tell nobody of your part in this. Will you take my word?'

He blinked, but then he looked at Phibae; she smiled, and his nervous eyes softened.

'I will.' But then his face fell. 'But there's not much to tell of, in truth. Only small things.'

'That may be all I need, Tacitus.'

''Tis about Mrs Howe, mostly. I've never seen her myself, because she lives away from Court, but one time Lady Herrick was with my mistress and her friends, and . . . it is those ladies you were interested in, wasn't it? Mrs Howe, Lady Herrick, and my mistress?'

'That is right.'

'Well, they talked about Miss Whent first, how she was foolish and . . . naïve. Is that the word?'

'It is a word.'

'And that her . . . looseness, I think . . . has – brought its reward? Forced her to leave the palace. Does that make sense? It seems unkind to me.'

'In the context of court prattle, I should say it does make sense. And it is unkind. Has Miss Whent been released, then?'

'Two days since, I heard, my lady,' broke in Phibae. 'And most upset.'

Mercia thought of her own interrogation. 'I am . . . not surprised.'

'Later, they talked of Mrs Howe.' More confident now, Tacitus leant forward. 'Lady Herrick was in a very bad mood. She said Mrs Howe had come to the palace to see Sir Stephen, in a panic.'

'Did she know about what?'

'Only that Mrs Howe was complaining about Mr Howe, my lady. But then Sir Stephen made Lady Herrick leave the room, she said, and I think that must have made her unhappy, because she called Mrs Howe' – he screwed up his eyes – 'an . . . upstart?'

'And that is another word.'

'Then they talked a bit more about Mr Howe. They said he's been trying to talk with Sir Geoffrey Allcot when he should . . . keep to his own concerns.' He nodded to himself. 'Yes, that's it. And they said Mrs Howe should look to her husband, or she'd lose him to some other woman. What did they say . . . that she was standing aloof because she'd travelled abroad, just like—' He swallowed. 'Oh, I mean . . .'

'Just like me?'

He glanced down. 'Maybe.'

'Do not be troubled, Tacitus. I care little for what those women think.' She gave him a smile. 'Please, continue.'

'They . . . said it wasn't her that was better, it was them. That she always keeps herself apart because they live at Court and she doesn't. And then they looked at me and said they couldn't imagine Mrs Howe owning a black, because her husband wouldn't let her.'

'I am sorry, Tacitus.'

'And that's all I know, my lady.' He bit his lip. 'I don't think 'tis much.'

'It may be,' she mused. 'And what of Lady Cartwright? Has she been anywhere unusual of late, done anything strange?'

He wiggled his head. 'She gets up late, meets her friends, sometimes meets Sir Geoffrey or another man. She goes to bed late. I don't think she's left the palace for days.'

She raised her head. 'Another man in particular?'

'Yes, but . . . I'm always told to go away when she meets him. Like that other man she used to meet, but she hasn't seen him for some weeks, I don't think.'

'Other man?' Her jaw twitched. 'Do you know who?'

'I'm sorry, my lady, but no.'

'You are sure you cannot remember?'

His eyes darted about, as though he were pained. 'I never saw him, my lady. Never heard my mistress talk of him.' He frowned. 'That's odd, because she talks to her friends about everything.'

'I wonder.' She sucked in her lips. 'Is there anything else? About the war, for instance, or the Dutch?'

'My mistress doesn't much talk of anything other than what happens at the palace. But Lady Herrick, I remember how she said no one need worry about the war, because she knew it would end quickly. I hope so.' He gazed into the corner. 'Fighting is not good.'

'Not usually, no.' As she turned from Tacitus, digesting his report, she became aware of the other residents of the safe house talking: her attention had been solely on the teenager this whole time. 'Thank you, Tacitus,' she said. 'You have been of great help.'

In truth, she did not know how useful his information would be, but at least he had been able to share some morsels of interest. That Cornelia Howe had been panicked intrigued her, and she wondered whether that could be related to events. But Cornelia was only one of her suspects, whereas following the trail of Julien Bellecour could lead her to whichever of the women Virgo might be. It had not escaped her notice that the tragic Frenchman had left his reports at a Southwark whorehouse and then been found dead in a stables in that same locale. And so she decided to return across the river, leaving the sanctuary of the safe house to brave the crowded streets.

After a hurried wash in a bowl of shallow water, she heaved up her dress to ascend the ladder, emerging into the unassuming room above with a little less dignity than before. One of the men who had brought her to the hideout was reading in a corner, a Bible it seemed, and he agreed to take her out into the city, provided she wear a blindfold and hide under a pile of empty sacks. He set off with his cart, but if she had hoped to learn her whereabouts by judging their route, she was disappointed: it took all of her effort to wedge herself in as the cart juddered over countless ruts and dips.

Eventually, they stopped. Pushing aside the sacks, the driver removed the blindfold and helped her out.

'You see that church?' he said, pointing to the entrance of the alley they were in. 'That's St Helen's. Be here when the clock strikes seven and I'll take you back. If you're late, I won't stay.'

The man was as sceptical as Phibae's husband, but she thanked him and waited until he trundled away before coming out of the alley into the shadow of the church. She pulled up her cloak to hide her face, looking left and right to gain her bearings.

To her left was a tavern, its sign a faded lion flecked with red, surrounded by a row of shopfronts. To her right the road was surprisingly empty, although a row of houses was packed the one atop the other on each side. She started in that direction, but an aged woman crouching near her feet reached up a scrawny arm to stop her.

'Woah, dear,' she whined through what blackened teeth she had left. 'Not that way.'

'Why not?' said Mercia, shaking her arm loose.

The old woman spat. 'See that door there, halfway down?'

'Yes.'

'Now see that cross on it?'

'The red cross, yes.' A chill came upon her. 'Oh.'

'That's right, dear. Man and wife, five kids, all locked away.' She coughed. 'Don't expect they'll last, but as long as they don't come out, we don't need to worry.'

Mercia peered down the street. 'Can no one help?'

'Too late for that. I'm watching to be sure no one goes in – and no one comes out.'

Appalled at her indifference, Mercia nonetheless obeyed her instruction and hurried the other way, past the tavern and the storefronts. It had rained overnight, and the shallow channel in the middle of the street was churned up more than normal; the stench from the filth was horrendous, and she kept to the left as far as she could, wishing she had iron pattens under her boots to raise her above the ooze. Still, the going was easier than it could have been, even if the obstinate hawkers lined up in her way made her weave in and out, left and right.

Wanting to avoid the squashed bustle of London Bridge, she was aiming for a wherry stand to take her across the river. She asked a passing sweep how to reach the nearest mooring; he nearly knocked the milk jug from a young girl's hands as he swung his brush towards a side street in response. Thanking him, she leapt the middle channel just before a convoy of drays came past, not without a curse from the driver up front, and a corresponding neigh from his horse.

Entering the side street, a rat or two scurried from her boots, and she crested a low rise, descending towards a patch of glittering sunlight. Forced to sidle sideways past an unmoving apprentice, she sent a trio of gulls flapping as she came out by the Thames. To her right, steps led to a creaking wherry, where she paid the boatman to take her across.

'Ain't you warm, love?' he asked, incessantly staring as he rowed.

'You mean my cloak?' She pulled her hood close. 'I am . . . unwell.'

He inched back, as much as he could. 'Not . . . that, is it?'

'Only a chill.'

Not looking reassured, the oarsman rowed faster, straining his arm muscles to speed them to the south bank despite the adverse breeze. When they arrived, he pushed off as soon as Mercia had both feet onshore, leaving a waiting peddler to shake his fist over his half-full basket of knives.

Mercia took advantage of the cutler's anger to slip unnoticed into the Southwark streets. Although the first stables she found were not the ones she sought, she was yet in luck, for word of Bellecour's death had spread fast. An excitable young stable hand was keen to discuss the gruesome news.

'Found him right in a bucket, Hal did,' he said. 'When he came to change the straw of the morning. Bastard foreign he was, too.'

'How could he tell? This Hal.'

The boy leant on his rusty pitchfork. 'You just can, can't you?'

'Can you? I . . . heard he had a knife in his neck.'

'Knife in his neck, face in the water. Nothing on him.'

'Sorry?'

'No coin, rings, nothing.' He smirked. 'He was wearing clothes.'

'Where did you say he was found?'

He hadn't, but he gave her directions to the stables she wanted all the same. Finding them quickly, she entered the yard to find a half-naked worker slugging a beaker of ale. In the midst of a band of placid horses, he set down his cup as Mercia approached.

'Morning,' he smiled, wiping sweat from his chest with a cloth. 'After a horse?'

She reached into her pocket and took out a shilling. 'I should rather learn more about the man who died here last week.'

He cocked his head, sucking in his layer of belly fat. 'Right warm today for that cloak.'

'So people keep saying. Do you want the coin or not?'

'I won't say no. Another of them lot, eh?'

She held out the coin. 'Them lot?'

'Them folk who like to hear about bad stuff. Murders, fights, that kind of thing.' He licked his lips. 'Don't matter to me who you are, ladybird. Could come from the palace itself and probably do.' Taking the coin, he pointed behind her. 'Where you're standing is right where I found him.'

She turned to look at the dusty spot. 'Would you describe it?'

'Keen, ain't you? Name's Hal, by the way.' He grinned. 'You one of them girls who like their men rough?'

'Shall we keep to the matter at hand, Hal?'

'I wager you are.' He traced a finger across his chest. 'It was cold, the morning I found him.'

'I do not care about the weather. Tell me about the dead man.'

'Very keen.' He dropped to the ground. 'He looked like this. Knife towards the left, here.' He jabbed at his neck. 'And his face covered in water in the bucket.' He made a bubbling noise, his cheeks vibrating on the earth.

'He had no possessions?'

Hal got to his feet, hay falling from his knees. 'Nothing but the shirt and breeches he was wearing. And his shoes. Told the harmans quick, but the man who came weren't a constable. Least not one who works round here.'

'Do you know all the constables in Southwark?'

'You . . . get to.' He puffed out his chest. 'No, that cove weren't no harman. He talked too fine. Came with another fellow and a cart and took the body away. Didn't say nothing, other than I should mind not to talk. Well, fuck that.'

'Nicely put.'

'I could see he was foreign when I lifted him from the bucket. Like that other woman who came to ask after him, couple of days back.'

Her head jerked up. 'What other woman?'

'Asking questions like you are. Talked funny.'

'Are you sure she was foreign?'

He blew out through his cheeks as if he were one of his horses. 'She talked strange,' he said, 'but I suppose she didn't need to be foreign. Might have been disguising herself. But why do that?' He winked. 'Besides, if nothing's going to happen, I think you've exhausted your coin.'

She felt inside her pocket for a second shilling. 'You can have this if you tell me how the woman looked.'

'I'd rather have something else. No?' He grabbed for the coin. 'She was a little shorter than you, but looked the same kind of age.' He grinned. 'Early twenties?'

'Try thirties.'

'Just being kind. She had brown hair sticking from under her hat. Not much on the chest, not that I noticed. Nose a bit crooked, small mark on her cheek. Far too thin, but not ugly neither.'

She stared at him. 'You are sure of this?'

'I ain't stupid, ladybird.'

'Please. Are you certain?'

'I ain't blind, either. I've a good eye for you women.'

Oblivious to his pique, Mercia gaped at the spot where Bellecour had been found.

Hal had just described Cornelia Howe.

Chapter Twenty-Five

There was one other place she needed to visit in Southwark. Once again drawing up her hood, she made the short walk to the last location she had seen Bellecour alive, the location where he had dropped his ill-gained intelligence.

She arrived at the whorehouse without incident, sticking to the river before heading inland at the bear pits. No women were waiting outside today, but then it was morning, and the rotten door was firmly closed. Steeling herself, she knocked, waited, and knocked again. And then again.

A window above opened with a grinding squeak.

'Fuck off!'

She looked up at the young face sneering through.

'I need to speak to someone,' she said. 'It is important.'

'And I need you to fuck off.'

'I have coin.'

The girl chewed on her bottom lip. 'How much?'

'Enough. Will you come down and talk?'

The mangling continued apace. 'What about?'

'I just want to know something.' She reached into her pocket and jangled her purse. 'Or do you not care for money?'

'Not as much as he does. Oi!' The whore leant through the window and screamed. 'Get it, you arseworm!'

Startled, Mercia looked round to see a hand pulling away from her dress, attached to a boy of no more than eight. She jumped from his reach, but the whore shouted once again, and with a rude shake of his fist the boy darted down an alley like a spider back into its hole.

'Got to be careful round here, see,' said the girl. 'You talk about money and they know it. Come running.' She looked up and down the street. 'You best come inside, then.'

She lowered the window and vanished. Still shocked by the boy's attempt, Mercia glanced nervously left and right as she waited with her back to the door. At the street corner, she could have sworn a face was peering in her direction, but by the time she could focus, nothing was there.

The door opened behind her. Finally, she thought, but as she turned to thank the girl for coming, she blinked, confronted by the madam of the whorehouse instead.

'What're you doing here?' she demanded, and then she stared more closely into Mercia's hood. 'You again? No, I'm not having this.' She stepped back inside, making to shut the door.

'Please, all I want is to ask a question. 'Tis of the utmost importance.'

The madam paused with her head through the door. 'We had the harmans here the other night, after all that trouble you caused. Then we hear Mellie's Frenchman's been found dead in a bucket. I don't need to answer more questions.'

'He attended the palace,' said Mercia, undeterred. 'The Frenchman. You can talk to me or you can answer to the King.'

The door reopened. 'Who are you?'

'Someone who will not close you down. Unlike the King's guards.'

The madam snorted. 'Some of those darling King's men of yours come here for their entertainment, my rum mort.' She ran her tongue around her lips. 'My girl said there was money in it?'

'There may be. You mentioned Mellie just now. 'Tis her I want to speak with.'

'Mellie ain't here. You can talk to me.'

'It is about her Frenchman.'

The madam stepped outside, pulling the door shut. 'Will this be the end of it? I can't cope with all these damn questions. Folk die round here all the time and no one cares. But when he's foreign, that's different, ain't it? Them who've lived here all their lives can go hang.'

'Please, tell me where Mellie is.'

'I know all Mellie's arrangements.' She held out her hand. 'The coin?'

Mercia reached into her pocket, but the only coin she had left was a guinea. Far too valuable for a common bribe, nonetheless there was little time to lose.

'Jesus Christ,' swore the madam. 'A whole fucking guinea?' Greedily, she snatched the golden coin. 'See, I love these. I love how they've put a damn elephant on them. Don't know why they have, but I love them.'

'They are made with African gold, and that is where elephants come from. Now, will you talk? And without asking questions back?'

'Ask away, my dear.' She bit the guinea and smiled. 'You should have said.'

'The Frenchman – Bellecour.'

'Belle-who?'

'Julien, then.'

300

The madam nodded.

'Did he only ask for Mellie?'

'Every time.'

'But he only sat with her? Never anything more?'

'How do you know that?' She shrugged, turning over her coin. 'That's right. Damn queer it was, him coming here and just . . . sitting.'

'He left papers behind?'

'Hell's teeth, love, if you know all the answers, why you asking? Yes, every time. He was using this place as somewhere to . . . leave things. Paid Mellie well, so I let him do it and took my share.'

'Then this is my question. Who came to collect the papers he left?'

'Ah.' She clicked her tongue. 'That's different. Don't know as I can tell you that.'

'Did you tell the constables when they asked?'

'If I told the constables everything the men who come here do, I'd be dead in a bucket myself. Men come here because they know they can trust me.'

'But you can tell me. Woman to woman?'

'God's truth.' The madam sighed. 'Very well, if it brings me peace. But I won't answer more questions, not from you or from anyone.' She leant in, although nobody else was near. 'He was around that night you were here. The man who collects the papers. I think the Frenchman was waiting to leave, but something was stopping him – probably that cove of yours.'

'My manservant?'

'Lucky you.' The whore laughed. 'Then the man you're after turned up, in that same hood he always wore. You could tell the time by him. Always five minutes after Julien left, he came to Mellie's room, paid her money for the papers, and scarpered. Course this time, he had to wait a bit longer, until you all fucked off too.'

'Was he Dutch?'

She screwed up her face. 'Why would he be Dutch? No, he was as English as I am. Talked a bit finer, course, said his name was Peter, though I doubt that's the truth.' She looked around the street. 'But paying a girl for nothing more than guarding papers for a few minutes, 'tis the sort of thing that gets you interested, ain't it? I set my man Gunner to follow him one time, all the way to that warehouse at the docks.' She chuckled. 'Whorehouse to warehouse. I should remember that.'

'Warehouse?' Mercia jerked up her head. 'Whose warehouse?'

'Gunner didn't go in, so I don't rightly know. But the sign on the front said it belonged to a man named Howe.'

'Hell's teeth!'

'But that ain't it, love. Oh, go on. I like that you've come here on your own. For that guinea, I'll show you something else.'

She disappeared inside, leaving Mercia to her startled thoughts. Why had the man who collected Bellecour's reports gone straight to Howe's warehouse? Had he always done so, or just the once he was followed? Who was he? Why was he English? Why not Dutch?

And with Cornelia, or someone like her, asking questions at the stables . . . could it even have been Howe himself? Then again, if Cornelia was Virgo, why would she pass Bellecour information her own husband went on to pick up?

She rubbed her aching forehead. What the hell was going on?

'Are you well?' The madam had returned. 'You don't look it.'

'Quite well, thank you.'

'If you say so.' She held out her hand. 'Here. Now Julien's dead I'd sooner not have it.'

'A piece of paper?'

'Part of his last lot.'

Mercia's eyes widened. She reached out, but the madam held back.

302

'Whenever Julien left,' she said, 'I looked at his papers before that other cove came for them. Normally it was rubbish, impossible to read, but sometimes there was something different. With all the commotion last time, I kept a sheet back.' She shrugged. 'You never know when you might need something to bargain with.'

'Or when you might be able to take advantage. May I?' Mercia nimbly took the paper and examined it. 'Why, 'tis a map.'

'And they say us women aren't clever.' She tutted. 'Course it's a map. Of England, too, the east coast. Don't know what most of them markings mean, though, along the shoreline. But I know what that one there is right enough.'

'Which mark?'

'That one, off Essex, or Suffolk, somewhere like that. Those places are all the same to me.'

'What, this cross here?'

'Yes, like they use when they want to show death. Like what they're scribbling on doors, with the plague.'

'That is the cross of our Lord, but . . . they have plague up there?'

'I doubt it. 'Tis only just taking hold in London. But I reckon it means death, for certain.'

She nodded. 'And what is this beside it? Very small, but it looks like the letters . . . R, and C. And then a word in code. I wonder what that means?'

'I thought I could make something off it,' said the madam. 'But not any more, not now he's dead. And with that other fellow coming round too—'

'Which other fellow?'

'Some other man, end of last week. Thought he could talk down to me, but I sent him on his way. And now you can get on your way too. I'm tired.'

Before Mercia could prevent it, the madam was through the door. Abruptly, it slammed shut. The interview was over.

There was nowhere to go now but Howe's warehouse. Nicholas had made a brief search during their last short visit, when they had discovered Bellecour had used Howe's company to ship to Amsterdam, but he had not had time for a thorough check. After what she had heard in Southwark, Mercia was determined to put that right.

Within fifteen minutes a wherry was depositing her on the north bank of the Thames; within fifteen minutes more, she was outside the warehouse, listening to a newsboy shouting to the dockhands, trying to hawk his pamphlets:

Fleet to leave this week! Battle expected soon!

Not that there were many labourers about, she noticed, still fewer than the last time she had come. Outside the warehouse, two men in dirty shirts sat swigging ale, a pile of uncomfortable crates providing a stiff backrest. They whistled as she passed, staring and calling obscenities, but aside from a quick glance she ignored them, and they went back to slaking their thirst.

There were two doors into the warehouse: a large opening, locked, for goods; and a smaller one, unlocked, for people. She pushed open that entrance, quietly, but she need not have worried; there was no one inside, at least not that she could see. A quick scour of the warehouse confirmed it, neither in the two small rooms by the entrance in which Howe or his supervisors must work, nor in the large open space that made up the bulk of the wooden structure, not so full of goods awaiting shipment as she would have supposed.

She circled the stockroom, its sparse contents lit by the sunlight falling through the windows above. Lying flat in the corner, three open crates made her shudder, for they were barely larger than coffins and looked just like, their lids propped up alongside. She studied the block writing that marked their intended destination: Rotterdam, in Holland. Interesting, she thought.

Her circuit of the stockroom complete, she returned to the small rooms by the entrance. The first was unlocked – still not fixed, it seemed, since when Nicholas had . . . paid his visit. Inside was the walnut desk he had described at the time, a couple of chairs, hooks for coats, and a bureau. She tried the desk drawers, but they held nothing save heaps of papers covered with figures and costs, the ledger Nicholas had found now gone. The bureau was open but unremarkable, nothing of interest within.

Unlike the first room, the door to the second was locked; a notice-plate on the wood read *Mr Thms Howe (Priv.)*. She returned to the office and searched for a key but without success, rummaging in the drawers, hunting in the bureau, finding nothing. Then she noticed how the piece of wood into which the coat hooks were nailed seemed to stick out from the wall, much more than was required. She felt along its edge, and smiled as she found a smaller rectangle cut into the top, even more when she pushed the hidden segment out to uncover a thin key.

As she hoped, the key fitted the lock to the second room, and she opened the door to pass in. The room was dark, no light of any kind, but her eyes soon adjusted – and well enough they did, for she was surprised to see what she found.

It was a printing press, a series of black letters laid out across its inky surface. Surrounding the machine were various woodcuts: scenes of London and of people, of animals and of birds. Discarded on the floor, ripped-off bits of paper littered the room; she rifled through the scraps, but it was mostly stray letters and words, a collection of meaningless references.

Alongside the press was a small cabinet of sorts, but it too was locked. She was about to give up and return to the stockroom when she saw how the floor in front was scratched. Recalling the room above the runaways' safe house, she leant down for a closer look, examining the feet. They were splintered and rough, as though . . . yes, as though they had often been dragged. And so she did the same herself, tugging on the cabinet until with a painful screech she forced it forwards, revealing an opening beneath.

She felt inside the recess to discover a pile of thin papers. She took out the top one and read it.

'My God,' she said to herself. ''Tis a Quaker tract.' She laughed. 'Howe is a Quaker.'

Although the tract was short, only two columns long, it was inflammatory to say the least. It could only be described as a call to arms, its writer demanding of his fellow Quakers that they resist the King's attempts to subjugate their freedom of conscience, describing such radical notions as the equality of women and men before God, and demanding an improvement in the condition of servants and slaves. Readers were exhorted to bide their time until the end of their persecution, which the pamphlet considered to be near. *Keep brave heart*, it said, *for the time of our acceptance is nigh*.

But it was strange, she thought, for from what she had seen of him, Howe did not behave like the Quakers she had heard of – and admittedly knew little about. He did not wear plain clothes, for one thing – his wife certainly did not – while he seemed perfectly at ease acquiring wealth, at odds with Quaker doctrine. Perhaps he sympathised with their cause, rather than worshipping as one of their own, but there would be time enough later to consider his beliefs. For now, she replaced the tract and pushed back the cabinet, locked the office door and returned the key, not wanting to leave any sign of her surreptitious visit.

Enthused by her discovery, she was about to take another look round the stockroom when she heard a muffled footstep from the wharf outside. The noise seemed quite near, right by the entrance, and she listened at the door to try to make anything out. But all she could hear now was silence.

And then the door pushed open towards her.

Pulse racing, she pulled back her head, but the man on the threshold had seen her. The angry look on his face told her only one thing: she needed to run, and fast. But her way out was blocked; she slammed the door into his face and retreated to the stockroom, searching for somewhere to hide. Her eyes caught the coffin-like boxes, but they were at the far side, too distant to reach in time. As she heard the man run in, she pressed instead against the interior wall that separated stockroom from office, trusting to the shadows to mask her presence.

Exactly as she had hoped, the man ran right past her, looking to his left and his right. Quickly she turned, stealing towards the exit, making it to the door before he knew she had gone. But as she opened the door to flee, she was grabbed from outside.

'Back,' ordered another man, even larger than the first, painfully gripping her arms. 'They said you'd be tricky.'

There was no chance of wriggling free. Her captor's powerful hold almost lifted her from the ground as he pushed her into the warehouse and halfway across the stockroom, where with minimal effort he swivelled her round and deposited her on a stool his fellow had already set down. She tried to stand, but he took a step forward, and that was enough to convince her she would do better to resume her place.

She looked up, and was startled to recognise the men as the two who had been drinking by the crates outside. A deep fear took her as she wondered what they might want, but they made no further move towards her, no attempt to engage her in talk of any kind, other than to tell her to wait. And so she waited, trying to keep calm, until a half hour later the door to the warehouse opened once more and her fear grew deeper still.

It was a large group of men, filing in one after the other, until soon there must have been ten surrounding her, but just like the first two they did little but stare. And then the men all stiffened, standing to the side as two more figures entered, slowly crossing the floor.

Two figures side by side.

One woman. One man.

But not the man and woman she would have thought.

Chapter Twenty-Six

'Uncle,' she exclaimed. 'What are you doing with her?'

Sir Francis hobbled forward. 'I believe you have met.'

The woman laughed, tossing her hat at one of the men. 'That we have. Quite recently, indeed.'

Mercia tried to hold her voice steady. 'I see your reputation is merited once again, Mrs Wilkins. You truly do have one eye on everything in the city.'

'I try.' One-Eye Wilkins, the smuggler-queen, came forward. 'With the help of your uncle, at least.'

The realisation struck her like a cannon shot. 'My God. He is your source at Court.'

'On this matter. A matter of revenge, no less.'

'And the servant who delivered your letter – my aunt's own maid?'

'I had you trapped,' said Sir Francis, his cane trembling in the dust of the floor. 'Caught as if you were Virgo. And then the King released you, claiming you had escaped. Does he think me a fool?'

'I do not know,' she dared. 'But as you are working with her . . .'

'I have been forced to deal with this – person. I have had her men searching for you since dawn, ever since the news of your flight came overnight. I have sent them everywhere I thought you might go, anywhere connected with the women you think you seek. I knew your arrogance would lead me straight to you.'

'I have sent them, I think,' said One-Eye.

He ignored her. 'And if the King makes clear that he needs more proof against you, I must take action to provide it.' His eyes widened, and he nodded to himself. 'Yes, I must. It is only right.'

'You talk strangely, Uncle. You do not seem well.'

His head snapped round. 'I am in perfect humour. Or shall be, once this is done.'

'He found me out,' said One-Eye. 'Came looking for me as soon as he was back from America. Quite ingenious, all told.'

Despite her words, she was peering at Sir Francis with little respect. He, certainly, did not return her stare with kindness.

'Can I not have a seat?' he snapped.

One-Eye's lips curled, and she clicked her fingers; one of her men began a search, until he found a second stool stored against the wall and brought it across.

Sir Francis sat without a thank you. 'When I returned from America, the King set that cursed painting in the palace and made everyone look. But I looked at this' – he shook his cane – 'and saw your face. The King was deluded. I had to make him see you for what you are – a plotter and a traitor.'

'A more perfect description for you,' she replied.

'I sent my man into the streets of London, asking questions about yours. It took him but half a week to find out where Wildmoor lived, who were his friends and his family.' He sneered. 'And they are the sort, Mercia, who will tell anything for coin. Soon enough, I found out your man had arranged a meeting with her, last year.' He raised his hand at One-Eye, the barest of acknowledgments. 'I wondered why. Would you care to explain?'

'Why need I, Uncle, as you clearly know?'

'I thought perhaps you would welcome the opportunity to show contrition.'

She laughed. 'You make a poor comparison to the inquisitor at the Tower.'

His cane slipped, but he caught it. 'Why do you think I have done this? That tone you take. That . . . shameful dearth of reverence.'

'A trait in your family, it would seem,' said One-Eye, for the present hanging back with her men.

Sir Francis closed his eyes. 'I believe I am speaking at this moment.' He took a deep breath. 'Mercia, you found out this woman to aid you in your attempts to disobey me. And now I have . . . sought her help . . . in making you see how that was wrong.'

'It was a most intriguing proposition,' said One-Eye. 'There was that promise you had made me, when I supplied you with the information you requested last year. And there was your uncle, offering me money to trap you into losing your newfound status with the King.'

Mercia looked at Sir Francis. 'If you think this woman will keep whatever word she has given, you are mistaken. She seeks only what is advantageous to herself. I see now how it must have been you who told the King's guards where we would be meeting, she and I, and yet when they came she fled, giving up two of her men without a thought. She took my manservant from the street and she tore off his fingernail, only to return him to the palace while I worried what she might have done. She is not worthy of anyone's trust – not mine, not yours, not her men's.'

'Those men had betrayed me,' said One-Eye, barely troubled by the grumbling that had arisen around her. 'They thought to keep for themselves a shipment they were sent to collect, and that was their reward. All these men here today are loyal – or they know to be.'

'And Jink?' she said. 'He was your second, I thought.'

'Jink had become . . . dissatisfied.' She nodded at the man beside her. 'Van is my second now.'

'These matters are irrelevant,' growled Sir Francis. 'When it became clear that the King intended you for his pet spy, I arranged for his guard to catch you as the very woman he had hoped you would find. It scarcely mattered if he truly thought you could be Virgo. Despite what you think you have achieved for him, if you cause him embarrassment he will not hesitate to cut you loose. He has done it to others before, promising them much and withholding their reward as it suited him.'

'And yet he has allowed me to go free,' she replied.

'Only so that he need not bother himself with the question. Now I shall resolve it for him.'

'I think you underestimate him, Uncle. The King, and Lady Castlemaine my patron.'

Sir Francis laughed out loud. 'You think she cares a jot for someone like you? She uses you to maintain her place at Court, and that is all.'

'As the Earl of Clarendon uses you, I hear.' Her face impassive, she switched her attention to One-Eye. 'What is your price for helping him in this? You do nothing for free, I know.'

One-Eye smiled, exposing a row of chipped teeth. 'The same price I demanded from you, my dear. But while yours was a pretence, to fit this . . . amusing act, his was most real. He promised me information that I could carry on my business with no interference from anyone at Court.'

'So this is the price for besting me, Uncle? You sell your dignity and collude with criminals. But if you think to discard her after, she will not permit it.'

'He will not discard me.' One-Eye came round to face him. 'He tried that once before, thinking he could change his mind so soon after seeking me out. But he suffered for it, as is my way. Actions lead to consequences, remember? Or, at least, his wife suffered.'

'You cannot mean . . . it was you who attacked my aunt?'

'Someone I employed to remind him of his promises, shall we say.'

'In the very palace?'

One-Eye shrugged. 'The King allows all and sundry to watch him strut to and fro. It is remarkably easy to smuggle someone into Whitehall. But we had already agreed on the scheme to disgrace you, and once agreed, it must be done.' She leant down to her uncle. 'Tell her, Francis. Tell her what sort of man you are.'

His face was entirely set. 'We agreed that—'

'What we agreed is not important. What I have decided counts.' She beckoned to her men, three of whom stepped forward to surround him. 'You see, Mercia, despite my warning, your uncle still sought to thwart me. When you and I last met, the King's men arrived peculiarly early.' She stared into Sir Francis's eyes. 'Could it have been that you hoped we should all be taken, and so removed from your way?'

Sir Francis paled. 'I . . . am sure that is not so.'

She looked up at Mercia. 'See how he blusters? At least you have more composure.' Then she turned back, pressing her face even closer; the smell of her breath must have been appalling. 'You thought to use me again today, did you not, to trap your poor niece? Whereas I intend to use this chance to rid myself of you. Get to your feet.'

He grew ever paler. 'What?'

'Get to your feet.'

She glanced at her trio of thugs, but Sir Francis stayed put. Unbidden, one of them wrenched him from his seat.

'What do you intend?' he shrilled.

The vindictiveness on One-Eye's face was absolute. 'Mercia's father was executed. I saw it myself. I am going to do the same to you.'

Mercia leapt to her feet, but the smuggler-queen cut her off.

'Those who seek to destroy me shall be destroyed themselves. I suggest, Mrs Blakewood, you sit back down.'

'You cannot mean to kill him?'

'I do as I please. My men have killed for him and received nothing in return, save lies and attempts at our arrest. As he sought to murder others, so I shall murder him.'

'No!' Sir Francis's cane shot out from beneath him. 'I will help you. I said I would!'

'Your actions prove otherwise. All you have wanted is to ruin your niece. I pity her, in truth. To have such an uncle as you, who would seize her property and presume to get away with it because she is a woman. Now I shall show you how a woman can be the equal of any vicious man.'

'One-Eye,' said Mercia, horrified. 'Do not make me your excuse. I wish nothing of the kind, despite what he has done.'

'I do it for me,' she said. 'Francis, on your knees.'

Two of her men grabbed him by the shoulders and forced him to the ground. He slipped, and sprawled out on his front, but they yanked him up so he was kneeling.

'Give me the powder and gun,' she commanded.

Another of her band produced a doglock pistol from a satchel, and handed it over with a pouch. One-Eye opened the drawstring, tipped powder into the barrel, and cocked the gun.

'Now,' she said, aiming at the back of Sir Francis's head. 'You will learn what happens to those who think to outdo me.'

'Please!' Sir Francis had become frantic. Tears were streaming down his face, and a puddle was forming on the floor. 'Please! Do not do this.'

'You were happy for me to order my men to kill Lady Allcot. You were happy for your niece to be taken as a traitor, with the consequences that would have entailed. If you care so little for life, why should I?'

'Killed Lady Allcot?' Mercia was transfixed by her uncle's ice-white face. 'Why?'

'Because he believed she was the spy you have been set to find. He thought killing her would leave the way clear for him to make you that spy yourself. He thought doing so in your presence would mean he could so control events that you would be the one accused of hiring those who shot her.' She laughed. 'When he learnt you were going to Hampton Court, he came to me straight away, pleading that I send my men to kill her there and then, as long as they were sure you were near. This now must be my payment. I shall put down this faithless dog.'

'This is madness!' Without realising, Mercia clasped her hands together as if in prayer. 'One-Eye, listen to me! His mind is addled. He blames me for his injury, and he seeks to deny me, but whatever he has done, he does not deserve death.'

'Such familial love, Mercia. Misplaced, I fear.' She extended her arm, the barrel of the gun resting on the tip of Sir Francis's hair. 'Now witness what happens to those who betray me and take care not to be so foolish yourself.'

'No!' screamed Mercia, but she was grabbed from behind, One-Eye's men holding her back.

'Oh, God!' said Sir Francis. 'Please, God, save me!'

One-Eye took a steady breath. She teased the trigger.

And then she shifted her aim two inches to the right and fired into the floor.

Sir Francis gasped, and crumpled to the ground. He was shaking uncontrollably, and a stench filled the air.

'You . . . bitch!' yelled Mercia, struggling against the overbearing strength restraining her. 'You . . . vile . . . bitch!'

One-Eye laughed, throwing the gun to her man. 'Temper, Mrs Blakewood. I have been called much worse than that.' She looked down at Sir Francis, whimpering on the ground. 'Do not cross me again, Sir Francis Simmonds. Nor you, Mercia Blakewood.' She clicked her fingers. 'Fetch the torches.'

Her men obeyed, half of them leaving the warehouse. Released, Mercia rushed to her uncle's side.

'What now?' she said.

'I intend to continue the lesson,' said One-Eye. 'God's teeth, that man stinks.'

She walked across the room and fell silent. Mercia busied herself with Sir Francis, but he responded to none of her entreaties, curled up in a ball on the dirty stockroom floor. Then an orange flicker caught her eye, and she looked up from her uncle to see One-Eye's men returning with lit torches.

'Set it there, and there,' said One-Eye, indicating piles of wooden crates. Her men circled the room, scattering some kind of fuel and lighting a fire after. 'I am going now, Mrs Blakewood. I shall tie you, but you will have enough time to undo the knots and get free. Whether you save your lamentable uncle is up to you.'

'But the warehouse.' Mercia looked at the flames, already accepting the life they had been given. 'Why burn it?'

One-Eye reached for her hat. 'Because it must be important in some way, or else why would we be here? And in truth, because it amuses me.'

As her men tied Mercia to the stool in a loose sequence of knots, One-Eye walked calmly from the building. Her men followed in a line, leaving Mercia bound, and Sir Francis rocking in his filth.

Once they had gone she squirmed in her bonds, undoing them in ten seconds they were so poorly done. She reached down once more for her uncle.

'Uncle, come. We have to leave. The warehouse is starting to burn.'

There was no response.

'One-Eye does not mean to kill us, just prevent us from following.' She tugged at his doublet. 'You have to come now.'

Still nothing. Nearby, wisps of smoke began to rise.

'Uncle, you will rouse yourself from this torpor and you will come. And once we are outside, you will explain to me what you have done.'

She pulled harder, but he remained immobile, snivelling a wounded squeal. In contrast, the flames at the end of the stockroom were beginning to take, and the smoke was swirling ever faster.

'Uncle!' Finally, she managed to twist him from where he lay, and he looked up at her, surprised, as he pivoted on the floor around his hip. She reached under his arms and pulled him up until he sat, and then continuing to coax, she walked him to his feet, thrusting his cane into his fist.

'Now take my arm and follow.'

She eased him towards the office, a popping of the fire behind hurrying them along. Passing from the stockroom, she kicked out with her right boot, forcing open the entrance and dragging her uncle into sunlight. She helped him towards the river, away

317

from the warehouse, and then she let him go. Utterly unsteady, he collapsed at her feet.

'Wait here,' she ordered, but Sir Francis was going nowhere. She glanced up, watching as the first thin pillars of smoke began to poke through gaps in the structure of the warehouse. But there was no need to seek aid: armed with buckets, a number of labourers were already running in. Others were removing straw and wood from around the building, hoping to contain the blaze.

Leaving them to their task, Mercia turned to Sir Francis. He was sitting up, seemingly recovered of some of his wits.

'Are you improved?' she rasped.

He stared at her as though still in a daze.

'Then you can talk. What did she mean about Lady Allcot?'

He remained silent.

'Did you order her death? Speak, Uncle! This is your chance to redeem some of what you have done.'

'She . . . she was Virgo.' He spoke in the same way he looked: Mercia wondered if he even knew she was there. 'What did it matter if I hired that smuggler filth to kill her? She would have hanged. Hanged anyway. This way she was stopped before she could do more harm.'

'But she was not Virgo, was she?' She shook him in an effort to rouse him. 'Was she? If nothing else, Bellecour's last report proves it. I know you must have seen it. It spoke of Lady Allcot as separate to Virgo.'

'That report . . . it was a lie.' He nodded vigorously. 'Yes, a lie, left to confuse us!'

'Is this what has become of you?' She shook her head in disgust. 'Now you will have to pay the price for your mania. But you can do something for your conscience first. You can tell me what you think you know of Virgo, in truth.'

318

'But she went to Hampton Court the whole time, to meet that Frenchman!' He looked up, his eyes wide, almost as if he were begging her understanding. 'She told my wife how she hoped the war would ruin her husband.'

'That is hardly conclusive.'

'Then how do you explain the letter I was sent?'

'What letter?'

'The letter that told me of Lady Allcot's treachery. It was sent to me in my chambers, denouncing her betrayal, explaining where I might observe her duplicity.'

'Yet Lady Allcot was innocent. Who wrote it?'

'There was no name given, but . . . yes, I concede it was strange, but I followed the letter's instructions, and I did observe her. Talking with that Frenchman, for one.'

She closed her eyes. 'God's teeth, Uncle. That letter must have been a ruse! Sent by the real Virgo perhaps, or someone close to her. She must have learnt of your investigations and set you on the trail of an innocent!'

He shook his head. 'I am not so foolish.'

'You were so determined to undo me you could not see it. And then you killed her.' She looked at him and felt utterly sick. 'Damn you, Uncle. Damn you to hell.'

Her vitriol seemed to work where all else had not. His eyes narrowed, and he turned to face her, the former animosity restored to his gaze.

'Then who is Virgo, if not her?'

'I . . . have my thoughts on the matter.'

'Well, you will not catch her today. All those women have gone to the fleet.'

She pulled back. 'When?'

'This morning, with the King and his council. They have made a pretty party of it.'

'The women have gone with the men? Even after what happened to the *London*?'

'So you do know something of events. But wives oft visit their husbands aboard ship before they sail to war. Children too. Even you must know this.'

'I know the *London* exploded while the women and children were still on it. Over a hundred died.'

'That was an accident. Some tar had stored the gunpowder poorly.' He shrugged. 'Many have gone to Harwich with the council, officers and womenfolk alike. The women are there to encourage the men. It reminds them for what they fight.'

'Then Lady Herrick and Lady Cartwright have travelled with their husbands?'

He scoffed. 'I doubt Lady Cartwright cares much for her husband, but yes.'

'And Mrs Howe? Why should she go?'

He fell sullen and silent, turning away. She crouched by his ear.

'Uncle, listen to me. You may hate me, but you do not hate England, I know. If you withhold anything that might affect the war, lives could be lost, and victory evade us. You must speak. It is vital that you speak.'

He flicked his wrist in irritation. 'Because her husband too has a place in the fleet. He will have asked Sir Stephen Herrick to secure him a commission.'

'Howe is at the fleet?' She thought of the printing press in his smouldering warehouse, of Cornelia visiting the stables where Bellecour had died. 'Hell's teeth! If Virgo has gone to the fleet, and Gemini is already there . . .' Then she thought of the map the madam at the whorehouse had taken from Bellecour's report, the map that marked the east coast with the cross signifying death.

She gasped. 'Uncle! Where did you say the fleet was assembling?'

'What does it matter? I will not help—'

'Damn you, Uncle! You will tell me again where it is.'

'Harwich,' he scowled. 'Harwich, on the North Sea.'

'The east coast.' She fished out the map and pointed to the cross. 'That is Harwich, there, is it not?'

'Why yes, but—'

'Then that is where I shall have to go too. I must prevent whatever she intends.' She got to her feet. 'We will finish this reckoning when I am back. I suggest you return to the palace and confess your crime, or else ready yourself for what must come next.'

'There is one thing alone I shall do now,' he called out, as she abandoned him on the quay. 'I have a matter of honour to settle with that . . . witch.'

'Then do what you must,' she said, already passed from his earshot. 'As I must follow Virgo – though she lead me to the very edge of war.'

Chapter Twenty-Seven

Public coach or privately hired horse? That was her first dilemma. The thought of a warm coach was appealing, but she was restricted by the timetable; moreover, she was still uncertain how much she should be seen in public. With a mount of her own, she had the freedom to set out whenever she liked, and could push the horse to the pace she needed. Then again, if the weather were foul, the country tracks churning into mud, the trip would be worse than misery, to say nothing of the highwaymen that could be lying in wait.

She looked to the sky. It wasn't raining yet. She knew how to ride fast.

And as for highwaymen, well. She had survived the arrows of the Indians.

A quick trip to her goldsmiths in Lombard Street, to raid her father's scant inheritance. A hard negotiation at a stables in the east of the city, failing to convince the wily owner she wasn't desperate for the swiftest horse she had. A promise to return the steed soon, and not to ride too fast. A successful deception on that score, at least.

After returning to St Helen's church to meet her transport back to Zion, she spent a second night in the safe house, asking Phibae to arrange an early start to take her to the stables at first light. In good condition, a horse might manage up to thirty miles a day: from experience, she knew it took two days for a coach to travel the sixty miles to London from Oxford. She was fortunate, then – the horse less so, perhaps – that May was turning into June, and the mornings began early, the evenings ended late.

She rode the eighty miles to Harwich in two and a half days: thirty-five miles on the first day, straight through to Chelmsford, with a brief stop of hours at an inn; twenty-five the day after, the horse tiring from its exertion, forcing her to stop at Colchester, impatiently awaiting the dawn. The final stretch brought Sole Bay into view, and by then she must almost have caught the King's party, settled into their quarters after what had doubtless been a swift ride of their own.

It was noon, the sun directly overhead, plenty of light in the bright, blue sky by which to enjoy the glorious sight further out in the bay: the massed English fleet, upwards of a hundred ships, waiting for the order to sail. Away in the distance, a blast of cannon fire echoed off the cliffs from an unseen enemy as if in mocking welcome: a brief skirmish off the coast, perhaps, before the real event.

The town was bursting with people. She tied her exhausted horse at a stables on the edge of town before pushing her way to the marketplace. A group of girls was blocking a narrow flight of steps, laughing at everything they saw, and she stopped to ask them where she might find a place to rest. But they merely laughed all the more.

'Haven't you seen how many's here, with the war? All the inns are full.'

Her heart sank. 'All of them?'

'King's at the Three Cups.' One of the girls stood up tall. 'The

King! Here in little Harwich. And all those ships in the bay . . . we're the most important place in England now!'

'I suppose you are.' She tugged at her collar, wondering what to do. 'If the King is at the Three Cups, what of the other noblemen?'

'Don't know.' The girl pointed across the square, where a red-robed official had his nose turned up and his neck chained in gold. 'Ask him.'

And the girls descended into giggles.

Mercia crossed to the officious man. 'Excuse me,' she said. 'Could you help me?'

A broad smile broke upon his face. 'I hope so, my beauty.'

'I have come from London with one of the King's war council. Could you tell me where they are based?'

'The Three Cups, my lovely. King and his council, Duke of York too.'

'Sir William Calde?'

'That's right, my precious.'

'Sir Stephen Herrick? Sir Geoffrey Allcot?'

He nodded his response. 'And that delightful young lady of his. Got her the best room, just as Sir Geoffrey demanded. The best after the King's, at least.' He scratched at his ear. 'And the Duke's. Do you know her? Lady Cartwright?'

'Indeed I do.'

'Then I trust we have assuaged her distemper. I know this is not the palace, but we do our best.'

'She is not staying with her husband, then?'

'Sir Geoffrey was most insistent, and I do like to oblige these best of men.'

'I am sure.' She chewed her lips, thinking: she did not want to be seen by the council yet, and there were other avenues she had to pursue first. 'What of the other noblemen?' she asked. 'Are they aboard their ships?'

'Some are. Most are still waiting. It was I, my sweet, who arranged all their affairs.'

She allowed him a smile. 'Then tell me, sir. Where may I find Henry Raff?'

Hood up, she waited on the edge of the square. Men were walking everywhere, dressed in all sorts of cloth, from the most sublime silk of the officers staying at the inns to the roughest hemp of the ordinary tars already billeted to their shipboard hammocks. There were women too, as Sir Francis had intimated: wives and children come for their loved ones, and a great many others of a less familial sort.

'Mercia?'

She looked up to see an elegantly groomed man standing above her, a puzzled frown marring his handsome face.

'Hello, Henry. Are you that surprised to see me?'

'Very. I had been told – in London – there was an altercation or some such?'

'Some such.' She got to her feet. 'Shall we talk somewhere more private?'

She led him from the busy square to the edge of town, where houses gave way to fields. In the corner of a meadow, a herd of lazy cows sat sprawled on the grass, merging into one loud bovine mass. It was shadier here, and nobody much was about.

'Where I want you at last,' he grinned. 'Alone, in the shadows.'

'Henry. This is not the time.'

'You mean you did not travel here to see me?'

'Stop laughing, Henry. I need to beg a favour.'

'Oh?'

'I know I have no right to ask, and I hope I can . . . I need to be able to trust you.'

'Mercia.' He swept to take her hand. 'You can trust me. You know it.'

'I would ask Sir William, but he is occupied, and quartered too close to . . . certain others.'

He looked at her a moment, his head cocked. But then he nodded.

'Pray, ask.'

'Thank you. When does the fleet sail?'

'As soon as the Dutch are descried off the coast. Perhaps you heard the cannon shot before?'

'Could it be tonight?'

'Very likely. We may put out at a moment's notice. To speak true, I am surprised the order is not already given. But from what I hear, we shall wait until this evening.'

'But the common sailors are already embarked?'

'Yes. Only the principal officers remain on land, especially with the King in town. Everyone wants to impress. And you know yourself what quarters are like aboard ships.'

'Henry, I need to get aboard the *Royal Charles*.'

His easy manner faltered. 'Whatever for?'

'I need to speak with my manservant. I cannot say much about it, save it is a matter of importance.'

His laughter turned nervous. 'Mercia, I cannot simply take you to the flagship. I know there are still women and children near, but with our departure imminent, most have already left. When I said the Duke is expected to give the order this very evening, it was not in jest. He takes command within hours.'

She squeezed his hand. 'Henry, if I do not get on that ship, men could die.'

'Well, Mercia, I know you are beautiful, but even so . . .'

'This is no time for merriment! Will you aid me or not?'

He raised an eyebrow. 'My, you are serious. But the *Royal Charles* is not my ship. I have to prepare to join my own, to serve as its lieutenant.'

'You must know someone on it. Or . . . shall I be forced to ask Giles Malvern for help?'

'Who?'

'You recall the sword fight in Hyde Park? He is in the fleet too.'

'Oh, him. Even so, I—'

'Do not tell me you lack the authority.'

'No, but . . .' He blew out his cheeks. 'How long will you need?'

'Not long. Please, Henry. Will you help?'

He looked at her for several seconds, but then he smiled. 'Mercia, you asked me once why I preferred you to other women.'

'Younger women, I believe I said.'

'Well, this is why.' He pulled her gently by the hand. 'Come, then. It will certainly be more interesting than playing at dice until the Duke finally leaves. Let us find a boat to row us out.'

The bay between shore and fleet was busy, men and provisions being ferried all the time, and it was not hard for Raff to appropriate a boat to take them out: used to obeying orders, the oarsman barely queried Mercia's presence.

'Here.' Raff threw her an apple from an overflowing crate. 'I wager you have not eaten yet.'

'That's for the men, my lord!' protested the oarsman, but Raff gave him a look and he fell silent.

'Thank you,' she said, crunching the unblemished green skin with relish. 'Apples and the sea. I would never have thought those scents matched.'

He smiled. 'We shall have to do this again. A day on a placid lake somewhere, in more pleasant circumstances.'

'Henry, after this, I shall join you on a boat anywhere.'

'I shall insist on it.'

She took a deep breath, for in truth the salty air was as evocative as it was intoxicating, reminding her of the long months she had spent on the ocean. Yet her journey today was not quite so long, a mere fifteen minutes before they came along the first of the lined-up ships – the *Mary*, the *Royal Catherine*, the *St. George* – until the massive bulk of the *Royal Charles* itself rose directly before them. Its creaking stern bobbed in the waves, the proud royal arms vaunting their colourful display, all lion and unicorn and *Dieu et Mon Droit*.

Pulling alongside, the oarsman called for a ladder. 'Will you manage, my lady?' he asked, and in spite of herself she laughed. But Raff still went first, helping her onto deck as she eased herself up. Her arms ached more than she would have thought; perhaps her weeks on land had made her complacent.

'My,' she said, stroking the smooth rail of the deck as she stared up the height of the mainmast. 'I never thought I should say so, but it is good to return aboard a ship.' She chuckled as Raff stumbled at a lurch in the waves while she managed to hold herself steady. 'You will become accustomed to it.'

'An unlucky turn,' he said.

'Luck has little to do with it.' She lowered her voice. 'Now could we find my man?'

She need not have asked. Seconds later, a sailor dropped from the rigging above and was about to hold out his hands in astonished greeting when he checked himself, busying himself instead with a length of rope near her feet.

'Mercia,' whispered Nicholas. 'I wasn't expecting to see you.'

She looked away, pretending to admire the ship's magnificence. 'Hold a moment,' she mumbled, hand before her mouth. 'We needs must speak.'

By now the ship's master had been alerted to her presence. His gait erect, he marched across the deck towards them.

'My lord,' he said, sizing up Raff's fine attire. 'I thought all the women had returned to shore.'

'I have invited this lady to the flagship myself,' said Raff.

'At this late hour?'

Raff raised an eyebrow. 'Take care how you address me, my man. This lady is no common hanger-on. She is the woman who travelled to America for the King.'

'Oh?' The master looked on Mercia with interest. 'I did not realise you were in Harwich, my lady.'

'Yes,' she said, looking at Raff askance, bemused at her unexpected status. 'I have come to have a strong admiration for the fleet, as well you might imagine.'

'And you wish to see the flagship.' The master nodded. 'I understand, my lady, but if the order is given, I shall have to demand that you leave.'

'Who is in charge of our ships, Master?' said Raff. 'We officers, I believe. Besides, the fleet is not due to depart for some hours.'

'I am aware of that, my lord, but still, I would have liked to—'

'Return to your duties, man. We shall stay only as long as my lady wishes, when I shall remove her offensive presence from what is clearly your ship, and not the King's.'

'My lord, I did not mean—'

'You must have cannon and powder to check. We do not want a repeat of the *London*, do we? Not with the Duke coming aboard at any moment.'

The master could not help but narrow his eyes. 'The ship, my lord, is perfect. As you will see when you look – quickly – around.'

He bowed and marched off. Leaving Nicholas with the rope and instructions to join her momentarily, Mercia accompanied Raff on a brief tour of the deck. After a few minutes' cursory exploration, they sidestepped capstan and winch to pass into that section of the ship where the officers' cabins lay. Checking at doors until she found one empty, she turned round.

'Henry,' she said. 'Could you get word to my man to meet me in here? While we speak, perhaps you could take the chance to learn more of this ship, for the upcoming battle. I am sure your captain will approve.'

He followed her inside the small room. 'I will, if I get something in return.'

He shut the door and hemmed her against it, his hand on the wall to the right of her shoulder. Then he pushed his body against hers.

'I will stop if you want,' he said. 'But surely, a kiss will not hurt?'

She widened her eyes. 'Henry, I do not expect—'

'Nor do I.' His face was hovering inches from hers, but he made no move to bring it closer. 'I simply ask, because you are beautiful, and sometimes I have been told so am I. And because tonight, I may sail to war.'

She looked into his eyes, and for that instant all she could see was the voluminous blue. She felt her breathing quicken, falling in time with his. And then she thought – thoughts unknown – and laying her hand on the back of his head, she pulled it towards hers, and she kissed him, deeply, feeling his warm lips, his slow tongue, smelling the scent of his skin. Then she pulled away, and so did he, and they stared at each other as if both needed more.

'That is the first time I have done that for years,' she said.

He breathed out and smiled. 'Then let us hope it is not the last for years to come.'

'It was a kiss, Henry. It does not mean anything more.'

'No.' He glanced at the small bed in the corner. 'But yes, it was a kiss. A kiss worth waiting for.' He gestured towards the door. 'Before I lose myself, let me fetch your man.'

As she waited, she smiled. What was she thinking? She was on a warship in the middle of the bay, on a matter of great importance to the King and to herself, the fleet about to sail to war at any moment, and instead she had allowed herself to kiss a man. The idea was absurd, and yet . . .

She shook her head, looking around the small cabin, listening to the sound of the creaking wood. There was a pile of papers on a desk, and she glanced at the sheet on top, but it was blank. The bed was unmade and unslept in, the officer destined for this room clearly still waiting in Harwich. Then the door pushed slowly open and she stiffened lest it were a member of the crew, but the sailor who entered was familiar.

'Nicholas.' A huge beam of a smile broke out across her face. 'It is wonderful to see you.'

He grinned. 'Did you miss me so much you had to ride all the way from London?'

'Still full of cheek, I see. How have you liked your few days as a sailor again?'

'Well enough. 'Tis good to be around . . . normal men again, and out of the palace.'

'I can understand that. The palace becomes stuffy, even for me.'

'How is Daniel?' he asked.

'Well. Hopefully it will not be long now until I can take him home.' She gestured to the bed, while she sat in the chair behind the officer's desk. 'Have a rest.'

He collapsed onto the bunk. 'My, this is less comfortable than my hammock. Quieter in here, mind.'

'Can you sleep?'

He pushed up on his elbows. 'We've been sailing around a bit. They expect us to put out tomorrow, this evening even. I don't think you'd best stay.'

She grew serious. 'Nicholas, I think Virgo and Gemini might be on the verge of some kind of attempt. I do not yet know what, but the King and his council are here, and they have brought the women with them. That is why I have come – to find her out and prevent it.'

'In truth? Did you not come with Sir William?'

'Since you left there have been . . . difficulties.' Briefly she summarised all that had happened: the Tower of London; Southwark; the warehouse.

'This is why I shouldn't leave you,' he said, his face pure dismay. 'You always find trouble.'

'I think 'tis more that trouble finds me. Have you seen Giles Malvern while you have been here?'

''Tis as he said, his ship is close. He's come to the *Royal Charles* twice, as far as I know, but he hasn't spoken to me. I think maybe he comes in case I've anything to say, though he's given me a signal to make if I need him.'

'And do you have anything to say?'

'Not really.' He sighed. 'Sometimes I can't help but feel I've been given a fruitless task. Nothing has happened – save I've been kept from you. Almost as if I've been got out of the way.'

'I do not think so, Nicholas. Why bother?'

'And all Malvern seems to do when he is here is watch Thomas Howe – while pretending that he isn't.'

'What?' She held up a hand. 'Howe is on this ship?'

'Spends most of his time in his cabin or in the hold. He's the purser, in charge of the supplies.'

'I know what a purser does.' She frowned. 'But a purser serves under the master. Why would Howe want that role?'

'He didn't have it to start with. The old purser took sick and had to be replaced. As I understand it, Howe agreed to step in, even though it brings him no pay. He wants to serve near the Duke, so he says. What I think is he wants to be noticed.'

'He wants to serve near the Duke . . .' She rubbed her chin in thought. 'Have you spoken with him, then?'

'I've listened in to his conversation, what there is of it. I've made it my business to, seeing who his wife is. It's not hard to find some task in the hold when the ship's stuck near port, with supplies coming all the time.'

'Has he recognised you?'

'We never met in London. I think he resents it, mind, being here. Even for one of them, he always keeps himself apart. Except whenever the Duke is around, and he just stares.'

She drummed her fingers on the desk. 'Nicholas, I think Howe might be Gemini. If he is taking a somewhat opportune chance to serve on the flagship, I think it all the more.'

'Howe Gemini?' He swung his legs round to sit up straight. 'With Cornelia as Virgo, perhaps?'

She nodded. 'If Malvern put you on the *Royal Charles*, he must have thought Gemini would be stationed here. And now Howe is here, and you say Malvern is watching him too.'

'But Howe didn't take up his post until about the time I came on board.'

'That I cannot understand. But I found plenty in London to

suggest Howe's involvement. A printing press in his warehouse, for one, and a hidden pile of tracts that were almost seditious.'

He whistled. 'Mercia, I was doubtful of Howe too. I've followed him as much as I can, but he hasn't done anything strange. When I said he keeps himself apart, I meant from the officers as much as from us tars. The only person he pays notice to is the Duke.'

A chill feeling set in as the ship rocked underneath her. 'Nicholas, what if Howe's interest in him is not to be noticed, but for something else entirely?'

'Meaning what?'

'Say he is Gemini. At first I assumed his role for the Dutch would be the same as Virgo's, to seek intelligence to pass on about the fleet. But the map I took from the whorehouse had a cross right here in Harwich, next to the letters R and C.' She slammed down her hand, making Nicholas jump. 'Hell's teeth, the *Royal Charles*! Nicholas, what if . . . what if Howe is after the Duke himself?'

'Christ.' He stared at her. 'If that's right, it would certainly shift the balance against us.'

'At the start of the first major battle of the war. It would send our fleet into turmoil and allow the Dutch an easy victory. There have been attempts on his life before, but even so . . . dear God, Nicholas. Could Howe be here to kill the Duke?'

Chapter Twenty-Eight

She waited in the cabin while Nicholas scoured the ship. Although nothing could have happened during those ten long minutes, still her nails were more ragged by the time he came back.

'No sign of him,' he said. 'Howe is nowhere on the ship.'

'How is that possible? Hell's teeth, Nicholas, could he have gone to shore?' She leapt up. 'The Duke is there now, not to mention the King. If Howe is involved, heaven knows what he plans. Come.' She opened the door. 'We must find Henry and return on the boat that brought me here.'

'I didn't see him either. Your new . . . friend.'

'Friend.' She waved a dismissive hand. 'He must be somewhere.'

But they could not find Raff either, and the master was in no mood to answer her questions. Then she looked over the side of the ship.

'The boat has gone!' Quickly, she looked around. Opposite the rope ladder that still dangled over the side, a wheezing sailor was coiling a heavy rope.

'You,' she commanded. 'The boat I came here on. Where is it?'

'It left a few minutes back.' The man let out a loud belly

laugh. 'Don't tell me you're trapped here with us?' He gurned at Nicholas. 'Hey, Wildmoor. I reckon she likes you.'

'Shut up,' growled Nicholas. 'Did you see who left on the boat?'

'How can I tell you, if you want me to shut up?'

'If you don't, I'll do more than just tell you.'

'Easy, precious! It was him. The new purser.'

'Thomas Howe?' said Mercia.

'Don't know his name, but he seemed right nervous. Think he heard some of the lads talking about you coming aboard, and the next thing I knew he was going down the ladder. I guessed he was taking advantage, heading back to shore to sort out these damned supplies we badly need. There's not much time left to get them.'

'And the man I came with?' she pursued.

'Look, I don't see everything that goes on. I have work to do.'

He went back to coiling his rope. Panicked, Mercia ran a frantic hand along her hair.

'Nicholas, if Howe has gone to shore, we need another boat. If I had known he was on board, I would have been more careful not to be seen.' She looked around. 'And where is Henry? I cannot believe he has taken Howe and left me here. Not after—'

''Tis not your fault. But I know what to do. Wait back in that cabin.'

He dashed off, leaving her alone on the deck – alone with what seemed like hundreds of sailors. 'Have you never seen a woman?' she snapped at their roving eyes. Uncomfortable, she did as Nicholas suggested and retreated to the empty cabin, ordering the sailor at the rope to tell him where she had gone.

'What, you want him to follow you?' he guffawed. 'It is his lucky day.'

Ignoring his lewdness, she hurried to the cabin, where she sat on the bed, waiting. Feeling hemmed in by the windowless space, she walked the two paces to the desk. Then she studied a chart on the wall, adjusted the lamp hanging from the ceiling so that it swung more freely, and sat down again on the bed.

Three-quarters of an hour passed. Beginning to worry that every shout she heard was the signal that the Duke of York had arrived to take command, she was about to brave the leers on deck when finally the door swung open. She looked up and was startled to see not Nicholas, but Giles Malvern come in, a finger to his lips.

'I got here as quickly as I could,' he said. 'Fortunate nobody over there needed my administrations.'

'How?' she said. 'Have you come across from your ship?'

He nodded. ''Tis anchored quite near. When he arrived in Harwich, I told your man to raise a certain pennant if he wanted me. As soon as I could get away, I used a boat to row across. The same boat I shall now use to row you to shore, as it seems is your wish.'

She got to her feet. 'Most clever. Where is Nicholas now?'

'Caught shirking in his duties by the master, thanks to us. He has been ordered to attend to some work in the hold. I fear you must make do with me.'

'Then shall we go? It could be urgent.'

'Yes, but . . .' He hesitated. 'Mercia, the last I heard, you were in the Tower, and then you were not. I cannot believe you simply walked free of that place, but nobody I can ask is willing to tell me the truth. It is as though they are pretending you do not exist.'

'That seems like the truth of it. Let us merely say I am still hunting for Virgo. For now, let us pursue Thomas Howe.'

'Why?'

'Because he has taken my boat. And . . . because I think he is Gemini.'

'Yes,' he said, disappointing her with his nonchalance. 'Wildmoor said as much. But he cannot be.'

'But he must! I found a seditious pamphlet at his warehouse, hidden near a locked-away printing press. Either he or an accomplice picked up Bellecour's reports from the whorehouse, and . . . Mr Malvern? Are you listening to me?'

'I suppose I shall have to admit it.' He sighed. 'Howe is working for me.'

'What?'

'In the same way that Wildmoor is. I did not want to tell you, because you did not need to know, but . . . it is all a ploy, Mercia.' He sat on the bed, holding his fingers to his mouth, before letting drop his hands as if coming to a decision. 'Initially, we were after Bellecour and Bellecour alone. We knew he was using Howe's company to ship items abroad, and so we asked Howe to help us entrap him. Then once Bellecour was dead, our attention turned to this so-called Gemini. We arranged for Howe to serve on the *Royal Charles* as we arranged the same for your own man. And before you ask, neither know about the other. But the chance to have a man in the crew and another among the petty officers was too good an opportunity to ignore.'

Her mouth was half-open in shock. 'Then how do you explain the tracts?'

'I do not. But his personal opinions are of no interest to us, if they are not treasonous.'

'They seemed as good as.'

'Mrs Blakewood, sometimes you have to . . . use those with whom you do not agree to find out about others whom you truly want to catch. Sometimes, we are instructed to turn a blind eye, as they say.'

'Then what of his wife? She is one of the suspects for Virgo.'

He shrugged. 'Another reason to keep Howe close.'

'And have you learnt much on that count?'

'I fear not. Let us say Howe works for us only unwillingly. He shares nothing of his wife, indeed nothing but what we ask of him.'

'And you will not tell me what you mean by unwillingly.' She sighed. 'Then what of the man who took Bellecour's report from the whorehouse?'

Malvern smiled. 'You are very good at this, Mercia. You notice much. Once this is over, I think we will have to employ your talents further. As for that man . . . it was me.'

The surprises were coming fast. 'You?'

'I told you when we met that night how I had been watching Bellecour for some time. What I did not say was that we had managed to make Bellecour believe he was leaving the information at the whorehouse for his Dutch contact to collect, when all the time it was we who were taking it, to find out what he was passing on. Then we would leave the information, mostly untouched, at the real location his true contact was using.'

'Why?' She frowned. 'Why not simply apprehend Bellecour and prevent his reports from leaving at all?'

'Because firstly, Bellecour is French, and any move on our part could have imperilled the King's desire for an alliance with our Gallic neighbours, and secondly, if we had halted the passage of information, the Dutch would simply have cast Bellecour adrift and used someone new. Then we would have found ourselves in the situation we are in now, prevented from learning what he was sharing. For all that time, we knew precisely what the Dutch were being told, and could respond accordingly.'

She shook her head. 'I do not believe this. Why did you not tell me when we discussed the message Nicholas took from the whorehouse?'

'Because I was so ordered. You will have to forgive my masters. They can rather lack trust.'

'Even after proof of Virgo's involvement? You make it seem as if they do not want her caught at all. Does Lady Castlemaine know?'

'I doubt it. And there is a point to what you are doing, Mercia. Now the war is truly starting, we should rather apprehend Virgo than allow her to continue. She is a spy, after all, and the Dutch will soon find her another go-between.'

'So who do you think killed Bellecour?'

'That I do not know. When the news came of his death, I was sent to remove his body, but there was no clue as to his killer. I assume it was his Dutch masters, who had somehow discovered the truth, or even Virgo herself. And so our careful plan was thwarted, after all.'

She pursed her lips, considering all he had said. 'Giles, are you certain? You say you were spying on the spy, but could Virgo have known all along? Could Howe, too, be playing some duplicitous game?'

'If he is, then he is good at it. I think I should know.'

'Then why did he take my boat?'

'Probably to be sure you could not flee while he went to the town to investigate your presence.' He shrugged. 'Whatever else Howe is, he is diligent. All he knows is you were committed to the Tower. I shall speak with him when we return to shore, if he is still there, for I have chosen to come to you instead. Now, Wildmoor mumbled something about that rogue Henry Raff?'

'Yes, God's wounds . . . Raff has gone missing. When Howe took the boat, he left us stranded. Unless Raff went with him, which would be most strange, I do not know where he can be.'

Malvern scoffed. 'Alas, I suspect 'tis not so strange. I believe Raff is a lieutenant elsewhere?'

'Yes.'

'And yet he brought you here, to the *Royal Charles*?'

'Again, yes.'

'Then I suggest the sight of the Duke's convoy heading this way might have panicked him into leaving when he saw Howe seizing your boat.'

'The Duke?' Mercia jerked back her head, crushing her topknot against the low ceiling. 'But Howe left an hour since!'

'The Duke is taking a tour around the rest of the fleet first. Showing his presence, no doubt to boost the men's spirits. Still, he will be here in minutes.'

'My God!' She laid a hand on the door. 'Why did you not say so? He cannot see me here.'

'Do not worry. The men are lining up to receive him as we speak. We will slip away unnoticed in the hubbub.' He smiled. 'But I would pull up your hood, all the same.'

They managed to leave the ship – barely. With a final, not-so-subtle word to Nicholas to keep an eye out for Thomas Howe regardless of what she had just heard, she jumped the last rung of the rope ladder into Malvern's waiting boat as the Duke's party appeared from around the bow of the nearest ship. Deftly, Malvern picked up the oars and rowed in the opposite direction, rounding the colourful stern and slipping out of sight.

'That was close-run,' she said. 'I hope Nicholas will come out of this unharmed.'

'He has served before,' said Malvern. 'Do not be uneasy on his account.'

Five minutes passed in silence as he manoeuvred them through the fleet. Only when they were in open water, heading back to shore, did she feel calm enough to resume their conversation.

'Mr Malvern,' she said, 'if you say Gemini is not Howe, then who is?'

'I wish I knew.'

'You must have some idea. Why else put two men on that ship?'

'I fear, Mrs Blakewood, I have told you too much today already.'

She sighed. 'But is the ship safe? The Duke?'

Water splashed against the side of the boat. 'I did not think you much cared for the Duke.'

'I may not like him, but I do not want him harmed.'

'There are many who would disagree.'

'Oh? What does that mean?'

'Merely that these past years there have been many plots against the Stuarts, most of them unknown to the people. Some are aimed against the King. Many are aimed against the Duke. He is not a popular man, not even among those who serve him, and yet he sits one illness or accident from the throne. The King is not likely to have a legitimate heir.'

'I wish men would cease saying that. Rather think of the poor Queen.'

'But is that not her duty? To beget an heir?'

'The realm has an heir. Several, indeed, if you consider the Duke's healthy children.'

'And yet he is avowedly Catholic. Do you not foresee the difficulties that lie ahead if he inherits?' He looked at her as he heaved on the oars. 'Do you want another war? Not a trade war with the Dutch, but another conflict of brother against brother, father against son? Assuredly, I do not.'

Something in his tone gave her pause. 'Mr Malvern, we—'

'Giles.'

'Giles, then. We all suffered in that war. There is not one Englishman or woman alive whose family remained whole. I should say you were taking this chance to assess me.'

He smiled. 'Not at all. I merely wonder what you think, while we are out here alone. Whether your father's influence has shaped your own beliefs, as my father's did mine.'

'Presently, my only belief is in the restoration of my manor house. Once that is done, then I can think on the right to rule, and who should have that right.' She raised an eyebrow. 'As much as I am permitted to, that is.'

'And yet the Duke pushed for your father's execution,' he pressed. 'Were it up to him, the King would ignore your claim on your house in an instant.'

Her face set. 'I am aware of that. But I would not condone his death merely to satisfy my own vengeance.'

'In no circumstances?'

She frowned. 'Why, no.'

'Then I shall speak no more on it.'

He dipped his left oar deeper in the water, turning the boat into the harbour. The caw of circling gulls replaced their talk as they gradually came into land. Soon the boat was bobbing against the side of a barnacled pier, and Malvern was extending his hand to help her out: useful when her boot slipped, catching on a damp patch of seaweed.

'Careful,' he said. 'You do not want to fall in.'

'I do not. Thank you.'

'Let me take you somewhere safe and then I must return to my ship. When the Dutch engage, I fear my surgeon's knives may be much in demand.'

She looked around. Although there was still a great deal of bustle, there were far fewer people than even two hours before, and far fewer supplies on the dock.

'Everyone has been busy,' she observed. Then she looked out to sea. 'My God, Mr Malvern. Are we truly ready for another war?'

'It is as the King commands it. One day, perhaps, we shall cease our arguments with Europe, but that day is not yet come.'

'I doubt it ever shall. The King remains on land, I trust?'

'Safe in his inn, I am told. Your friend is there too.'

'My friend?'

'Sir William Calde.'

'Ah, indeed. But as much as you have duties on your ship, I have duties here. Nicholas would have told you Virgo is in Harwich. I cannot believe she will give up this opportunity to spy on the council away from the palace. When she does, I mean to find her.'

'Then I wish you luck. We are both England's soldiers, in our way. Now follow me.'

He led her around the edge of the town, ducking into a side street where the houses overhung the roads as grimly as they did in London: certainly, the stench of effluence, animal and human, was the putrid same. Towards the end of the narrow lane, a timber-framed building projected from the rest. Malvern passed in through the door.

'This is where I have been lodging with some others while not on the ships, but no one will need it tonight. We go back and forth, but . . . no longer. If you wish to stay in town, stay here. There is a well nearby for water, and a privy. Let me show you where to hide if you need it.'

She followed him down a small set of stairs to a pantry of sorts. A trapdoor was set in the floor, but unlike at Zion, this one was fully exposed.

Malvern swung it open. 'If anyone arrives you do not much trust, you can drop down here. Have a look now, if you wish.'

She shook her head. 'I do not need to see it to know what it must be like. Is there a room where I can wash?'

'Please, I insist. If only to be sure you know where to go.'

'Giles, I can see where to go. Why would I need . . .'

She trailed off. His arms were folded, and he was blocking the way from the pantry. He took a step forwards. But then he smiled.

'As ever, Mrs Blakewood, I expect you will please yourself. But I would perhaps take a candle with you if you do need to descend. I would light one now, from the fire in the front room, if it is still burning.'

She realised she had been holding her breath. 'Thank you, Giles.'

'Take any of the beds. I cannot say they are comfortable, but they serve a tired man. A tired woman, indeed. Throw the belongings on the floor, such as remain. I do not like leaving you on your own like this, but my ship cannot wait.'

'I have been in worse positions. I will cope.'

'Put the door on the latch.' Turning to leave, he looked her up and down. 'And please, Mercia. Keep safe.'

Chapter Twenty-Nine

Who was Gemini? Despite what Malvern had said, she still did not trust Thomas Howe. Who was to say he was not deceiving Malvern, as Virgo was deceiving all around her? Maybe Gemini was just a common tar, and the Duke was safe, but whoever he was, she would have to leave him to Nicholas for now. She was in Harwich with the three women she thought could be Virgo, and that was the mission she had been entrusted, where her efforts needs now must lie.

Early evening was upon the town, but the sky was still blue, and would be for some time. After a quick wash, she went out into the streets, for she realised she was hungry. Keen to walk where the air was fresh, she wandered along the road that led out of town until not far down she found the inn she remembered passing on the way there, a white building with a pleasant aspect that reminded her of some of the hostelries back home. Now quite ravenous, she went inside to find a table and order dinner, a tasty dish of the freshest green peas and the most succulent roasted pork.

She was sitting back, enjoying the crunch of perfect crackling, when a cloaked man sat down beside her.

'I followed you from the town,' he said. 'Please, do not call out.'

Well, she thought. *This was unexpected.*

'Good evening, Mr Howe. Are you not meant to be on your ship?'

Howe peered from under his bulbous hood. 'I am securing our final supplies. Ensuring we have enough powder is part of my office.'

'I suppose it is. Should you not then be doing it?'

'The task is almost complete.' He turned to face forward. 'I wanted to warn you to keep away from my wife.'

'A threat, Mr Howe? I have little to do with your wife.'

'You know of what I speak. Cornelia's will is weak. She should not be disturbed, or her humours will suffer.'

'So you say. But whenever I have seen you together, you only seem to argue.'

On the table, his hand flinched. 'How I comport myself with my wife is not your affair.'

'That is the second time I have heard a man say that of late. May I ask you a question?'

'By all means. My quarrel is not with you as a person.'

'Most gratifying.' She looked at him askance. 'What is your relation with Giles Malvern?'

She noticed him swallow. 'With whom?'

'You are not a very good dissembler, Mr Howe. Mr Malvern has told me that you and he . . . know each other, shall we say?'

'Malvern has . . . ?' His eyes fell on her knife, set atop her half-finished meat. 'Yes, I know him. As it seems do you.'

'But up until now, he has told neither of us of his association with the other. And yet somehow, Mr Howe, you appear to think I have an interest in your wife.'

'Just leave her be, Mrs Blakewood.' He got to his feet. 'She has nothing to do with any of this.'

'With any of what?' she tried.

But he was already halfway to the door.

She traced her knife about her plate, chasing the peas around the final slice of pork. Then she drained her weak ale, threw down some coins, and followed Howe from the inn. If this had been winter, he would already have vanished into darkness, but there he still was, on foot in the middle of the road ahead, striving to avoid the many ruts.

Sticking to the grass at the side of the road, she tailed him, her full stomach tingling in anticipation that he might turn his head and spy her pursuit. But she kept far enough back to remain unnoticed, and the one time he did look, she made sure to hold herself with confidence, continuing to walk as though she could be anyone else.

He passed into town, and she quickened her pace, for fear she would lose him in the streets. But he stayed within sight, and once inside the gate she spotted him turn towards the harbour. Peering from a corner, she watched as he was met by another man who bowed and showed him a series of parchments. Then pulling down his hood, Howe seemed to nod as the man pointed out two heaps of barrels, the one much larger than the other. Soon enough, more sailors appeared, hauling the larger pile onto a waiting barge onto which they embarked once their task was complete. Howe climbed into a separate boat and cast himself off, speeding past the delicate barge in the direction of the fleet.

Curious, she remained where she was, the evening sea breeze blowing at her face, watching to see if anything further should happen. But the remaining pile of barrels stayed unclaimed, and she sauntered to the seafront, feigning she was taking a stroll. When she reached the barrels, she looked for any mark that might reveal their contents, but there was nothing. Then a gruff shout barked its disgust.

'Get away from those barrels! They're mine!'

She turned to see a small dray making its way towards her. A young man was driving, while the older man at his side was almost on his feet.

'Get away, I say! That's our ale!'

She stood to one side. 'What, did you think I was going to carry one off?'

He spat as the driver reined in his horse. 'You could have a gang hiding. Plenty of smugglers in these parts, to say nothing of Bill Steer at The Crown!'

'Sir, I have no gang of any kind. It is always just me.'

'Still, this is our reward, and I'm not about to lose it to anyone who might have heard of it.'

'Be quiet, Dad,' said the younger man. 'She's no harm.'

'How do I know 'tis not you taking someone else's ale?' she said in jest. 'There is no mark.'

'Shove aside, and let us through,' growled the father. 'This is part-payment for hosting the King. Check with His Majesty, if you like.'

'His Majesty – whom I know.'

'Begging your pardon, my lady.' The son doffed his hat. 'My father is a little . . . aged.'

She inclined her head. 'There is no offence. I shall leave you to your ale.'

She stood to one side, watching the father snarl orders at his son and the two other men who had come with them. Gingerly, they eased the three barrels onto their dray, and with another doff of his hat, the driver steered his horses back towards the town. With no more to do at the harbourside, she followed the cart up the shallow hill, pausing at the same corner as before to see the dray stop outside the gate that led into the yard of the Three Cups.

It was getting cold. Wishing she could enjoy a tankard of ale herself, instead she pulled her cloak about her and considered her next move. If the King was staying at the Three Cups with his war council, so too, she assumed, would be the women; indeed, the pompous red-cloaked official she had met on her arrival had told her as much about Lady Cartwright. And Lady Cartwright knew Lady Herrick: they were probably in a bedroom of the Three Cups now, gossiping about all manner of subjects.

Perhaps the one learning from the other what she herself did not yet know.

She leant against the wall. What would she do if she were Virgo? The King and his council were an easier target away from the palace. It was an irresistible opportunity, surely. How would she take advantage of that – if she were Virgo?

Listening in? Too public – and too risky. What if she were caught with her ear to the wood of the King's door? Hiding in the King's room, or else in one of his councillor's? She shook her head. Too absurd. Taking advantage of the time away, to say nothing of the council's anxiety at the impending battle to try to . . . relax the man she was with? More plausible. And more likely, given that anxiety, to succeed in learning things she otherwise might not; or if the man were complicit, that he would have something useful to tell.

What of Cornelia Howe? Although her husband's threats had confirmed she was in Harwich, Mercia was not about to let those threats dissuade her. More tricky was to find where she might be. But if Cornelia were Virgo, and wanted to profit from events, she would surely find some way into the Three Cups herself.

Mercia looked at the inn's vibrant sign, its paint recently touched up, swinging in the breeze. Whatever she considered, everything seemed to point here. But she could hardly walk in through the door unnoticed. There were guards posted, for one.

But there was another way in, perhaps.

She strolled up to the dray by the gate; the two horses were brushing against the inn's stone wall, pushing each other's heads as they shared a bag of oats. Two of the barrels from the harbour had already been unloaded, but the third remained to be taken, and she waited for the workers to return, hoping the elderly owner would have entrusted the heavy task to his younger counterparts.

True enough, the owner's son soon appeared, jumping onto the cart. He rolled the barrel to his two waiting helpers, before looking left and right and taking a swig from a flask stored at his hip. On the other side of the gate, she noticed two guards were standing aside to allow the work to proceed apace.

'Hello again,' she said to the young man. 'Looks like you have to be strong for that kind of work.'

He smiled, flexing his arm muscles in the same boastful display she had been confronted with countless times before.

'You do,' he said. 'And it is our ale, you know. The King himself said we might have it.'

Out of sight of the guards, she leant against the cart. He was smooth-faced, not far into his twenties, she supposed. Around his neck he wore a woollen red cloth.

'I did not doubt it,' she said. 'I was merely curious to see it left on the harbourside unclaimed.'

'Well, now it is claimed, and safe in our cellar. 'Tis good stuff, too.' He gestured towards the inn. 'Do you want any? Or a glass of sack, perhaps?'

'I am not thirsty.' She inched a little closer. 'It must be an honour to have the King stay at your inn.'

'Aye, it is. You'll have come with an officer yourself, I wager?' He leapt nimbly to the ground. 'Don't worry, my lady, the Dutch have no chance. Every day I've seen our ships gather. 'Tis quite a sight.'

'You were not pressed to fight yourself?' she asked.

'Too busy making sure everyone had their ale.' He glanced down. 'My brother's out there, though, on the *Charity*. He's only sixteen.'

'Then I'm sure he'll be safe too.' She gave him a reassuring smile. 'Is it just the men here now? Or are there women with them?'

'Some women. Not many.'

'Ladies of the court?'

'Looks like it. And . . . one or two of their maids.'

'I suppose you have been talking with them?'

'Don't get me wrong, my lady. I behave.'

'It matters not to me.' She pushed off from the cart to face him. 'What is your name?'

'Oli. Oli Moss.'

'Well, Oli, do you think I might go inside your inn and sit?'

'Everyone's free to, my lady. No need to ask.'

'Even with the King here?'

'The King seems to like people to see him.' He raised his head. 'I even heard, my lady, folk in London can go and watch him get up and go to bed. Is that true?'

She nodded. 'It is. The *lever* and the *coucher*, they call it.'

'Must be a sight. Have you seen it?'

'No.' She pictured the scene in her head. 'Nor do I much wish to. Oli, I should like to go in through the back, if I may. There will be someone inside who would not want to see me enter. Someone's wife. I fear she becomes jealous.'

He scratched at his neck. 'I don't know, my lady. 'Tis not that slipshod here. We're not supposed to let people in without them at least being searched.'

'Then search me, if it eases your conscience.'

His eyes fair popped from his head. 'I can't do that!'

'Well, then.'

'I mean I—'

'Come, Oli, I do not want anyone to know I am here. I have arranged it with the man I am meant to meet.' She reached into her pocket. 'And I would hate you to lose out on this.'

Moss stared as she twisted a silver coin in her fingers. 'You can't just bribe me, my lady.'

'What harm am I going to do?' She pulled at the folds of her dress. 'Look at me. I am sure the King will be safe. Please, search me if you like.'

'I don't need to do that.' He sucked in through his teeth. 'Oh, give us that coin. If they ask, I'll say you're with me. But slouch a bit, as though you aren't such a lady.'

Heart racing, she pulled up her hood, but she supposed it hardly mattered. The worst the guards could do was send her on her way, unless they recognised her face and thought she should be in the Tower. But she need not have worried.

'Who's this?' one said to Moss, scarcely bothered as he propped himself against the wall, sipping a beaker of ale.

'Friend of my ma's, ain't she?' said Moss.

The guard wiggled his beaker. 'Got any more for when I get off?'

'For the King's guard? Of course.'

And they passed into the yard. Although it was still light, one or two torches had already been set, but their flames were almost invisible, in that way fire loses its brazen confidence in the presence of the sun, somehow aware it can never compete. The two workers from the harbour were slumped cross-legged beside the open cellar hatch: hidden behind her hood, she was nonetheless greeted by their unsuspecting whistles.

At the door, Moss grinned. 'Easy, no? If you want to get to the rooms, it's through the door, dead ahead.'

'Thank you, Oli,' she said.

'Watch out for my old dad, though, eh?'

She smiled and, leaving him in the yard, entered a small passage that looked to be recently scrubbed. Immediately to her left was the kitchen, where two red-faced cooks were stirring large pots, from which an equally heated serving woman was plating trenchers and dishes. Behind their worktop, a wooden trapdoor in the floor provided interior access to the cellar, while to her right in the passage, a bucket and mop were stacked against a closed cupboard door.

Straight in front, an opening led to a wider corridor in the main body of the inn. She put her head through, and immediately retracted it as she saw the elder Moss, but he was walking away from her, towards the main hall. Waiting for him to disappear, she pondered where she should go herself.

Presumably the King was in the bedrooms upstairs, as surely Lady Herrick and Lady Cartwright would be as well. Would that she could catch one of them in the act of spying . . . but it was more likely, she thought wryly, that one of them would end up catching her. And so she edged into the corridor, feeling all the while exposed, thankful her hood was so concealing.

A guard was posted at the bottom of a staircase, and she cursed to herself. How would she get up now? But as she dithered, Oli Moss's voice sounded from behind.

'Hey, Paddy,' he called. 'You want some ale?'

She ducked back as the guard peered round.

'Not right now,' he said.

'Then come get it for later. I'll leave it here, by the door.'

Moss retreated outside, not before giving Mercia a knowing smile: the sort of smile that might listen at guestroom doors, she thought. But she was thankful for it then, as the guard rubbed his hands and passed her by to retrieve his ale, giving her enough time to dash up the stairs hardly noticed.

She came out onto a carpeted landing, a series of fine paintings lining the papered walls. Was the inn always this grand, she wondered, or had the finery been installed for the King's brief visit, to be removed as soon as he had gone? In front of her, a galleried landing formed a wide rectangle around an open space below, four doors giving to bedrooms on each long side. In one of those was the King, she supposed, perhaps pacing his room, worrying for the fate of his fleet and his brother. In one of the others, for all she knew, awaited Virgo.

Tentative, nervous, she inched along the right-hand side, her body tingling with the excited anticipation that one of the doors might open. But none of them did, and as the tension grew to an almost physical barrier, she forced herself forward, towards the first room.

And then – chaos.

Without warning, an enormous explosion powered through the inn; the whole building shook, shattering the immaculate hangings. Her hearing howled in agony, her vision turned white, then black, and she found herself hurled off her feet, flying back towards the top of the stairs as the landing in front caved in.

Thrown against the wall, she lay dazed, unknowing, contused. For a moment, all was silent. And then the screaming began.

Chapter Thirty

She sat up. Her ears were ringing with pain, and the building appeared hazy, as though it were underwater. She took a panicked breath, unclear if she were still alive; the dusty air filled her lungs, and she began to cough, worsening a wrenching ache down her back and her side. She looked at her legs: intact, no blood, no damage that would not heal.

The same could not be said of the inn. What before had been perfect was now devastation, masonry hanging from the ceiling, the left-hand side of the landing collapsed to become a steep ramp to the indiscernible hall beneath. Smoke was filling every small space, and she tugged her hood around her neck to cover her stinging mouth.

The doors off the landing were beginning to open, those that could; something swift ran past her, a rushing of air, and as her vision began to clear, she looked up to see a host of guards breaking down the end door of the right-hand side. 'Your Majesty,' they called. 'Your Majesty!'

A woman fell out screaming from another door on the right, limping towards Mercia to flee down the stairs, and even in her current state, she recognised Lady Cartwright, but she looked somehow different, as though her face was black. Then a guard ran into the chamber she had left; moments later he swore, and he emerged, his helmet greying with dust, struggling to drag out a misshaped bundle. Then she realised the bundle was a man, too heavy for the guard to remove by himself. And then a face appeared, bending down to address her.

'My lady, do you live? My lady!'

She nodded, and immediately cried out in pain; the headache that coursed through her temples was more painful than any she had known. Unable to speak, she allowed the guard to aid her to her feet, and she leant on his shoulder, descending the battered staircase step by terrible step. He led her past the kitchen into the yard where she had entered, and slowly walked her to the other side.

The yard was unrecognisable. The door to the cellar was gone, a thick, black smoke rising from the hole that had taken its place. The dray in the entrance was on its side, and one of the horses was whining, its flank caved in, thrashing about in agonised panic. The other did not move at all, what was left of it. At its side, a young man lay blackened and still, his legs . . . she looked away. His legs were gone.

Holding her breath, she managed to reach the street, until the guard set her on the ground a short distance down, assuring her she would live. But he had to return to help others, and he left her on her own, unbelieving, uncomprehending, staring at the thick smoke enveloping what had once been the happy inn.

Then she thought of the young man in the yard. Oli Moss, she thought, and she could not get his name out of her head. Oli Moss, she thought, scolded by his father at the harbourside. Oli Moss, she thought, her uncertain accomplice who had sneaked her inside. Oli Moss, she thought. So young. So dead.

She willed herself to cry, but the tears never came. Instead a deep and violent anger took their phantom place. She got to her feet, barely remarking how she staggered against the wall, barely noticing the pain all down her back and through her head. She felt her arms – they were there – her legs – the same, still. She could see, and she could hear. She had survived.

Unlike others.

She forced herself towards the inn, stumbling amidst the downcast scene, to a frantic group of people gathering apace outside the entrance. A tall, bewigged man was pushing away a pair of guards, waving his arms in protest, but they bundled him into a waiting carriage and he was soon sped away, leaving the destruction behind. Another man followed in a second carriage, someone she could not make out, while at the centre of the growing crowd, an imposing figure was shouting orders at the guards and the people of the town who had fast become volunteers. Drawing nearer, she could see it was Sir William Calde. His face was bloody, his doublet was torn, but his spirit was utterly intact.

She looked around. To the left of the group, a young woman – a maid, she thought – had draped a shawl around a shaking pair of shoulders, her arm embracing the elderly woman in total disregard to the difference in their class. While the older woman was trembling, the maid was rocking her gently, talking into her ear. She looked up as Mercia approached; Mercia nodded, indicating the maid could see to others who were hurt, for she recognised the woman as Lady Herrick.

She sat beside her and took her hand. 'Lady Herrick. You were inside?'

The ashen-faced woman nodded. 'In a room near the King.' Her eyes watered. 'I am . . . I could have been killed.'

'You are safe now. Whoever has done this will not do the same again.'

'Thank the Lord my Stephen is on his ship.' She took in a

sharp breath and whimpered. 'Sir Geoffrey . . . poor Sir Geoffrey.'

'What happened to Sir Geoffrey—oh.' She stroked Lady Herrick's hand. 'He is gone to our Lord.'

Lady Herrick nodded, then swivelled her head, as if only now noticing Mercia was there.

'Mrs Blakewood? How are you here?' She gulped, her throat doubtless as dry as Mercia's own. 'No matter. Suffice that you have not been blown to nothing by this madman.'

She bit her lip. 'Not madwoman?'

'Would a woman do this?'

'If she had sufficient cause.' Softly, she squeezed her hand. 'Tell me, Lady Herrick, were you with Lady Cartwright? I saw her coming out.'

She shook her head. 'I was in our room – mine and Stephen's. Alone. I was praying, truth be told, that he would be protected in the battle to come. I did not realise I needed to pray for myself.'

'And Cornelia, your niece?' she said quietly.

'Of course not. She has rooms at another inn, I am told, where her husband was staying before he went to sea with the rest.'

'Mercia!' Of a sudden, Sir William was standing above them. 'What are you—are you well?'

'I am,' she said, looking up. 'But Lady Herrick is not. Can she be taken somewhere to rest?'

'The ladies are being cared for in a house just there.' He clicked his fingers and a boy ran up. 'Take Lady Herrick next door,' he ordered. 'And you, Mercia. You had best come with me.'

Handing Lady Herrick to the boy, Mercia followed Sir William across the street, but when she stopped walking, a pain shot through her head and she had to grab at the wall.

Sir William clutched her sleeve. 'Mercia, you are not well. You should follow Lady Herrick.'

'I need but a moment,' she lied, trying to steady her quivering legs. 'Sir William, Virgo must have done this.'

'Virgo? How?'

'She is here, is she not?' Of a sudden a deep irritation overcame her, fuelled by the throbbing in her head. 'A fool idea of the King's to lure her close, was it? To lure me after her also?'

Sir William blinked. 'I scarcely think so, Mercia. He thought there was a chance you might come, with your man in the fleet, and that bringing the women here would lead Virgo to take a risk. But she is only one of his concerns. He thinks more this day on the fleet, or else he did. And it was not his idea to come here.'

'Yet it seems as though that risk has truly been taken.' She held her hand to her forehead; the agony came and went, in sharp waves of dizzy torment. 'Where is Cornelia Howe?'

'Why her?'

'That inn has been blown away by an explosion of gunpowder – hidden in the cellar, yes?'

'It would seem so.'

'Then even if Lady Herrick set the fuse without being noticed, she could not have returned to her room in time. And I saw Lady Cartwright come out of hers myself.' She coughed, banging on her chest. 'Please, where is Mrs Howe?'

He did not seem to be listening. 'You were in the inn, Mercia?'

'I was carrying out my task. God's truth, Sir William, I have been out to the fleet.'

'What?'

'Never mind that now. Cornelia Howe – find out where she might be!'

The urgency of her words made him sweep round and hurry into the wreck of the inn. As she waited for his return, she supported herself on the wall, catching her aching breath. The smell of powder filled the darkening air, and smoke still rose high over the surrounding buildings. Everywhere she looked, people were wailing or shouting, but most were also helping: tending to those who were hurt, or forming a chain to pass buckets down the line until the man at the end could hurl water on the flames. All except a figure on the opposite side of the street, but when Mercia looked again, the figure had gone.

Sir William was back. 'The Howes were staying at the Tar and Feathers,' he said. 'On the edge of town, down the street over there. I had best go for you.'

'No,' she objected. 'You are needed here.'

'Mercia, I—'

'Look around you, Sir William. There is no time to debate it.'

'Then I will send someone else.' He beckoned over a guard dressed in the King's livery. 'Powell, I have a task for you. Go to the Tar and Feathers and see if Cornelia Howe is in her room. If she is, bring her to me. If she is not, find out where she is.'

The guard hesitated. 'I don't know who that is.'

'God's wounds, man, ask the innkeeper there! Someone will know.'

The guard saluted and set about his orders. Mercia made to follow but Sir William grabbed her arm.

'Not this time, Mercia. The guard will see to it. And if you will not follow Lady Herrick, then sit down here and rest a while. You are not well.'

'Sir William, I am quite . . .' She held her forehead as the pain raced through the back of her eyes. A ringing was filling her ears, and a nausea was rising through her chest. 'Very well. But five minutes only.'

'You need five days, more like.'

He turned aside as another guard ran to seek his advice. Mercia eased herself down on the edge of the street, and as she sat, her head swam, blurring her vision. Ignoring the filthy surroundings, she lowered her head as much as she could, closing her eyes and taking deep, slow breaths. A tiredness almost took her, but she kept herself awake, and soon the nausea had passed, although the pain in her temples was stubborn.

An approaching scuffle of boots made her open her eyes, and she lifted her head to see the guard Sir William had dispatched running towards them, alone.

'Well?' said Sir William.

'Mrs Howe is not there. The innkeeper said she left two hours ago.'

'Did you look in her room?'

'It is empty. It seems when her husband left for the fleet, she left at the same time.'

'To go where?' said Mercia, forcing herself to speak. 'There was not much between here and Colchester, as I recall.'

'In two hours, she could not ride far,' said Sir William. 'There are likely other inns on the road, but . . . I do not know.' He nodded at the guard. 'You may go.'

A sickening thought struck her. 'What if . . . what if Cornelia left her inn, came to set the explosion, and killed herself with it?'

'Deliberately?' He frowned. 'Why?'

'Not deliberately. If she made a mistake with the powder, it could have exploded when she did not wish it. She will not have been trained in its usage. Then again, she could have set the fuse and escaped in the aftermath.'

He was shaking his head. 'I do not know the woman, Mercia, but I do not think she could have done this.'

'Why not? Someone did.'

'Perhaps the other spy? Gemini?'

'I do not think Gemini was in the town.' She rubbed the dust from her eyelashes. 'Whoever it was, they had to get the powder into the cellar. I doubt they could have done that without collusion from within the inn itself. I should arrest that innkeeper and make him speak.'

'I think I had best arrest all the inn.'

'Those that live.' Suddenly the tears came all at once; her whole body heaved as she cried out a painful sob.

'Mercia . . .' Sir William crouched down and rested a hand on her arm. 'Oh, Mercia. Please, go to where the women are being cared for.'

She shook her head, ignoring the pain as she forced the tears to stop. 'No! Virgo must be caught.'

'You said yourself, she might be dead.'

'We need to be certain.' She pointed behind him. 'And you have guards that require your attention.'

He looked round. 'You are right. But please, join Lady Herrick. I will be back for you as soon as I can.'

With a squeeze of her arm, he got to his feet and disappeared into the carnage. Forcing herself up in her turn, Mercia moved away down the street to escape the roar of the fiercest noise, and began to pace.

'Think,' she said to herself, caring little if anyone could see her. 'Virgo and Gemini are both in the vicinity of Harwich.' Pace. 'The fleet is about to fight the Dutch, and at the exact same time, the inn where the King is staying is blown up.' Pace. 'Gemini is meant to be aboard the *Royal Charles*, where the Duke of York is commanding.' Pace. 'Thomas Howe is aboard the same ship, and his wife has now gone missing.'

And then she stopped. On her last to and fro, a figure had appeared, blocking the way.

'Scarcely missing,' the figure whispered.

Obscured by the fading light, Cornelia Howe stood directly before her. She looked Mercia in the eye. And then she turned and ran.

Mercia tried to keep up, but it was impossible. Her head throbbed too much, and her legs were weak. Within two streets, she had lost her. But then a silhouette bobbed from behind a storefront ahead, and as if taunting, she waited until Mercia could resume the chase before she sprinted on.

The same happened at the city gate, abandoned of guards now the explosion had drawn them away. In the gateway itself, Cornelia hung back, waiting just long enough for Mercia to draw near. Then she ducked outside the gate, and awaiting Mercia's approach, she strode out once more.

The pain in her head was almost overwhelming, but Mercia made herself run on, or else stumble and walk. She knew she could be staggering into a trap. She knew she should go back for the guards. But she could not put Oli Moss from her mind, and she knew she could not risk Cornelia getting away. So she willed herself on, ignoring the pulses of agony, pursuing Cornelia around the edge of the town. The setting sun was disappearing behind her, and as she rounded a windswept knoll, the shadows that had stretched over the sea before her lengthened until they were gone.

They came out onto a narrow beach to the west of the town. Cornelia had stopped on the edge of the sea, the wind whipping around her dress as the waves splashed almost to her feet. She was standing, looking on, waiting as Mercia neared. Her hands were at her sides, and she appeared tranquil. A boat bobbed in the shallows behind her. Nobody else was about.

Breathing fast, Mercia walked towards her. She made no move to flee.

'Mrs Howe!' she panted. The water lapped calmly on the beach. 'My God, what have you done?'

She was close enough now to see Cornelia's face. And yet where she had expected anger or bitterness, tears were rolling down her cheeks.

'I am sorry, Mrs Blakewood,' she said. Her hood was down, and her unkempt hair lay tossed about her cheeks. 'I did not want to do this. I hope you can forgive me.'

'Forgive you?' A fury rose, threatening to consume her. 'How can I ever do that?'

But then the air sang behind her, a blow struck at her head, and the shore seemed to spin at her feet.

Chapter Thirty-One

She was more drowsy than unconscious. The blow had not hit hard. But she recalled the stones of the beach swiftly coming towards her, the blood rising painfully to her head as she was turned upside down and carried to the waiting boat. She recalled being placed gently inside, two hands taking up two oars, and a dark figure crying on the beach. She recalled the sharp smell of salt and of seaweed, and a picture of smoke rising over the silhouette of a torchlit town. She recalled the breeches, the grunts, the splashes of the oars, the vague memories of a man's voice urging her to be still.

For some minutes, she fell asleep, or maybe an hour – there was no way to tell. Then she was jarred awake as the boat ran aground. She looked up, the scent of the sea stimulating her mind until her vision cleared. The town was now some way distant, on the other side of the black bay. A hand reached down, helping her up, and she stepped from the boat onto a pebbly shore, eyes drawn to a light in a fisherman's hut. Not far off, the shape of a fort sat protecting the harbour, although the defences did not appear substantial.

'Come, Mercia,' said the man. 'Let me take you inside.'

His voice was familiar. 'I should have known when you brought me back. I did know, I suppose. And yet I did not want to believe it.'

'There are more of us than you would think,' he said. 'Come into the hut, and we can talk. I am sorry for our deception. I am more sorry for the blow. But I did not want you to struggle. I am trained . . . it should not have been hard.'

She raised her hand to feel the throb on the back of her head, a dull balance to the sharp pain coursing through the front.

'Hard enough, Mr Malvern. Hard enough.'

He stood back to allow her into the hut. He had no gun to force her, but she doubted he would let her run away, and nor did she have the strength. Besides, she wanted to hear what he had to say. Needed to, more like.

The hut was simple, a table and stools, a selection of fishing tackle stacked in a corner. A single candle was set on the table, its flame lending the shelter an eerie appearance.

'Is someone here before us?' she asked.

He smiled. 'Will you sit? I think you should need to.'

'Still refusing to answer my questions, I see. But you are right about needing the stool.' She collapsed onto the nearest. 'And yet wrong about so much else.'

'Why say that?'

'Setting powder to fire an inn. The murder of innocents. I should say that was wrong, if wrong is sufficient a description.'

'Here.' He reached behind him for a hidden tankard, filling it from a pitcher of ale. 'You must be thirsty.'

She took the beaker and set it on the table.

'It is not poisoned, Mrs Blakewood. And I am as pained about the inn as you are.'

'Curious, when it was you who set it. Or perhaps that was Cornelia? Tell me, how did you meet?'

'In a roundabout fashion. But Cornelia is not the person you think she is. Neither am I.'

Again, the anger pulsed through her mind. She bore the pain, because she had to.

'Then explain how the innkeeper's son is lying dead in his father's yard. Explain how Sir Geoffrey Allcot is pulled from his room, slain. Explain how a knife found its way into Julien Bellecour's neck.'

He looked away. 'Julien Bellecour was unfortunate. There is only one person we ever intended to kill. At least at the start.'

'Then I suggest you begin there. At the start.'

'I do not know as I can.' He sighed. 'But now I fear our long-held plans may be lost. It depends on what happens tonight.'

'Tonight?'

'At the fleet.'

'Where you should be, should you not?'

'I shall row the boat out soon. If it is to be the last time I serve, then I will take comfort in knowing I did my duty. I hope we may yet succeed in at least one significant part.'

'You speak in riddles, Mr Malvern. I thought you wished to talk.'

'I wish I could.'

'Then let me talk for you. You said Thomas Howe worked for you, but in what? In your role as the King's spy, or your role aiding the Dutch? Are you Gemini, or is he?'

He took in a long breath. 'We both are.'

'What does that mean?'

'That Gemini is both of us. It makes sense, once you realise.'

'Both of you?' She closed her eyes. 'Of course. The sign of Gemini is that of the twins. Two men, indeed. A jest as part of the deception?'

'It was Virgo's idea. Howe and I are not related, but she chose that name as she chose her own. I suppose in a way she bewitched us. We had our ideas, and then she came. I did not know she would take her revenge to such extremes as to destroy the inn.'

'Wait. That was not part of your plot?'

'Plot? I suppose you could term it that. But you should know, neither Howe nor I would betray our country to the Dutch.'

'Then you have a peculiar loyalty, Mr Malvern. Are you a Quaker too?'

'No. But Thomas's beliefs are what sustain him.'

'And Virgo?'

'Not as such. But you can speak with her yourself. When she arrives I shall return to the fleet and face whatever judgement God might impart.'

He got to his feet and opened the door. A swift breeze rattled in, bearing the whinnying of a horse.

'Yes,' he said. 'I think I see her riding now. She likes that. She says it helps her think.'

'She could not fit in the boat with us?'

'She was not on the beach. She had already come across.'

'Then what of Cornelia?' She pushed off the table, rising almost to stand.

'All Cornelia ever wanted was to help her husband. She has no true part in this.'

'Then why did she go to the stables in Southwark?'

'How do you know of . . . ?' Softly, he laughed. 'I meant what I said on the ship before, when we were on the *Royal Charles*. You are good at this.'

'Do not seek to flatter me. Answer my question.'

'Cornelia went because Thomas asked her to.' He turned his head. 'I had to kill Bellecour. There was no choice.'

'Why not?'

'I fear because of you. When your man went into the whorehouse, Bellecour realised he was being watched. When you gave me the papers Wildmoor found, I thought a disaster had been averted. But when you had gone, I searched again for Bellecour, fearing what he had seen. But he was waiting in the shadows, observing. There was a . . . confrontation. I panicked, I suppose. Me. But there was no time to remove the corpse. I had to make it look like a common murder.'

'And Cornelia?'

'Thomas made her go back a few days after to find out if anyone had seen. He never told her why, but she did it all the same.' He shrugged. 'She loves him, Mrs Blakewood. They argue and they fight, but she loves him, as he loves her.'

By now she could hear the rider reining in her horse. 'What of tonight? Why did Cornelia lead me to you?'

'Because you had found her husband out. You told me you suspected he was Gemini. And more, I was wary of what . . . Virgo had planned. I was waiting as long as I could, and I asked Cornelia to do the same. When the explosion happened, I knew my fears had been realised, and that in time you might deduce it all. I wanted to speak to you first. And so I sought Cornelia's help.'

'So she is not Virgo. Then who?'

'Can you not guess?'

Falling back in her seat, she clutched at her aching head: if anything, the pain was getting worse.

'I thought she was one of five, but . . . not Lady Herrick, or Lady Cartwright, for I saw them in the inn after it was fired. Not

Lady Allcot, nor Lavinia Whent, because Bellecour's final message to the Dutch spoke of them as separate. Not Cornelia Howe, because you say not.'

'Because I say not,' he repeated. 'As I said not about another before.'

She rubbed at her forehead, trying to think. Then she jerked up her head and regretted it.

'God's truth! It was you, was it not, who gave me the translation of Bellecour's final note?'

He nodded. 'It was my role to follow Bellecour and collect whatever notes he left. My role as the King's spy, that is.'

'An expedient role, all told. I cannot imagine that was chance.'

'No doubt. But in the plot, as you term it, things were similar. Virgo gave him a wealth of information, to convince him she was sincere. He left his summaries at the whorehouse, thinking a Dutch spy would come to take them. But instead it was me. I took his notes and burnt them, leaving a shortened account for his true associate, with enough detail so the Dutch would not suspect. You must understand, we never wanted to aid them as much as to use them for ourselves.'

'But why go through Bellecour at all? Why not simply pass the information straight to the Dutch?'

'To cover ourselves if ever we were found out. We knew Bellecour had spied for them before. So we used him for our own ends, ensuring he would be the one to take the blame if things went wrong . . . until he realised the truth.'

'My God.' She looked up. 'Then I know who Virgo is.'

'I do not doubt it. And now, come to greet her. She is here.'

A figure passed behind him, pausing in the doorway. A woman, familiar, whom she had not seen for some days.

'Good evening, Mercia,' she said. 'It is pleasing to see you again.'

'I am not so sure.' For that instant, all the pain besetting her counted for naught. 'I am not so sure . . . Lavinia.'

'Do you like my new rooms?' Lavinia Whent walked into the hut, dropping onto a stool as she set the gun she was carrying at her feet. 'I found this shelter unused. It is not quite the palace, but it provides a dry place to hide – and now to talk. Did you really not guess until now?'

'Your deception fooled me,' Mercia replied. 'Or Mr Malvern's did. For a moment, at the house in Harwich, when he showed me the door to the cellar, I thought he might be involved. I should have listened to my instinct.'

'But me?' Lavinia was looking on with interest. In contrast to the fine attire she always wore at the palace, her outfit tonight was simple and black. 'You never guessed about me?'

'Thanks to Mr Malvern's ruse. You have a good ally, Miss Whent.'

'I told you before to call me Lavinia.'

'I am not certain I can. It was you who set the explosion at the inn?' She remained silent.

'Answer her, Lavinia,' said Malvern. 'I should like to know more of what happened myself.'

'I told you I would do it,' she said, looking away. 'Why so surprised?'

'Because we ordered you not to. We hoped you would have learnt the sense to behave.'

Lavinia laughed. 'See how he speaks to me, Mercia, as if I am not a woman, but a thing to coerce. Giles, why do you think I joined you in the first place? I told you I would get what I wanted, as you will get what you want later tonight.'

'If you have not ruined the whole business.'

'Giles. And here I was thinking you cared.'

'I do care.' His eyes quivered. 'You know I do.'

Mercia looked from the one to the other, at the unspoken messages passing between them. 'Do not tell me you two are together?'

'Scarcely,' said Lavinia. 'We have shared a bed, that is all.' She rested an elbow on the table, her long fingers dangling down. 'Poor Giles thinks it should be more than that. But he is married and so . . . that is that.'

Mercia looked at him. 'I did not know you were married. All that talk in the eating house . . . that was a pretence also.'

He managed a smile. 'It was no pretence to call you beautiful.'

'You called her that?' said Lavinia. 'Well, you are right, she is. I hope I look the same when I reach her age.'

'I am scarce ten years older, nothing more. But you will not reach it if you have killed those innocents tonight.'

'Innocent?' She narrowed her eyes. 'What is innocence?'

'Lavinia.' Malvern came round to her. 'I must return to the fleet. Already I have spent too long away. You will have to keep Mrs Blakewood company until all is over.'

'And then?' she said.

'We will see. It may not matter that she knows.'

'I agree, but . . . she is the only one who knows of my part. The only one who knows of yours.'

'Of our part, yes. The conspiracy could have held, but . . . damn it, Lavinia! Why did you have to fire that inn?'

'I did not. Not directly. Something must have happened when those men were storing the barrels in the cellar. I was not even there when the explosion occurred.'

'A nice distinction,' said Mercia. 'Which men?'

'There were two of them, I think. They took some powder that had been left for them on the shore. A lot of money, besides. I think because their master was always demeaning them. Still, their incompetence sealed their fate.'

Malvern stared. 'They could only have gotten that powder from Thomas. He assisted you in this?'

Lavinia glanced at Mercia. 'Then she knows about . . . ?'

'About Thomas, yes.'

'Oh. Then yes, he left the powder.'

'But he said he would not! Hell's teeth, why?'

'Because he agreed with me, Giles. Because he was fed up with you . . . giving him orders.'

He set his face. 'If ordering is striving to keep the plan intact, then yes, I ordered.'

'Giles, you worry too much.' She shooed him away with a flap of her wrist. 'And you will be late back to the fleet. I will oversee matters here.'

'Will you?'

'Yes. And Giles. Do not fret. All will be well.'

He took a long look at her and sighed. Then he reached his lips towards her cheek, but she shook her head. Pulling back, he smiled sadly at Mercia and left without further word.

'Finally,' said Lavinia. 'Why do men think they must be needed?'

'That depends on the man,' Mercia replied. 'It seems Mr Malvern is needed by you.'

'He will get what he wants. Thomas will ensure it.'

'He means to kill the Duke of York?'

'Very good, Mercia.' Her animated face appeared pleased. 'So you know.'

'Some of it. I do not know why.'

'You seem quite calm about it.'

Renewed pain throbbed through her head, but she was battling to hide it. 'Lavinia, there is nothing I can do. I must leave preventing that to others.'

'Like your man?' She laughed. 'Rest assured, Mercia, no one is in danger of Thomas save the Duke. And even he need do nothing if the Dutch play their part. Either way, the Duke will not return from the battle alive.'

'The Dutch play their part?'

'Virgo – that is, I, have told them precisely how the fleet will assemble. Which ship will line up next to which, and on which the Duke will serve. Where he will stand on deck as the Dutch cannonball flies across to strike him dead.'

'That is your plan?' scoffed Mercia. 'How can they know where on deck he will be? They have some special telescope?'

'He will be encouraged to stand in a certain, exposed place. His pride will compel him.' She stood and mocked a salute. 'All hail glorious James, splendid Admiral of the fleet!' She smiled. 'He will wear the sash he is given, because he trusts the man who will give it, the gleaming, new sword, and when the Dutch are in place, they will recognise his vain decorations, they will aim and they will strike.' She jiggled her head. 'Of course, the Dutch think we mean to help them win the battle. Whereas all Giles wants is to eliminate the Duke, by making his death appear an accident of war.'

'Meaning no one in your group need be blamed.' She found herself nodding. 'Most ingenious, if it works.'

'And if it does not, your man Wildmoor will turn his gun on the Duke before he is gunned down himself. I hope it does not come to that, but . . . he has been prepared.'

'What?' Mercia leapt to her feet, and a horse seemed to ride through her head. 'Nicholas will not do that.'

'That depends how loyal he is to you. I should say just about now Thomas is letting him know you are captured and threatened with death if he does not comply.'

'Captured?' She looked at the door. 'I could walk outside now and take your horse.'

'I do not think so.' She took a swig of the ale Mercia had refused. 'There is a man on the beach. If you leave, he will shoot.'

'I am supposed to believe that?'

'Try it, if you wish. I should rather you live, but I can hardly prevent you from seeking your own death.'

Mercia opened the door and looked out. She could no longer see as far as the bay, let alone the town opposite. It was possible a shooter could be lying in wait.

'It matters not,' she said. 'Nicholas would never kill the Duke, not even for me.'

'I think he would. He most certainly would for his daughter.'

'No! You have not taken . . . ?'

'Of course not. But he only knows what he has been told.'

'Let us both hope that is true.'

She shrugged. 'Thomas said he saw you on the ship together. He listened at the door when you were talking. He took your boat to row to Giles to get him to go over and . . . restrain your enthusiasm, shall we say. He says he told him to lock you away, but he obviously did not. Giles is, above all, a man of deep honour. A strength – and a weakness.'

'Then you must know I was accompanied by Henry Raff. What happened to him?'

'I would not be concerned for that preening jackanapes, Mercia. He is often in the Duke's displeasure for the way he behaves, not to mention he has certain secrets he would rather remain unknown.

All Thomas had to do was suggest the Duke might not take kindly to his presence, and that his means off the ship was about to be taken away.'

'But he is safe?'

'On his ship, I should wager. He has no idea about any of us.' She got to her feet, rubbing her arms to ward off the descending chill. 'You may not think so, but this is a noble endeavour. We want to free the country from the tyranny of the Duke. If aught happens to the King, he inherits the throne. We want to prevent that.'

'Mr Malvern has said something similar. Why?'

'For Giles and Thomas, it is because they are convinced the country will prosper without the threat of his rule.' She inclined her head. 'Who is next in line, after?'

'His son, the Duke of Cambridge, who . . .' She nodded, ignoring the flash of pain. 'I see. The baby in whose nursery your own duties fall.'

'They believe that, over time, the young Duke can be raised to be the King his father could never be.' She shook her head. 'Can you imagine England under the Duke of York? A land that countenances despotism, Catholicism . . . the abhorrence of the trade in slaves. If his son were to take in any of his father's bigotry, nothing will change for a generation. But if the child is raised a true Protestant, a believer in the rights of men to live free, then England will thrive.' She smiled. 'That is their argument. Kill the Duke and save the nation.'

'And the current King?'

'Giles is too innocent, but the King profits from the foulness of slavery in the same way his brother does. Only a child untainted by such horrors can end it when he accedes. And so yes, I intended to blow up the King. I intended to blow up the whole vile council. If I did not kill the King, it seems I killed Sir Geoffrey Allcot, the worst of that foul breed. There, at least, I have my revenge.'

'I thought you said this was a noble cause.'

'Satisfaction, revenge, call it what you will. You should see it in the Barbados. Hundreds of children die there, women and men too. Thousands. Solely for being born African.' Her fist clenched. 'It is disgusting, against God. I will no longer see it go unpunished.'

'And you think destroying the men who profit from it, raising the Duke of Cambridge to be different . . . that will set things right. I understand, Lavinia. I do. But death? You have killed innocent men tonight.'

'Are not the men of Africa innocent? Who speaks for them?' She leant on the table, staring into Mercia's eyes. 'You are a woman who has seen something of the world. You know of what I speak. Women like Lady Cartwright think these men are as meaningless as jewels, to be worn as it suits them and then tossed aside, like so much wasted flesh. But not even you know what I have seen!'

'Then tell me,' she said softly.

'I knew a boy, back home, in the Barbados.' She drew herself up. 'When I was fifteen. I knew a beautiful, clever boy, whose crime was to be black. He worked on my father's plantation. We used to talk, when we could, of the sun and the sea, of the plants and the animals and the stars. We danced in the fields and he beat his drum, and we laughed, and we cried, and . . . once we kissed.' Her eyes clouded over. 'But my father had set a woman to watch me. He found out I would talk with this boy, and do you know what he did? He bound his wrists, strung him on a tree, and commanded his men to whip him.' Of a sudden, her fist crashed on the table. 'Not just whip, but mutilate! He made me watch, Mercia. His own daughter! He made me watch, telling me, this is what the blacks are worth, pigs to be hung up for slaughter. He made me watch, blow after blow, until my

378

boy's skin had gone, and all that was left was blood and bone and he was dead.' Her jaw shook. 'He made me watch.'

Mercia swallowed, a mixture of disgust and sorrow joining her throbbing pain. 'Lavinia, I do not know what to say. Truly, no child should have to suffer such a sight.'

'At least I live. They left him hanging to be picked at by birds, rotting in the wind as a lesson to those around him. But still my father was not finished, for he rounded up my boy's friends, and he put them in a line, and he ordered his men to shoot them, the one after the other, for having kept his secret. And what was his secret?' She beat at her chest. 'He had talked with me. He had beaten his drum with me. What is wrong with that?'

She took a deep, hysterical intake of breath. Despite all she had done that night, Mercia reached out her hand.

'Lavinia. I am here. Please, try to be calm.'

'How can I be calm?' She flung away Mercia's hand. 'How can I be calm, when I am born to a race that thinks itself better, when all those who rule it are the worst kind of evil! My father sent me back to England to learn from my own kind. But it is they who will learn from me. I will kill them all if I can!'

Her whole body was trembling. Mercia looked at her pale face, and felt pity.

'Lavinia,' she said. 'You do not mean that. Murder is not the means of assuaging murder. Think on your own soul. The cycle of death has to stop somewhere.'

'Not with me.' Violently, she shook her head. 'Thomas understands. He is close with the Quakers, do you know that? That is where I met him, at a meeting of such folk. I am not sure I am one myself, but . . . they understand. Or at least, Thomas does.'

'You met him first, before Malvern?'

'Thomas and Giles knew each other from their service in the fleet. It was in that service when they sailed to the Guinea coast, on a mission against the Dutch, where they found the forts crawling with terrified Africans and saw them being forced onto those . . . trading ships. They were appalled at it, and grew ever more appalled as they talked on the long voyage home. They thought it was . . . not English, but not many would listen. And they saw the Duke of York planning to increase his disgusting profit, and they resolved to prevent it.' She grabbed Mercia's hand. 'You see, this is a noble cause. Once the Duke is dead, and the King, the child will inherit and see the truth!'

'Perhaps,' said Mercia. 'Or perhaps that is merely an ideal. Where the Duke of York and Sir Geoffrey Allcot fall, others will take their place. Wealth, Lavinia, is what encourages these men. They care nothing for who suffers.'

'Have more faith, Mercia. Or at least, say nothing of us. Let us succeed!'

'Lavinia, murder is never the way, whatever the reasons.'

'Not even for this?'

'Not when there is a young man in a Harwich inn who is dead tonight.' She closed her eyes. 'I knew nothing of the world until I saw it. I knew nothing of the peoples that live in it. But then I travelled the ocean, and saw the smallest amount, and now I know. That is how you change things, Lavinia. By talking to people, by sharing the truth and convincing them of its worth. Not by killing and death!'

'Then you are against us.'

'It is not as simple as that.'

'It is to me.' She reached down for the gun she had dropped when she arrived. 'The powder may have failed at the inn, but I will not fail now. When the Duke falls this night, so too will his brother. He must.' She nodded to herself. 'Events must be forced, to make matters right. But I cannot leave you here. You will have to come with me.'

'Lavinia, please,' she begged. 'Think on what you do.'

'Oh, I have. Ever since the martyring of my beautiful boy. My Charles.' Waving her pistol, she beckoned Mercia to follow her out. 'Strange, no? That he shares his given name with the King? And now the King will join him in the places beyond, although he shall not go to heaven. If he thinks this night to elude the death of which I have long dreamt, he is mistaken.' She stepped onto the beach. 'Come, Mercia. Come and watch me kill the King.'

Chapter Thirty-Two

A hidden wave crashed against the beach. Leaves rustled in the unseen trees.

'Lavinia,' implored Mercia, following along the shore. 'Please stop this.'

Lavinia tightened her grip on her gun. 'Have you forgotten that man on the beach? All I need do is call out and he will come.'

'I doubt that. There is no man, is there?'

There was no reply.

'Then where are we going? Lavinia! Put down that gun and let us continue to talk.'

'Why?' She swivelled round. 'Stay back. I should rather not waste my shot.'

Mercia looked at the pistol. It was difficult to make out now it was dark, but it did not seem to be cocked. It may not have even been loaded, but for the moment, she did not want to take that chance.

'Then tell me what you intend,' she said.

Lavinia gestured in front of them. 'Over there is a fort. Landguard, it is called. Giles says it is due for repair, but for now, it is little more than so much crumbling earth and splintering wood. Yet that is where the King was taken after he was swept from the inn.'

'How do you know this?'

'Suffice that I do. Whenever the King leaves London, there is always some device planned to rush him away should his whereabouts turn unsafe. The powder may have failed, but this is more pleasing. I shall be able to see him as I shoot.'

'Lavinia.' Mercia was panting, struggling to keep up. Her whole body was aching, and the nausea had returned. 'If you kill the King, you will burn for treason. And not only that.'

'It does not matter. Things will only change if people take notice. I intend to make them take notice.'

'You will be portrayed as a madwoman. A madwoman who will be burned at the stake, most like not even strangled to ease your pain, on view for all the mob to despise. How does that help your poor boy?'

'Then I will die as he did, in defiance of those who would deem his death right.'

'Lavinia, you will not even—'

'No more talking. Else I call for the shooter.'

They fell silent, continuing along the seafront. Not far out over the waves, a lost gull called its monotonous cry, adding its low pitch to the whispering of the sea. Holding herself together, Mercia stumbled over pebbles until soon a dark structure loomed into view, lit here and there by a number of quivering torches. Lavinia sidled behind an outcrop of rock, signalling that Mercia join her.

'That is Landguard,' she said. 'Just inside, a tent has been erected for the King's accommodation. He was to come here tomorrow to witness the battle, as much as he could until the fleets sail further out. But now he has arrived sooner, and so have I.'

'Lavinia, this is madness. You will not be able to walk in there and shoot the King! He will be guarded.'

She gripped the rock with one hand, her pistol with the other. 'Most of his guard remains at the inn in Harwich, ordered to deal with the explosion. The purpose at Landguard is not to guard the King, but to hide him somewhere safe. Or where he thinks is safe.' She brandished her gun. 'And so we wait until he comes out.'

'What, out here?' Mercia looked around; the only land between their outcrop and the fort was an exposed segment of shoreline. 'Why should he do that?'

'Because this is the best view of the bay. He is a man, Mercia. When the battle starts, he will come out to watch. And that, I am told, will be just before dawn.'

'I still do not know how you know all this.'

'No?' She smiled. 'I am sure you will work it out.'

They waited the long hours in silence. Mercia's headache had grown steadily worse; perhaps she had inhaled more smoke than she had thought. Her eyes were continually drooping, and from time to time she was sure she fell asleep. But every time she came round, Lavinia was alert, a focussed zeal in her eyes she recognised well enough from others she had known before.

'Why Virgo?' she said of a sudden, to try to keep awake.

'What?'

'Why choose that for your code name?'

'Why not?' Lavinia never wavered from her watch. 'Because it amused us. I am an unmarried maiden, so Virgo. Giles and Thomas together make Gemini.'

'And yet . . . you are hardly a maiden, Lavinia.'

She laughed. 'You will not rile me into giving this up. I am what my father's attempts to constrain my life have made me.'

'Then do not let your father destroy your life now.'

'I shall see my father in hell. I shall enjoy watching his torment.'

A brief quiet descended. From the fort, the wind carried over snatched murmurs of activity. The half-moon shone its rays across the silvered shore. Mercia's head felt as though the powder from the inn had been exploded in her mind itself, but she could see no other recourse than to try to keep Lavinia talking. At the least, she might learn more.

'When you were with Bellecour,' she tried again. 'When you passed him your information. Were you learning all you knew from Sir Peter Shaw?'

'Does it matter?'

'It matters when Sir Peter is still in the Tower. It could be the difference between his survival and his execution.'

'Do you think I much care?' She sighed. 'No, he is no part of this. But he is a foolish and lonely man. It is very easy to make such men speak when they feel flattered. Especially an older man who is scared he has lost his appeal.'

Mercia sidled an inch closer. 'And yet I cannot imagine he told you whatever you asked. I begin to think there may be another involved in your scheme.'

Lavinia's eyes were ever forward. 'Do you?'

'Because 'tis convenient, is it not, that you have a position in the Duke of Cambridge's nursery? If his father is killed in battle then 'tis nobody's fault, and as he grows up, he thinks nothing but good on all those who helped him. Men never forget those who were kind to them as a boy.'

'I suppose not.'

'And when he is older, and needs male tutors? I wager someone is already thought of for that task. And who will rule the regency while he is a child? Someone must.'

'Those matters are not for me to choose.'

'Then let us consider Mr Malvern. 'Tis convenient, too, that he was the very man tasked with following Bellecour. And Mr Howe, granted at some short notice a commission aboard the Duke's very flagship. It seems to me, Lavinia, that someone most elevated must be complicit in this endeavour. I wonder.' She grabbed her pounding head: her hypotheses were making her mind hurt. 'When you were arrested, how were you so easily released?'

'You need speak of arrest.' Finally, she turned to face her. 'I have known why you are at Whitehall for longer than you probably assume. We have suspected it ever since the death of Lady Allcot. You think we did not question her murder?'

'It was you who made it appear she was Virgo. My uncle has told me of the letter he was left. Clever, Lavinia, until it led to her death.'

For an instant, she glanced down, but not long enough: no chance for Mercia to seize her gun. 'That . . . was not meant to happen. We knew Bellecour was hoping to use her, in the same way he thought he was using me. It would have been a useful distraction if ever he had been caught. But . . . I did not realise your uncle was so taken with his hatred for you that he would kill her. I am still not sure I know why. But it meant we discovered your involvement.'

'So it seems. But I think there was someone pleading your case, when you were taken yourself. In the end, that piteous confession too must have been a sham, designed to throw your pursuers until it was too late. And . . . oh!' She clutched at her head. 'How it hurts . . .'

She fell back against the rock, fighting to settle her wild breathing. Lavinia looked to the fort, and they spoke no more.

A thunderous roar ripped apart the night. In and out of troubled sleep, or troubled unconsciousness, Mercia jumped. Out at sea, bright lights shot across the sky, and a series of frenzied, cacophonous bangs rent the air itself.

'It has started,' said Lavinia.

'Dear God,' said Mercia. 'Let those men survive.'

The clamour was unbearable. Fire swarmed the dark, sparks of orange and white bursting from a thousand cannon. The fleet was too far out to see the ships themselves, but that scarcely seemed to matter.

Mercia winced at the pain racing through her. 'The noise! They will hear this in London.'

'Perhaps it will serve to wake them from their slumber. And look, I was right. Here they come.'

As hell rained down at sea, a group of figures poured from the fort, heading for the spot opposite. Torches bobbed in their midst, and as they drew closer, a tall man at their centre came into view – the King, a number of his guards around him. But in the din of the battle, they were less concerned with keeping close than with running to the shore.

'May God have mercy on us,' she thought she heard him say.

And then as the King was looking out to sea; as his guards were dodging each other in the hopes of an impossible view; as the cannons roared their power across the burning night – Lavinia stole from behind the outcrop and began to creep towards him.

Mercia jumped to follow, but she almost fainted, her head hammering with the ferocity of what had happened that night. She opened her mouth to call out, but nothing sounded but an agonised croak. The more she tried to raise her voice, the hoarser it became.

'Lavinia,' she rasped. 'No!'

Voice muted, she had little option but to try to run. Ignoring the rush of dizziness without and within, she pushed from the outcrop and pursued as swiftly as she was able. But the gap between them did not lessen, and by now Lavinia was in range of the King.

And still, all his guards were looking out to sea. Still, the violence of the cannon fire was masking Lavinia's approach. Still, Mercia pressed on, calling on the depths of her strength to grant her one last effort. Then as an enormous bang seemed to split earth from sky, Lavinia raised her arm and cocked her gun.

Finally, the nearest guard turned his head and swore. But by then it was too late. The King was directly in her sight.

'Stay back,' she ordered, although it was uncertain who could hear. 'Stay back!' she repeated, louder now, as a second's silence calmed the sea. The guard held up his hands in a signal of compliance and moved away.

Her finger was on the trigger, but she did not fire. As the rumour of her presence made its fast circuit, the King turned from the sea-fire and seemed to gasp, standing utterly still. Then the guard beside him raised his musket, but Lavinia thrust out her pistol and he was ordered to hold.

As battle raged behind them, nothing further happened. Guards held steady their weapons. One or two were cocked. And then the cannons fell momentarily silent.

'Miss Whent,' called the King, his voice carrying on the wind. 'Put down the pistol, and we can talk. See, my guards are lowering their own.'

'He is not,' she shouted back, aware of the soldier beside him.

'Then it is one against one. Let you both disarm together, and we shall talk.'

'Do as he says,' said Mercia, now within reach, coming as close to Lavinia as she dared.

The King flinched. 'Mrs Blakewood!'

'Lavinia,' she said, ignoring him. 'Please, do as he says.'

She held her weapon steady. 'Come nearer, Mercia, and I will fire.'

Mercia held up her hands and backed slowly away. Out at sea, the ships remained mute.

'The fleets will be sailing in lines,' called the King. 'Taking the measure the one of the other. But battle will soon recommence. There is some little time to talk.'

'You will not shoot,' said Mercia, her eyes on Lavinia. 'Do you want the others to be taken? Because I know now, Lavinia. I know and I will speak.'

'Then I shall kill you next.'

'You know you have only one shot.'

'Do you not recall the man at the beach? He is still here, Mercia. He has followed us.'

'I do not think so. Please, put down the gun.'

Lavinia's jaw began to shake, and her eyes grew fearful. Her free hand curled up into her side.

'You have changed your mind, I can see,' said Mercia, arresting her retreat and daring a step forward. 'You can stop in this course. Please, throw down the gun and you will be given your chance to speak. Your chance to explain.'

'How?' she said. 'I have come too far. My God. I have . . . come too far.'

'Then ease the burden on your soul, at least.' Her head feeling as though it would shatter, Mercia walked round to put herself directly before the King. 'Beseech God to save it.'

'No!' said the King. Urgently, he signalled to the guard to lower his gun. 'Do not risk yourself!'

'She trusts me,' said Mercia, looking only at Lavinia. 'She trusts me, and she will do as I ask.'

Lavinia's arm was still outstretched. 'Mercia, I no longer have a choice. I should rather revenge my boy than betray him now.'

'But Lavinia, you are no traitor. Not to your boy, not to the King, not to yourself. You are a woman overwhelmed with sadness at the horrors you have witnessed. I understand. But please, put that fury to better use than this. Please, Lavinia. Lower the gun.'

A tear dropped onto her face. 'Move away.'

'Lavinia, please. This is not the answer.'

'I said, move aside!'

Somewhere to Mercia's right, she heard the renewed cocking of a gun. Frantic, she raised her hand towards it.

'No,' she said. 'No, wait!'

She glanced aside to see the guard lower his barrel. Then she turned back to Lavinia to resume her attempt.

'Lavinia, I will not let you kill this man. This King. I know why you wish it, and I believe you think yourself right, but please. Tell him your grievance. Tell everyone. If you kill him, all that will happen is you will burn, a traitor indeed. A regicide, the same as the men who killed his father before him.'

'But they were heroes, were they not?'

Her aim faltered, dropping a half-inch. In the corner of Mercia's eye, she saw the guard again raise his gun.

'It could all be different,' she said. She realised her whole body was trembling, and she sobbed as she managed a smile. 'Do not be remembered this way.' She took a step forward, and behind her, the King gasped. 'Please, Lavinia. Lower your gun.'

Lavinia blinked. Tears were now running down her face, just as they were starting down Mercia's own. She hesitated, her hand shaking on her gun. And then she lowered her arm.

'Thank you, Lavinia.' Mercia put a hand to her mouth. 'Oh, dear God. Thank you.'

Lavinia nodded. All around, the guards seemed to relax.

'I am sorry, Mercia,' she said.

Mercia held out her hand. 'That is no matter. Give me the gun.'

'I mean I am sorry I cannot do as you wish.'

With unnatural dexterity, she jumped to Mercia's right and raised her gun once more.

'For my boy!' she cried. 'For my boy Charles, more worth to be a king than anyone!'

With a scream of pain, Mercia leapt towards her. The guard to her right aimed his gun and fired.

The shot rang through the air. Lavinia's arm jerked, her pistol spiralling to the ground.

And Mercia . . . Mercia fell beside it, clutching at her side as blood began to pour from the gash in her dress. Feeling faint, and scared, she looked up to see the guards surrounding Lavinia, until they faded into a blur. And then a face peered down, or what she thought was such, the King's it seemed, but how could that be? He reached behind to ease her close, tearing at her dress to try to staunch her wound.

'Mercia,' he said. 'Dear God. Brave Mercia.'

She stared into his eyes. She managed a terrified smile. And then she tumbled once more into the clawing realms of darkness, certain she would never again wake.

Chapter Thirty-Three

'She is up! Nicky, she is up!'

There was a bright, white light. A cannon was roaring through her head. And she thought she could hear a child's voice.

'Mamma, you are awake!'

The room came into focus. There was a pleasant breeze wafting through an open window. On the other side, the chants and cries of the city sounded out. A church bell rang, she thought.

'God's truth.' She clasped her head as she attempted to sit. A small hand appeared, grasping her arm.

'Mamma! Hurrah, Mamma!'

'Danny?' She turned her head to look at him, but then winced at the pain in her side. 'Danny, is that you?'

'Yes, Mamma. And here is Nicky too!'

'Nicky?'

'He's started to call me that.' A man's voice cut in; in the corner, he rose from a chair. 'I thought you were going to sleep forever.'

'Nicholas! I wish I still could sleep. But . . . I was in Harwich. I was . . .' She looked down at her side.

'The King's guards tied a tourniquet.' He looked at Daniel. 'It was only a graze.'

'And the King?'

'He's well, as far as I know.'

She fell back. 'Thank the Lord.'

Daniel was dancing around her bedside. 'Mamma, are we going home now? Someone said we are.'

'They did?' She tried to smile. 'Danny, could you wait outside for me a moment?'

He pulled a face. 'You only just woke up.'

'Please.' She squeezed his hand. 'I need to speak with – Nicky. Just five minutes.'

'Very well.' He mocked a sigh and skipped through the door, shutting it behind him.

'Was that a fake sigh?' she asked, staring after him.

'I think it was,' said Nicholas. 'Best get him away from Whitehall as soon as you can.'

She looked up at him. 'Thank you.'

'For what?' He came beside her. 'I wasn't even there.'

'You are here now. That is what matters. And I do not think this was merely a graze.'

He sighed.

'Now you are doing it.'

'It was more than a graze,' he admitted. 'A few inches to the left, and . . . But you will recover.'

'How did I get here?'

'You were kept at Harwich for a while. I stayed with you, when I got off the ship. Then they put you in a coach and brought you back here.'

'I remember none of that.'

'You wouldn't. You've been in and out of sleep all the while.'

'And Lavinia?' A sadness filled her mind. 'I remember her, at least.'

'She's in the Tower. I'm afraid . . . I wouldn't hold out much hope.'

Lavinia's terrified face seemed to float before her. 'Why is it when women – when men – are scarred by life as she was, then they are the ones who must suffer? Yet those who profit from the hatred that drives them live.'

'That's the way of life, Mercia. The question is, how you go about your own.' He smiled at her. 'I don't think you have anything to worry about. Despite your wounds, you seem to be talking quite well already.'

'I do, do I not? It hurts, though, here.' She rubbed at her side. 'I know now how my uncle must have felt when he was run through with that sword in New York.' Uneasy, she bit her lip. 'Do you know what happened to him?'

'In a cell next to Lavinia, I should wager. His wife – your aunt – confessed it all when he came back to the palace, threatening to go out into London to shoot smugglers on sight. I think she feared for his soul. The palace guard had to be sent to restrain him.' He shook his head. 'I can't believe he was working with One-Eye.'

'I think he was mad, in the end. But he has to pay for the death of Lady Allcot.'

'I heard the King was thinking of locking him away. But Lavinia . . . she tried to kill the King. She won't find any mercy.'

The image of the awful night came back to her. 'I am not sure she would have done it, even at the end.'

'Then why did you jump at her?'

'You know of that?'

'It's the talk of the palace. I'm told even Lady Cartwright has had to admit it was brave. That, or foolish.'

'You seem bruised yourself.' Of a sudden she sat up straight, and wished she had not. 'Dear God! The battle! And the Duke!'

Nicholas laughed. 'That's a story for another time. Suffice to say, thanks to your visit I had one eye of my own on Howe, and the other on the Duke.'

'Please, Nicholas, I need to know what happened.'

'Always so curious! At one point in the battle, the Duke came on deck for no particular reason, and I tell you, he nearly died. A cannonball came right over and killed the three men he was standing with – but the lucky bastard lived. Then he's wandering around, covered in gore, throwing up on his precious red sash, and all of a sudden Howe seems to make up his mind and draws a gun. But I was watching him, and so . . . well. He was disarmed.'

'By you?'

'Maybe. But it was too much for the Duke. Later in the battle – which we won, by the by – he had the chance to pursue the Dutch, but instead he turned on his heels and came back to port. I think he was shocked from his skin.'

'Lavinia told me Howe was going to make you kill the Duke, if he had to. She implied they had threatened your daughter.'

'Truly?' He frowned. 'Howe never said a word to me. Perhaps he lost the will, in the end.'

'Or perhaps Lavinia had grown too used to telling lies. Where is Howe now?'

'Locked away too, as is Giles Malvern. I do not fancy their chances either.'

'Cornelia?'

'Why mention her?'

'Oh. Does nobody know?'

He shook his head. 'Howe says he and Malvern acted alone. With Lavinia, I mean.'

'I see.' She looked towards the window, towards the light. 'Then let us say no more about it. But . . . I do not think they acted alone.'

A week later, when she was recovered, she went to see the King. Not during his getting up, or his going to bed, when the people could come. But in a very private room with only herself and one other as witness. A beautiful woman, all silk, radiance, and smiles.

'Mrs Blakewood.' Lady Castlemaine was beaming from ear to ringed ear, animating the fabulous face patch she was wearing: a canary fleeing its cage. 'Come in, come in.'

The King was more decorous. 'Mrs Blakewood. It is gratifying to see you are much improved.'

She tried a curtsey, but she could only manage half of it. 'Thank you, Your Majesty.'

'Please, it must be uncomfortable for you.' He indicated one of his high-backed chairs. 'Will you sit?'

'How fares Your Majesty?' she asked as she complied.

'I am well, thanks to you. Certainly, I am pleased you came to Harwich.'

'The Duke also?'

'He won the battle,' said the King, and that was that.

'Mrs Blakewood,' said Lady Castlemaine. 'I knew I had made the right choice in selecting you for this task. And Lavinia Whent . . . she fooled us both for a time, did she not, but we caught her in the end.'

'Indeed we did,' Mercia replied, looking on through knowing eyes.

The King raised the slightest eyebrow and smiled. 'Well, then,' he said. 'This painting above me hangs where it should, a revolt in the colonies has been averted, I am told, and you have unmasked our spy. A threefold success, Mrs Blakewood. I shall have to consider you in the future for other endeavours.'

Her heart sank, just a little. 'I am honoured, Your Majesty.'

'But for now there is the matter of your manor house.'

Her stomach churned. This was the moment. After all she had done, would he help her, or would he not?

And then he rose. 'Mrs Blakewood, while you were recovering, I instructed the relevant authorities to investigate your claim on the manor house at Halescott, lately belonging to Sir Francis Simmonds, your uncle, and before that, to Sir Rowland Goodridge, your late father.'

She waited.

'I have to tell you, the points of law debated around the ownership of the manor were reportedly of no small interest.' He licked his lips. 'But Sir Francis is now imprisoned for his part in abetting murder, colluding with smugglers, and attempting to thwart the King's will. You, on the other hand, have also colluded with smugglers, which transgression we have seen fit to pardon, given the circumstances in which that collusion arose. And so I have come to a course of action.' He took a slow breath. 'I have decided to appropriate Sir Francis's estates, such as is permitted me by law, including the Halescott manor house – for myself.'

She let out a gasp. She could not help it. Was this how everything was going to end, with the King taking what should be hers?

But he was smiling. 'And so I can inform you, that in view of your service . . . and as soon as the legalities are finalised . . . I shall see fit to transfer the manor and its lands into a trust, for your son, Daniel Blakewood. Such trust to be held by yourself as his guardian until he comes of age.'

For a moment, she could not speak. The strife of the past year came upon her all at once, and just as quickly it was gone. The relief was too intense, the magnitude of her accomplishment too great, and all she could do was nod, battling to hold back the thankful tears. But then she took a deep breath, and she performed her half-curtsey, and she looked at the King who had set her on such trials.

'Thank you, Your Majesty,' she said.

'I hear Daniel performed well with the other boys while he was here,' he continued. 'I shall expect to see him play his part, when he is older.' He pointed to his left. 'Barbara here mentioned something about a title, I believe. Let us see how his mother comports herself in the years to come and . . . we shall see.' He gave her a meaningful glance. 'We shall see.'

'And now you may go,' said Lady Castlemaine. 'You must need to prepare to leave.'

Mercia looked at her patron, recognising the dismissal for what it was. But she was not about to leave just yet.

She bowed. 'There is something else, Your Majesty, if I may be so bold.'

'There was never any fear of you not being so. Please, speak.'

''Tis my maidservant, Phibae. She has served me well these past weeks. If I am to return to the manor, I shall need a new helper. My current maid there is an excellent cook, a marvellous housekeeper, but she is growing old. In such a big house, she will need assistance, at least until I can employ someone else.'

'And you wish this – Phibae, did you say – to provide it?'

'Only if she and her husband are willing, and if she can be released from her duties here.'

'If her mistresses are favourable, I do not see why not. Barbara will insist on it.'

'Thank you, Your Majesty. There is . . . one other thing.'

'Merely one more?' he joked.

'Lady Cartwright has a boy, Your Majesty. Tacitus, her . . . servant of sorts. I should like very much if he could be removed from that service.'

'I cannot speak for Lady Cartwright, Mrs Blakewood. Her business is her own, or her husband's.'

'This is my last petition, Your Majesty, and then I shall cease. I should like his service, also, transferred to me.'

'To you?' He frowned. 'I thought your opinions . . . conflicted with such a request?'

'I know I am unusual in those opinions, but I should like his service all the same. Lady Cartwright has suggested she does not require it for much longer. And I believe she could have compensation, if I may call it that, for losing him?'

'What form of compensation would you suggest?'

'There are enough traitors in the Tower, Your Majesty. There must be some jewels, or some such she would like?'

'Indeed, Charles,' said Lady Castlemaine, a sparkle in her eyes. 'Take the boy and give him to Mrs Blakewood. But let me tell that harlot Cartwright myself. I should so like to see the look on her wounded face.'

She hobbled through the palace, taking in the finery of Whitehall. The scale of what she had achieved refused to sink in, and she was still anxious that the King might change his mind. Only when she had the deeds to Halescott firmly in Daniel's name would she truly be at rest.

Up ahead, a man stepped from a side passage to block her path. She looked up, surprised.

'Mr Raff,' she said. 'I did not think to see you again.'

He bowed. 'I came to see you when you were sleeping, but that maid of yours chased me away. I wanted to beg your forgiveness for leaving you on the ship.'

She pursed her lips, but it was hard to feel animosity. 'It was rather awkward, yes.'

'That rogue Howe said he had to leave on a matter of importance to the Duke. I told him to use another boat, but he said the Duke was on his way there and then, and that he would have to take mine.'

'Was that the reason, Henry?' She raised an eyebrow. 'I was told it might be something else.'

He flushed. 'Well, I . . . perhaps . . . but . . .'

'It scarcely matters, after all that has transpired. Think no more on it.'

'Damn that Howe. But he did say, Mercia, you would not be abandoned. I should never have left you otherwise, believe me. And if I had known what was to come . . . I wish I had struck Malvern down when I had the chance.'

'He fooled us all, Henry. He was in a position of trust, where he could pretend to be something he was not. But there is someone who earned him that position.'

'Oh?'

'You will soon find out.'

'Then I shall wait, intrigued. In the meanwhile, will you let me make up for my lack of chivalry? As you are leaving soon, perhaps a reminder of who I am, and a promise to make amends and to see you again?'

He reached across to pull her towards him, and for a moment she allowed it. But then she pushed away.

'Henry, you must learn you need to ask before you do that.'

'Do I?' He smiled. 'Then you do not like it?'

Her eyes roved his handsome face. 'Some of it, Henry. I shall grant you that.'

* * *

There was one final matter to resolve. Before returning to what would soon no longer be her chambers, she made a detour to a different set of rooms, steeling herself to knock. In spite of what she knew she must do, she felt as little appetite for it as she had for condemning Lavinia Whent. But finally she rapped her knuckles on the wood, and a deep voice within bade her enter.

'Good morrow, Sir Stephen,' she said.

'Mrs Blakewood.' Sir Stephen Herrick, advisor to the King's war council, looked up in some puzzlement. 'What brings you to my apartments?'

She decided not to advance too far into the darkened room: not from fear, but from respect.

'It is over, Sir Stephen. Howe and Malvern are captured and Lavinia is caught. I do not think they will keep their peace for long.'

'And you come here to tell me this.' His eyes darted for an instant to the pistol on his desk. 'Why?'

'I hold you no malice, Sir Stephen. But I have a duty to the King, and . . . I have a duty to Lavinia too. She and her fellows could not have planned their attempt without help.'

'Could they not, indeed?'

'The information she passed from the war council had to come from someone. And I do not think that was Sir Peter.'

He remained silent.

'I think you are too noble to let another man languish in your place,' she continued. 'It would be well if you would speak yourself. But if not, I shall do so for you. I have not told His Majesty yet.'

He turned to look on a portrait of his wife that was hanging beside the window: captured at the age she was now, in a beautiful green dress, with a low, adorned neckline.

'It was worth the gamble, do you not think? Worth the risk that events might have ended differently?'

Her shoulders relaxed, just a little. 'You were careful, 'tis true.'

'But not too careful for you, it seems. The King is right to value your ability.' Unconsciously, he stroked the lion's head that finished the armrest of his chair. 'When did you know?'

'Howe and Malvern served together in the fleet on a mission to Guinea. In Harwich, Lavinia said it was there that their ideals took hold. Your wife once said you had also sailed to the Guinea coast.' She looked at him. 'When you were their captain.'

'Yes.' He sighed. 'That is right.'

'I am willing to wager that what repulsed them repulsed you too. Evening discussions in your cabin over a glass of rum or ale, all three sickened by what you had seen. It would have been a relief to discuss it.'

'It was.' He stroked his chin. 'Our antipathy developed on the voyage home. We came to believe the soul of the nation was in jeopardy. The very idea that the Duke of York could become King . . . it was important to prevent that from ever occurring.'

'It was you, also, who placed Lavinia in the Duke of Cambridge's nursery.'

'Thomas met her at a Quaker meeting, but I suspect you know that by now. He recognised her from Court and they began a friendship. She wanted to be involved, and it was a silly thing, I know, but even at the Duke's young age we thought it prudent he have a loving influence. One he would remain fond of as he matured to his older years, who could speak to him of decency and honour as he grew. Was that so wrong?'

'Not in itself, Sir Stephen. But it was you, also, who secured Howe his commission in the fleet, close to the Duke of York. It was you who earned Malvern his position amongst the King's spies. You have all the right connections at the Admiralty to be able to have done it.'

His eyes turned again to his gun, and now they were full of sorrow. 'Think, Mrs Blakewood, what was at stake. One illness. One successful plot against the King. And the Duke of York with all his bile would have inherited the sacred throne. But only remove him before that occurred, and then his children would inherit. Children who could be raised to know the true meaning of the honour it is to be the English King.'

'I doubt the present King will agree with you.'

'He will take me as a traitor with the rest. He will execute me without hesitation. Still, the throw of the dice was worth it. *Alea iacta est.*'

'Pardon me?'

'*Alea iacta est.* The die is cast. Caesar said it on crossing the Rubicon, before he invaded Rome.'

'You are not Caesar, Sir Stephen. But perhaps you thought to create one.'

'It is what this country needs. An honourable and firm King who will take our nation into the world in defiance of our enemies. An honest ruler, not some hated Catholic. You cannot owe the Duke any love.'

'Perhaps you would have succeeded, had Lavinia not been so intent on her own revenge. She only wanted to take vengeance for the sins she had witnessed in her past.'

'She wanted to destroy anyone involved with the Royal Adventurers. The slaving company, I mean. I did not think she would try it. Perhaps Giles trusted her too much. Perhaps I did.'

'They were sharing a bed.'

'I do not doubt it. There was ever a certain tension between them. And oh, poor Cornelia. She loved her husband too much, I think.' He tugged at his doublet. 'Thank you for coming to speak with me, Mrs Blakewood. I had already made up my mind not to run from what I have done. I was merely . . . preparing myself. But you should know, nor do I lament it.'

'I did not think you would.'

He got to his feet. 'I wish you well, Mrs Blakewood, in your life. I am glad you are to be restored to your manor house. Your father would have been most proud.'

She held his keen gaze, and with a short bow she took her leave.

Thirty seconds later, the gunshot rang out behind his door.

Epilogue

It was truly a beautiful day. The Oxfordshire sun shone down its benevolence as she rode her horse into Halescott. She progressed with Daniel along the lazy street, passing cottages made of the local stone she so loved, its warm orange glow the perfect welcome home.

She reined in her horse, waiting for her followers to catch up. The first to pull alongside was a young, teenage boy, staring in amazement at the village surroundings. More slowly, Nicholas trotted up, bearing Phibae beside him on his horse.

'Very good, Tacitus,' said Mercia. 'You ride that horse well.'

'Thank you, my lady,' he said, his eyes taking everything in.

'So this is it,' said Nicholas, staring just as much. 'What everything has been for.'

She smiled at their excitement. 'Yes. This is Halescott. My home.'

A girl had appeared at a gate behind them. She stared up at Tacitus and frowned, and then her eyes took in Phibae, and Nicholas, and then she looked at Mercia and gasped.

'Mamma,' she called. 'Mamma, 'tis Mrs Blakewood!'

And then the door opened, the mother emerged, and the cries of astonishment began.

She held out her hand to the iron gates, pausing to take her time. She was not about to rush this moment. Taking a steady breath, she pushed, and as the gate squeaked open, she looked up. There, before her, stood Halescott Manor, its doors, its windows, its familiar stone. The gravelled drive, the bushes and the trees. The grand house was empty now, save for one elderly woman, her uncle's tenants dismissed before she had arrived.

She passed in through the gate, relishing the crunch of the gravel beneath her feet, feeling the sun's warmth on her face. She walked slowly, enjoying every second, and it was only the knowledge of the company behind that stopped her falling to her knees to touch this sacred ground. And then the door to the manor threw itself open, and the elderly woman belied her age, hurrying towards her with a tear down her face.

'Mistress!' she cried. 'Oh, mistress! It is so good to see you. And Daniel too – my, you have grown!'

'Bethany.' Mercia opened her arms to embrace her. 'My dear old maid.'

'Mistress, you did it. You won back your manor!'

'Did you ever doubt that I would?'

Bethany reached down to ruffle Daniel's hair. 'I hope you behaved for your mamma, young man.'

'Of course he did,' Mercia beamed.

'And, Mistress, your mother will return next week. As you instructed in your letter.'

'Very good, Bethany. Now allow me to introduce some people.' As Daniel skipped ahead, she turned around. 'First, this is Phibae, who will be joining us at the manor for a while, as long as she can bear to be separated from her husband. Under your instruction, of course.'

Bethany did not flinch. 'Very good, Mistress.'

'This is Tacitus, who has helped manage my belongings all the way here. They should arrive by cart this afternoon, I am told. And Tacitus, now you have done that, I have some news.'

'Yes, my lady?' he said.

'The King was so gracious as to grant me your service. But I think you can make up your own mind now.'

'My lady?'

'I discharge you from my service, Tacitus. Should you wish it, you can voluntarily rejoin it, and help me here. Should you not, you can return to London and find other work. But the choice is yours, and yours alone.'

He glanced at Phibae, who was looking on expectantly, her hands clasped beneath her chin. 'Then I choose to stay, for now,' he said. 'There are people in London I should like to help, people you have met. But now I am here, I shall help you until you no longer need it.'

'Then I thank you, Tacitus.'

He shook his head. 'Kwadwo. My name is Kwadwo.'

She regarded the boy's keen eyes, and she nodded and smiled. 'And this, Bethany, is Nicholas. He sailed with me to America and back.'

Bethany bowed, as well as she could. 'Will Nicholas be joining us also?'

'I had to come to see Halescott for myself,' he said. 'But I'll be going back to London soon.'

'I said you can stay here,' said Mercia, 'if you want, if the plague gets worse. You could bring your daughter.'

'No, London's where I belong. A couple of days' rest to help you settle in won't hurt. But I doubt I shall ever want to say goodbye to you for good.'

She looked at him, the strangest of companions, and in defiance of all decorum, she reached over to give him a hug.

'Thank you, Nicholas, most of all. I would not be here without you.'

'And Nathan?' said Bethany, looking around. 'Mr Keyte? Has he not returned with you?'

'Not yet, Bethany. I shall tell you about that. And I shall write to him again soon. For now, I want to enjoy this moment.'

She walked the last few steps to the front of the manor and laid her hand upon its stone, scarcely believing she was there. But she was. And it was glorious.

'Well, old friend,' she whispered. 'I am back.'

Historical Note

In early 1665, King Charles II declared war on the United Provinces of the Dutch Republic, starting the Second Anglo-Dutch War. Much like the first such conflict (and the third to come), it was in large part a war about trade, about who had the right to dominance of the sea routes and colonies that would fuel the development of empire in the centuries to come. New Amsterdam on the eastern American seaboard had already been captured and swiftly renamed New York; there had been skirmishes on the African coast. But while the surrender of New Amsterdam, as documented in *Birthright*, had taken place without a fight, the upcoming conflict would witness all the deadly firepower of war.

The Battle of Lowestoft, the sea battle that forms the backdrop to the end of this novel, must be one of the most unknown in British military history. Perhaps its very nature makes that inevitable, the difficulty in visiting a maritime battlefield obvious. But it was of crucial importance at the time, a massive engagement involving well over a hundred ships, the cream of both fleets. King Charles's journey to be near at hand is made up for the purpose of this fiction, but the Duke of York, as Lord High Admiral, did lead the fleet, and he did so to a celebrated victory. One of the mysteries of Lowestoft is why he failed to consolidate his success by pursuing the beaten Dutch. It is recorded, at least, that the three men on deck beside him were struck down by a well-aimed cannonball: covered in their gore – and why not shaken from a plot on his life? – it is perhaps not so surprising that he instead headed back to shore.

Already in early 1665, five years after King Charles had been restored to his throne, there were grumblings, often horrified ones, that the unpopular (and Catholic) Duke would most likely inherit. While Charles's religious beliefs were private and pragmatic, James's were brazen, as were his uncompromising attitudes to all manner of subjects. Although Charles had fathered eight children already (by the age of thirty-four), none of them were by his Queen, and with the simmering tensions of the civil war still lingering, plots against him were scarcely uncommon. Remove the Duke, and remove the threat of his accession – this is the premise behind *Traitor*. Alas, the poor child the conspirators had hoped to elevate in his place – James, Duke of Cambridge, the happy boy Lavinia cares for in his nursery – died in 1667 just short of his fourth birthday. It would be his sisters, Mary and Anne, who would one day both become Queen.

If plots were commonplace, so too were spies. Under the Earl of Arlington's auspices, Joseph Williamson was creating a vast espionage network for the King; in counter, there were plentiful informers working against them, aiding causes both domestic and foreign. Charles II often employed (read 'used') women for this, among them the renowned Aphra Behn – and now Mercia Blakewood too, with Virgo a supposed agent for the Dutch. Since *Birthright* was published, I have been asked by some readers whether Mercia would have been able to do much of what she does, or be present at certain events, on the grounds she is a woman. I respectfully submit that women like Behn – incidentally also a great playwright (*The Rover*) – most definitely did have such intriguing lives, along with others like Margaret Cavendish and of course Lady Castlemaine. And besides, Mercia is Mercia. The idea of reneging on her and Daniel's inheritance would assuredly have been an affront.

The feud of Lady Castlemaine and the Earl of Clarendon as referenced in this book is well documented. Not content solely to play the King's mistress, she installed herself at Whitehall as the real queen of the Court; she may have been Lady of the Bedchamber to Queen Catherine but everyone knew where the real influence lay. She bore six children with the King in all, and would have been in the very early stages of her fourth such pregnancy when the action of this book occurs. Certainly she was shrewd – and, it would seem, incredibly beautiful – involving herself in politics to a great degree, turning her ire on all those who would oppose her, and as far as Clarendon was concerned, ultimately emerging victorious.

After the great triumph at Lowestoft, events ceased to favour the King. The guns from the battle were reportedly heard in London, where a menace of a different sort was taking hold. The first case of death from plague was recorded in May 1665, when Mercia ventures into the streets of London in search of Virgo. Of course, matters worsened significantly after then, and over the course of the summer, thousands were to die. That, the subsequent defeats of the war, and the Great Fire the following year contributed to a loss of public confidence; the crowning humiliation is still visible today: the standard of the *Royal Charles*, captured in a later reverse, on display for all to see in the Rijksmuseum in Amsterdam. Charles needed a scapegoat: Clarendon was it. And so finally Lady Castlemaine got her way, although she too would not be immune in the years to come.

Horrific to us now, the moral implications of the burgeoning slave trade did not seem to trouble many at Court at the time. Officially known as the Company of Royal Adventurers Trading to Africa (and later the Royal African Company), the Royal Adventurers were a real and serious concern, sending ships to the west African coast to seize men, women and children for enforced labour in the plantations of Barbados and Jamaica, as witnessed by Lavinia Whent. Significantly involved with them was the Duke of York, and neither was the King opposed. There were those who were, including among the Quakers, but their influence in opposition was negligible.

By the time this novel is set, there was a significant black community established in London, many in domestic service. Unlike in the colonies, it was a principle long held to (if not categorically laid out in law) that no person in England could be a slave, but that did not stop abuse. When masters forgot their humanity, safe houses like Zion (an invented name) existed to protect those who chose to run away. Equally disturbing to us now, it was fashionable at this period for women of the Court to use black boys as accessories in their entourage. Go to any art gallery that displays portraits of the time and you may see their young faces peering up at their mistress. History, perhaps, but a history, like all else, those in the present should not forget.

As in *Birthright* and *Puritan*, most of the characters in this book are fictional. The King's war council as described did not exist, nor did any of its principal members. The only real-life characters are those of the Royal family, Lady Castlemaine, and the Earl of Clarendon in his brief appearance. Most of Whitehall Palace is lost to us now, save in the name of the street of government buildings where the massive structure once stood. The sole surviving element is the Banqueting House, the scene of the masked ball in chapter four, the scene too of Charles I's execution in 1649. Hampton Court of course still stands, although it has a different aspect now, thanks to the renovations of a later king.

As ever, any errors of historical accuracy are mine, but I hope readers will bear with them, in the event that any such mistakes may be intended. History is a beautiful and intricate backdrop, a marvellous canvas on which to paint countless tales, but it is the characters that live amongst it who must drive their own fate above all.

Acknowledgements

I would like to acknowledge the support of a number of wonderful people who have been instrumental in the genesis of Mercia's adventures. In particular my agent, Jane Conway-Gordon, for believing in Mercia in the first place; Lesley Crooks and Susie Dunlop at Allison & Busby, as well as all the amazing team there, for giving her life; my husband Matthew Jackson, for every single 'yes', and for all those *awesome* road trips and fun times in New York; my parents, Keith and Pauline, the staunchest of my rocks forever; and finally a big thank you to all the readers and readers-to-come who are starting to discover Mercia Blakewood and finding pleasure in the discovery, just as she does.

Originally from the Midlands, DAVID HINGLEY worked in the civil service for eleven years before moving to New York with his husband, where he passed his days in Manhattan fulfilling his long-term ambition to write and penned his debut novel, *Birthright*. He has since returned to the UK.

davidhingley.com
@dhingley_author